Ahnalian: The New Beginning

The Prophecy of Korham, Volume 1

Timothy E. Collins

Published by 45-1 Properties, LLC, 2024.

AHNALIAN: THE NEW BEGINNING

First edition. October 28, 2024.

ISBN: 979-8227681621

Written by Timothy E. Collins.

Table of Contents

DEDICATION

To my beautiful wife, Colleen
In the past, I have written pages of poetry and lyrics
But most have come from a place of pain.
By comparison, you have brought only joy to my life
So there are no lyrics or prose for you
But, without you, without your love and support,
This book does not exist, does not get written.
Your understanding and attention to my creative needs
Ensured that my thoughts and ideas made it to paper
For all the world to enjoy.
So to you, my beautiful wife,
I dedicate this book.
With all my love,
Tim

THANKS

NO BOOK EVER GETS COMPLETED and published without a TON of encouragement and help along the way.

First and foremost, I want to thank my step-son, Ryan Champlin, who is as much a son as the one I fathered, for all the time and effort he put in to editing this book. Without his input, it never would have been ready for publishing. For every grammatical correction, every thought and opinion on how things flow, for every change I made as a result and even for those I did not, I offer you my most heartfelt thanks.

To Sandra Romaniello and the late Joanne Grzelak, two school teachers from my youth: thank you for encouraging me and supporting my writing. That encouragement and validation fueled my efforts from the late 1970's until today. The love for writing that you helped develop has given me the drive to push through every rewrite, every change of direction, that eventually brought me to the book that the reader holds in their hands right now.

Although far too many to mention, to all the individuals whose personalities and names inspired some of the characters: you may never know who you are, and our interaction may have only been fleeting, but the many inhabitants of Xerses do not exist without you.

And to each and every one of you that made the choice to purchase my book and took the time to read thus far. I hope you enjoy the story I have to tell in the following pages. If you find this book at all enjoyable, please look for the future installments. There is so much more to tell.

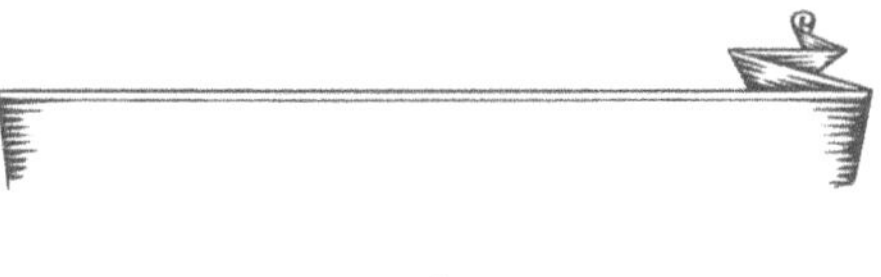

1
AHNALÍAN

IN THE FAR OUTER REACHES of the Triangulum galaxy, in a planetary system of eight circling a giant white star, there exists one of the few oases of sentient life in the universe. On the fourth planet from their sun, life had evolved independently from our own, into a whole host of species, some very much like those on our Earth, some strange and exotic, and some beyond the imaginations of the most prolific of fantasy writers. And within this natural structure, an intelligent apex predator, a humanoid species so identical to our own, that one could only call him "man." "Man," with all the characteristics and frailties of our own: good and evil, charity and greed, trust and dishonesty, happiness and anger, life and death. It is here, in this world, a world parallel to our own, that our story takes place.

Even in a place so distant, so foreign to that of our own small world, it must hold true that, no matter how good things are or for how long, evil still exists. The laws of nature, as well as the laws of statistical probability, establish that there is equal opportunity for evil to occur as there is for good. Even *Ahlok*, the Creator, or, if you so choose, nature itself, is unable to guide the events of time in a manner that precludes evil.

And so it is on the planet Xerses. But, unlike Earth, evil has been dormant for decades, much to the thanks of a cleric who sacrificed his own body to be the vessel for everything evil. With the help of another mighty and good cleric, he is put to an eternal rest, forever trapping evil within his sleeping body. Good has since thrived and the people have grown complacent. Only the most experienced in life remember how it once was when evil touched their daily lives, and how the struggle to maintain a balance between the good and the bad was commonplace.

The Prophecy of Korham speaks of Evil's long slumber and its awakening as an irritated beast, overwhelming those entirely innocent to its ways. From the *Loritae Eyieritu*, the Song of the Chosen One:

And he that preaches right from wrong
Shall swallow that which can do harm
And gently lay his head to rest
A sacrifice for all that's best
The seven clans shall come together
And the vessel shall be put to slumber
To remove Evil from the land
By the cleric's sung command
He shall be awakened as time does pass
As an angry beast, a spell that's cast
By the voice of a woman-child
And the work of a serpent's guile
The sister stars of dusk and dawn
Shall bring to life, one praised, one scorned
Cousins lost but bound by fate
One shall live to guard the gate
To Korham by another name
The Chosen will return again
To bring a good to the land
And balance off the evil hand

Pendiro ahc olenitur, and so the prophecy speculates.

The year is 6093 *Eeja Korham,* since Korham. And here this tale begins.

2 THE BEEKEEPER

6093 E.K.

The dark orange sun hung heavy in the deep blue sky, like a discarded, over-ripe melon floating in a placid garden pool. Rays of heat stretched to the ground, dripping from the orb like rivulets of sweat. The parched earth below eagerly drank from the mirage created by the heat, desperate to slake its thirst, only to be further desiccated. Deep cracks formed in the earth's surface, creating a puzzle-like appearance. The true puzzle was when the oppressive sun's heat would, once again, give way to rain. *Or if it ever would.*

"CORA, I'M OFF!"

Zephraim's wife responded from within. "Be careful, my love... and be home for dinner."

"I will."

Historically, the Souliban countryside was a rather barren place, iron red gravel covering low stony plateaus with nothing but scrub growing between the crags and rocks. However, things had not been normal for quite some time. Times were tough. Dry conditions made the land nearly impossible to cultivate. The rain had not fallen for months. The only people able to eke out any semblance of success were those who possessed the fortitude and persistence to continue working the land and those that exploited innovative, less pedestrian activities. Zephraim was a member of the latter, a man with the keen ability to find a productive niche in an otherwise sterile environment: the tending to one of nature's most industrious creatures, the honeybee.

Zephraim was approaching his 40's, tall and lean, with a pate of close-cropped, dusty brown hair and a clean-shaven face. Although patched in places, his clothing was clean and surprisingly well maintained, and his leather boots were freshly resoled. It was obvious he was not a man of means, but Zephraim had the look of a well-kept husband with a caring wife.

Zephraim's house was a small, domed mud-brick hut with a single door and no windows. It was clearly not sizeable enough to have more than one room. A small flue poked through the rear of the dome; a thin wisp of gray curling skyward. The hut was neatly kept and in good repair. A small, orderly-stacked pile of firewood stood propped against the side of the hut. Zephraim took pride in the few possessions he owned and the presentation of his property. Another source of his pride became evident as two small children, a boy around eight and a girl about five, ran out from behind the hut, giggling.

"Gotcha!" He reached out and grabbed both children, one in each arm, twirling them about before placing them back down on the ground. He mussed up the tow-headed boy's hair and lifted the little blonde girl onto his hip, planting a kiss on her cheek. She smiled at her father with her crooked grin, a little rag doll firmly clasped in her hands. Zephraim placed his daughter back on the ground and bent down to address his children.

"Don't you two give Momma any trouble, OK?" he said with a smile. "Daddy's gonna go milk some honeybees!" He let out a deep chuckle and the children giggled in response. Donning a wide-brimmed hat with a hand-made net as protection from the sun as well as his bees, Zephraim stood and began his journey to his hives, pulling behind him a large wheeled cart burdened with all the tools of his craft. The children chased after him for a short while, then stopped and waved as he continued on, slowly becoming just a blur on the stark, heat-ravaged horizon behind him.

ZEPHRAIM CAME UPON his first hives nearly half an hour later. Sweat dotted his forehead behind the net veil and perspiration created a wide wet streak down his back and circles under his arms. Stopping for a moment, he produced a gourd from his cart and drew a long pull of water from a small hole at the top. As he drank, he noticed a dark storm cloud stretching across the horizon. "Finally," he thought to himself. "Rain!" Perhaps some much-needed moisture would produce a fresh bloom of flowers to help increase the output of his hives. Replacing the gourd to the cart, he began to gather the supplies necessary to collect his honey.

A few dozen bees swirled around the hive, some leaving in search of flowers, others returning, laden with nectar and pollen. Several bees buzzed about his net-covered face as he pulled on long leather gloves to protect his arms from their sting and grabbed his bee smoker. Skillfully, he lit a handful of dry pine needles with an ember struck from a flint and stone and placed the smoldering mass into his smoker along with a wad of damp wool. After a moment, a hint of white smoke began to wisp from the smoker's nozzle. Zephraim gave the bellows a few squeezes and thick gray smoke began to billow out. He pumped the bellows while aiming the nozzle at the openings to his hive, causing the bees to disperse and allowing him access to the combs within.

Zephraim lifted the top section off the hive to get access to the honeycombs inside. Turning to set it on his cart, something unusual about that storm cloud caught his eye. He turned back squinting a little to focus on what might simply be a mirage in the heat of the afternoon sky. As the image became clear in his view, his eyes widened with alarm and he began to slowly back-pedal from his open hive.

"For the love of *Ahlok*!"

Catching his foot on a loose stone, he fell backward, dropping the section of hive to the ground and landing on his back. A swarm of angry honeybees poured from the dropped section, forming a cloud that obscured his view. As the insects began to disperse, he refocused through the bee cloud on what had originally caused him such alarm. A look of absolute terror fixed on his face. Scrambling to his feet, Zephraim ran towards home as quickly as his feet would take him, leaving his tools and his bees to whatever had chased him away.

3
THE SWARM

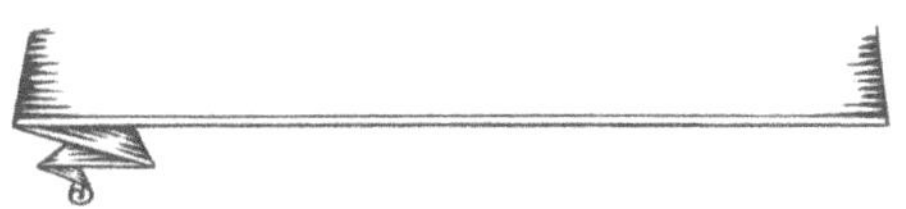

THEY CAME BY THE HUNDREDS, over the horizon and as far as the eye could see, like an immeasurable swarm of honeybees. It was a horde of biblical proportions; draconian locust belching flaming acid and laying waste to the land below. The skies were thick with wings, blotting out the sun like a fast-moving rainstorm and beating the air like thunder, the skies slashed by the lightening flash of flaming acid breath as it etched the land below, leaving only scorched earth in its wake, the smoke from the destruction below as thick as a hard pouring rain. What little life that may have been left upon this parched and desolate landscape now lay in smoldering ashes.

These were the creatures that legends and nightmares were made of. No one from the Tendira Confederation had ever seen such creatures before. The flying reptilian beasts were of enormous proportions, thirty feet long from snout to tail and as big around as a small sailing ship. Gossamer wings extended out from the shoulder girdle twenty feet to either side along arm-like appendages, finger-like stays holding the near-transparent membrane taut when extended and folded neatly for later use when brought tight against the body. A strangely equine shaped head swiveled atop a serpentine neck that extended eight to ten feet ahead of the shoulder and a ten-foot tail followed behind. Along the top surface of the tail, triangular scutes stood tall, one fitting neatly into the next, to form a rudimentary rudder to aid the creature in turning. Scales covered the remainder of the body, shiny gray like graphite. With wings fully extended, each appeared like an angel of death in the sky.

Upon each beast, a heavily armored warrior sat in a small leather saddle, strapped tightly to the shoulders of his dragon, directing its every move.

A slight pull on the reins, a gentle nudge with a knee, or a short, barked command was all that was needed to guide his demonic winged steed towards each intended target. Man and dragon working in unison, like a single entity, in an unbreakable bond between creature and rider.

What set these beasts aside from any other creature was the extraordinary adaptation that they utilized to hunt down their prey and exploited by the handlers for their own devious designs. The dragons belched a phosphorus-based acid that accumulated in one of its stomachs, an evolutionary trait enhanced through breeding to be deftly utilized by their human handlers. It burst into hellish flames as soon as it exited the mouth and hit the air, liquid fire raining down on the earth below. When directed by the riders, this trait was extremely precise and particularly lethal.

Whether legendary or plucked out of a childhood nightmare, the destruction these creatures wrought was very real. Nothing escaped the flaming, corrosive acid that rained down from above. Below the marauding swarm, people and animals scattered in every possible direction, doing their best to avoid the siege from above. Never before had anyone seen such beasts or, for that matter, any creature in such numbers. Unique was the unbiased and total destruction. The attack took them entirely by surprise, quickly creating chaos and terror everywhere. There was no time to mount a defensive counter to the aerial bombardment. Refuge was nowhere to be found as every man-made structure was being targeted from above and destroyed before their eyes. The attack was as precise as a doctor's scalpel and as devastating as a volcanic eruption. Every rider sought out an individual target and directed his dragon to remove it from existence. His steed would locate the targeted quarry with extra-spectral vision, hurl forth a regurgitated gob of searing ejecta and then move back to the swarm to await the next assault. Any movement below was quickly targeted and disintegrated. Creatures large and small suffered the agonizing torture of fur, flesh, feather, and scales being eaten away by the unprejudiced malice of the dragons' fiery destructive bile. The pungent odor of the dissolving chemical and burning tissues filled the air. The Tendirans did not stand a chance against this onslaught. This was a raiding party the likes of which no human had ever experienced before. Even the trees and plants fell victim to the horror wrought from above; resembling melted candles after the acid had worked its destruction upon their leaves, flowers, and stems, and the ground itself was scorched to dust; the stones and boulders that made up most of the landscape crumbled to powdery nothingness.

The noise within the swarm was deafening. A Wagnerian symphony of intense and disharmonious noises filled the air. The low rumble of the creatures, communicating with one another and their masters; the commands issued by riders, both to their creatures and the other riders; the sound of huge powerful wings beating the thick afternoon air into submission; the roar of each dragon as it belched corrosive hellfire onto its targets far below; the hissing of the acid as it met the atmosphere and ignited into a fiery waterfall cascading from the skies. The cacophony produced by the aerial horde overwhelmed the clamor of destruction below. To anyone not accustomed to the uproar within a gaggle of marauding dragons, the volume and dissonance could easily make the average man go mad.

As grotesque a sight as they were, the dragons moved individually with the subtle grace of a well-studied dancer and interacted as a whole, with the unison of a school of reef fish, as if in a well-choreographed aerial ballet. Hundreds of dragons flying en masse and then individually turning and spiraling downward from the swarm to scorch the earth below with molten sputum expelled from within, returning to the spot amongst the swarm that they had previously occupied awaiting its next attack. It was as if the swarm acted with one mind.

Flying high within the swarm astride a noticeably larger and darker beast, a noble figure in black leather barked out orders to the warriors below. Roga. Warlord of the Khogians. This was his mission, his guerrilla attack. He had carefully studied the Prophecy of Korham for years, intently reading every word. The ancient tomes foretold of a great battle between good and evil that was to be waged upon this land, and the victor would have power above all. Roga was intent on destroying anything that would stand in his way. He would be the victor and would control everything upon this land. Responding to an unspoken cue, Roga directed his steed to dive. "*Shuh*!" The beast rotated left and dove down through the swarm and locked onto a target below, a small, domed mud brick hut sitting alone on the barren wilderness. "*Domae*!" The beast let loose the deadly bile from its fore-stomach, aimed directly at the hut, and quickly rotated left and upward to return to the swarm. From out of the corner of his eye, Roga spied a female figure running with two children in her arms but lost sight of them as the next dragon sped by him on its way to eradicate its target. Returning to their position in the swarm, Roga leaned forward and patted his dragon on the shoulder and smiled. This was going to be a victory that changed the history of Xerses and would place his name prominently upon it.

The onslaught continued around him as dragon after dragon twisted and turned down towards the land below. With no counter, this incursion would be over in a mere hour or two, and Roga and his aerial forces would return home.

A LONE FIGURE APPEARED over the top of the rocky knoll. Zephraim. He just barely managed to evade the onslaught of the dragons. A small grotto beneath a rocky outcropping had protected him from the extra-spectral vision of the dragons and the death being rained down from above. He had huddled deep inside the rock for what seemed like hours, waiting for the maelstrom to end. Now, he was headed back to his home, wading through the death and destruction that was once a vibrant, albeit poor, community. Not a single landmark produced by human hands was recognizable. The few natural features of the landscape that had been left untouched by the onslaught were the only way posts that gave Zephraim any indication of where he was. On his way, he encountered no one, not a living thing. Everything that had existed before on this arid countryside had been exterminated. As loud as the dragon attack had been, the silence now was even more deafening. Even the wind had died. The air hung heavy, the faint smell of acid and burning flesh still apparent, dust and ash slowly settling to the earth below, wisps of smoke rising from the charred remains of... the Creator only knew what it once had been. Zephraim plodded along slowly, making his way back to his home.

What he saw made his heart sink. Where his small mud hut once stood was now just a pile of rubble. A wisp of gray smoke wafted into the air above the pile. Nothing was recognizable in the place where he once made his home. Zephraim quickly ran to the spot, calling out the names of his wife and children.

"Cora! Wilhem! Agnes!"

There were no answers to his cries. Zephraim fell to his hands and knees and began rummaging through the rubble on the site, searching for something, anything, to indicate his family was alive and had found safety elsewhere. Nothing remained. He rummaged a bit more before slowly standing in defeat. He kicked at the half of a pottery jug lying on the ground. It shattered into tiny fragments and dust, scorched to nothingness by the dragons. From beneath, a flash of color caught his eyes. Stopping, he bent down and brushed the dust away, revealing the singed remains of the rag doll his daughter had been clutching as he had left to tend his hives earlier that morning. He fell back to his knees, sobbing. The sorrow of a man that had lost everything of meaning in his life poured forth. Sorrow followed by self-pity and despair and, finally anger.

Kneeling on the ground, the rag doll in his hand, Zephraim contemplated what to do next. His family and his home and all that was important to him were now gone forever. The community he had once been part of had been removed from the face of the land. The anger boiling in his gut urged him to seek revenge. But what could one simple man do to avenge the death of his family against such a formidable force? Nearly reconciled to accepting the events of the day and moving on, a honeybee landed on the back of his hand. Bringing his hand up to eye level, he examined the creature closely. Something other than himself had survived the onslaught, something he could connect with; a simple honey bee. Without warning, the bee plunged its stinger into the skin on his hand. Zephraim shook his hand to dislodge it. The bee went flying to the ground, but the stinger remained in his hand, the venom sac still unconsciously pumping its poison into his flesh. Zephraim looked down at the bee, realizing what it had just done. It had given its life in defense of its family and community from what it saw as a threat. Casting his eyes over the rubble that was once his home, Zephraim knew what he had to do.

4
THE DEAL

6054 E.K.

The castle sat high upon a hill, its enormous outer palisade shielding the inner court and keep from the eyes of any invader with the poor judgment or the foolhardy self-confidence to attempt an attack on such a formidable edifice. The base of the outer wall consisted of stones so large they had to have been placed by the hand of the Creator. The outer surface of the wall had been polished smooth to prevent scaling by invading armies and reflected the sunlight back upon the fields that surrounded the fortress. The common people called it "*eht Vilna Sahnah,*" the Beacon Castle. Eight square towers sat evenly spaced upon the outer palisade. Even in these times of peaceful co-existence, the king preferred to keep the towers well manned. Three sets of eyes constantly peered into the outside world from each vantage.

King Olen was loved by his people. At 45, he had led his kingdom for almost five years. In his youth, he had worked hard for his father, King Heidel, forging peaceful relationships with the surrounding kingdoms and even those many days travel away. At a young age, his father had brokered a peaceful alliance between *eht Vilna Sahnah* and the six surrounding kingdoms, forming the Tendira Confederation, which continued to this day, each kingdom benefiting from the cooperation born out of the alliance. Upon his father's passing, Olen took over governing *eht Vilna Sahnah*. His rule was defined by peace and prosperous enterprise. The outer courtyard of the castle housed some of the finest artisans in the known world and travelers and traders alike came from miles away to purchase and barter for their wares. The fields beyond the outer palisade produced abundant harvests every season and the stores in the undercroft of the keep were always stocked to capacity. *Eht Vilna Sahnah* had become a center for commerce and all the Confederation kingdoms brought their wares to the marketplace.

Queen Isella was of noble blood. She was the daughter of Earl Montfort, a member of King Heidel's court and one of his closest advisors. Although 40, she could easily pass for Olen's daughter; near-perfect alabaster skin, eyes like two pools of the softest rainwater, a youthful smile capable of lighting up a room with the slightest flash, and a curvaceous but well-toned figure that belied her age. She had grown up with the then-Prince Olen until she was about 10 when her parents sent her off to school. To her, the Prince was just the odd-looking older boy that lived in the main castle keep. He was pushy and bossy and she did not much care for him at all. It was no major consequence to her to be sent away to school. All her female companions would be cast off from the castle as well. Such was the practice. Girls of noble blood did no work around the castle and were more of a burden than anything else, putting demands upon the staff that was simply unnecessary. It was a way of thinning out the "estrogen pool," especially during their adolescent years, before their bodies had become used to the natural cycle. It was far easier for the men of the house, let alone the servant women, to conduct business without the irritation of spoiled, premenstrual pubescent girls lingering about.

Isella had left for school still a little girl, but she returned an extraordinarily beautiful young woman of nineteen. Upon her return, she became the focus of attention for nearly all the males of the castle, garnering stares and whispered comments dripping with double entendre. Yet she found herself attracted to but a single, particular young man who daily practiced the arts of warfare, falconry, and horseback-riding in the fields just beyond the outer palisade. He had broad strong shoulders, large hands and piercing gray-blue eyes that could be seen one hundred yards away. Although they had yet to be introduced since her return from school, Isella would sneak her way to the East Tower, where she and her lady-in-waiting, Ebby, had befriended one of the watchmen, Seamus. Hidden in the shadows, they would watch for hours on end as the young man practiced his craft. Just the sight of him, his tunic stripped off, sweat glistening from his muscular frame in the bright sunlight, stirred feelings within her that she had never felt before.

"That, my dear Princess, is Prince Olen, son of King Heidel", whispered the watchman. Isella looked back at him quickly, a perplexed look on her face. She found it very hard to believe that this was the same peculiar teenaged boy from her younger years that she could not have cared any less for. How had that spoiled brat grown into such an incredible specimen of a man?

Turning her attention back to the young man, she whispered under her breath, "Prince Olen."

Soon thereafter came a day when the two passed innocently in the courtyard marketplace. Olen flashed a quick wink and a smile her way as they approached each other. Isella blushed noticeably. She turned in front of one of the many shops, a purveyor of fine linens, silks, and lace, and pretended to be interested in the wares, hoping that Olen would continue on his way and allow her heart to return to its normal rhythm. Instead, he stopped and stood beside her appearing not to notice her in any way, as if disinterested. Her heart skipped a beat when she realized where he had chosen to stop. To her surprise, he addressed her quietly, without turning to look, so as not to draw attention to their discourse.

"Do you enjoy the performances from the fields in the evening?"

Her heart leaped to her throat and she turned her glance towards him ever so slightly in response, and just as quickly returning to stare forward. Her face was now a bright crimson. He had somehow noticed her in the East Tower, where she thought she had herself a very secret vantage point.

"Or do you prefer the matinee?"

She quickly turned to stare at him wide-eyed, and, as before, just as quickly turned her head away. He was, obviously, well aware that she had been watching him at all hours of the day.

Olen picked up a piece of fine lace and silk lingerie. Fondling the material gently in his fingers he whispered to her again. "Lucky be the man to gift someone so lovely with such an elegant piece of intimate apparel and then be so privileged as to remove it, himself, in private." He nonchalantly tossed the nightgown down in front of her, turned, and walked away, a wry smile on his face that she could not see. Isella felt her knees buckle and struggle to remain on her feet. *Oh,* she thought, *he is quite the Lothario! He has cast his spell on me, capturing me; heart, mind, body, and soul.* Isella stood, unsteady, in the weaver's shop for another few minutes, trying to compose herself before moving on to her initial destination.

That evening in her quarters, Isella gave up the details of the day to her best friend and most trusted of ladies-in-waiting. "Ebby, he addressed me today, in the market! Not openly, but discretely so no one else could hear. And the words he spoke to me! If the spoken word were a carnal instrument, I would have become a woman right there, in the middle of the market! Him standing so near aroused me so. Oh, I was fearful that my heart would race clear from my breast!"

"Oh, please! Do tell!" Excitedly, Ebby sat on the bed to face Isella.

"He came through the market this morning as I was on my way to see the pastor for tea. He was staring and smiling at me, so I turned into the weaver's shop to let him pass, but he stepped into the cubicle and stood beside me. He was so near as to fill my nose with his most masculine scent. I tried to ignore him, but I am quite sure he knew I was aware of him. He addressed me directly and made mention of me watching him exercise and practice from the watchtower. I thought I would die! He knows I have been watching him! And then he picked up a piece of lingerie and said he wanted to give it to me so he could see it on me, and then remove it with his teeth before he ravished my body, making mad passionate love to me throughout the night."

"Oh my! M'lady, it sounds to me as if this handsome young paramour has his eyes set on you." The two young ladies giggled.

"I wonder if he knows what he does to me, how he arouses feelings within me that I dare not speak about except in private? He knows I have been watching him from the shadows of the East Tower. What else could he know about me?"

"I know not, m'lady, but I could possibly persuade information from his groom. He and I have... an understanding."

The pair giggled again.

"Oh, Ebby, you are the devil's little mistress, aren't you?"

"One has her ways, m'lady. One has her ways."

The two, falling over each other with laughter, continued discussing the young prince long into the night. It was that night that Isella had made up her mind: this was the man she was destined to marry.

Isella made every effort, in the following weeks, to ensure she and Olen would cross paths. She continued to watch him exercise from the East Tower, but in full sight from the battlements, not from the shadows. Innocent meetings in the courtyard or marketplace soon became private luncheons and intimate dinners for two. Their courtship became the talk and envy of all in the castle. Every move, every meeting, every moment, was the subject of microscopic inspection and dissection but the couple failed to fall into the traps of the envious. All gossip was simply ignored and they continued to live their lives, seeking only to gain the affections of the other. Olen proposed later that year and plans for a wedding were soon under way.

Olen and Isella were married to much fanfare. The finest of produce, baked goods, wild game, and livestock were prepared. Musicians and performers of all styles were present to entertain the guests. King Heidel ensured only the finest of all possible accouterments were made available for the festivities. They were a handsome couple, very much the talk of the land. Even after the fanfare surrounding their marriage had subsided, the couple remained the darlings of the kingdom. Olen ascended to the crown at the age of forty upon the death of his father. King Heidel had grown frail in his later years and, although his father was still king, Olen was attending to most of the affairs of state. The king's passing was a blow to the people, but the presence of Olen and Isella helped maintain a continuum that precluded chaos. After the appropriate period of mourning for King Heidel, things quickly returned to their normal rhythm with Olen now leading the kingdom.

Although happy and obviously very much in love, one issue seemed to cloud their otherwise perfect relationship. The couple had yet to produce an heir. Lady Isella had not been able to conceive. Advice, requested or not, was provided by nearly everyone they would encounter. They had tried every potion and position, every idol and fertility prayer, but to no avail. The couple had finally settled on the fact that they would not be blessed with progeny. Finally, as she approached the age of 40, a proud King Olen announced to the entire kingdom that his beautiful wife was with child. It was an announcement that the people had long awaited. A cheer erupted from the crowd as Olen finished his announcement. People danced and sang. It was another reason to celebrate, another omen of good. This family, this kingdom, these people were truly blessed with all that was good in the world.

That evening, a proud Olen brought his wife to bed and held her close. Sounds of the celebration could still be heard outside their room. He smiled at her as he drew her near to him.

"You have made me the happiest and proudest husband in the world. I cannot imagine a life more complete."

"And you, my love, have made me happier than any woman has the right to feel. You and your affection mean everything to me."

Olen kissed her gently on the forehead and drew her closer to him. The two snuggled quietly together, happy to be at rest in one another's arms, happy that their lives would now be complete.

Isella had fallen asleep beside him, but Olen remained awake, staring at his beautiful wife, as she lay contently wrapped in his arms. He reached down to scratch at an itch on his leg and felt a sharp pain on the back of his hand. Quickly withdrawing his hand, he noted two small puncture wounds. He grabbed the edge of the bed sheet and flipped it off his body, exposing the cause of both the itch on his leg and the puncture wounds on his hand. It was a snake! And not just any snake. It appeared to be a cobra. The snake raised its head and flared out its hood. The king stared in terror at the serpent.

Gathering his senses, he carefully reached over and gently shook the queen never allowing the snake out of his sight. "Isella, wake up. Wake up, my dear."

Isella lifted her head groggily. "What is it, my love?"

"Just get out of bed, carefully and slowly."

Isella did not realize at first what was happening, but it quickly became apparent as she wiped the sleep from her eyes and adjusted to the dim light.

"Oh, my gracious! Olen! A snake! Are you alright?"

"Just get out of bed slowly. I've been struck, but I do not want him to bite you as well. I will not endanger you or the baby. Just get out of bed. Then go get someone to care for this wound."

Isella was shaken but followed Olen's directions. She carefully got out of bed, wrapped herself in her night coat and grabbed a cloak. She turned as she got to the door. "I love you."

"I love you, too, my dear. Please, make haste. Find someone to bind this wound. Seek out the Lady Illsinga. Some claim her to be a witch or a healer. She may possibly know what to do about the snake bite."

"Yes, m'lord. I will go to her directly." Isella rushed out the door and down the hall.

Olen turned his gaze back to the snake. "Stay calm, serpent. No one is going to harm you," he said calmly and quietly, trying his best not to further aggravate the creature.

To his shock, the snake hissed back at him. "Rest assured that you shall not be the last," and struck him again, this time in the thigh. It happened so quickly that Olen could not react fast enough to stop him. He could see the fangs enter his flesh and could feel the venom pump into his veins. He grabbed the snake behind the hood and ripped it from his leg, throwing it hard against the wall. Grabbing at the puncture site, he squeezed, trying desperately to keep the poison from traveling up his leg and into the rest of his body. The snake slithered towards the bed. It rose up, flaring his hood out again, and looked directly at Olen. "The star that signals the setting sun shall sow the serpent's seed. The sibling's spawn shall seek to suppress so that he shall not succeed. Sleep peacefully, your majesty."

The snake began to slither away. Much to the disbelief of Olen's eyes, it turned into a wisp of vapor as it approached the wall, which wafted into the cracks between the stones and then disappeared into nothingness.

Moments later, Isella returned with the Lady Illsinga in tow. The medicine woman approached the bed. "Your lordship, may I?"

"Please, woman, this is no time for pleasantries and titles. I am relying on your knowledge, be it natural and supernatural, to bring this situation to a satisfactory close. Do whatever you must, without regard for my status."

"As you wish, m'lord. Your lady has told me of your plight. I understand you have been struck in the hand by a poisonous serpent."

"Yes, I was struck in the hand, and then, later, in the thigh. The pain is all but unbearable. Is there anything you can do?"

She turned to the queen and started giving orders. "I will need a clean tunic and a shaving razor. Have someone boil some water. And I will be in need of a lit candle."

Lady Isella had been staring blankly at her husband, in a daze over what was happening. Hearing the woman bark orders at her snapped the queen back to reality. She quickly turned to gather up the supplies that Lady Illsinga requested and had one of the maids begin boiling water. The queen quickly returned with the requested supplies.

"Tear the tunic into long strips. I will need them to tie off the wounds." Isella did as she was told. Illsinga took two of the long strips and tied them off to the king's thigh and arm above the snakebites. Taking the shaving razor, the medicine woman ran the edge of the blade within the flame of the candle to sterilize it and wiped off any soot with another strip from the tunic. She looked at the king. "Forgive me, m'lord." He nodded and she brought the razor to the flesh of his thigh at the site of the punctures. Over each, she made a deep 'X'-shaped cut. "I need that water now." The queen went to fetch the water, into which the medicine woman soaked more of the strips. She placed the boiling strips on the site of the wounds. The king tensed up, air whistling through his teeth as he inhaled deeply, as the boiling hot cloth touched his skin, but relaxed soon thereafter. The cloth became bright pink as blood seeped up from the wounds. After a few moments, the witch removed the cloth and placed her mouth over each wound, suctioning out the poison mixed with blood and spitting it out on the bedroom floor. She then repeated the procedure on his wounded hand.

"I pray that we were in time to prevent the poison from spreading throughout the body". She looked at the queen. "I fear that there was something more than just a snake here tonight. I sense the presence of something dark, something.... evil."

Isella shot a quick look at the witch. "Evil? There has not been a word spoken of evil in this land since my husband's father helped establish the Confederacy some 40 years ago. How can it be possible that it has returned here on this night?"

"I know not, m'lady. The ways of *Ahlok* have no reason, for only He knows the justification for what happens and when."

Queen Isella was beginning to lose patience with this line of conversation. "Enough with all this talk about evil! What of my husband? When shall he recover and rise from this unfortunate accident?"

"I have done all I can do for him. What happens now is out of our hands. All we can do, now, is wait."

The queen and the medicine woman stayed at the king's side all night and into the next day. He slept fitfully, shivering and sweating profusely, uttering nonsense about a star and a seed and the serpent. As day turned into night, the king's condition worsened. Fits of dementia accompanied by seizures filled the next few days as the king slowly slipped away. Isella never left his side, vowing to remain in the company of her declining husband as she suspected every good wife would do. On the king's final day, Isella removed everyone from the room. She requested a guard, her trusted ally Seamus, be placed at the door and ordered that no one was to enter the room until summoned. She wanted to remain with her husband, uninterrupted, during his final hours. At long last, the king took his last breath, succumbing to the effects of the snake's powerful poison. She sobbed uncontrollably for quite some time, and then she collected herself, kissed her husband, offering her final goodbyes, and left the room. She would never enter the room again.

Outside, Ebby, Seamus, and Lady Illsinga were waiting. All were quite astonished at the queen's composure.

"It is done," she said. "Have the priest come to offer final prayers and blessings. Once the priest is done, have the funeral preparations begun. And I want the room closed. No one is to disturb the contents. I want it to forever remain as it is now."

Escorted by the guard, Lady Illsinga and Ebby quickly left to attend to the Queen's wishes.

6055 E.K.

Queen Isella gave birth to, not one, but two, twin girls, nearly nine months after the king's death. Their birth helped buoy the mood of the kingdom, still reeling from the untimely death of their beloved ruler. They came into the world with the pomp and circumstance typically associated with the most royal of weddings. The celebration and feasting lasted nearly three weeks. Delegations and noblemen were sent from nearby kingdoms, bearing gifts and marriage proposals. Although each proposal was graciously entertained, the Queen had a distaste for arranged marriages and firmly believed there was no place for romance and the sanctity of the institution within the realm of politics. Indeed, her daughters were still infants, and there would be time enough in the future for such arrangements to be made. She respectfully declined each offer, deferring such decisions to a later place and time when her two girls would be capable of making those choices on their own.

Ahlāan, the Morning Star, was first born, emerging from her mother's womb at daybreak. She was named after the morning star that stands proudly on the horizon, greeting the coming morn and bidding the evening farewell before fading into an ever-brightening morning sky. The second child delayed her emergence, enjoying the fleeting solitude of the womb, by herself for the first time in her existence. Born nearly twelve hours later, as the last wisps of twilight faded into night, Shahlāan, the Evening Star, was given the name of the first star that appears high in the evening sky, announcing to the world that evening was at hand.

The young girls were identical in every way with one very notable exception, their hair. Ahlāan's, as black as onyx and as shiny as the full moon on a clear, starless night, cascading over her shoulders and down her back like a river of blue-black India ink. Shahlāan's hair, orange-red like the flame within a blacksmith's brazier, an inferno of flaxen sunbeams that identified her easily from across the courtyard, dazzling bright and all about like the mane of a lion. Their hair belied the personality of each girl. Ahlāan, calm and gentle, but purposeful and steadfast. Shahlāan, quick to temper, often irrational and prone to flights of fancy. It was these personality traits that would ultimately dictate the course of their lives.

The twins would grow up in a world of privilege, nursemaids and ladies-in-waiting at their beck and call. The finest silk and lace protected their skin from the harshness of the outside world and they dined on the best that came from the fields and the forest. The Queen brought in the best educators available, for, unlike her own adolescence, Isella could not bring herself to send them off to school. After the death of her husband, she did not want them out of her comfort zone. She would see to it that they stay within the walls of the castle proper, at least until the time arrived when they would take a husband and move on to a new life, potentially beyond the palisades.

Ahlāan grew to be her mother's darling. She was never known to indulge in anything overtly controversial. She was content to be primarily a homebody and practiced the skills of a refined lady: sewing, tying fine lace, embroidery, and cross-stitching. In many ways, her mother considered her the perfect child and she did little to cause her to feel otherwise. And those actions that her mother might look upon with disapproval, she kept discretely hidden.

Shahlāan was never satisfied with the more mundane aspects of life. She was often out and about, without her mother's consent or knowledge. She had no use for the more lady-like skills. She and the queen were often at odds and those within the castle were familiar with their frequent verbal skirmishes. Shahlāan had neither need nor desire to hide anything, whether it was upsetting to her mother or not. And she had a penchant for the dark arts, something that the queen objected to most vehemently.

6071 E.K.

It was a cool, crisp evening. The tower watchmen kept a careful eye on the castle and its surroundings. The silence of the evening was arbitrarily broken by the bark of a dog, the murmur from the cattle in the outer court, the giggling and soft moans of an adolescent girl from the stable. The watchman smiled and shook his head. Oh, to be so young and so full of life again!

Queen Isella and her ladies were sitting in the Great Hall. A large fire was blazing in the grand fireplace. It was the one place in the large, dank castle that the Queen found some peace and comfort so many years after the death of her husband. She often spent hours in the evening by the fire reading a book or just conversing with Ebby. Most of the ladies were tending to small chores; sewing minor repairs to clothing, preparing the evening meal, tending to the younger children, while others were utilizing their skills at tying fine lace, embroidery, or cross-stitching. It was a quiet, pleasant atmosphere, with a few of the ladies humming a tune and others engaged in near-silent small talk.

Unlike most members of the castle, Ahlāan was outside of the castle proper. Secretly, she had a thing for the boys in the stable and how they made her feel, and she would take advantage of any moment she could steal in their company. Tonight, as she was often wont to do, Ahlāan was attending to the affections of a particularly handsome young man in an empty stall at the back of the stable. Although they were careful to keep their actions private, an occasional giggle or stray outburst emanated from their hiding place. Ahlāan knew their time was short, enough for some heavy petting and a few lustful forays of his wandering hands. As he pressed for more, she playfully pushed him away and jumped up, pulling her bodice back up over her breasts. She kissed the stable hand one last time while straightening her gown and petticoats, quickly checking herself and, removing any straw that she could find, quietly emerged from the barn and into the shadows outside the castle. From her sister's window she saw a flicker of light, then a flash followed by a wisp of smoke. Shahlāan was doing it again, playing at being a sorceress. Well aware that their mother would disapprove, Ahlāan headed straight for the castle. She bounced into the Great Hall, breaking the quiet, a huge smile on her face. Skipping up behind her mother, she straightened her clothing and quickly removed a carelessly overlooked piece of straw from her hair.

"Mum-ma! She's at it again!" she chimed, almost singsong.

The Queen slammed her book into her lap. "Damned that girl! Ebby, whatever are we going to do with her?"

The nursemaid half looked up from her sewing. "Girls will be girls, Mum. If you wish, I can find my way upstairs and put an end to it. Nothing that a firm swat or two on the backside wouldn't cure." She stopped her sewing for a moment, looking directly at the Queen. "In some ways, I suppose you should be grateful. She could be passing time with one of the stable boys. Now that would put some gray hairs on your head!" Behind the Queen, Ahlāan nervously bit her lip, pulled another piece of straw from her dress, and unconsciously drew circles on the floor with her left foot. Ebby stole a quick glance at the princess and smiled. "You know how boys can be. I remember a certain young princess..."

Isella quickly cut her off. "Enough! I think there will be none of that for the present time. Just leave her be with her little spells and incantations for the moment. She will find far less mischief in that than she will in the company of a randy, young stable hand."

A few of the ladies giggled. Ahlāan blushed, noting she had become the object of attention for many of the ladies in the room. Unconscious to their reactions, Isella went back to reading her book.

Unlike her sister, Shahlāan had no interest in the young men about the castle. Her interests were much more self-centered. She was only interested in moving up and out, up on the ladder of notoriety and out of the castle and kingdom. Nothing about this place appealed to her. What did appeal to her was witchcraft and sorcery. By becoming a powerful sorceress herself or employing the graces of an omnipotent being, Shahlāan knew she could fabricate her own destiny. That was the way to bigger and better things.

Shahlāan spent hour upon hour scanning the books on the shelves of the palace library. Both her father and grandfather had been firm believers in the power of knowledge and had stocked the library with volumes from far and wide. The young princess had scanned through hundreds of historical texts, religious tomes, and writings on spells and incantations. She had found a quotation from the Prophecy of Korham that defined the snake demon as being the key to the most powerful and balancing force in the universe. He was the portal through which this great power would pass and begin to establish itself on Xerses. She was determined to call upon the snake demon and offer to serve him in exchange for freedom from the castle and the insular world within which she currently resided. But first, she would need to find the identity of the demon and the proper incantation by which to call him to her.

From the pages of an ancient tome, Shahlāan had found reference to a snake demon known as Sutek. The accompanying narrative discussed his banishment to the form of a snake and his return at the 'Castle of Light.' Could this 'Castle of Light' be *eht Vilna Sahnah*, The Beacon Castle? Was this the sign she had been searching so long for? Knowing her own familial history, she surmised that the demon may already have ties to the location. She hastily grabbed the tome and several books describing incantations and headed off to her room. Tonight could quite possibly be the night that set the stage for her inevitable deliverance from the confines of this castle and the deprivations of the life that she had been forced to live within its walls.

A swirling cloud filled the small room and the fireplace exploded in a fireball of sparks and flames. Shahlāan sat in the corner, a large tome on her knees, mumbling incantations. A large candle still burned, though overturned, on the mantelpiece. Books littered the floor in front of the bookshelves.

Shahlāan mumbled something and three books launched themselves from a shelf and landed on the floor. "Damned! That wasn't it!" She flipped over a few pages, carefully scanning the contents of each page before proceeding to the next. "There must be something here."

Incantation after incantation brought explosions and the scattering of items throughout the room. At one point, she conjured a small rabbit that hopped about her room until she became loathe of it and diverted from her original intention to its removal. Finding the proper spell, she sent the poor creature back to the ether. Taking a breath and tossing aside the volume she had been searching, she chose another book and began to explore its contents. The results were predominately the same. She managed to clear the contents of the mantelpiece, light and later extinguish candles and even change the color of the bed linens, but she had still yet to summon the snake demon. Exhausted, she fell asleep, the book of incantations still cradled in her arms.

After a fitful hour or two of sleep, Shahlāan awoke. It was still dark out, so she knew she had not been asleep for long. Snippets of a dream remained in her head, a dream about a book with the spell she had been searching so long to find. She examined the book she had fallen asleep with, but she did not recognize it as the book from her dream. Tossing it aside, she moved across her room to the pile of books she had brought up from the library. Surely, she would find the book from her dreams in this pile. One by one, she carefully examined the binding of each book, attempting to match it to the image from her dream. She closely examined each and every book in the pile but could not find it. Frustrated, she plopped herself on the floor, placing her head in her hands and tearing at her hair. It was then that she saw it. The book she had tossed aside after ridding her room of the rabbit. It had slid beneath her bedside table. Crawling over, she pulled the book from its hiding place and carefully looked over the binding. This was it! This was the book from her dream! Now, she simply had to find the correct incantation. How difficult would that be?

In her eagerness and excitement, Shahlāan could not remember which spells she had uttered when she had previously begun searching through the tome. Starting carefully at the first page, she began slowly reading the text, trying to determine what the result of each bewitchment would be before uttering the words. With each page, her excitement continued to build. She knew she was only pages away from being touched by a power greater than she had ever experienced. And, if the Fortunes smiled upon her, she would be graced with a wonderful new life, a life of power and stature in the world beyond the castle's stifling walls.

Shahlāan recognized the chant that had created the rabbit, followed by the one that sent it back to whence it had come. Next, a spell that appeared to produce boils on the face; a spell for some form of precipitation, although she could not tell which; a spell to entice the loyalty of a feline familiar, a cat, she assumed. And, then, there it was! An incantation to summon a demon! It did not make specific mention of the deity it may produce, but she knew she could summon the snake demon by somehow inserting his name or reference into the chant. Her heart was beating furiously and a lump formed in her throat.

Shahlāan silently said the words in her mind, inserting the name of the snake demon, Sutek, where she thought it should be, silently rehearsing to ensure she got it right. After a few practice runs in her mind, she took a deep breath, closed her eyes, and prepared to recite the words that would change her world forever.

"From the moons above to the land below and the shadow realms beyond, I call out to you, Lord Sutek, to come to me and extend to me your favor. Powerful and omnipotent mentor, show yourself to me."

Shahlāan opened her eyes and scanned the room. Although everything appeared out of focus, she saw nothing. Lack of sleep must be getting the best of her, she thought. And then, to her surprise, a blurred image began to appear as a mist in the center of the room. A figure appeared gather itself from the mist, yellow slit eyes penetrating the darkness like two beacons from a foggy shore. A black leathery cloak enveloping his body, the maroon lined hood standing up behind his head like the hood of a cobra. She had been successful! She had summoned Sutek, the snake demon!

Shahlāan dropped to her knees and bowed before him. "My Master, you finally show yourself to me. Ask of me whatever you will for I am but your humble servant."

"You have done well, little one," he almost hissed. His eyes carefully scanned the room, recording every feature of his surroundings, his forked tongue periodically reaching out from between his lips to taste the air. "I praise you for your persistence. It is through your efforts that I am able to present myself to you at this place and time. Because of you, I have broken the bonds of magic that had me imprisoned and can now transcend the boundaries of my serpent form to carry out the will of the Master. Once events have been put in motion, the Chosen shall pave the way for the Master to return and ensure a balance of the powers that control the universe. You are the key to setting events in motion. Arise, child, and accept your proper place in the history of all that is yet to come."

Shahlāan got up from her knees. "I am honored to be in your presence." She bowed to Sutek. "I am here to do you bidding, Master."

Sutek slowly walked around his liberator, sizing her up as if she were his quarry. "But if only I were the Master. I am but an instrument, the conduit by which the Master interacts with this world. I serve as his itinerant proxy, engaging with those he chooses to be brought into the fold."

"Then I am here to do the bidding of the Master, as instructed by his most capable proxy."

"The Master has a task that only you are able to complete. It is your destiny to fulfill that which was prophesized at Korham so many years ago. We have waited long for this moment when the actions shall be put in motion to awaken him of his eternal slumber and relieve him of his bonds. Your incantation has released me from my serpent form. It brings immense pleasure to me to know I must no longer wander the land slithering upon my belly. For that, I am most gracious, and at the Master's command, I have a gift for you. It will ultimately release you from the bonds of this castle and free you of this claustrophobic world."

Shahlāan beamed. Her mind began to race with thoughts of the future. Finally, she would be able to go beyond the prison that was this castle and her life within it. Never again would she feel inferior to anyone. She was to be revered and powerful, a force to be reckoned with, and all those from her past that had shown her any disrespect would now cower before her.

Sutek's words brought Shahlāan out of her thoughts. "Come. It is time. The Master has empowered me to present you with a token of his power; a power that shall grow within you; a power that, in time, will change the world." His cloak parted slightly and what appeared to be the head of a cobra appeared from between his legs. "Give yourself to me, now, my child. The rewards of my pleasure shall be yours."

Shahlāan gasped slightly at the sight of his grotesquely misshapen manhood and stepped back. Her eyes quickly moved up to his, fearfully questioning what it was he wanted of her. Unlike her sister, Shahlāan had yet to experience a man.

"Relax, child. There is nothing to fear." His eyes pierced through her being, captivating her. "Our union shall be a new beginning for the universe. It is as the words of those that preceded us describe. You shall bear the seed from which the *Ahnálian*, the New Beginning, shall grow."

The demon reached out with his hand and gently placed two scaly fingers along the curve of her jaw. His touch sent shivers throughout her body. Slowly, he retrieved his hand, maintaining contact with her cheek, and she unconsciously followed. Shahlāan let her robe fall open exposing her milk-white skin. Shrugging it off her shoulders, it fell to the floor, forming a silky puddle of royal blue at her feet. The demon scanned her exposed body up and down, an evil smile forming on his face.

"I must thank the Master for this most pleasing opportunity." Sutek quickly regained his composure. "But, now, it is time for us to seal our arrangement," he hissed.

He wrapped her naked body in his cloak and pulled her close, her soft virginal-white skin juxtaposed against his hardened smoke-gray scales. Shahlāan placed her hands over his shoulders and around his neck as he drew her closer. Placing her head on his shoulder, she could feel his breath upon her neck. His smooth, scaly fingers stroked the small of her back and up to her shoulders. Picking her head up, she looked into his eyes and then kissed him. The smooth scales of his lips were oddly arousing, his strong muscular shoulders comforting. She let her hands slide across his chest and down to his belly. What would be his pectorals and abdominals in a normal man were well defined by smooth but stiff scales. She instinctively wrapped her hands around his back, pulling herself closer to him, letting her hands drop to his scuted buttocks. Sutek wrapped her tightly in his embrace. His scaly hands groped at her naked flesh, now flush with desire. Her breathing quickened as her arousal intensified, heightened by his every sensual touch. She felt a special warmth from within that she had never experienced before and it felt good. Overcome by the moment, she did not notice the phallic snake wrap itself around her upper thigh and nudge its way slowly towards her sex. When she felt the snakehead part her labia, she did nothing to stop it. She wanted the power the Master promised would come from a union with the demon, but, then again, she was fearful. She had always been taught the propriety of one's virginity, but the desire to give herself up to this union and the power it was sure to bring was stronger than any teachings she had received. Her mind was racing with conflicting thoughts of what she was doing but her body was giving itself to him willingly as if it had a mind of its own. She felt the serpentine phallus enter her sex and a rush of warmth enveloped her body.

Sutek could see in her eyes that she was his. She had cast away all her inhibitions and released herself completely to him. He coiled his arms around her tighter and tighter, bringing her body ever closer, squeezing her until she could barely catch her breath. Now that she was acquiescent, it was time to plant the seed.

The demon thrust himself deep inside. She felt a sharp, quick pain as his persistent efforts tore her hymen followed by the intense burning pain of what felt to her like the piercing of a needle deep within her. The phallus swelled within her, locking her to the demon like a bitch in heat. Shahlāan was overcome by the pain of countless 'snake bites,' over and over, inside her womanhood. She had always been told that sex was not necessarily pleasurable for a woman, but had thought the warnings were just a means to persuade her not to indulge. Why would her sister sneak off to be with the stable boys if it was like this? Connected to her newfound lover, she would have to endure this experience, pleasurable or not, until their arrangement was full consummated.

A SHRIEK ECHOED THROUGH the cavernous halls of the castle. Startled, the Queen and her ladies turned to face the direction of the sound. The ladies looked at each other, searching for an answer for what they had just heard.

The Queen dropped her book to her lap again in disgust. "What has that child done now? Ahlee, go fetch your sister. See what sort of mischief she has done to herself now."

"Yes, Mum-ma!" Ahlāan skipped off up the stairs, a mischievous smile etched across her face. Whatever her sister had done now would certainly raise the ire of their mother.

AHLĀAN FOUND HER SISTER, passed out, naked on the cold stone floor of her room. "Shah! Shah! What have you done?" She fell to the floor and cradled her sister's head in her lap.

"Shah, wake up!" She gently slapped her sister on the cheeks, desperately attempting to rouse her. "Shah!" The more frantic she became, the more forceful her slaps became until finally Shahlāan's hand snapped out and grabbed Ahlāan by the wrist, ending her frantic buffeting.

"Stop hitting me, you crazy bitch! I'm fine. Just leave me be."

"Fine? I come to find you passed out on the floor, naked as the day you took leave of the womb and you tell me you're fine? How did you come about to be this way? What have you done this time?"

"I have done nothing. Just leave me be!"

"No! I will not leave you be, not when I find you here, like this. Your dabbling in the art of sorcery will surely be the death of you and I intend to make sure ***that*** does not happen."

Shahlāan picked herself up off the floor. "Fine. If you must know, then I will tell you. But it has nothing to do with sorcery. And what I tell you in this moment must remain a secret between two sisters. Do you agree?"

Intrigued, Ahlāan did not hesitate to agree. "Yes, yes. Of course I agree. Please, tell me what happened here."

"If you must know, tonight, I have become a woman. I have experienced carnal pleasures such that you could only dream of, the union of two souls in a bond that is only exceeded by the forces that move the universe." She retrieved her robe from the floor, and draped it over her shoulders.

"A man? In this castle? In your quarters? Without the knowledge of anyone else in this house?"

Shahlāan scoffed. "Don't be silly. How would I ever get a man into this castle without someone, somewhere, seeing him?"

Ahlāan stared at her incredulously for a moment. "Well, someone was up here tonight, by your own admission. This room, and you, smell of sex! You were up here with a man. I know it!" She wagged a finger at her younger sister. "Wait till I tell Mum-ma about ***this***!"

Shahlāan grabbed her sister by the wrist and sharply pulled her back so that their noses were nearly touching. Glaring into her sister's eyes, she hissed through her clenched teeth, "Remember our pact, dear sister. Do no such thing, or I will tell Mum-ma of ***your*** indiscretions with the little stable boys! I'm surprised you can identify the smell of sex without the intermingled odors of horse shit and bedding straw! I, dear sister, have been with a man. A man of such power and stature, the likes of which you shall never know. Far and beyond any of your illicit adolescent rendezvous. I dare say Mum-ma would not look so approving of your promiscuity, wiggling your naked little ass in the hay, and offering your cunny to every stable hand that flashes you a smile."

Ahlāan snatched her hand away, rubbing at the imprint of fingers left by her sister's firm grip. She conceded, grudgingly. "As you wish, then. I will honor our pact. But, damned you, Shah, be more careful! If Mum-ma was to find a strange man about the castle, it would surely be the death of him and, quite possibly, you."

Shahlāan reached over to her sister's dress and smugly removed a stray piece of straw, holding it up for her sister to see. "I am not the only one that should practice a little discretion, Ahlee. Use care, dear sister. It would be quite embarrassing if you were to be found naked in the stables knotted like a bitch to a common stable boy, grunting about like a pig and smelling of horse excrement."

Ahlāan shot an angry stare at Shahlāan and stormed out of the room. Shahlāan wrapped herself in her robe and cinched it up. Walking over to her bed, she lay herself down, haughty with the events of the evening, a perverse smile etched upon her face.

IN A SMALL, STONE WALLED room, a magician sat hunched over a table reading a book of spells and incantations. Abruptly sitting straight up, he cocked his head and blinked. He could feel it. The time was now at hand. The seeds of darkness had once again been sown on Xerses.

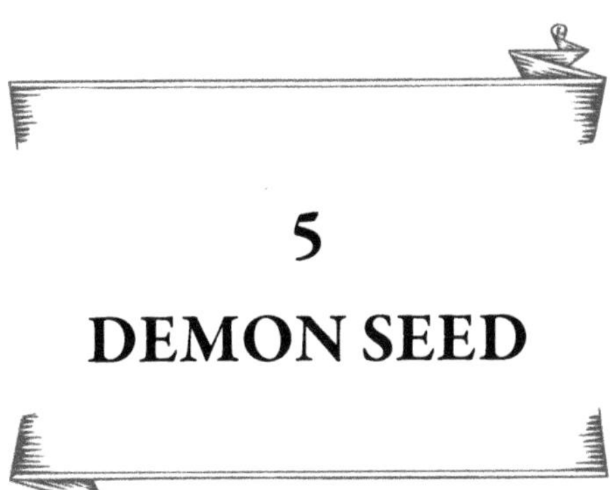

5
DEMON SEED

FOR ALL OUTWARD APPEARANCES, it seemed no less than a typical evening in *eht Vilna Sahnah*. A huge fire roared in the immense fireplace of the Great Hall. The ladies were all attending to their sewing or needlework, and the staff was busy cleaning and preparing for the day to come. However, a tension that had everyone on guard hung heavy in the air. Although the date of conception was unknown to all, since the Queen's youngest daughter's pregnancy had begun to show, the feeling about the castle had changed dramatically. Shahlāan had become miserable as soon as her belly had begun to grow, which, rather unusually, had been a mere few weeks into her pregnancy. With each advancing week, her mood had become fouler. She was far more demanding than ever, often asking the impossible of the staff and then belittling them when they failed to produce. Now, a mere nine weeks into her pregnancy, she looked as though nine months pregnant, and her mood was beyond tolerable. Indeed, life in the castle had become almost unbearable. No one could predict when or if she would fly into a rage or if she would simply brood, remaining silent to everyone and everything.

Shahlāan spent her days and nights wandering the halls of the castle keep, carrying her burden before her like a massive pumpkin. It had been mere weeks since her encounter with the demon but it was more than apparent to anyone that her belly was full of new life. Although she felt as if she were carrying a boulder within her, it was alive and kicked and moved of its own free will. Her discomfort increased daily, as the being within her seemed to grow by the hour, stretching the flesh of her abdomen to near breaking. Only walking had the effect of temporarily settling the unborn child, making her burden almost bearable.

"I have never seen such a pregnancy, Mum. The child has grown so quickly within her. It's unnatural. A number of the ladies are terrified to be near to her. They fear it the work of *Uglebdek* himself." Ebby herself was fearful, not of demonic possession, but of Shahlāan, her vicious disposition, and her penchant for lashing out violently at anyone and anything. She spent as little time as necessary in the presence of the princess. It may simply have been the unusual circumstances of her pregnancy, but the princess was constantly in an especially foul mood. She was with child, she was uncomfortable, and she wanted everyone in the world to suffer along with her.

"Ebby, I know not what to make of it myself. It is indeed very unnatural, although I have nothing but my own pregnancy and common knowledge to judge it by. Most certainly it is her condition that makes her particularly frightful. It must be intolerable. Even with twins, I had not grown to such size until the few days immediately before childbirth. I fear for her well-being."

"I fear for the wellbeing of the entire castle, My Lady. The girl may indeed be in a frightful state, but the way she has been treating the staff has put everyone on edge. No one knows if she will erupt and lash out or simply storm off to be with herself and her own discomfort. And what should happen if she decides to cast one of her incantations? Which one of us is bound to disappear in a flash of light and a wisp of smoke?"

"I understand, Ebby. I will see what I can do. Perhaps the Lady Ilsinga will have a remedy for her hardship. I will call upon her in the morn."

"The mistresses of the household, myself included, will surely appreciate your efforts, my Lady. I pray the witch has a cure to make your daughter's hardship more bearable."

Early the following morning, Queen Isella called for the healer, Lady Ilsinga. Since the time of King Olen's death, Ilsinga had remained a trusted servant and advisor. The healer reported to the Queen immediately.

Ilsinga entered the room with a slight bow. "You have requested my presence, my ladyship?"

The Queen rose to meet her. "I appreciate your immediate attendance, Madame healer. There is a problem and I need your advice. It concerns my youngest daughter and the circumstances surrounding her pregnancy."

“I must admit I am not the most knowledgeable of the concerns of childbearing, my ladyship. Perhaps a consult with a doula is in order?”

The Queen took Ilsinga by the hand and led her to a chair, motioning for her to sit. “I am not certain a midwife would be able to assist in this matter. Shahlāan had only begun to show a mere nine weeks ago. Today, as if full-term, her belly is distended like she is carrying a prize pumpkin. I am beside myself, not knowing what to do. She is miserable and in great distress. Perhaps you could examine her and the child, to make sure everything is as it should be.”

"If that is what you request of me, my ladyship, then I shall do as commanded. When can I see the expectant mother?"

The Queen stood from her chair, the sorceress immediately following in reverence. “Allow me to find her and see if she is amenable to an examination. I shall be but a few moments.”

Lady Ilsinga bowed. “Of course, my ladyship.”

The Queen left the medicine woman and went to find Shahlāan. She found her, in her room, pacing the floor, trying to support her unborn child in a way that would provide some relief.

“Oh, my dear girl. It pains me to see you like this. I have called for Lady Ilsinga and she is willing to try to help you. Come. Let her take a look.”

“That crazy witch? Are you mad?” Shahlāan pulled away. “I think not! Why would I let that lunatic touch me?”

The Queen implored her daughter to listen. “Shah, do not be like that. Just let her look. It doesn’t matter to me if she is the best doctor in the land or a simple midwife. If she can ease your discomfort, I think it is worth looking into. Would you not want some relief from this?”

Shahlāan sat down on the edge of her bed, exhausted. “Yes, Mum-ma. You are right. I will let her look, but I do not want her chanting over me and I will not take anything from her that she is not willing to eat or drink herself!”

“Agreed, my child. May I bring her up?”

“Yes, Mum-ma, but please hurry. I cannot remain seated for too long or it becomes more than I can bear.”

The Queen left and returned with the medicine woman. “This is my daughter, Shahlāan. She has agreed to allow your assistance.”

Shahlāan stared intently at the witch as she approached.

"I sense I am not trusted. Please, calm yourself, child. I mean you no harm."

Shahlāan did not let her guard down, remaining vigilant to the witch's every move. "I do not want you chanting over me, witch! I have studied incantations and I understand the power that the simplest of words possess. You will not be placing me under any of your spells."

"Please, child, I will not be chanting over you. I am simply going to examine you and your condition to try and figure out why you have advanced so quickly and ensure the babe is fine." She held her hand out towards Shahlāan's belly. "May I?"

Shahlāan nodded, anxiously allowing the witch to touch her belly. Her touch was gentle and placed the expectant mother slowly at ease.

As she gently probed Shahlāan's belly, Lady Ilsinga suddenly sat straight up, eyes wide open as if in fear. The Queen noticed and questioned her. "Is everything alright? Is there a problem?"

The witch quickly removed her hand and stood up. "No, there is nothing wrong. The babe is nearly full term and appears to be healthy."

"Then what of her discomfort, what might you be able to do for my daughter?"

"Your daughter's misery is nearly at its end. The birth is imminent. I suspect in the next few days. I suggest she continue walking and not to sit, but to lie on her side, instead. That should support the babe and provide some relief. But I must be going now." Lady Ilsinga hastily left the room. The Queen watched her leave, perplexed.

Once away from the room, Lady Ilsinga quickly made her way out of the castle and back to her home. Something was not right with that pregnancy, something not human. She could sense evil, a feeling she had not felt since the death of King Heidel. This pregnancy and the birth of this child could not lead to anything good.

LITTLE KNOWN OUTSIDE of the family, except to the most trusted of servants, her sister was also with child. But, unlike her twin, Ahlāan had yet to exhibit any of the outward signs of pregnancy that were so evident with

Shahlāan, save the occasional bout with nausea that was easily explained away as an aversion to the previous evening's meal. The Queen was led to believe the father had been one of a number of courtiers from neighboring kingdoms that had come to call last month, but Ahlāan knew better. She had rebuffed each and every advance from the self-absorbed young noblemen that had come to call. Ahlāan knew it had to be one of the stable boys, just as her sister had accused her of the night she found her passed out on her bedroom floor. Their strong athletic frames were the only bodies with which she desired to have intimate contact, their strong, rough hands the only hands she wished to touch her skin. Certainly, Shah felt the same. And not one of them would pass up the opportunity to lie with a beautiful princess. But which one may have fathered her unborn child... she did not know?

SHAHLĀAN WAS ROAMING the halls of the castle as had become her daily practice. Ebby came upon her in one of the castle's large stone staircases. Her struggle to climb the stairs was evident. Ebby reached out to help her. "Here, child, let me help you."

Shahlāan swatted her hand away. "Let me be, woman! What help could a withered old hag like yourself be to the likes of me?"

Shocked and offended, Ebby struck back. "As you wish, princess, but hear my words when I tell you, the day will come when you need the aid of your tired old nursemaid and she will no longer be on this earth to carry your brazier to your quarters, braid your hair, or assist you up and down these stairs. Maybe then you will understand the folly of your sour attitude. Until that day, be mindful of the enemies you create with your acid tongue."

"And you should be mindful of whom ***you*** are addressing as well, for I am the last person in this kingdom, no, on this ***earth***, that you ever want to become your enemy!"

The two women stared each other down for a moment before Ebby, realizing the precarious position she was putting herself in, broke her gaze and continued down the stairs to the Great Hall. Shahlāan continued her way up the stairs.

At long last, Shahlāan reached the top of the stairs and started her way down the hallway. Laboring with every movement, she shuffled her feet along the stone floor, slowly working her way towards her quarters. Every few feet, she would stop and prop herself up against the wall, trying to catch her breath, both hands beneath her greatly distended abdomen in a vain attempt to provide some support to her burden and relief from the stresses it was placing upon her back. A few moments rest and she would shuffle along again.

As she stopped to rest once more, a searing pain slashed across Shahlāan's lower abdomen, sending her to her knees. Unable to right herself, she bellowed for help.

"Ebby! Ebby, you lazy ignorant whore! Why aren't you by my side when I need you! Ebby! Mum-ma! Ahlee! Why doesn't anyone answer my call?"

"Insolent child," Ebby hissed beneath her breath as she struggled to get her old bones up from her chair and on her way back up the stairs to where she had last seen Shahlāan. "Knows not where she is going or where she has been. Only knows what she wants ***now*** and as quickly changes her mind as she receives it."

Ebby turned to the Queen. "I will attend to her, Mum," she huffed, and began making her way towards the stairs.

Shahlāan felt something parting deep within her body. The pain was beyond belief. Blood began to spot the front of her smock and her mood quickly changed from anger to shock to absolute terror. Something was definitely not right, not normal, and she had no idea what to make of it or how to handle the situation. Her initial screams for help elevated to more frantic screams of terror laced with every imaginable profanity.

Queen Isella cocked her head as she listened to her daughter's rampage in the hallway above. Her demeanor had changed, but the Queen could not place how. Her eyes widened as a long, blood-curdling scream punctuated the string of foul epithets emanating from up the stairs, stopping everyone in their tracks. And then all was silent.

The old nursemaid quickened her pace to as near to a run as her old legs would carry her. Something was not right and, no matter how petulant the young girl might be at times; this was no time to hold on to past transgressions.

Ahlāan had stopped what she was doing along with everyone else when she first heard Shahlāan start her rant but quickly rose from her seat in the Great Hall as her sister's screams became silence and rushed to be by her twin's side. She passed the elderly nursemaid, bounding up the staircase, two and three stairs at a time, to where her sister's screams had been coming from.

EBBY REACHED THE TOP of the staircase and peered down the long, dimly-lit hall. Nearly a third the way down she could make out a huddled mass on the floor. As she approached, she could see Ahlāan on the floor, Shahlāan's head cradled in her lap. She was rocking back and forth, sobbing, and stroking her sister's hair. Unintelligible mumbling abruptly interrupted by the staccato of her uncontrollable sobbing was all that Ebby could make out. Shahlāan stared lifelessly from her sister's lap, her face ashen with the pall of death, her mouth slightly agape as if contemplating her next expletive-filled diatribe. But there would be no more words. Shahlāan's smock was bloodstained and torn to shreds in the front, revealing a large gaping wound. Beside her lifeless body, in a pool of blood and viscera, lay a perfectly formed baby boy, normal in all aspects save his piercing yellow eyes. The babe cried not once, but was oddly alert, those eyes seeking out and absorbing all that was within his sight.

"Ahlee, what is the meaning of this? What have you done to your sister?"

Ahlāan struggled to compose herself enough to communicate. "Nothing, Ebby, nothing. This is how I came upon her, torn open and bleeding with her babe upon the floor."

Ebby looked down at the baby. As their eyes met, she thought she observed the eyes change from yellow to ice-cold gray, but she passed it off as a figment of her imagination, born from the chaos of the moment. No human being possessed yellow eyes.

Presently, the Queen arrived, immediately hysterical at the sight of her lifeless daughter on the floor. Falling to the floor beside her two daughters, the Queen began to cry out for help. "Shah! Shah! My baby girl, my little princess, what happened here? Who has done this to you? Somebody, please help her! Ebby! Ebby! Do something!"

"Mum, I'm afraid there is nothing anyone can do. The wound is far too large, the bleeding far too great. She has passed too far from this life to be brought back. I am sorry. I wish there was something I could do."

Imploring, Queen Isella begged her trusted servant for answers. "But why? What happened here? Who did this to my little girl?"

"I can only assume that the discomfort of carrying such a large child within must have driven her mad enough to attempt to rip it out and free herself of the burden. I have often questioned her mental stability, but I would have never predicted her to be capable of this. But it must be the case, for there was no one else in the hall when Ahlee arrived."

The infant moved and cooed a little, attracting the queen's attention. Ebby's stare moved from the babe to the queen.

"Ebby, remove that thing from my sight. I cannot bear to look at it a moment longer."

"But, M'lady, it is your daughter's child, your grandson."

"I said remove it from my sight! It is neither my grandchild nor the child of my little girl! It is *aszadha*, and I want it out of my sight!"

Ebby wrapped the babe in her apron, wiping away some of the mess from his face and hands. In doing so, she noticed the child had oddly well-formed fingernails, beneath which she could clearly see small shreds of flesh. Shahlāan had not removed the child to relieve herself of the discomfort. The babe had removed itself! It was all beginning to make sense to her; the unusual pregnancy, the yellow eyes now steel gray, the wounds, and the fingernails. This was not a mortal child, but the offspring of something evil.

"Mum, where shall I take the child for the time being?"

"Take it nowhere! That ***thing*** is the reason my dear Shah took her life! There was something unnatural about it from the beginning, and I care not to know what it might have been. Dispose of it. I do not want it in my sight, nor do I want it in this castle!"

Ebby took the child from the hallway as quickly as she could without causing suspicion. She knew the Queen was right, the baby had to be removed, but how could one dispose of an infant and have any satisfaction in it? She left the queen and Ahlāan to their mourning and began to contemplate what needed to be done and how things would be explained away. First, she would have to deal with the child. The queen had obviously no desire to be anywhere near it. From her perspective, her daughter had taken her own life because of the babe and she harbored no desire to provide it with the basic necessities for existence. Ebby was best off disposing of it as quickly as possible. And, second, how to explain the death of the princess as well as what happened to her unborn child. All within the castle were aware of her pregnancy. Quite simply, it would be told that the princess had succumbed to complications of the pregnancy and that neither she nor the unborn babe survived. All the while, as she made her way, the babe remained surprisingly silent.

Ebby called for her old friend, Seamus, now Master of the Watch.

"By order of Queen Isella, this child must be cast out of the kingdom in absolute secrecy. No one must ever know that it was ever here, from whence it came, or the circumstances behind its demise. Is that understood?"

"Yes, ma'am."

"If anyone should ever ask, this baby never existed. You know nothing of it. Understood?"

"Yes, ma'am. If it is the wish of the Queen, I shall take knowledge of this child with me to my death."

"Then, together, we shall harbor the agony of that knowledge for the rest of our days."

Ebby handed the bundle to the watchman. He placed it securely beneath his cloak and retreated through the bowels of the keep so as not to attract any attention. Once outside, he made his way back to his post upon the outer wall. Reaching his post, he walked several yards away from the tower and prepared to toss the infant from the parapet.

"Forgive me, child," he said as he peeled the blanket away from the baby's face. "Know what I do is in fear for my own life, for if I do not carry out the orders of the Queen, I may not see the light of the next coming day. May *Ahlok* watch over you."

Seamus cast the infant over the outer palisade and into the darkness. There was an audible thud and the sound of something rolling off into the rushes, but he did not hear the wail of a babe at any time. The impact of the fall had apparently killed the infant instantly. He would be able to take some solace from that fact.

As he walked back along the palisade towards the tower, a nearly inaudible noise caught his attention, almost like the sound of something sliding through the rushes below. Dismissing it as a fox or other nocturnal scavenger dragging off the small corpse, the watchman returned quickly to his post.

6
THE RISE OF DARKNESS

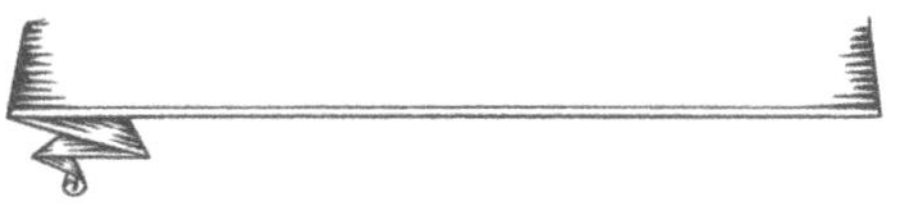

6093 E.K.

Roga entered his office. The room, with its large, vaulted ceiling, was carefully hand-hewn from the dark-gray basalt of the now-dormant volcano that housed his aerial forces. The doors, cabinetry and decorative touches were carefully crafted in exquisite detail from wenge and purpleheart. A central wrought chandelier above his mahogany desk and dragon-leather upholstered chair illuminated the otherwise dark space with its two-dozen oil lamps. The room's construction exuded testosterone and entitlement. He walked straight past his desk, the sound of his footsteps on the stone floor harsh, regular, and deliberate. As he approached a great tome lying open on a pedestal in an ornate alcove at the opposite side of the room, he clicked his boot heels together and gave a curt bow. *Eht Olheb Ahnan*, The Book of Beginnings. It was one of many known volumes containing all the stories and songs that composed the Prophecy of Korham. Roga had selected the book to be the guide by which he intended to gain control and rule over the entire mainland.

However, the book was not his ultimate destination. He had more pressing business elsewhere. Stepping around the bookstand, he approached the ornately decorated wall behind it. Pressing a hidden mechanism, a panel in the wall unlocked and pivoted on its center, revealing a darkened hall behind. A few oil lamps dimly lit the space, barely enough to see. As he entered, the panel closed behind him without a sound.

Roga shuffled slightly towards the area lit by the oil lamps, his eyes slowly adjusting to the darkness. His scuffling footsteps echoed out of the dark recesses. The space was obviously much larger than it seemed. As he approached the dimly lit space, a deep voice addressed him, unheard in the room but loudly booming within his head.

"*Roga, my faithful and loyal child, you honor me once again with your presence.*" Immediately before the warlord, the vague silhouette of a prone figure on a bier was barely discernible. "*And to what do I owe the pleasure of your return?*"

"Master, the siege has begun. We made our first foray to the mainland near Tendira today and laid waste to all we could see with absolutely no resistance. I predict it shall not be much longer before we have completed your mission."

"*Very good, my child, but use care. Never are things exactly as they seem. A haughty warlord may soon find himself confronted by a surprisingly cunning adversary. Over-confidence has been the downfall of many a promising crusade and I prefer that this is not one of them. Discretion and caution are, at times, the best strategy.*" The figure upon the bier never so much as twitched, lying completely still as he addressed his servant.

"I shall take your words to task, Master. I will not underestimate the abilities of the Tendirans. I have no intentions of failing you."

"*I trust you shall not. If you keep your head about yourself, our ultimate goals shall soon be at hand. You have done well, but there is one more thing that I must ask of you. I sense a kindred soul amongst the Tendirans, the seed of Sutek, the snake demon. His energy has only recently become known to me. He was born under the eye of the Purple Wanderer, the child of the Evening star, the sister star of dusk. His mother died during childbirth and the babe was cast out to die. The snake demon was able to ensure his survival. He should be brought to you and nurtured, for as the son of the Evening Star, he is a key element spoken of in the songs. Under your tutelage, he shall become a great warrior and serve our cause well.*"

"I will have him sought out and brought to my side immediately, my liege. But, how shall I know him?"

"*I can sense him, but I cannot see him. His location among the Tendirans remains a mystery to me. Send a contingent to the Speaker. There you will learn all you need to know. Find the young man and educate him in our doctrine. Teach him our ways. Most important, make him feel welcome and wanted.*"

"I humbly accept your command to find and train the snake demon's progeny, and I will begin by seeking the wisdom of the Speaker. You shall not be displeased."

"*Good, my son. After you have learned how to find the Tendiran, ask the Speaker about the means to secure domination over the mainland. Listen well and victory shall be yours.*"

"It shall be as you ask, my Lord."

"*I sense there is another, a family member, possibly a cousin. This one is not a candidate for our cause and may indeed become an adversary.*" There was a moment of silence. "*You are a loyal servant, my child. I am always pleased with your accomplishments. Keep your wits about you and your emotions in check and you will achieve our goals with ease. I know you are more than capable.*"

"I am humbled by your confidence in me. It is my duty and pleasure to serve you well, my Lord. It shall be as you wish."

"*I would expect nothing less. Now go. Seek the wisdom of the Speaker and find the Tendiran.*"

Roga bowed. "With pleasure, master."

The figure on the bier slowly faded into the darkness, as Roga remained standing with his head bowed. As it faded from view, the warlord turned quickly on point and walked towards the exit, his heels once again resonating upon the stone floor.

ROGA THE INTERROGATOR, Warlord of the Khorgian War Machine, was born to an aristocratic family in the city of Oro, the lone metropolitan domain on the Isle of Khorgia. At an early age, he was sent off to a boarding school that molded young men through the use of military discipline. Not wanting to be away from home and everything he had known; his first years were tough. His peers exploited this weakness, teasing and pushing him around. The humiliation fueled a fire within him to become the strongest, the smartest, the best at everything he experienced. He would avenge his ignominy and make his tormentors pay. He practiced every lesson until he excelled, read every book he could get his hands upon, and worked tirelessly to strengthen his body. By his mid-teens, Roga was head of his class; highly regarded by his instructors and well respected (some would say feared) by his peers. He joined the newly formed Dragon Guard upon finishing school and quickly rose up the ranks. The Dragon Guard grew into the elite fighting force of the Khorgians, and the smartest and strongest among them became commander: Roga.

But what good was an elite fighting force when everyone was at peace? Battle simulations and war games were boring playtime activities. Roga aspired for more. He wanted to lead more than the Dragon Guard. He wanted to govern all of Khorgia... and beyond. He made a smooth transition from military to political leader and was readily accepted by the masses. His rule was characterized by a structured and orderly regime, military in nature. He understood that defensive armies risked complacency, allowing their skills to winnow away. The Khorgians would not become a complacent military under Roga's watch. They needed an adversary and he needed a means to which he could aspire to greatness. The populace would naturally accept a victorious commander as a great and exalted leader.

A great leader should not only be highly educated and trained in the ways of warfare, but worldly and wise as well. Roga began to gather ancient books and read, increasing his knowledge of the past and understanding of the present exponentially. He found a compelling interest in the words of the prophets and how their predictions had come to reality. It was through his study of the old tomes that Roga became better aware of the world around him and began to formulate a plan for his own rise to great power. From the pages of the *Olheb Ahnan*, he found the recipe from which he would create his future. A man of greatness would come to a city named Korham and be greeted by the Gatekeeper. This man would lead Ahnálian, the new beginning, a time of change and promise. Roga was intent on being that man of greatness.

ROGA EMERGED FROM THE hidden chamber. The secret panel closed behind him as before, concealing everything beyond from view. Stopping before the *Olheb Ahnan* he clicked his boot heels together and gave a curt bow once again. He had his instructions and he would be sure to implement them to the satisfaction of his Master. Sitting at his desk, he beckoned for his assistant.

"Minarik, I require your presence."

Roga's manservant appeared in the doorway. "Yes, My Lord. You called?"

The warlord's eyes did not leave the book upon his desk as he addressed his servant. "Yes, I have several tasks that I need you to complete for me. I am confident that you can carry them out as intended."

"Of course, My Lord."

"Good. I need you to gather a contingent to travel to the Speaker and seek an audience. I have become aware of a comrade, a brother, in a far-off land. He is the offspring of the Snake Demon, Sutek, and is residing somewhere in Tendira. Have the contingent request from the Speaker the means to locate him so that I might bring him into the fold."

"It is as good as done, My Lord. Is there more?"

"The contingent should ask of the Speaker what the keys to victory in our battle against the mainland might be. I am certain we will encounter more strenuous resistance at some point in the future. If we are aware of the challenges before us and can plan accordingly, such resistance will be easily thwarted."

"As you wish, my Lord. I will instruct them to gather the information necessary to defeat the Tendirans through counsel with the Speaker. Is that all?"

"No. I have one more thing I wish for you to take care of. Arrange a meeting with Governor Zea, here, in my quarters. I have some things I need to discuss with him."

"At your command, My Lord."

Roga looked up from his desk. "When he arrives, make sure Zea is well taken care of until I am free to attend to him. This meeting is of the utmost importance and I require his... undivided attention. I'm sure you understand and can manage that."

Minarik bowed and clicked his heels. "I understand, My Lord. I will ensure Governor Zea is... well prepared for your meeting." Roga's manservant turned and left the room, duty-bound to complete the tasks assigned by his master, leaving the warlord alone to his thoughts.

FOUR DRAGONS CROSSED the Touphorus Sea in tight formation under the cover of darkness, heading for the mainland north of the Souliban. In the distance, a single, snow-capped peak was visible, sprouting forth from the desert wasteland. The Silver Mountain, known to locals as the Wailing Mountain, was the home of the Speaker and the dragons were making a beeline for the foothills.

After flying to the base of the Silver Mountain, the four riders dismounted, secured their beasts, and began their climb to the Speaker. The trail meandered upwards through the crags and hollows of the foothills, well-worn but treacherous. In the distance, magnificent waterfalls cascaded from high ledges to the depths of the valleys below. The verdant slopes and valleys were a stark contrast to the desert waste that surrounded the mount. The beauty of the scene masked how dangerous this journey would be.

The warm temperatures of the foothills quickly gave way to the frigid rarified air of the heights. Snow and ice replaced the greenery and made traveling on the trail precarious. The persistent wind wicked away body heat as fast as a man could generate it, quickly chilling to the core, and the constant buffeting worked endlessly to disrupt a man's balance and send him careening to his death in the crevasses below. This was as inhospitable of an environment as any of the men had ever encountered, and they were far from reaching their final destination. Snow and sleet blew up with the wind, coating them in thin icy cocoons. Their eyes, noses, and mouths were the only features evident to the outside world. With steadfast determination, they continued to their journey's end.

As they approached the cave of the Speaker, the explanation behind the name locals had given the mountain became evident. The constant wind blowing into and across the mouth of the cave generated a sound reminiscent of the wail a widow makes at the grave. The noise echoed down the mountainside, reverberating through the valleys. The four riders entered the cave, as much to seek shelter from the elements as to gain an audience with the Speaker. With a mere step inside the cave, the wind disappeared and the temperature rose to a level resembling comfortable. Quickly shaking off their shrouds of snow and frost, the riders proceeded further, following lit oil lamps that hung on the cave walls, eventually rounding a corner to encounter an ornate entranceway. Two immense wooden doors flanked by four heavily armed behemoths prevented further access. From a small alcove, the figure of a man in silken robes appeared. He was old with scant white hair, a tuft of white that was barely passable as a beard, and an unkempt mustache. Slightly bent over, he approached the four.

"Welcome, weary travelers. I am the high priest and curator of the temple. You must be weary from your travels. May we offer you respite?"

The leader of the riders stepped forward to address the priest. "We appreciate your very kind offer, but we are charged with a task that requires immediate attention. I am Bengt of Khorgia. My fellow travelers and I seek audience with the Speaker for the clarity and vision only his insight may provide."

"If you would excuse me, I will address the Speaker for you. Please make yourselves comfortable for the time being."

The priest bowed curtly and entered the room behind the doors, which closed with a deep echo behind him. The riders found themselves seats on the simple wooden benches that lined the walls of the entranceway, awaiting the priest's return.

Nearly ten minutes passed before the priest returned, approaching the four riders.

"The Speaker informs me that he has been expecting you for some time now. He will grant you an audience presently. If you are ready, I must ask you to remove all weapons, talismans, and religious articles before you enter. The Speaker will not entertain an audience that is armed, be it with blade, spell or the Omniscient."

The four looked at each other, removing their swords and amulets, and forming a small pile on one of the benches. Fully disarmed, they approached the priest, who stood steadfast before them, harshly eyeing one of the four, the one known as Mordock. Sensing the tension and the attention the priest had for him, the others turned to look at their comrade and then back to the priest.

"Is there a problem? We have removed all that you required, have we not?"

The priest pointed to Mordock's hand. "The ring. It bears the stone of blood, a talisman. It must be removed."

"But it cannot! I have worn this ring for more summers than I can recall. It is stuck firmly for it is far too small to escape the knuckle beyond it. And I shan't remove the finger." He looked back and forth to his compatriots, imploringly.

The priest closed his eyes and pressed his palms together before him. After a moment, he brought his hands apart in large circles and back before himself again. Whispering beneath his breath and extending his arms abruptly downward, his fingers towards the floor, he once again brought his hands together before him, palm to palm.

Mordock gasped in astonishment as the ring slipped from his finger and clattered upon the cave floor. Reaching down, he examined the ring and then his finger, finding no defects on either. He stared blankly at the priest, mouth agape.

"If you would kindly place it with your other belongings." He motioned to the pile. "Please be mindful that you will be allowed only three questions. And the Speaker shall answer any question that he can hear." He looked each of the four in the eyes. "If you are ready, we can proceed to the Speaker."

Mordock placed his ring upon the pile, still in shock, and joined the others as they followed the priest through the great doors.

Beyond the great doors was an immense, dimly lit room. Directly opposite the doors was a wide dais upon which a massive wooden chair stood. In perfect dichotomy, seated in the chair was the diminutive figure resembling an elven troglodyte, Pada Vona, the Speaker of Truth. Wiry hair hung down from his balding head, a strong jaw jutting from his clean-shaven face, and two piercing steel gray eyes sought the arrival of his guests.

"I was beginning to wonder if you would ever arrive." The Speaker made a motion for them to advance. "Come, I have been expecting your appearance for some time now."

The four slowly edged closer, looking back and forth amongst each other for approval. Their leader broke the silence.

"We are humbled by this audience, Pada Vona. We have come to seek the answers to questions concerning one of our brethren and the future of our clan."

"Be aware, my guest, that I only speak the truth in response to the questions that you ask. I do not temper my answers for your benefit, for I cannot do so. My gift from the Creator is truth, and for those that ask the truth of me, the truth shall be theirs. Prepare your questions carefully, for not only will the response be precisely honest and truthful, but you will not be afforded a response to the same question twice. Any question that may be answered with a multitude of responses may not result in the answer you desire, even though the response is truthful. You may present your queries when you are ready."

Bengt took a deep breath and collected his thoughts. "Our master has told us of a kindred spirit that lives on this land. He desires to bring him into the fold, but we must locate him. Where might one from our clan be able to find him and bring him into the fold?"

The Speaker closed his eyes for a moment, appearing to be deep in thought, then opened them and spoke. "The young man shall journey to Korham. Your clansman shall encounter him there."

The four looked back and forth at one another, whispering amongst themselves. After a few moments, the leader turned back to the Speaker.

"How will our clansman identify the young man in question?"

The Speaker smiled. "The young man shall be identified by his eyes. They change to near-glowing yellow with a black vertical slit for a pupil when he becomes enraged. They are a representation of his father, the Snake Demon, Sutek."

Mordock turned to the leader of the group and whispered loudly, "How are we to be sure we stir the ire of the correct young man? Confront every man in the city?"

"He will be found in the marketplace, trading his labor for sustenance. Unlike many, he is not seeking refuge from you."

Unsure if the Speaker was simply continuing his previous answer or if he had actually answered Mordock's question to the leader, Bengt asked his final question.

"Once we have the young man within the fold, what will be the keys to ultimate victory over the people of the mainland?"

Pada Vona simply looked at the four and smiled. His expression did not change, and he did not utter another syllable. The high priest stepped forward.

"The Speaker has answered your allotment of three questions. It is respectful to offer appropriate thanks prior to taking your leave."

Bengt looked from the priest to the Speaker. "Pada Vona, we thank you for granting us this audience and for the truths you have bestowed upon us. We have no oblation to present. We are merely humble soldiers, here at the behest of our master. Please accept my most humble apologies for our ignorance. We mean no disrespect."

"Bengt, you and your friends have been most respectful. I harbor no ill towards you or your master."

"You know my name, Pada Vona?"

The Speaker smiled. "Another question, but this one I am at peace to answer freely. I know all that is true, Bengt. I have been blessed by the Creator with the knowledge of everything past, present, and future. I know your name, the names of your friends, your enemies, your ancestors, and your progeny. I even know the name of your master, Lord Roga. No knowledge escapes me."

Bengt and his colleagues bowed deeply. "Thank you, Speaker. Your understanding and kindness are greatly appreciated." The four turned to the priest. "If you would kindly show us the way."

Pada Vona addressed the group as they turned to leave. "Prepare your story for Lord Roga well. If you waver, he will surely know you are not being truthful. Fear not, I do not judge. I may not have the capacity to utter untruths myself, but mortals must often bend the truth to ensure their freedoms and existence. At times, the truth presents itself as an impediment."

Bengt tried to look back, but the priest gently guided him to the doors. The four exited the audience chamber and gathered their belongings to prepare for the long journey back. Mordock turned to the priest and handed him his ring.

"I have no use for it. I have been a slave to it for decades, as I could not separate from it. I know not whether it brings good or ill will, but I am sure I am capable of living an honest life without it. Present it to the Speaker as an oblation. It will certainly come to better use here than with me."

The priest accepted the ring and bowed in acknowledgment. Mordock rejoined his comrades and the four headed towards the cave entrance.

TWO KNOCKS RESOUNDED from the outside of Roga's office door.

"Come!"

The door opened slowly to reveal Minarik closely followed by a group of four riders. "My Lord, the contingent has returned from their audience with the Speaker."

Roga turned in his chair to face them. "Of course. I will see them immediately."

Minarik showed the four into the room to a place immediately before Roga's desk. They stood at attention before their master.

Roga addressed the group. "Relax, my faithful acolytes. You have just returned from a long journey. Be at rest."

The four relaxed slightly but remained standing.

"Have you obtained audience with the Speaker?"

Bengt addressed Roga. "Yes, my lord. We were granted audience with Pada Vona and were granted the truth to three questions."

"And what information do you bring to me in your return?"

"The Speaker informed us of our comrade on the mainland. The young man shall be found in Korham, now De'Aarna, laboring in the marketplace in exchange for food and shelter. He can be identified by his eyes, which disclose the identity of his father when anger is aroused. The Speaker also made mention of him not seeking refuge from me. I am unsure of the meaning to this."

"We must have someone sent to De'Aarna to gather him up and return him to me. Minarik, see to it that he is found and brought here to my office. Perhaps the Speaker intended Bengt as the one. His response was that the man will not seek refuge from him."

"Of course, my lord."

"You did well, Bengt. And what of the keys to victory over the Tendirans? How did the Speaker respond to your inquiry?"

Bengt turned slightly to look at his friends through the corner of his eye.

"He did not, my lord. The Speaker would answer only questions regarding a single subject. We chose the subject of the young man, the first task given to us. Based on that, and the fact that your superior tactical intellect has easily directed us towards victory, evident in the fact that we have been so successful in our initial attacks, we determined that finding our brethren, crucial to the realization of prophecy, far exceeded the necessity of acquiring the keys to victory. Certainly, victory will be easily attained through your competent leadership."

Roga was irritated that the Speaker had not proffered specific information regarding a successful campaign against the Tendirans, but he would not argue with a man exhibiting such unflagging resolve in his abilities as a leader.

"Be it as it must. You have done well. Minarik, see to it that these four men are fed from my personal larder. Have their dragons rubbed down, fed, and rested. They have earned their reward. Prepare Bengt for a journey to De'Aarna tomorrow. It would appear he has a comrade to track down."

"I will see to it immediately, My Lord." He bowed towards Roga and then motioned for the men to follow him. "Come. I will take you to the master's dining hall where you will be fed, and I will inform the warren master to attend to your rides."

The four bowed towards Roga and followed his attendant out of the office. Roga sat back in his chair, lost in a moment of contemplation. He would soon have the spawn of Sutek by his side, confirming another element of that which has been foretold. Perhaps he would have all the keys to victory at his disposal shortly. He was, at least, not the slightest bit uneasy about his prospects for reigning over Tendira and the entire mainland. The Khorgians would not become a complacent military under his watch. They needed an adversary and he needed a means by which he would aspire to greatness.

7
THE INTERROGATION

TWO FULL MOONS HUNG lazily in the night sky, painting the ground below with an ethereal luminescence. Stars punctuated the darkness of the sky like diamonds randomly strewn across blue-black silk. From a distance, over the trees on the horizon, the shadowy outline of a flying creature appeared, possibly a large bird, but then, as it drew closer, quite obviously, the hulking figure of a dragon. The silhouette of a single rider could be seen straddling its shoulders. Wings laboring from the effort, the dragon flew in, just above the treetops, headed for a huge spine of rock that ran north and south as far as the eye could see.

The mountain range slashed across the countryside; a huge wedge of the planet's crust heaved up millennia ago standing tall above the forest canopy like colossal scutes on the tail of a dragon. A huge wall of stone, rising from the forest, walls straight and sheer, magnificent snow-capped peaks reaching for the heavens, a natural obstacle to anything or anyone trying to travel further east. The forest before it was lush and green, the benefactor of weather halted by the immense barricade of stone that was the Khorgian mountain range. It was within this ridge that the Khorgian Dragon Warriors lived, housed within the warrens and grottoes carved out by eons of seismic upheaval and human sweat. Unreachable from below, the location of the caves, high above the forest canopy provided a natural defense to any ground attack.

Near the completion of its approach, the dragon quickly gained altitude in order to reach the entrance to the warren, more than halfway up the face of the monolith. The reptilian beast landed on a small outcropping beside a low, wide cave mouth and folded its wings along its sides. The rider slid off the dragon's shoulder and down to the ground. Two men scrambled from the cave and began to lead the beast in. The rider shouted to them. "See to it that she is fed and groomed well before bedding her down for the night. An extensive rub down shall do her well. She has more than earned her keep today."

The animal squatted low and ducked its head down, shuffling to get inside the cave. Another man, tall and confident, wearing the dark leather breeches and jacket of a rider, marched out to meet the dragon's master. It was Roga's assistant, Minarik. He gave a curt bow.

"My Lord. It is good to see you have safely returned. The other riders have arrived before you and are in the process of feeding and grooming their beasts. I am confident the campaign went well."

"Yes, very well, if I should say so myself. It wasn't as much of a challenge as I had hoped. Mostly desert with a few sparse settlements. And the Tendirans are not the most cunning or challenging adversaries, but they do make the most dreadfully wonderful sound when the dragon fire first sears their flesh. It is the most divine music to my ears. I am sure you would agree, wouldn't you, Minarik?"

"Yes, of course, my Lord. Surely, one day, I too will be granted the pleasure of such an experience."

Roga placed his hand on the man's shoulder and smiled. "Ah! You aspire to be a rider, do you? Your time will come in due course, my most loyal assistant. I will see to it. And to what do I owe the unusual pleasure of your greeting my arrival on the apron?"

"Your guest precedes you and is awaiting your arrival in your private dining hall, my Lord." He motioned for his superior to lead.

"Ah, yes. I had summoned Governor Zea to sup with me tonight if I recall correctly. Well then, we shouldn't be inattentive hosts now, should we? That would be exceedingly poor etiquette. Besides, I am feeling a bit peckish. These forays to the mainland can drain even the greatest of men of his energy. I dare say I could go for a bite or two of pheasant and a glass of wine before retiring."

"Perhaps you will enthrall the Governor with tales of your great victories or how thrilling it is to fly home under such beautiful full moons in the evening sky."

Roga looked at his assistant, imploring. "Beautiful moons?"

"Yes, my Lord. Look." He pointed over Roga's shoulder and off into the night sky. "Eos and Nyx hang together low and bright in the evening sky. I'm sure their beacons make for a picturesque ride as you fly back home after a glorious battle."

Roga turned to look at the two moons. "Picturesque?" He cocked his head slightly. "I had never noticed. Perhaps they do have some sort of..." He paused a moment in search of the right word. "... some sort of... aesthetic appeal."

The warlord continued to stare at the two bright orbs in the sky, overcome with a sudden, strange fascination.

Minarik put his hand on his Master's shoulder and motioned toward the caves. "Shall we, my Lord?"

Roga stalled a moment, entranced by the vision in the sky before him. Turning, but quickly shifting his gaze back to, and then from, the pair of moons, he refocused his attention to his attendant. "Yes, let us make our leave."

The two men turned and ducked through a small opening in the cliff face, the rider preceding the messenger.

Roga's private dining hall was a long, vaulted room apportioned with a monstrous banquet table, nearly thirty feet in length and six feet wide, with but two ornately carved high-back chairs, set at either end. Between the two chairs, a most elegant feast was laid out. Pheasant and duck, roast piglet and meat pies; the finest breads and pastries; vegetables of every imaginable type and origin; wine and milk and mead; a feast large enough to feed a score of men. A fire roared in the large fireplace at the far end, casting a flickering light over the room accompanied by distorted shadows upon the dark wood-paneled walls. Three candelabra spaced along the table provided the only other light.

Lord Roga entered from a door at the far end of the room, followed immediately by his assistant. He removed his gloves and jacket and handed them over to Minarik, who placed them over the back of a chair against the wall. He walked back to the table and stood at the far end, closest to the fireplace, to address his dinner guest. Roga was still in his riding gear, dusty from his recent journey back to the fortress from their latest assault upon the

Tendirans. His guest was barely visible from behind the opposite chair, his unkempt black hair sticking over the top of the chair back.

"Governor Zea, I am so glad you could be persuaded to join me for dinner this evening. I am graced by your presence." Roga nodded slightly in his guest's direction. "Please excuse my appearance, but I have just returned from a raid across the sea and I have yet the opportunity to change. A dirty job, for sure, but someone must ensure it is carried out properly." Minarik pulled Roga's chair out and he sat down. The acoustics of the hall were such that Roga need not raise his voice to converse with his guest, even at such a great distance. "I have been informed of some rather exciting circumstances that have presented themselves, events that you may very well play an integral part in." Roga carefully placed his napkin on his lap. He clasped his hands together, placed his elbows on the edge of the table, his hands meeting fingertip to fingertip, and continued to address his dinner guest. "I have been carefully studying the pages of the Book of Beginnings and have found verses of the manuscript that may implicate your own involvement in our future. Notice the two full moons in the evening sky? The time of the New Beginning, *eht Ahnálian*, is now at hand and the writings of the prophets appear to have described you, my dear Zea, as the Gatekeeper. The teachings, as written in the *Olheb Ahnan,* states '*The eyes of the Creator shall shine high in the evening sky, signaling the time for the cleansing of the earth to begin. It shall come to pass that the beneficent hand of the Chosen shall appear outside the Kingdom of Korham as a man, and he who holds the seat of power shall assume the role of Gatekeeper, opening the way for Eyieritu, the anointed one.*' You, Zea, are the leader of the people of De'Aarna, once Korham, and, as such, would seem to be the most logical choice as the Gatekeeper, by my interpretation. I am sure you are familiar with the teachings. The prophecy claims the time for the anointed one is at hand. The city gates at De'Aarna are apparently an impediment to the completion of his task and only the Gatekeeper, ***you***, can open the way for him. What a privileged position you hold, my friend. I am quite sure you must be enraptured!"

His guest remained motionless and silent. Roga's discourse had, strangely, produced not one response, neither vocal nor physical. Only from his host's vantage point could the reason for the lack of response be seen. Roga's guest was, in fact, a captive. Tightly bound and gagged as to permit no movement or speech. The man tried vainly to move his arms. Perspiration beaded on his forehead, revealing his efforts to gain his freedom.

Roga was keenly aware of Zea's struggle to respond and he relished in his guest's discomfort. "You must excuse the bonds. It's not necessarily a reflection on any feelings of mistrust I may harbor for you. I simply prefer a . . . captive audience. I find it easier to maintain their attention that way. I'm certain you must agree."

Presently, the wine steward appeared with a bottle of red wine and, opening it, poured a glass for his master. Roga first inhaled deeply from the glass, took a drink, offered a gesture of satisfaction, and continued. "The prophets write '*following the Vivification of the Immured, the eyes of the Creator shall walk across the evening sky together in all their glory. This shall signal the Ahnálian. Behold, the coming of Eyieritu, the Anointed One, is nigh!*' I have been told that this is the first night since the Immurement, in a time long since passed, that both moons sit side by side, full in the sky. According to the writings, it is a signal of the Vivification. It is written that the *Ahnálian* follows shortly thereafter. That is why I invited you to be my dinner guest tonight. You are the Gatekeeper. You occupy the seat of power in what was once known as Korham. You hold the power to begin all that was prophesized. You shall open the gates of De'Aarna to the Anointed and initiate the time of *Ahnálian*, the New Beginning, when all that is known shall be refreshed and begun anew. I can only imagine how honored you must feel! To think, you hold the key to when the next great event in history, the New Beginning, shall come to pass. You have the power in your hands to shape history, to shape the future of all! You must promise me, Governor, to send notice when the time has come. I would be most appreciative of the opportunity to be present when history is made!"

Zea struggled vainly at his bonds, intent on freeing, at least, his mouth in an effort to respond to Roga's rhetoric. But the bonds were too well tied and the gag too large to dislodge from his mouth. His face was nearly beet red and the sweat was pouring off his forehead.

Roga continued with his interpretation of the prophecy. "It is written that Eyieritu will release the sleeping magi from his confinement. '*Upon the Gatekeeper's command, the walls of Korham shall open and Eyieritu shall cross the threshold, breaking the enchantment containing the Immured within and liberating all that has shared in captive slumber. Truth shall once again encompass the land and all collaborators shall enjoy the fruits of their assistance...'* "

His struggling became so intense, the Governor faded in and out of consciousness from time to time during Roga's rambling discourse.

"...*'and He shall reign, supreme, from the mount, as the right hand and loyal servant of the once-captive corse...'* "

Suddenly, in obvious disgust, Roga took pause from his prophetic manifesto to address his guest once again. "Damned you, Zea! Wake up! Look at yourself! Would you at least express some gratitude? Your lack of attention and your vulgar gruntings and groanings do nothing to proffer appropriate respect to the honor which has been bestowed upon you or even that of your host!"

Zea's face was so red it appeared that his head was preparing to explode. His body tensed and relaxed in rapid succession in near seizures as he continued to struggle against his restraints. His frantic attempts at discourse had now intensified from grunts and groans to high-pitched nasal whining accompanied by nearly epileptic shaking of his head.

Exasperated, Roga called upon his manservant once again. "Minarik, would you come to assist our guest? I believe he may be trying to tell me something and I am beginning to become most irritated with his incessant animalistic vocalizations."

Minarik appeared from an archway that led into the adjoining kitchen. He walked over to Zea and slowly turned the small handle that stuck out of his mouth, reducing the size of the pear-shaped object that gagged him for removal. In obvious relief, Zea spat out the distasteful remnants of the gag, stretched his aching jaw side to side, and licked his parched lips. His breathing was labored but relieved as he tried to calm down and address his host.

"Honestly, Lord Roga, I meant no disrespect towards you or that which has been taught by the ancients, but I have no knowledge of what you are speaking. I am familiar with the Prophecy of Korham, but me? The Gatekeeper? Opening the way for the Anointed One? These ideas are foreign to me. I am far too unassuming a figure to be selected by the Creator to serve as an instrument of the Chosen. I do not believe I can be of any assistance to you in this matter."

Roga slowly shook his head. "Such a pity, my dear Zea. It pains me so to see people like yourself with such little self-confidence. You simply do not understand your potential, your power over the events that unfold before you on a daily basis, your ability to change and create what is to become the future. If you never aspire to greatness, surely you will languish, forever, in your mediocrity." Roga sat forward and poured himself another glass of wine. "Would you care for some wine?"

"Uh, yes, yes. I would find that most hospitable of you, Lord Roga."

Roga called to the wine steward. "Friederich. Some wine for our guest."

The steward appeared from the archway into the kitchen area with another bottle and opened it. He poured a glass of red wine and brought it to Zea's lips who eagerly sipped at the liquid as it was offered to him. The steward took the glass away, Zea's mouth greedily seeking more, and placed it on the table, leaving the room.

"You disappoint me, Zea. I envisioned such great things for you. A shame, you refuse to be a party to such grand events. I fear you shall not see the master plan come to fruition." Roga paused for a moment, then continued with a sneer, "Such a vile thing, disappointment, is it not? I loathe being disappointed."

Changing subjects without as much as a breath, Roga took a drumstick from a pheasant and began to eat from it. "The pheasant is very well done, I'm sure you will agree. We do employ the finest kitchen staff. Have you enjoyed your wine?"

"Yes, Lord Roga, it is indeed a very fine vintage."

"I am so glad you enjoyed it." Roga called through the archway. "Friederich! Please see to it that our guest has as much wine as he cares to drink."

He turned back to face Zea. "You must excuse me for I must take my leave. It has been a very long day and I still have much business to attend to." He snapped his fingers. "My steward will ensure you have enough wine and there is certainly enough food to satisfy any particular taste or appetite you may have. It's a shame we could not come to a mutual understanding concerning this matter of prophecy, but so it must be. Surely that is how it was predetermined to be at the beginning when this timeline was fashioned by the Creator. I'm certain it is of little consequence in the grand scheme of it all. Surely it is written that we will both be justly rewarded in the end. I bid you good evening, Governor Zea. I expect the remainder of your stay with us shall be as pleasant as possible. My staff will ensure that you are... well taken care of." Roga got up and walked from the hall, nodding to Minarik as he exited.

The steward presented himself shortly thereafter with a very large bottle of wine, which he expertly uncorked in one motion. He allowed the Governor to sample the cork.

"Ah, yes, a most eloquent Merlot. Lord Roga certainly maintains a fine cellar." Zea looked up to the wine steward. "Do you think we could dispense with these bindings now? Master Roga has had his audience with me. I am sure you see no further reason to have me remain in this condition."

The steward blankly looked down at Zea. There was an awkward moment of silence. It was then that he noticed a wide, jagged scar along the man's neck, nearly running ear to ear. He had suffered a severe injury at some point in his life and it had obviously taken his ability to speak. Zea quickly redirected his own question. "Perhaps I should ask Minarik. Your specialty is obviously the wine cellar and not the affairs of your master." Motioning to the bottle of Merlot with a nod of his head, "May I have a taste?"

Bringing the bottle to his lips, Friederich allowed a small amount trickle into his mouth. Although not expecting to be served directly from the bottle, Zea greedily swallowed the offering. He had not noticed Minarik approaching from behind. In one swift motion, Roga's aide grabbed a handful of the Governor's hair, pulling his head down over the back of the chair, forcing his mouth open and aligning his throat straight up. The steward deftly rammed the neck of the bottle down his throat forcing a seal between the bottle and his lips. Zea gagged and struggled, attempting to breathe and swallow all at the same time as the liquid quickly rushed into his mouth and down his windpipe, rapidly flooding his lungs. The crimson liquid bubbled and sprayed from his nostrils as he attempted to expel the liquid and make room for air. Zea's body began to shake and quiver, his hands clenching and releasing, as he struggled to release himself from his situation. Guttural sounds emanated from his throat, half choking, half attempts at screams. His eyes bulged, seeming to approach the point of popping out of their sockets. The steward held the bottle down tightly, all his weight bearing down upon the punt, allowing the wine to spill from the opening, continuing down Zea's throat, and into his lungs. A few short moments later the Governor's body tensed one last time. Then the frantic movements and noises of the guest slowly subsided. Minarik released the Governor's hair and the steward relaxed, removing the entirety of his body weight from the base of the bottle. Their deed complete, both men silently exited the room leaving the lifeless body behind, the magnum still upturned and lodged in their victim's throat.

OUTSIDE HIS DINING room, Roga approached Worren, his Man at Arms. "Find someone that is trustworthy and loyal to the cause. Assign them to De'Aarna in replacement of Governor Zea. It would appear that he has an alcohol problem. He cannot handle his wine, and I will not tolerate anyone that shows such weakness in a position as important as the city seat. He is unfit to govern an area as sacred as old Korham. It is most important that whomever you send assumes Zea's position as Governor within the community immediately. If I cannot trust those that are already there, I shall place someone of my own in the position of authority. The *Olheb Ahnan* simply states '*he who holds the seat of power shall open the way for the Anointed One*.' Nowhere does it say that I cannot choose who that person shall be. Perhaps General Canthus would be a good fit for the role. He bears an air of authority about him and is most definitely loyal. Send him to De'Aarna."

"I shall see to it immediately, my Lord." Worren clicked his heels and bowed to Roga before turning quickly and attending to his new task.

Roga, too, walked away, talking quietly to himself. "Why must the world be populated with so many inferior minds? It places such a burden upon those of us that have been born into greatness."

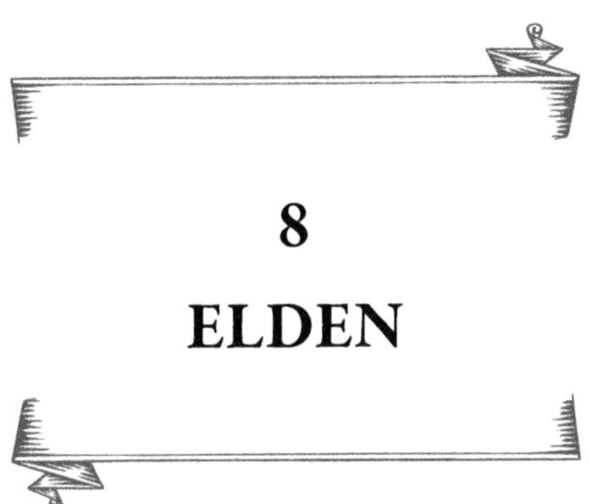

8
ELDEN

6072 E.K.

Ahlāan gave birth to a son on a damp and cold spring morning, months after the death of her sister. It was as joyous an occasion as could be expected for a family and community hit so hard by misfortune. Queen Isella had lost a husband shortly before the birth of her twins. Her youngest daughter had passed, unexpectedly, along with her child due to the complications of the pregnancy. Now her eldest daughter had given birth to a son amidst an aura of trepidation. The entire castle community was awaiting the next misfortune to befall the family. To make matters worse, her grandson had no father. He was a bastard child, with all the innuendo and stigma that is inherent to that circumstance. The inhabitants of *eht Vilna Sahnah* were deeply enamored with and devoted to their royal family and disparaging remarks were far beyond the norm, but this particular situation managed to raise more than a few eyebrows. To the best of the queen's knowledge, Ahlāan had fallen victim to one of the many royal courtiers that had attempted to woo the princess. He had obviously come to court with the selfish intent of an intimate meeting with the lovely princess and nothing more. Her daughter was simply a notch on his belt, a story of a noble sexual conquest to be shared amongst his sophomoric comrades. It pained her, particularly, as she had been the impetus behind entertaining potential suitors for her daughter's hand. The castle needed a strong masculine appearance and she had hoped to achieve that through Ahlāan's marriage to a fine young man of royal blood.

Unbeknownst to the queen, the child was borne from an illicit relationship between her daughter and a common stable hand, although which young man could not be named as the father was unknown, even to the princess. She had found the enticement of the forbidden, a tryst with a rough and uncouth stable boy, a drug so exhilarating that she had given herself to any and all of them who showed the slightest interest. It was an act that her mother had no control over and the feeling of empowerment along with the sheer erotic thrill was intoxicating to her. It had consumed her every thought and action to the point of addiction and, to satisfy her own carnal desires, she had taken every opportunity, no matter how risky, to offer herself in the hay for the pleasure of the boys. To her ultimate dismay, knowledge of her 'condition' resulted in immediate disinterest. An intimate rendezvous with the princess was no longer a desirable encounter. Ahlāan would suffer the consequences of her illicit relationships alone.

The unfortunate circumstances surrounding his conception and birth had little effect on Elden as he was growing up. Things had fallen into a normal rhythm by the time he was old enough to be cognizant of his parentage. There was the occasional teasing from the other children in the castle regarding his not having a father, and he would, at times, question Ahlāan about it. She would simply tell him that his father was a wonderful person and had made his mother very happy, but he could not manage to be near due to circumstances beyond the control of anyone in the castle. It seemed to provide the young boy with the answers he needed at the time.

As Elden grew into an adolescent, the teasing became much less, almost non-existent. The few that dared to mention his father were oftentimes treated to a face full of knuckles. Elden had grown into a strong, tall, athletic young man. Although he never took liberties with his royal status, he did take advantage of the training that his social position afforded him, much the same as his grandfather before him. He had become quite proficient with his hands and had trained extensively in the study of combat, especially with the flamberge, his weapon of choice. The serpentine wave of the massive blade had enticed him, and the sheer enormity of the weapon made its command an accomplishment of only the most well trained and physically adept men. From a young age, Elden was determined to become one of those men. He had heard the stories of his grandfather, King Olen, from his grandmother, a strong and intelligent leader of men, and knew he wanted to be spoken of in the same manner.

Queen Isella knew the importance of having a strong male figure as the leader of the Confederacy. Her husband, King Olen, had used his countenance to great advantage, bringing together the seven kingdoms and ensuring the peace and prosperity of all that came under his influence. Their grandson would be afforded all the training and tools necessary to evolve into a man of similar stature and influence. Elden was taught by the most learned of scholars that the Confederacy had to offer, in language arts and grammar, politics and relations. He was trained in the fine arts of warfare and strategy, and in the maintenance of his chiseled physique. As it was with his grandfather, he was the object of desire for every young maiden in the castle and the envy of every young man. His manner, though, was the antithesis of envy, as everyone he encountered grew to respect and admire him. He treated everyone he encountered as his equal, forgoing all airs for the promotion of the common good.

6093 E.K.

As part of his duties and daily ritual, twenty-three-year-old Elden would walk the castle grounds, attending to the people, the vendors, the farmers in the field, and every visitor. Everyone knew him and he knew all the inhabitants of his realm. He worked hard to maintain an approachability that fostered good will and respect between himself and the castle community. No one entered or left the bailey and nothing occurred about the kingdom without Elden hearing about it.

In the market, Elden approached a produce vendor. "Good morning, Duggan. How is business on this fine day?"

"Elden, my boy! A pleasure to see you this morning, as always! Business is fine. The tomatoes have begun to ripen. I will save a nice red one for your grandmother. Have her send the cook down for it in a day or two."

"I will do so. The Queen always appreciates your generosity."

"The Queen has been kind to the lot of us and I have found her especially congenial. A mere tomato is far from adequate compensation for the kindness and stability that she and your family has offered over the years."

"She is a very special lady, Duggan."

"That she is. And can I assume there is a special someone in your life right now? I know of a secret spot where the desert lilies have begun to bloom.

I am sure I could manage to procure one if you desire to impress a special someone."

Elden chuckled. "If only that could be true. Unfortunately, my heart and mind are currently betrothed to this castle community. It would take a woman as fair as my mother and as venerated as my grandmother to steal me away, and a woman of that cloth would be near impossible to find in our little corner of the world."

"I would not be so sure of that, my young man. *Sibu* has definite plans for us all and has created for each a partner of perfect compatibility. She is out there, somewhere. I am certain of it."

"I will take your word on the matter, Duggan. Perhaps you are correct, and might I not bump into her during my daily rounds about the castle someday, perhaps at this very stand." Elden stood on his toes and scanned the marketplace, half mocking. "Alas, I fear today is not the day. It was nice to catch up, Duggan, but I need to be about. My presence is always in demand, even if just for a chat. I will have grandmother send the cook for that tomato. And if the woman of my dreams should be by today to purchase the same, inform her I will return tomorrow."

Duggan reached out his hand. "That I will, my lord. And should it not happen the morrow, do not be surprised if you bump into a beautiful damsel in the market someday. The Queen may be a most wise and respected woman, but I dare say, with no disrespect intended, she may not be the sole possessor of those qualities."

A SHOUT RAINED DOWN from the parapet. "Quick! Open the gates! A messenger approaches in full gallop!"

There was a sudden beehive of activity below as guards rushed to throw open the huge wooden doors and raise the portcullis. The heavy metal gate had barely risen to the height of a man when the rider and his steed rushed beneath it and struggled to stop quickly in the square.

The rider dismounted and, winded, stammered to get his message out. "Sound the alert! The Sou... the Souliban has been attacked! Quickly! Close the gate and sound the alarm! The Souliban has been attacked... by... by dragons!"

His final word drew a gasp from the gathering crowd.

"By the Mother's light, what are you stammering about, man?"

"The Souliban, it was attacked, devastated. There is nothing left."

"Nothing left? What are you talking about? And what is this foolishness about... about ... dragons?"

The crowd began to encroach upon the messenger and his inquisitor, eager to hear more.

"They flew in, over the Touphorus Sea and into the foothills. They had flaming breath and laid waste to everything... everything. There... there is nothing left."

A familiar voice rose from the back of the crowd. "Make way! Let me through! Let me through!" It was Elden. "Make way, please. I wish to question this man."

The crowd parted to give Elden ample room to approach the messenger. As he met the man, he extended his hand. "Welcome to *eht Vilna Sahnah*. We are graced with your presence. Relax. Take a breath and let's figure out what has happened, from the beginning."

As the messenger took Elden's hand, there was suddenly a noticeable ease in his demeanor. "Thank you for your hospitality, but this matter is urgent and requires immediate attention. Civility can wait for a less emergent situation. The Souliban was attacked by dragons this morning. They flew in over the Touphorus Sea, hundreds of them, and began spewing forth balls of flame as soon as they were above land. They burned everything, homes, trees, even the stones. There is nothing left."

"The people. What has happened to the people?"

The messenger lowered and shook his head. "I may be the only person to make it out alive. I have not seen nor heard of anyone else on my travel here."

A pall fell over the crowd as jaws dropped and eyes groped about for answers.

"Are you certain of this, sir?" Elden questioned quietly

"Only as certain as what my own eyes have experienced. I have not seen another soul recognizable from the Souliban, but I cannot claim absolutely that someone else may not have managed a way out. What I can say for certain is the number of possible survivors could not exceed the fingers on a healthy man's hand."

A murmur began to make its way through the crowd. Eager to maintain some order, Elden decided it best to remove the messenger to a more controllable environment.

"Make way once again, people. Let us through. This man needs some respite from his journey. Please, someone, rush to the keep and inform the housekeeper that we have a guest that requires some nourishment and repose." Elden began to walk the messenger towards the castle keep. "In the meantime, I promise all of you that I shall conduct a full inquiry into the news brought by the messenger. You will all be informed as soon as we have the entire story. But, I daresay, be prepared for the worst. The truth may show we are indeed under attack and at odds with an unknown aggressor. Go about your business, find your way back to your homes and prepare for what might be to come."

The crowd began to disperse as Elden and the messenger made quick work of the distance to the doors of the keep. Elden escorted the young man through the kitchen to a small stairwell at the back of the keep and up to a private room.

“Please, make yourself comfortable.” Elden motioned to a divan against the far wall. “I will have one of the maids bring you something from the kitchen. It will be quiet here and you will be afforded time to rest. I must first ask that you divulge to me all that you know about the attack. Collect your thoughts while I call for your food.”

Elden ducked back down the stairwell, returning shortly thereafter. “You shall have nothing shy of a feast in but a few moments. Are you feeling up to speaking about the attack?”

“Most certainly, sir. The sooner the details are known, the sooner a plan can be devised by which we might defend against another such attack.” The messenger leaned forward to ensure Elden heard every word he was about to speak. “It was a typical hot morning, the sun high in the air, not a cloud in the sky...”

"THE DRAGONS CAME IN over the Touphorus Sea by the hundreds, thick enough to block the sun. Their attack was well orchestrated and precise, targeting every structure, every tree, every animal. They flew in, destroyed all that existed below them, and flew out, entirely within a matter of minutes."

The Queen focused intently on every detail of her grandson's report.

"Do we know where the attack originated from?"

"The dragons came in from the east, over the Touphorus Sea. It is speculated that the only possible origin is the Isle of Khorgia. It seems rather perplexing as we have had no evidence of discord or provocation with the Khorgians, but there is no other land mass that is within flight range and large enough to support such a large number of creatures."

"News from Khorgia is indeed scarce. An occasional story from a sea-faring merchant, but never anything overtly indicative of aggression towards the mainland. But, again, I have little personal experience of the Khorgians at all. I cannot remember the last time there was any formal discourse between the Confederation and the island. Elden, what do you propose?"

"I suggest all members of the Confederation be informed immediately. We must be prepared in the event that this is more than a single incident. And, perhaps, we should send an envoy to Khorgia to discern the reasoning behind this sudden turn of events."

"Agreed. Send out the word immediately. Request all Confederacy member be prepared for the worst. Inform the people that there is no other attack known at this time and no reason to expect we will find the same fate but, as always, be prepared. We will react accordingly if it is found that this is more than an isolated occurrence. Seek a contingent of volunteers capable of sailing to Khorgia. With luck, they may be capable of negotiating a political solution to these events."

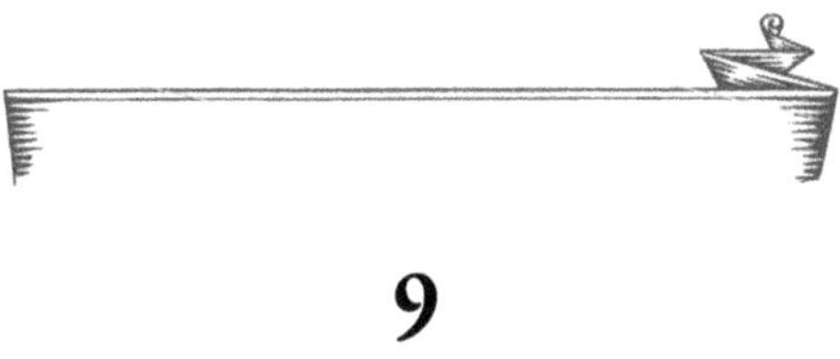

9
THE VANQUISHED

UNDER A CANOPY OF TWINKLING stars, two young lovers lay curled together atop a pile of straw stacked in a farmer's cart. Engrossed in one another, the pair were unaware as a veil of darkness encroached, slowly devouring each star in its path leaving complete darkness in its wake. The young girl pointed a finger towards the heavens.

"Look, Arvid, look! A shooting star! Make a wish!"

The tranquil darkness of the night sky was split in two by a flaming ball crossing overhead. It was quickly followed by another. Both splashed like liquid lightning in the bailey below, igniting everything they touched. The startled young girl screamed. From a watchtower, a lone sentry stumbled to grab a dusty old horn to signal the alarm. The castle guards snapped from their slumber as the frequency of the flaming balls increased, raining down upon the castle from above. *Eht Vilna Moht*, the Black Castle, was awakened to the reality of an attack, breaking not only the silence of the night but breaking the decades of silence that had become the norm for this and every other kingdom south and west of the Souliban. As archers rushed to their places upon the ramparts, the sky took on an eerie glow, reminiscent of the evening twilight, although the midnight hour was nearly at hand. Arrow after arrow streaked aimlessly into the darkness, the archers unable to see their adversaries hidden in the hollow darkness of the evening sky and further masked by the smoke and fire that had engulfed the castle. The castle defenses were ill-equipped to withstand any attack even under the best of conditions let alone marauders hidden in the darkness above. The inability to focus on a target made it all but impossible.

Chaos ruled the moment. Shouts of the guards attempting to organize and establish an advantage and the screams of women and children seeking shelter from the attack filled the air. The sulfurous odor of the flaming bombardment mixed with the pungent stench of burning flesh wafted about the compound, floating upon the smoke being generated by the burning edifice around them. The amalgam of sights and sounds and smells coupled with the inability to see the enemy quickly disintegrated any organized defense into a state of total confusion and fear. Even the most stoic and die-hard veteran was hard pressed to stand his ground and hold his post in the morass. The confines of the castle were quickly becoming a living hell, embodied by the visage of a single, winged, devilish beast appearing through the darkness and smoke as it flew just low enough to be seen. Both man and beast fled in sheer terror at the sight. With little resistance, the Khorgians' aerial attack made quick work of the castle guards, securing a rapid and decisive victory.

SCORES OF DRAGONS SAT perched upon the parapet like a flock of grotesquely misshapen and over-sized ravens keeping keen watch over those on the ground below. Riders scurried about beneath their gaze in the bailey, removing items from the castle and loading them aboard other dragons. One by one, the mighty beasts flew from the castle, laden with the fruits of victory, every fifteen to twenty minutes. As each dragon left the confines of the outer walls of the castle, another would take its place, ready to be loaded up for the flight back home.

A large centipede scampered across the damp stone floor of the hallway, its legs moving like waves from front to rear, searching for an evening meal. From around a bend in the hall, a column of men, two by two, dressed for battle, marched down the passageway. The centipede darted towards a crack in the wall, barely avoiding being trampled by one of the many leather-soled jackboots that stomped by in perfect cadence as the column of soldiers passed through.

The castle had succumbed rather quickly to the onslaught of the invaders. For as far back as anyone living could remember, there had been peace.

War and evil were things of legend and horror stories conjured up around a roaring campfire. Unlike *eht Vilna Sahnah*, *eht Vilna Moht* had been ill-prepared to handle an attack of any sort, let alone an aerial onslaught from a force as mighty as the Khorgian dragons. Lord Darden had inherited his position of authority and the castle from his father, who had done likewise. The cost of maintaining a contingent of guards, equipped with the weapons of war, seemed exorbitant and unnecessary. Why protect yourself from an enemy that no longer existed? Complacency had replaced the diligence that had been necessary in centuries past. But now, the calm and silence of the world had been shattered by the loud clanging of the gong that was the Khorgian Dragon Guard. Peace would be gone forever.

Inside, the castle was now a beehive of activity. Some soldiers were scouring the hallways and rooms, searching for inhabitants that may be hiding in the corners while still others were busy assessing the value of everything and anything that was to be found. The sound of leather soled jackboots marching on the stone floors echoed throughout the castle. Orders were loudly barked above the din caused by all the fervent activity. The cries of women and children stripped from their husbands and fathers filled the courtyard.

Outside the main castle keep, not a single building stood whole. Everything that could be burned was either ablaze or a pile of smoldering ash. Everything built of stone was in the process of being knocked down. Livestock ran loose everywhere. Soldiers were busy looting anything that was of any value, destroying anything that was not. Nothing of any use would be left behind.

Amidst the flurry of activity, a single stoic warrior, flanked by two aides, walked calmly from room to room. Lord Roga, dressed in full battle gear was inspecting the spoils of war. Every room he walked into was in a state of disarray. As he entered each area, all activity would stop. Every soldier quickly stood at attention and waited for him to pass before resuming their activity. At least a dozen men were working each room, one man assessing the value of everything, the others segregating it. Anything of value was stacked carefully in the center; everything else was thrown into a pile in a corner. Roga approached Aramas, the man in charge of the room, questioning him as to what was found.

"Aramas, what do we have here?"

"This appears to have been a sitting room, my Lord. We found furniture and a few tapestries, but nothing much else of value. Would you care to inspect the contents?"

"No, I do not believe so." Roga kicked a few items lying in the center of the room. "Nothing here appears to catch my eye." He turned back to the soldier. "But I do trust that you will carefully inspect everything to ensure nothing of worth is left behind."

"Of course, my Lord."

"And destroy anything that will not be returning with us. I want nothing of any usefulness left behind, not even a child's toy. Do you understand?"

The soldier clicked his heels. "As you wish, my Lord! I will ensure nothing of any value is left behind and everything left behind will be destroyed. I will not disappoint."

"Good." Roga turned to leave, quickly glancing over the men, still standing at attention. "As you were."

As the warlord stepped back into the hallway a young soldier approached and stood at attention before him, clicking his heels as he did. "My Lord, your presence is requested by Marshall Octrall. He is beneath the castle proper."

Roga motioned for the messenger to show him. "Lead the way."

The two quickly marched down the hallway followed by a detachment of soldiers. Roga had been summoned by one of his marshals to the undercroft. It had to be something of importance, for no one would dare to request him for a trivial matter. The consequences for such a request would most certainly be a slow torturous death. The marshal met him at the bottom of a winding stone staircase. Two heavily armed men could be seen down the hallway, guarding an inconspicuous small wooden door.

"My Lord, I requested your presence immediately upon finding him. It would appear he is the castle wizard. He is detained within. I respectfully suggest you be on your guard. He has not attempted any trickery yet, but we have not ascertained the extent of his abilities."

Roga looked at Octrall, attempting to discern the level of concern in his general's eyes. After a tense moment, he broke his stare and turned to duck in through the low door.

The small wooden door creaked as it opened into what appeared to be an equally small room. The actual size could not be truly calculated from the vantage point of the doorway, so cluttered was the space. A desk and a table and bookshelves were strewn with books and papers and paraphernalia of every imaginable sort. Whoever occupied this space certainly had a very odd sense of organization and an even more bizarre sense of decorating.

Seated in a high-backed wooden chair was a withered old man. He had bushy white eyebrows, a poorly kept mustache, and long, thinning white hair. His cloak was worn and patched in many places. He sat staring blankly into nowhere.

"So, this is the castle wizard? I'm not particularly impressed by his countenance." Roga spoke as if the wizard was not there. "And what of a sorcerer that cannot conjure his way around two guards and a little wooden door?" Roga paced back and forth around the old man, carefully examining the figure in front of him. "So, what do you have to say for yourself, old man?"

The magician sat silently, still staring blankly into space. Roga wheeled violently and struck the man in the face. "Look at me when I address you! I asked you a question and I expect an answer! What is it that you have to say for yourself, old man?"

The mage slowly brought his eyes up to meet Roga's. "I am Taygen, the castle wizard." Taygen spoke in the tone of an old and beaten man. "I have served my Lord Darden for these past twenty-odd summers, providing him with services that filled his wants and needs. But, a sorcerer, I dare say, I am not. A simple magician, equipped only with trickery and sleight of hand, some simple magic tricks and chemistry, and knowledge of the natural world. I simply provided Lord Darden with the information he wanted to hear, and I convinced the people of his kingdom into believing he had the strength of a master sorcerer at his command by performing simple tricks and predicting the occurrences of natural events. All things any mere mortal could do, given the correct knowledge. I am embarrassed to say I am a fraud, only a simple, but well educated, common man. The title 'sorcerer' is one, I daresay, I do not qualify for."

"Spare me the self-pity and endless diatribe. It annoys me. I do not care very much for things that annoy me." Roga quickly lashed out with his hand

and caught a bee that had been buzzing about his head. He squeezed it in his palm and cast it hard upon the table. The severely contorted creature bounced once and lay dead. "I do not condone untruths, either." Spinning the magician's seat to face him, Roga bent forward, hands on the arms of Taygen's chair, and stared directly into the old man's eyes. "Keep that in mind, magician. If you have been untruthful with anything you have said to me or my men, now would be the time to cleanse your soul." Roga stared the magician in the eye for a short while longer, waiting for him to change his story, then turned and marched out of the tiny room, his entourage of soldiers in tow.

As he exited the room, Roga turned to Marshall Octrall.

"Keep a close watch on the magician. I do not trust he has been particularly truthful in his responses. And find me this Lord Darden he was speaking of. I believe he and I should have a little chat"

As the small door closed behind Roga and the noises outside subsided, Taygen gently reached over and, mumbling something under his breath, touched the dead insect. As he pulled his hand away, the bee quivered and righted itself. Straightening its legs, it began preening and working the kinks out of its once-mangled wings. Within seconds, it appeared as before its unfortunate encounter with Roga and flew off the table. Taygen watched as it flew away into the far recesses of the room, a smile carved across his weary face.

Roga continued his tour of the castle. By now most every room was completely torn apart. A constant flow of men was carrying items out of the castle and into the courtyard to be packed on dragons and returned to Khorgia. Roga glanced at the items as they were carried by him. Suddenly, he reached out and stopped one of the soldiers.

"What have you there?" he demanded.

The young soldier stopped in his tracks, frozen with fear. He stammered his reply. "It...it's a glass globe, my Lord. It has water and fish in it. Decorative, I assume."

Roga looked up at the young man's face and then back at the globe. "Decorative, hmmm? Fish?" Roga stooped down to see the fish swimming about in the vessel. "I have never seen such a thing." Roga continued staring, enraptured by the calm, gentle movements of the fish.

Two to three awkward minutes passed, Roga staring at the fish bowl while the young soldier stood at attention. The young man finally coughed to get warlord's attention. "My Lord?"

Roga snapped out of his trance and stood straight up. "Yes. Indeed." He fumbled a bit, annoyed at his moment of vulnerability. "Place it in with the items for my personal quarters. And use caution! I do not want it broken during the flight."

The young man straightened himself up, clicking his heels. "Yes, my Lord. As you wish." He continued on his way with the globe.

Roga looked about, searching out Aramas, the officer in charge of the area. "Aramas, that young man there." Roga pointed at the young soldier as he carried the globe out into the courtyard. "There. What are his name and his position?'

"A new recruit, my Lord. Ursen, I believe. Has he done something wrong? Something to offend you? I will deal with it immediately!"

"No. Quite the contrary. A fine young soldier. See to it he gets moved to a higher position. Is he one of yours?"

"Yes, my Lord."

"Fine job, Aramas. Keep up the good work."

"Thank you, my Lord!" Aramas began to leave and resume his work.

"Aramas."

"Yes, my Lord?"

"Better yet, see to it that the young man is sent to Minarik, my assistant. I am quite sure we can find him something to do on my personal staff."

Aramas smiled broadly and puffed out his chest. "With pleasure, sir!"

Roga dismissed Aramas and went back to inspecting the valuables as they were removed to the bailey. "Fish?"

"Fish, my Lord?"

The voice came from behind Roga. It was Marshall Octrall. Roga turned to face him, quickly changing the subject.

"You have a report for me, Octrall?"

Octrall snapped to attention. "Yes, my Lord. It would appear that the master of the castle, Lord Darden, did not manage to survive our attack. His remains were identified in the courtyard."

"And we are sure it was Lord Darden?"

“If the wails of his widow were any indications. She was quite inconsolable.”

“And what of our new acquaintance the magician?”

“The magician has been secured. He has no items of value or concern about his person. He, in fact, appears to be quite harmless. Shall we place him with the others?”

Roga grabbed his chin with his thumb and forefinger. "No, I think not. Place him in a wagon and take him to a place far from here. Release him to his own methods, but make sure he is left with the memory of who we are and what we are capable of. I do not trust him. I believe he is much more than he appears to the eye. I want reports on his activities, especially anything that seems out of sorts. If this magician reveals any powers of the supernatural, I want to know at once. Understood?"

“Understood, my Lord. I will attend to the magician immediately. And the others?”

“The others?”

“The other people of the castle, my Lord. What should I do with them?”

“Round them all up. Place them under guard in the stable.”

“As you wish, my Lord. Shall we begin interrogations?”

Roga chuckled. “Of course not, Octrall. Interrogation would be such a waste of time. Herd them into the stable, Darden’s body as well, and, as soon as I have left, burn it to the ground!”

FLAMES SHOT HIGH INTO the air as the castle’s stables quickly burned. The screams of the dying had subsided and only the roar of the flames could be heard. Marshall Octrall watched the scene with several of his guards.

“It is done. Let us leave this place. We have no more business here. Besides, the smell of victory is not as sweet at the place that it was won.”

The group turned and headed for the castle keep, seeking to make their dragon-borne escape to the fresh air above. Across the bailey, a lone figure slipped silently from shadow to shadow and out the gate, racing for the nearby forest as soon as he was beyond the castle walls. As he reached the underbrush, Arvid quickly scanned the only home he had ever known, his eyes flickering from the flames that tore through the stables and with the intense anger and disgust of a man stripped of his livelihood and history. After one last gaze, he faded into the shadows of the forest, never looking back.

10
REFUGEES

ELDEN WALKED THROUGH the market in awe. Hundreds of people of unknown origins occupied every corner. They sought refuge from the dragon attacks in the one place legendary for its stability, *eht Vilna Sahnah*. People had trekked from the kingdoms south of the Tantallon Forest and *eht Vilna Turega*, from the edges of the desert wasteland north of the Souliban and the lands beyond the Oryon River. All order of people were arriving; the injured and infirmed, the frightened, and warriors making their way southward. Nomads, vagabonds, countrymen and royals – all were equally represented. Elden did his best to greet all that passed through the gates for the first time. He approached individuals at random, asking their name, homeland, and situation. Most were not victims of the attacks but simply seeking a place where they felt safe. Sadly, he had yet to find a single refugee from either the Souliban or *eht Vilna Moht*, both completely devastated by the dragon attacks.

Elden approached a tall, lean fellow who appeared particularly disheveled. "Good day, sir. I am Elden, a royal agent of this castle. May I ask what parts you have journeyed from and what I might be able to do to help you now that you have arrived here?"

The man stood in respect. "I am called Zephraim. I am a beekeeper. I seek refuge from the dragon attacks."

"You shall have refuge here. May I ask your home?"

"I have traveled from the Souliban..."

Elden cut him short. "The Souliban? A messenger informed us all were lost. Can you offer us different news?"

"Sadly, I cannot. All I had and all that I have known is gone, melted as if ice and left to seep into the parched earth. I was spared by a hollow deep in the ground but emerged to find everything laid waste. The dragons left little if anything behind. This messenger you speak of is the only other I have heard of that may have survived. I know of no one else. I lost everything." Zephraim's voice trailed off. "Everything."

Elden placed his hand upon Zephraim's shoulder as a show of support. "Come. Walk with me. I must attend to the people here but would ask you to join with me and return to the castle. Perhaps you would be kind enough to grant me the wisdom of your experience. From what I see before me in this marketplace, the time for action is at hand. Any knowledge of the attacks and the assailants would be of great assistance in creating an appropriate plan of action."

"I will gladly tell you all I know with but one request. I seek vengeance for my losses, my family, my home. I pray you allow me that opportunity when you set your plans in motion."

"That is a request I cannot deny, Master Zephraim. I would be honored to have you beside me when we confront the dragons. What skills do you bring? What specialty do you offer?"

"I was a beekeeper by trade but the dragons have ensured I no longer have hives to care for. Beyond that, I have but my hands and my mind and my heart to offer. I have nothing else."

Elden smiled and extended his hand to Zephraim once again. "Sounds exactly like what we are looking for. No matter the skills brought, if a man has no heart to offer, he is of little value to this army. We need committed souls if we are to be successful. Committed souls and intelligent minds. Please, walk with me."

Elden and Zephraim walked together amongst the mass of humanity that was once the marketplace, talking between stops to comfort the injured and confused. As they approached Duggan's produce booth, the figure of a badly beaten elder caught Elden's attention. Duggan was attempting to help the older man, comforting him to the best of his abilities.

"Duggan, who is this man? What has happened to him?"

"Master Elden! I am not sure. When I arrived this morning, he was here, propped up against my booth. He is rather battered but I am not sure if by the journey or by the hand of some unscrupulous soul. He has no more than the clothing on his back so I fear the latter. He has not been conscious enough to tell his story."

Elden knelt down beside the old man, brushing the thin white hair from his face. The man's eyes fluttered suddenly and then slowly opened.

"Be still, old man. You are in good company. We are here to help you. It would appear someone has done you a world of mischief."

The old man nodded his head slowly in affirmation.

"Were you robbed?"

The old man shook his head. "N... no. What I carry is all I own."

Elden placed a finger on the old man's lips. "Shhhhh. Relax. Do not speak. You are weak and need your wounds attended to." He turned to Zephraim and Duggan. "Duggan, take my new friend Zephraim and find something to use as a bier. We need to carry this man to the castle keep. I will see to it that his injuries are cared for."

Duggan took Zephraim to find some wood and a skin or canvas from which to fashion a litter. Elden propped the old man up and attempted to tend to his wounds.

"Easy. Relax. Try not to move. When my partners return, we will take you inside and have your injuries looked at. Are you well enough to tell me who did this to you?"

The old man spoke softly. "I was at *eht Vilna Moht*. The dragon riders interrogated me and then took me away. They brought me to the forest, beat me, and left me to die. I believe they were trying to send a message. What happened to the rest, I have no knowledge."

"You are one of the few I know of that has survived the dragon attacks. The Souliban, *eht Vilna Moht*, they were annihilated. I can count the known survivors of those two attacks on one hand. The dragon riders have not knowingly left a single witness. That is what makes your case particularly strange to me. Why were you spared?"

Presently, Duggan and Zephraim returned with a makeshift litter.

"This is the best we could do on short notice, my lord."

"It will do just fine, Duggan. Come. Help me get him into the bier and to the castle. He needs care and rest. He will have both beneath the same roof that shelters me."

Carefully, the three men moved the old man to the litter. Duggan and Zephraim each grabbed an end and Elden parted the crowd, making way to the castle. Elden wished to further talk to the man but realized his need for medical assistance surpassed his own need for information. He would ask for the man's story at a later date.

Elden spent the next few days meeting with the refugees, asking their stories and helping those that needed assistance. So much fear and tragedy surrounded him.

Most difficult was the fact that the exploding population within the walls of the castle was taxing the resources. Food and water were readily available at the moment, but the massive influx of people would soon deplete whatever reserves were in storage. Far less available were places of lodging. Many refugees were simply living on the streets and in the marketplace. Sanitary facilities were also at a premium. If things did not change in the near future, life at *eht Vilna Sahnah* would become troublesome. Something had to be done... and soon.

ELDEN POKED HIS HEAD into his mother's sitting room and, seeing she was alone, let himself in.

"Good evening, mother. How was your day today?"

Ahlāan looked up from her needlework and smiled at her son. "Elden! What a pleasant surprise! And to what do I owe the pleasure of your visit this evening?"

"Why nothing. Can't a son just come to see how his mother is doing for no reason other than the sight of her smiling face?"

"Yes, a son can do that, just not my son." Ahlāan laughed. "Elden, you are a good son. You never once caused me trouble, but you have more important things in your life now, adult responsibilities, obligations to this castle and its inhabitants. And, although I might be one of the inhabitants, I am far more capable of care within the walls of this keep than those that live on the outside. Quite frankly, you are far too busy to spend time with your boring old mother so, when you come to visit, I know it is more than just to wish me a good evening."

“I could never fool you. You know me better than anyone, mother.”

"Yes, I do. And I do not hold any of it against you. You have grown into an important figure in this kingdom and your time is valuable. And, to be truly honest, I have no desire to be kept informed of the minutia of daily life within, or beyond, this castle. Politics and matters of state and the price of wheat in Cameron do nothing to stir my interest. So, what have you come to ask me?"

“I’ve come to ask your opinion on a matter of great importance before I approach the Queen for her approval.”

“Ah! So, you need your mother’s advice regarding how to present your case to your dear grandmother? I appreciate your trust in my powers of persuasion over her, Elden, but if anyone knows the mind of the Queen, it is you.”

"Of that, I am well aware, mother, but this is far more grave than a simple matter of state or how to garner another pet plains rat. It involves my leaving the castle and taking arms against the dragons. Even with my insight, I cannot wrap my head around how the Queen shall react."

“Ah! Now it has all become crystal clear! You need your mother’s advice on which deception will work best against the Queen in order to garner her approval for your plans.” Ahlāan put down her needlework and flattened the wrinkles on her lap. “Well, then, I guess you have come to the proper place. Who better to give advice on swaying the mind of Queen Isella than her own daughter? I daresay I have had the opportunity to use my wits against Mum-ma on occasion, and, I might add, with some modicum of success. And I believe it was I that provided you the proper argument by which you were able to procure another plains rat for your menagerie. I am ready. Present your case.”

“Mother, the resources of the kingdom are being stretched to the limit with the influx of refugees. We will not be capable of sustaining them long term. Something needs to be done if we are to survive the consequences of the dragon attacks. I have determined the need to take the offensive. We are no match defensively for the dragons. They simply overwhelm any resistance. Only a well-planned offensive will strike the enemy and show them we are a force to reckon with. If we continue to huddle in our castles like frightened children, they will devastate the mainland, one kingdom at a time, until we are all but gone."

"And how do you plan to implement this undertaking?"

"I will head south, likely to De' Aarna, and try to gather forces. The dragons appear to be working from the Souliban southward, striking each population center in separate attacks. De' Aarna is well south. I should have a few weeks to put together a small army."

"How can you be sure of your safety or the safety of this castle?"

"I have studied warfare and strategy for years, Mother. How the attacks have progressed follows a particular logic. They are working their way south along the coast, attacking every few days. This allows for any missed inhabitants to seek refuge in the next kingdom. Then they attack that kingdom. It is a logical assumption that they will continue south along the coast until all cities have been destroyed and then they will follow the same pattern, in reverse, attacking the next tier inland. It minimizes the chance of being surrounded as they slowly move inland."

"IF I AM WRONG AND THEY begin moving inland, they open themselves up to being surrounded. Their dragons can fly only so far before setting down to rest. Once they set down, they become vulnerable. Somehow, I fail to believe their leader is that much a fool."

Elden repeated his intentions to the Queen, exactly as he had explained it to his mother. When he finished, he let his arms fall to his sides and stood quietly before the throne awaiting his grandmother's response.

Queen Isella looked at him long and hard, slowly stroking her arm. "Your mother has coached you well, grandson. You often know the strings to pull to gain my favor or obtain yet another creature that your mother and I end up caring for, but you have surpassed even your best with this argument. Clearly, you have joined forces with her on this occasion." The Queen paused for a moment. "The two of you have crafted a most eloquent and persuasive line of reasoning. Let it be so. When will you need to leave?"

"At daybreak. I wish to reach De'Aarna in as short a time as possible and begin recruiting men."

"And you will travel with a contingent of soldiers from the castle?"

"No, I will not leave the castle without protection. Besides, a large contingent will only draw attention."

"You intend to travel alone?"

"That would not be a prudent decision either. There is a man from the Souliban, a beekeeper. He is the only survivor known to us from that attack. He seeks to avenge the loss of his family. I would be happy and honored to travel with him."

The Queen nodded. "As you wish. My sole request is that you send word when you reach your destination."

"That I can promise, my Queen. And when we have assembled an army, I will send word. You can call for a conclave of the Confederacy to convene in De' Aarna where we may discuss the best posture to assume against the dragons."

11
ORAN, THE DEMON CHILD

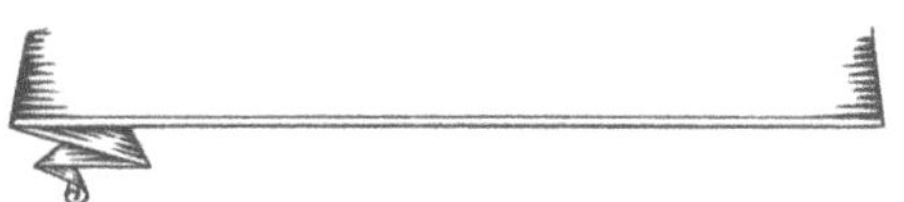

6071 E.K.

Timmol and Vidro sat around the fire, greedily gorging themselves on the corn and turnips 'creatively acquired' from the castle fields the previous evening. The *borundahli*, a nomadic tribe that traversed the lands outside and between the castles, had settled down and set camp in a small clearing deep within the dense evergreen woods between *eht Vilna Sahnah* and the mountains to the west. Time to eat, pass stories amongst themselves, and settle down for a quick evening's sleep before breaking camp and moving again. Such was the life of a nomad. Moving quietly by day, sometimes stopping at the outskirts of a town to offer their skills or barter and trade for goods, taking what was needed to survive by dawn or twilight, and settling down overnight in places out of the way of the 'normal' population. A close-knit family, even if there were few blood relations, the nomads relished their vagabond lifestyle, happy to endlessly roam the countryside, as opposed to settling down to the more mundane work-a-day lifestyle of the general populace, unfettered by the chains of familial, political, or commercial associations.

"A fine nosh this is, I must say, eh Vidro?"

Vidro took another large bite from the turnip he held. "I dare say you are right Timmol, but I could do for some meat soon. Maybe we could roust some game come the morn."

"Agreed. A spot of bird or possibly a hare would make a fine meal. And who knows, with some luck, maybe a damned fine buck will cross our path. What a fine feast that would be!"

"Well, if the Good Mother decides that tomorrow is not the right day for us to be blessed with some game, so be Her will. We will just have to make do with the sustenance She provides for us." Vidro took another bite from his turnip then hesitated for a moment, coddling an idea in his head. He turned to his companion. "Timmol, have you ever given second thoughts to the manner by which we take from the gardens and stock pens of the villagers?"

Timmol took a moment to mull the question over himself. "Vidro, the Good Mother *Sibu* has created all that we see before us, the trees, the plants, the mountains and all the animals. They are Hers to withhold or give, as She sees fit. If we are not stopped from procuring those things that we require for survival, then they are there for us to use as we see fit. If we take beyond our needs and hoard the fruits of Her labor, then She will no longer be so gracious to provide for us. Besides, those foolish blue-bloods fail to adequately protect what they rear or cultivate. If they are that foolish, then they deserve to have it taken away. Remember, the ancient writings tell us '*A fool quickly loses the fruits of his labors while a meticulous laborer reaps the rewards of his efforts.*' Those of the inbred aristocracy have not the good common sense to safeguard their goods, what with all that bowing and genuflecting they do to one another."

Both men chuckled loudly as they went back to their meal. At the edges of the firelight, the faces of possibly two-dozen others flickered in and out of view. Two or three women stood up presently and began to gather the children in preparation for bed. They would all sleep well tonight with bellies full of vegetables and their minds full of the stories and wisdom of their elders' fireside chats. A young boy ran up to Vidro, wrapping his arms around his neck.

"Good night, Papa. I hope you catch a fine buck in the morning."

Vidro smiled and hugged the little guy back. "Get yourself to bed, Yockeff. Your Papa will see what he can do to get that buck for you tomorrow. If I can get him, you can have the antlers to make a knife handle or two with your playmates." Yockeff smiled and gave his father another hug before running off to his mother to be put to bed.

"A fine little boy you have there, Vidro."

Vidro continued to watch his son head towards the wagon where all the children slept. "Thank you, Timmol. I have his mother to thank for that. She's the one that has raised him so far. My day will come when he is ready to begin hunting and fishing. Then, I will teach him those things most important, like all there is to know about being a man." He bent closer to his friend and whispered, "But don't tell his mother I said that, or I'll get a swift bat up beside the earhole!"

The two men laughed.

"That is true for all boys, Vidro. Pulling at their mother's apron strings for their first ten years. Once they get older, they start to learn from their dads all the skills needed to be a man. Your day will come."

Vidro nodded his agreement and then turned to face his friend. "Timmol, why haven't you and Mari had any children?"

Timmol took a moment to answer. "Mother *Sibu* has never graced us with a child. Not for lack of trying, I daresay. I'm surprised my ding hasn't been worn down to a nub! Perhaps *Sibu* has other plans for Mari and me. We do not question what Her intent may be. We have been too involved in leading this clan, making sure everyone was fed and safe. All of the children of the clan are our children, Mari, and I. We care for and love each and every one as if they were our own. What matters to us is family, this family. The success of the clan is our reward."

Timmol pulled a small stoneware jug from behind the boulder on which he was sitting and held it high. "And this is *our* reward!" he said, smiling. Pulling the cork out with his teeth, he offered it up to Vidro. He took a large mouthful of the clear liquid and grimaced as he swallowed. He passed the jug back to Timmol.

"That will make a man out of you, Vidro!" Timmol took a large mouthful and swallowed. "If it doesn't kill you first!" He laughed, wiping his mouth with his sleeve.

Both men continued talking for some time, passing the jug back and forth between them. With all the children safely tucked in and asleep, the women were quietly cleaning up the pots from the evening meal, often glancing up at the two as they broke into raucous laughter. The fire had long since burned down to a mass of glowing embers.

Timmol's wife, Maricol, stopped what she was doing and walked over to the two inebriated men, standing before them with her hands on her hips. Maricol was a beautiful woman of about 35, flaxen blonde hair pulled back from her face exposing two soft, expressive green-blue eyes, currently glaring at the two men sitting on the rocks in front of her. She was Timmol's conscience and the glue that held the group of vagabonds together. One could quite easily say that *SHE* was the leader of this family, not her husband. Gracious to a fault, she instead gave all her love and support to Timmol, allowing him to stand before their clan as their leader. Only he was truly aware of how big a part Maricol played in the governing and direction of the group. The two men looked up at her standing before them.

"Oooooo!" The two men began giggling and falling over each other. Timmol pointed at his wife, speaking into Vidro's ear in a very poor attempt to whisper. "It looks like we have been very naughty boys. Matron has come to spank us." The two laughed like children.

"Time for the two of you to get yourselves to bed, before you cause any mischief." Mari dumped the dishwashing water on the remains of the fire. "Come. The dawn will arrive before you know it. If you have any plans for hunting game in the morning, then it is time to be in bed. Two giggling, drunken fools will more likely scare all the game away."

Still sniggering, the two men struggled to gain their feet, leaning against each other to maintain their balance. Timmol dropped the now-empty bottle. He placed his arm around Vidro's shoulders.

"Come, Vidro. Let's retire. A few hours of sleep will take the edge off and get us back on our feet for the hunt."

Arm in arm, Timmol and Vidro shuffled off to their respective tents, giggling loudly along the way.

A deep silence hung over the nomads' camp as two moons in a cloudless sky lit the ground from above. A thin wisp of smoke still curled above the now dormant fire pit, the only movement to be seen. The mules, goats, and dogs were all bedded down for the evening. All the members of the clan were fast asleep in their respective tents and wagons. Even the nighttime insects were silent. Altogether, it was a most peaceful scene.

Timmol woke to the prodding of an elbow into his side. Maricol, still half asleep mumbled at him. "Timmy, go take care of the baby."

Timmol rolled out of his bedroll with great effort, his eyes still full of sleep, his head clouded and pounding from the after-dinner drinking binge he had with Vidro. He picked himself off of the ground onto his hands and knees and began to crawl to the door flap of the tent, not anywhere near awake. He mumbled to himself, "Take care of the baby." As he reached the tent flap, he realized that he and Maricol had no baby. Stopping in his tracks, he turned back to his sleeping wife. "Baby? Maricol, we don't have a..."

Just as he was about to say it, he heard it - the cry of an infant, just outside of the tent. Timmol quickly wheeled around and stuck his head outside the tent flap, looking left and right. Then he heard it again to the right of the tent, a distinct baby's cry. Suddenly sober, he scrambled out of the tent and to his feet, stumbling around to the right side of the tent. There, on the ground, and wrapped in an apron, was an obviously newborn baby. The child was still covered in the white, pasty vernix caseosa from birth, little bits of leaf, stick, and dirt sticking to the slimy goo. Timmol snatched the baby up, checking him over carefully. He seemed no worse for wear, with no obvious injuries. Timmol looked back to the spot where he had picked up the child, hoping to find a clue as to his origin. What he found brought a chill up his spine. Quickly grabbing the item from the ground, he looked about to see if he had been noticed and ducked back into his tent.

Inside the tent, the babe continued to cry. Maricol began to stir.

"Timmy, what in the name of *Sibu* is that infernal racket?" She turned over, wiping the sleep from her eyes, to find her husband kneeling before her with a child in his arms. Not even *Sibu*, the most holy Mother of the Land, could have prepared Maricol for the vision that was now before her. A look of astonishment froze on her face. "Timmy! Wha...? Where?"

"Mari. It's a baby. It was against the side of the tent."

"I can see it's a baby! How did it get there? Why was it left beside our tent? No one within the clan is with child, so it is not one of ours."

Timmol held up the item he had found outside, a large snakeskin. Maricol's face went ashen, a look of total fear in her eyes.

"He has come back for you! I thought you had repaid your debt to him! I cannot live on with him terrorizing us again!"

"Mari, please, calm down. My debt has been paid. He said himself that he would not bother us again."

His wife was not encouraged by his words. "Then, why this? Why would he drop this baby off at our tent?"

"Who knows the mind of a demon? Why this? I cannot say. Would he not afflict me with boils if he could, or cripple me, or smite me down in my tracks? For some reason, he has chosen me to watch over this child. Maybe I am the only human he has had contact with that can be found in this area of the land. Whatever the reason, the child is here now and I will not cast it out into the world."

"No. We cannot cast him out. Whatever the reason for him being here, it is not because of anything he has done. We cannot leave him. Surely the demon would come back to haunt us if we left the child to die in the wilderness. Timmy, give him here. He needs to be kept warm."

Timmol handed him over to his wife who quickly wrapped him in her blanket. As she cradled him to her breast, the infant calmed and began rooting around for a nipple.

"Timmy, he's hungry. We're going to need to figure out a way to feed him as I am certainly in no condition to do so."

Although still not completely clear, Timmol's mind went to work, desperate to find a solution to their quandary. After a few minutes, he had the answer. "There is goat's milk in the wagon and I can fashion a nipple for a wineskin. That should be suitable." His eyes eagerly sought affirmation from his wife.

"Yes, my love. That should be more than suitable. But, please, be quick about it. He is very hungry and far less gentle than you. I fear he will suckle my nipple clean from my breast. If he is not fed soon, I would expect him to wail through the night until he has awakened the entire camp."

Timmol left the tent to gather the milk and wineskin. Upon his return, Maricol dripped milk onto her breast to satisfy the babe while he altered the wineskin spout to create a makeshift nipple. Handing it to his wife, she managed to release the babe's suction on her own nipple and replaced it with the wineskin. Greedily, he drank nearly half the contents before drifting off to sleep.

Maricol rocked the babe gently in her arms. "How do we explain the sudden appearance of the child to the clan?"

Timmol mulled the question over in his mind for a bit. "We simply tell them the truth or as much of the truth as they need to hear. The Good Mother has miraculously blessed us with a child. We announce it to the clan as such and convince them how blessed we are to be given such a gift from Her. No one will dare to debate the validity of a gift from *Sibu*."

"And he truly is a gift, Timmy. Look how peaceful he is now. This is where he is supposed to be." She smiled as she looked down at the sleeping child. "We must name him, Timmy. We need to present him to the Good Mother and offer thanks. She will guide us to the proper name." She handed the child to her husband. "Go while he is still quiet and his belly is full. You do not want to wake the camp."

Timmol carefully took the child from his wife, trying not to awaken him. Cradling the babe against his chest, he left the tent and walked into the wilderness away from camp. In a clearing surrounded by large evergreens, he stopped. Looking up to the sky, he held the babe out and called to *Sibu*, the Mother of the Land. "Most gracious Mother *Sibu*, we thank you for the blessing of this child and seek your guidance and favor. Grant us the knowledge to raise him properly and offer a sign of his name." Staring into space, a twinkle caught Timmol's eye. Oran, the Purple Wanderer, the largest planet in the Beta Trianguli system, blinked high in the sky directly over the clearing. This was the sign he was looking for. "I present to you, Good Mother *Sibu*, my son, Oran. May he always be graced with your favor."

A cold breeze blew through the clearing. Timmol brought the baby back to his chest and hurried back to his tent.

6093 E.K.

Life for Oran was not necessarily the easiest. Growing up as a child in a band of nomads could be harsh. There were strenuous chores that had to be completed and skills to learn if one was to be a productive member of the clan. Every member, even the children, was expected to contribute somehow to the communal good of the clan. Being the child of the clan chieftain, it was even tougher for Oran. Timmol could be quite the task master. As the leader of the clan, he and his family had to live up to a rather high standard. Timmol would accept no deviation from that standard, not for himself, nor his wife or his son. Frequently during his childhood, Oran had felt the business end of the switch or a slap across the face. Many an evening, the young boy had plotted his revenge, typically in the most fanciful of plans. He would become a magician and turn his father into a cricket that he would keep in a little cage and torment by pulling his legs off one by one only to regenerate them with a spell, or he was to fly off into the sunset on a grand white Pegasus and never return. As he grew older, his thoughts became less fanciful and more defiant. He would dream of the day when he would finally stand up to his father and push him aside, conjuring up the inner strength to challenge him and leave him in defeat. That day would come.

Oran would often seek solitude in the forest in order to be away from the clan. Careful to have his chores completed, he would slip away for hours, walking the hunting paths and deer trails, happy in his isolation. Here he could conjure any of a million scenarios to release himself from servitude to his adoptive parents and familial tribe.

As Oran quietly moved through the forest, he was startled by the figure of a man suddenly standing in the path before him. Veiled by a dark cloak, the young man was unable to make out any distinguishing features. He took a defensive pose and addressed the figure.

"Hail! Do not startle. I walk alone and in peace." Oran presented his hands to the stranger. "I intend no harm."

The figure turned its hidden face towards him. "No harm has been inferred." The figure's voice was booming and hollow, but somehow strangely melodic, resounding through the forest as if projecting directly from the wood. "I travel alone and in peace as well. Give your name and station as we might converse as equals."

"I am Oran, son of Timmol and Maricol, leaders of a small tribe of nomads native to this forest and adjacent lands. I seek solitude in the deeper ranges of the forest, to think quietly and be at peace with the natural realm. And with whom am I to be acquainted?"

"I am hailed Sahk Tett by the few that know me. I, too, have sought the solitude of the deep forest. Perhaps this meeting was foretold somewhere in the songs and writings, two like minds brought together by fate. And from what reality do you seek isolation?"

"I seek a separation between myself and my clan. I am truly not one of them and do not prescribe to their way of life. They work for the benefit of the whole even at the deficit of themselves."

"So, if I understand your comments correctly, you would prefer to work for your own benefit and reap the fruits of those labors? Again, I find the two of us to be of common mind. Those I have chosen to surround myself with also labor towards their own aspirations, whether they be common to the others or not. We seek influence and power to control our own destinies, forge our own lives. We embrace that which provides advantage and shun weakness and submission. Perhaps you would join us?"

"I am intrigued. May I ask that you walk with me and tell me more of your group. Perhaps I shall find reason to change the company I keep."

"It will be a pleasure, Master Oran. I will gladly share the philosophies of our following. And, should you decide, we would be honored to accept your accompaniment."

"And where would I locate you should I find the desire to leave and seek my own fortunes?"

"We often take leave at the mouth of the great river in the place known as De'Aarna, just a few days trek from where we stand presently. Come to visit us. There is always room at the table for one of like mind."

"I may just take you up on that offer."

The two men walked and talked, discussing life and philosophy and the meanings found in the songs and prophecies. An hour, and then another, had easily passed before they approached the edge of the forest near to where the clan was encamped.

Oran pointed through the trees. "There. Beyond the trees is where we make camp." He turned to look at Sahk Tett, but the cloaked man was no longer beside him. He wheeled around, scanning the forest behind, but the man had disappeared as if ether. He took a few strides back towards where he had come, desperately seeking any sign of his newfound acquaintance but the figure was nowhere to be seen. Confounded, he turned to go back to the encampment.

AN INTENT ORAN SAT at the small table that occupied the center of the family tent, carefully running a stone across the blade of his knife.

"Oran! What for the love of life are you doing? Did I not tell you to clean up after the mules?"

Not removing his focus from his knife, Oran addressed his father, monotone and distant. "Yes, father. I know what you told me to do, but I do not see why I need to pick up after mules that are not even ours. I will tend to the mules when I have finished."

Timmol was infuriated. "When I give you a task to complete, I expect you to do it! Those mules belong to all of us. We in this clan are family and everyone works together for the benefit of the whole, you included!" Enraged he slapped the knife out of his son's grasp with one swipe of his hand.

Oran jumped up, spilling the chair behind him, and got up into Timmol's' face. Before he could say anything, Timmol struck him across the jaw with an open hand. "Do not challenge me, young man! I am your father and the master of this clan. Out of respect for me, you will do as I have instructed! I gave you a task and I expect it to be completed!"

Oran turned his face slowly back towards his father, his brow furrowed with anger. But what caused his father to startle were his eyes. They had become bright yellow with vertical slits for pupils and full of hostility. Timmol curled back slightly in fear.

Oran addressed Timmol in a barely audible whisper. "You will never strike me again, old man. Do not *ever* raise your hand to me again or I will surely strike you down. I choose what I do from now on, not the likes of you. You forget one important fact; I am NOT of this clan!"

Timmol backed into the corner, shivering in fear. Pointing to the flap of the tent, he screamed at Oran. "Leave us! Leave this tent, leave this camp. Just leave and let us be. You are the demon's child! I should have known better than to take you in when you were left at our tent all those years ago. I knew there had to be a reason for it. I just failed to put all the clues together. It was Sutek's way of getting back at me, having me raise his evil spawn! You are cursed. Get out! Go out into the wild and never return!"

The color of Oran's eyes had returned to their normal brown but his stare had not left Timmol. "I shall leave of my own accord, but mind me when I tell you, this is not the last time you will think of me. The memory of my face shall haunt you again and again, and I shall take pleasure in the fact that you will never be free of me." Oran grabbed his things. "Sleep with one eye open, father, for the days of plenty and happiness that you have enjoyed are soon to pass."

Oran ducked through the tent flap and out into the night. Maricol bolted towards the opening, intent on stopping her son from leaving, but Timmol held her back.

"Let him go, Mari, let him go. He is right. He is not one of us and does not belong here. Let him go to find his own way, and himself, in the world."

Maricol ceased her struggling and pushed the tent flap aside. The shadowy figure of her adoptive son slowly disappeared into the night, causing her to break into heavy, silent sobbing. Timmol wrapped her in his arms gently consoling her.

Oran left the encampment under cover of darkness. He was determined to get as far away from the vagabonds as possible before dawn. He never wanted to cross their paths ever again. It was time to make his own place in the world, separate from the family that had raised him. Heading east, he sought the great river that the cloaked figure had told him about. It would take him to De'Aarna and to a better way of life. Never giving so much as a glance back, he slipped into the forest and was gone.

Oran spent most of the evening and the next day working his way eastward through the forest. He had encountered not so much as a remnant of mortal existence the entire journey and only a few denizens of the wood. He fed on berries and plants, drinking water that had pooled up on large leaves or in the hollows of tree trunks. It was enough to keep him going, but barely. By nightfall, after a night and a day of travel, he was in need of rest. Finding a thicket, he crawled within and buried himself in the leaves to conceal his whereabouts and maintain some of his body heat.

ORAN ROSE FROM HIS earthen bed in the morning and continued on his way towards the rising sun. Repeating the pattern, he traveled by day and settled in each evening for sleep. Three days of travel brought Oran to the Oryon River, a wide, fast-moving ribbon of water. Unable to cross and having been taught all rivers and streams eventually lead to the sea, he followed the waterway downstream, through the wood. Another day of travel brought Oran to the edge of the forest where the land opened up to a hillside meadow. As he crested the hill and looked into the distance, the sea enveloped the entire panorama. In the center, along the shoreline directly before him sat a sprawling walled city. Cautiously, Oran headed for the roadway that led towards the shore and the metropolis that rested alongside.

As he approached the edge of the sprawl, he was surprised to see it bore no resemblance to the castle he was familiar with. Surrounded by a high wall with a single well-guarded entrance, the city lacked a central castle or keep. Instead, a large market occupied the hub. Low buildings lined the narrow streets, packing the space surrounded by the wall to the point of bursting. People were everywhere, walking, doing business, or simply sitting around waiting for a handout. He stopped a man as he walked by.

"Excuse me, sir. Could you tell me the name of this wonderful place I have stumbled upon?"

The man gently pushed him away slightly. "You are in De'Aarna, once known as Korham. You and thousands of others that were not here a mere fortnight ago."

"Please, tell me, why have so many descended upon the city?"

The man glared at him, pure bemusement on his face. "How have you not heard? Dragons have attacked. First in the Souliban, then *eht Vilna Moht* and last at *eht Vilna Antessara*. These people around you are all refugees. And if not dragon attacks, what has brought you here?"

Oran looked perplexed. "I have come here on my own, seeking the company of like-minded people and a safe haven from my past. I know nothing of these dragon attacks you talk about."

Disgusted, the man walked away. "First it was refugees, and now it is vagabonds. What is next, tourists?"

Oran watched the man in disbelief as he quickly disappeared into the mass of humanity that walked the narrow streets of De'Aarna.

And then reality set in. What was he to do next? He was here, in the city of De'Aarna, but he had no means to earn a living, no place to rest his head at the end of the day. He had no idea where to begin looking for the cloaked man or his associates. He did not know the lay of the land. Then his stomach grumbled and reality struck him again. He was hungry and he had no idea where to find something to eat but he knew he needed to have something in his gut. Scanning the market, he found a booth with a produce vendor. A tomato or bunch of carrots would hit the spot right about now. He approached the vendor and cleared his throat.

The vendor looked up from his work. "If you are not here to buy, just keep moving. No free samples or handouts here."

"I would not accept a handout, sir, but I would be willing to work for a few tomatoes or a bunch of carrots."

The vendor looked him up and down. "Are you for real or are you playing me for a fool?"

"I am most certainly for real, sir, and I do not know enough of you, yet, to consider you a fool. Unlike the majority, I have sought this place of my own will, a city by the sea. I wish to make my own destiny, through my own hard work and good deeds. I will accept neither pity nor charity, but I will work the remainder of the day for you in trade for three of your tomatoes and a bunch of carrots."

The vendor looked him over carefully, not sure what to make of the young man. He tossed Oran a tomato. "Quell your hunger a moment with this and follow me. I have crates I need to get down from my wagon and have them brought to the stand, but I cannot retrieve them and watch my merchandise at the same time. When you have finished, I will have more for you to eat, and then, if you like, we can talk about tomorrow."

Oran took a bite of the large, ripe red tomato and followed the vendor to his wagon, a smile on his face. Mere days on his own and only moments in the city and he was well on his way towards making a life for himself. Certainly, this would be much more to his liking than scraping a living out of the forest or stealing from the castle. And whatever he earned here would be for his own benefit, not the benefit of others. Here in the city by the sea, a man could earn a proper wage and, while doing so, earn respect.

Oran spent the day with the vendor, helping him move produce back and forth from his wagon and his stand, stacking the produce for all to see, and even trying his best at sales every now and again. The vendor would toss him a carrot or two or even a tomato or potato throughout the day. As the day wound to a close and the crowds subsided, all the merchants began collecting their wares for another day. Oran and the produce vendor crated up the remains of the produce and transferred them back to the wagon.

The vendor tossed Oran another potato. "Kid, you did well today. It would be far from a lie to say you were quite helpful. Would you care to meet me here at dawn for another day of this?"

Oran smiled. "Gladly, sir."

The vendor extended his hand. "I am known by most as Pennik."

"I am Oran. It has been a pleasure making your acquaintance today."

"Well, Oran, tomorrow will be another hard day of work. Do you think you're ready for it?"

"Most certainly, Mister Pennik. I will await your arrival at dawn, ready for another day."

Pennik rummaged around in a wooden box beneath the wagon's seat. He tossed something towards Oran. "Here. It's some dried fish. You will need meat if you are going to be moving crates all day."

"Much obliged, Pennik. 'Til tomorrow." Oran closed the gate to the wagon and Pennik turned and rode off.

As the wagon disappeared, Oran realized he was once again alone in De'Aarna. Not knowing anyone and having no place to go, he began to wander, looking for a place to rest his head for the night. Perhaps he would encounter the cloaked man and his colleagues and would be offered a place to stay this evening. Oran walked the streets of the city, scanning the crowd for the faceless cloak, but, as night began to fall, he had yet to meet with success. In need of a place to rest his head, he returned to Pennik's produce stall and curled up in the corner.

ORAN STARTLED AWAKE. Rubbing the sleep away from his eyes, he looked up to see the figure of a cloaked man standing above him.

"Master Oran. I'm glad to see you have found your way to De'Aarna. Come. I have friends who are anxious to meet you."

Oran rose from his makeshift bed. "You! I have been seeking your acquaintance for the entire evening. I was beginning to wonder if we would ever cross paths again. Our discourse in the forest intrigued me enough to direct me here, to De'Aarna, when I left the clan. I often wondered what happened to you that afternoon. You... disappeared."

“That is in the past, Oran, and we have no means to change the past. What matters is that you are here now. Come. Follow me. We can talk more on our way. I have much to tell you.”

Oran joined the cloaked man and, engaged in conversation, walked off into the darkness of the evening.

IN A MAKESHIFT MEDICAL facility in the bowels of a shining castle, an old man lay asleep on a litter. Suddenly his eyes opened and he was awake. A chill overcame his body, from head to toe. There had been a change in the balance of nature. Another soul had been enjoined with the side of darkness, a strong soul. The events predicted in the Prophecy of Korham had been set in motion. Gathering his meager belongings, the old man slowly pulled himself to his feet, joints creaking, and shuffled to the doorway that led out of the hold. Pushing the door to the side, he stepped into the night, disappearing into the ether before he completed his third step.

12
THE MEETING

THE SUN WAS SLOWLY sinking in the sky, muting the vibrant colors of the surrounding world into grays and blacks. Two figures strode purposefully in the twilight along the path leading to De'Aarna. Rounding a corner, they came upon a small group of travelers collecting supplies to settle in for the night. One of the pair shouted forward to the group.

"Ahead! May we approach? Is there room for two more in your party this evening?"

The apparent leader of the group stopped foraging and approached them with another.

"Come. Yes, we can find room for two more, but be on notice, if anyone in the group finds a reason to doubt your intentions or sincerity, you will be asked to leave us. If those conditions meet your approval, please, come help us prepare for the evening."

"Your conditions are fair enough." The pair approached the camp. "I am Elden. My traveling companion is Zephraim. We have come this far from *eht Vilna Sahnah* with hopes of arriving at De'Aarna soon, answering the call to arms. We hope to be of assistance in turning away the enemy."

"I am Quoregg. This is my cousin Dorian. We come from the Northern Plains at the headwaters of the Oryon and answer the call like yourselves and many others. It would appear that we are all intended for De'Aarna. The cleric and the cook join us from *eht Vilna Moht*; Angus and Tomas from *eht Vilna Antessara*; the farmer, Rubert, and Dubro from Cameron. We have encountered a number of others who have either hurried ahead of us or lagged behind. I would expect to see many more along the way. If everyone we have seen makes it there, I would presume there to be thousands when we reach the city."

"We, too, have encountered many, both on the road and at *eht Vilna Sahnah*. Most at the castle were simply refugees seeking safe haven, but there was a handful intent upon striking out against the enemy. That is where I met Zephraim and now we seek our own revenge against the dragons."

"Please, Elden, Zephraim, join us. I pride myself on being a good judge of character and your story sounds genuine and true. You are welcome to bed down with us for the night and continue with us to De'Aarna, provided you carry your own weight and your intentions remain true. What skills might you bring to our band of refugees?"

"My companion Zephraim was a beekeeper from the Souliban before the dragon attacks and I... I am an administrator for the castle at *eht Vilna Sahnah*."

"An administrator?"

"Yes, an administrator, a clerk for the castle storehouse. I... I kept the inventory of the castle food supply."

"There is no disgrace in such an occupation, Elden. Everyone has a need to eat. Surely a trusted servant to the lord of the castle. Speaking of food, have you eaten?"

"We have scraped a meal together along our journey, but a bite of something warm would settle the stomach for the night."

Quoregg pointed to the fire. "Sit. Make yourself comfortable and take something to eat."

Elden and Zephraim joined the group around the fire, sharing congenial nods with them as they each found a place to sit. The cook handed them both a trencher with a chunk of meat and a few greens on it which they thanked him for and ate slowly while listening to the fireside conversation. The cleric was addressing the group.

"Evil has returned to Xerses and has begun to permeate our everyday lives. Soon, we will be subjected to its whims at every moment."

Dorian interjected. "Evil has been with us forever. Do we not endure death and disasters wrought by nature on a regular basis? There is certainly nothing good about them for they bring suffering and pain upon us all."

"Do not be fooled by those things that happen naturally but are presumed to be bad, such as the end of a long life and floods and windstorms. They possess no conscious malice towards man. But know the balance of nature is changing. What you have been experiencing these past few weeks is true evil, something none of you have ever seen or heard of before. Man, deliberately killing man, carefully calculated, planned, and executed. There is nothing natural about that; it is true evil. Read the words of the ancients, listen to the songs. Know the difference, for it will keep you safe from that which is truly evil. There was a time in our deep past when both good and evil coexisted in balance. But the evil that men often do carries with it a sadness that is pervasive and afflicts everyone that it touches. Men sought power over others through ways of evil and it brought misery to many. Reacting to the ever-increasing evil, a conclave of the most powerful wizards and wise men gathered together to devise a means to keep evil at bay. Their desire was to make this world a better place to live. Together, they carefully constructed two spells, one that would draw everything evil to a single entity and a second that would entrap it within. A particularly powerful and gracious cleric, known by the name of Braeden, offered his body as the vessel to collect and hold the singularity of all that was evil within his body. His face began to contort and his body began to convulse and twist in all directions as, slowly, everything that was truly evil came to reside within him. And as the last vestiges of evil were absorbed by his person, one of his fellow clerics uttered a spell that placed him in an eternal and confining slumber. All that was evil was now trapped in his sleeping body, never to be released to the world again. Unfortunately, no spell is eternal. Although Braeden still sleeps, the evil within him has managed to pass influence into the conscious world."

The group stared intently at the cleric, completely engaged by his tale. Quoregg finally broke the silence.

"I am not familiar with what has been foretold, but I cannot deny the words of a learned man such as yourself, magus. You speak true about the good and bad of nature, for death and storms are merely part of the natural cycle of things. These dragons may have been created by He That Has Made All, but what they do is far from natural. And their riders seek pleasure from the misery of their victims. My question to you is: What can we do to stop this evil? How do we stop the dragons and how do we stop Braeden?"

"I am sure there is a wise and fearless warrior amongst us that will devise a strategy capable of ending the scourge of the dragons. For Braeden's part, he has no control over the maleficence that evil does. He is merely a vessel and that vessel, over the many years, has developed cracks and fissures and no longer holds the contents completely within. Perhaps evil will slowly continue to find its way back to the natural world until the vessel becomes empty. It is surely inevitable, something we cannot stop. If that is true, then we must begin learning how to recognize it and be on guard to prevent it from controlling our lives, or, for that matter, our very existence."

The group was once again silent, intent to absorb the words of the cleric. Quoregg poked at the fire. Tomas shuffled his feet a bit and repositioned himself on the log he sat on. One of the men coughed. No one dared to speak for fear of ending the wise man's discourse. Finally, Quoregg spoke.

"Your words have us all captivated, magus. Even I would welcome your learned dissertation most evenings, but we have another long day of travel ahead of us. Perhaps we should turn in for the night and save the continuation of this narrative for another evening. Elden, a few more logs for the fire, if you would. It will keep the night creatures at bay. I bid you all a good night's rest. The morning will be soon upon us."

Elden dragged a few more logs into the fire as the group dispersed and then joined them all for a restless evening's slumber.

DAWN BROKE WITH ALL eight men ready for the day's journey. Morning evolutions completed, every last evidence of anyone ever being there was erased. Quoregg addressed the group. "Leave not a trace of our night-stop here. We know not who or what may be lurking about, seeking details of our movements for the benefit of the Khorgians. Trust nothing, for our lives may depend upon it." Quietly, the men completed their clean-up and prepared for another day's journey. Quoregg nodded his approval. "Let us be on our way."

As they methodically marched towards De'Aarna, Elden found himself paired alongside the priest.

"Did I hear correctly that you have joined us from *eht Vilna Sahnah*? I have had the pleasure of resting my head within the walls of the castle on at least one occasion. I must say that I was treated very well during my short stay."

"It is indeed a very hospitable place. I would not speak harshly of the place nor the people." The two walked along quietly, side by side, for a while longer before Elden broke the silence once again. "Magus, your words last night by the fire, they intrigued me. You are clearly educated in the prophecies and their history. Perhaps you may be able to direct us in how we are to stave off the evil that is to confront us."

"I appreciate your misguided faith in my abilities, but I am merely a preacher of what has been taught for centuries. I recite what I have studied. I have no more control over the events that we will endure than you have. Perhaps a man more learned than myself could gain insight into the future from careful study of the teachings, but I am most certainly not that man. Prophecy does tell of such a man. Perhaps that man is you, Master Elden."

"Or, perhaps, Quoregg or Dorian or Zephraim, magus. I am, like yourself, but a man, simple and honest. I travel to fight for the protection of those dear to me; my family, my friends, and the values I hold dear. I have no time for didactics. There are men far more studious than myself to learn all that the ancient manuscripts have to teach."

"It was once said by a very wise man, 'Do not overlook the abilities you possess, nor the abilities of those that surround you, whether they are apparent or not, for everyone is capable of, and can be inspired to, greatness.' You would be wise to keep your mind open to such notions."

"I will keep your words under advisement, magus. Heroes are made in the moment, I believe, and the future will surely afford many moments for us all."

The group trudged along purposefully, steadily making progress towards De'Aarna. Each step brought the group closer to their destination. They passed, and were passed by, many similar groups of travelers along the way, often stopping to question them about their journey, eager for information about the happenings of the surrounding world. They would trade the information they had and whatever supplies they could spare to build their knowledge of the current affairs. Each tidbit added to their understanding of Khorgians and their dragons and of the unusual city that was their final destination.

As the group traveled, Elden began to get anxious. The pace was too slow for his liking. A large group with an elder cleric in tow traveled much slower than a pair might. Elden approached Quoregg as the group stopped to rest.

"Master Quoregg, I do not wish to sound unappreciative. Your hospitality has been exemplary. Zephraim and I could not have ventured upon a better group of men, but I fear the pace is much slower than what I would prefer. I am anxious to get to De'Aarna and begin developing a strategy to eradicate the dragons from our skies. We must go ahead or the wait will drive me to insanity. Please accept my apologies."

"No apologies necessary, Elden. I understand and empathize with your desire to arrive at the city. A smaller group tends to move more quickly. Go, with our blessings. May we meet at a later time and stand alongside one another against the Khorgians."

"Seek us out when you reach De'Aarna."

"That we shall."

The men exchanged handshakes and pleasantries before Elden and Zephraim made their way alone.

For three days more, Elden and Zephraim traveled south along the trail, through forest and field until the land before them opened up to the sea, an endless expanse of water extending out beyond the horizon. The sun, high overhead, glinted upon the clouds reflected on the surface of the water below. The crisp, fresh sea air rose to meet their nostrils, reinvigorating minds and bodies exhausted from the journey. And there before them, sprawling across the shore of the sea, a great walled city – De'Aarna! They had reached their destination.

Elden stopped and put his arm out to bar Zephraim from moving further forward.

"Now is the time to be most cautious, beekeeper. Many travelers are making their way to the city seeking shelter and safety, but there are those that are seeking opportunity for personal gain even through the loss of others. The unscrupulous may try to intercept us prior to gaining entrance to the city and take from us our weapons, our supplies, and even our lives. We must be wary and vigilant, watch out for one another. Together we are strong enough to stand up to any adversary, but, as individuals, we may be easily overmatched."

They made their way along the road to the gates, carefully watched by others camped alongside the road. A less worldly pair might have been naïve enough to engage with the charlatans outside the gates, but Elden and Zephraim knew better. Unless the city was beyond capacity, only those seeking to avoid an encounter with authority would set camp in the lawless lands outside of the city walls. Any involvement with this lot would surely result in a less than satisfactory outcome.

The massive wooden gates to the city lay open but were flanked by a battalion of well-armed guards, eyeing each traveler that entered, stopping most to question them and inspect their belongings. The dragon attacks had created an air of diligence not previously known in the city. As the two travelers entered the gates, Elden scanned the city in awe. Never had he seen a compound like this. There was no bailey, no keep, just structures sprawled about within the confines of the city walls. To the far side was a seaport opening to the ocean beyond.

"It is probably not in our best interest to split up and explore the city. It would be advantageous to know the lay of the land, but first, we need to seek out a place for us to shelter."

“Agreed, Elden. We can search for supplies and places to enlist recruits later. For now, it is probably best to remain paired.”

“I must agree. Even in a city as well guarded as this one obviously is, a certain less desirable element can sneak through the cracks. Do you believe you can endure my company for another day?”

Zephraim chuckled. “Possibly for one more day unless, of course, you can find us a place at which to bathe. Although days of travel are good for building morale and friendships, it is not very kind to the nose.”

“I will see what I can do.” Elden laughed at his friend.

Elden and Zephraim headed toward the center of the compound, searching for the seat of the city. After walking the city streets for nearly half an hour, they came upon a large plaza. Stopping a man, Elden asked about the city seat.

“My good man, we are new to your city and seek a representative of your government. Can you direct us to the city seat?”

"The Governor's manor is across town, down that boulevard. It is a large structure of pink limestone. The Council Hall sits beside it. But, be it known that Governor Zea is no longer among us. He left soon after the first attacks in the north and has yet to return. It is feared he may have fallen with those at *eht Vilna Moht*, but it has not been proven. No successor has been chosen. If you require a decision from an authority, you may be able to inquire of the Council."

"My gratitude for your assistance, sir."

The two proceeded in the direction the man had pointed. They had traveled several blocks when they came upon the large pink building they had been told of and, beside it, a large granite structure which was presumably the Council Hall. They scaled the steps to the main entrance and proceeded inside.

The interior of the Hall was dark, as there were no openings other than the doorway. A single column of light from the portal stretched across the smooth granite floor to the far wall some fifty feet beyond. The two men entered slowly, allowing their eyes to adjust to the darkness. The main hall was flanked by four small arched openings that allowed access to two rooms on each side. The rear wall also had an arch in each corner that opened to an area behind. The high barrel-vaulted ceiling focused any sound back to the center of the hall. Long low granite blocks lay on the floor, apparently to serve as seating for the Council. An immense torch chandelier hung from a thick iron chain, offset towards the rear of the hall to provide artificial light to the areas not bathed in the light that encroached from the outside.

Elden announced their presence. "Hello?" His voice echoed slightly in the emptiness.

From beyond the far wall, another voice echoed a response. "Hello?" A slight man in a long white cotton vestment appeared from an arch on the far wall.

"I am Mican, the Council foreman. May I ask your name and your business?"

"I am Elden of *eht Vilna Sahnah*, grandson of King Heidel and Queen Isella, and this is my traveling companion, Zephraim. We have come to your city as warriors, seeking refuge and to formulate a strategy against the dragon attacks. Many others are here or en route. We seek shelter amongst you."

The foreman stood and bowed to Elden out of respect for his royal position. "Your lordship. The blessings of our city are yours. Please feel free to seek shelter in the Governor's manor. It is currently unoccupied."

"I appreciate your offer counselor, but I must decline. My status is unknown within the walls of De'Aarna and I will not take advantage of it while others suffer the miseries brought upon us by the dragon attacks. A simpler shelter is more than adequate."

"As you wish, Master Elden. Let me ponder this for a moment." Mican lowered his head in thought and stroked his chin. "I believe I have a place where you can find shelter. My brother, Jonas, has a shop in the marketplace. There is room beside where a shelter might be easily constructed. I will inform him of your need for a place to set down for the night. He and the other vendors will be able to assist you."

"Your assistance is appreciated, counselor. Perhaps we can repay your kindness by sparing De'Aarna from the wrath of the dragon attacks."

"Perhaps, together, we can spare all of Xerses."

"Well put, Mican. If I have any say in the matter, your wish will be realized."

"Seek the tanner's shop in the marketplace. That is my brother. I will send word to expect you. You may shelter there for as long as you require." Mican summoned a young boy and instructed him to bring a message to the tanner. Obediently, the boy took off like a rabbit, out the main entrance to the Hall, instantly lost in the brightness of the sunlight.

The three continued to discuss details of the city, where certain features could be found and the general lay of the land. The men exchanged final pleasantries and Elden and Zephraim exited the Hall into the same blinding sunlight that had enveloped the young messenger. As they began to descend the steps, Zephraim stopped Elden.

"What was that all about? Grandson of the Queen? Was that all some grand ruse to gain favor amongst the locals? What other secrets have you held from me?"

"It is all the truth, but I have nothing else to divulge. I regret having been dishonest, but I wish to be treated as any other man seeking vengeance against what the dragons have done to our people and our land. My station should not afford me any greater privileges than those afforded any other person. I am as you, a warrior, a man. So, you must swear to me that you will not tell anyone of my status."

"I shall do as you wish, my Lord."

"Please, Zephraim. Do it out of respect for me as a man, not out of reverence for my position. I ask that you dispense with the royal salutations. I will have far more respect for you if you would consider us equals."

"Of course, Elden. I respect your wishes as a man, and as a friend and equal. You are truly a very good person. Your grandfather would be proud."

"That is kind of you to say. Thank you. Now let's go find this marketplace and the tanner. We need to set up a place to settle down."

ELDEN AND ZEPHRAIM slowly made their way to the marketplace, fighting their way through the throng of bodies that occupied nearly every empty inch of the city. Surprisingly, as they approached the market, the pace increased dramatically. What would be expected by most to be the most disorganized and congregated area was, in fact, a place of order. Much like a traffic circle, the occupants moved in a single clockwise direction around the plaza, entering and exiting the carousel of humanity via the many side streets and alleys that dumped into the marketplace plaza. The two men merged into and moved with the crowd until they came upon the tannery shop where they exited the human carousel to address the owner.

"Are you the tanner Jonas?"

"That I am. And might you two be the travelers my brother sent notice of?"

"We are."

"My brother's message-bearer has informed me you seek shelter and shelter you shall have. If he were to suggest I place an army in bivouac, then that is what I would do. For you, I have a space behind the market stall. It was once a sort of stable within which my father would keep some of the stock from which he acquired his hides, but it fell into disrepair and now barely stands, empty. It may not quite be the Governor's manor, but it could be a fine, serviceable shelter with a little work."

"We appreciate your generosity, master Jonas. With little to offer in trade, we cannot expect residence in the royal castle. I am Elden, stores clerk from *et Vilna Sahnah*, and my companion is known as Zephraim, beekeeper from what once was the Souliban. Ask of us what you may, for, if nothing else, we possess strong hands and backs and a willingness to offer labor in exchange for accommodations."

"Quite honestly, by not doing anything, you could save me a great deal of labor."

Elden and Zephraim eyed Jonas with befuddlement.

"Allow me to explain. Daily, I must pack in my wares before the light of the morning and pack them out in the evening darkness. If there is a presence here overnight, I can leave my skins in place and save a fair amount of time and effort every day. Use what skins you may to bed. I will return come the morn and you are free to explore the city and attend to whatever business you have. All I ask in exchange is that you return before nightfall to serve as my eyes overnight."

"A more than fair exchange, beneficial to both parties, if I say so myself. I think it right to say I speak for both of us when I accept your offer." Zephraim nodded in agreement. "But I do have one last request before you make your leave. Would there be means to acquire nourishment for the evening?"

"The produce vendors typically have some damaged goods. If you are not overly particular and can manage to overlook a bruise or a split, I can certainly rustle up a basket full."

"I would appreciate the opportunity to accompany you and introduce myself to the other vendors. We must make contacts if we intend to survive here."

"I can entertain one of you but request the other stay with my skins to prevent any pilferage."

Elden looked to his friend. "Zephraim, do you mind?"

Zephraim waved him on. "Go! Do whatever business you need to for the benefit of us both. I shall be pleased to be rid of you for a moment, having spent nearly half a fortnight with you as my sole companion. Solitude, even for a wink, would be a welcome diversion."

Elden chuckled. “Be careful what you wish for. I pray you would miss my charm and my wit should I be far for too long.”

“Your wit, possibly; your waft, I would say not. While you are out and about making new friends, you might possibly enquire of a place we might be able to bathe. I fear we have both become quite ripe.”

Jonas laughed. “I will show you the public well. You can gather fresh water there and bring it back here. There is a trough in the stable that is still serviceable. It may prove to be too small for a bath but should be adequate for a wash basin.”

Elden and Jonas made their way around the marketplace while Zephraim began to clean up and sort out the old stable, making it a suitable space for repose.

FRESHLY BATHED, WITH bellies full of local produce, Elden and Zephraim settled in for a well needed night of slumber.

“Come the morning when Master Jonas returns, we should seek a place to begin recruitment. It will be far better to have a single, unified force than many splintered factions. I feel it will be likely that we encounter Quoregg and the magus once again. Quoregg might prove to be a very good leader.”

"I must agree with you, Elden. A man of his quality would serve well as a leader of men. We should be sure to find him and rejoin forces with his little group once again."

"It is decided then. We begin recruitment tomorrow, but, for now, we should get some much-needed rest. ‘Til the morning, Zephraim."

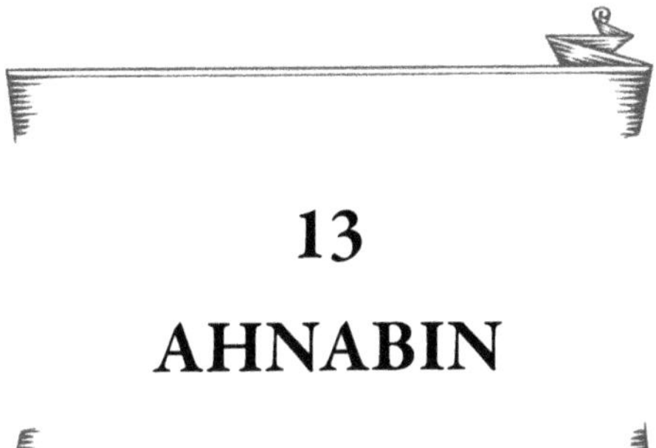

13
AHNABIN

6093 E.K.

Eht Vilna Antessara sat high on a craggy piece of rock on the edge of the forest. Partially obscured from view by the tall fir-like evergreens from which it took its name, the castle had a perfect view of the valley below. The Lord of the castle and his wife, King Maob and Queen Vivien, were well respected by their people, much the same as King Olen and Queen Isella were at *eht Vilna Sahnah*, although not quite as fastidious and critical in their preparations for all eventualities. King Maob was a most amazing tactician and had a well-trained contingent of Royal Guards.

Their daughter, the Princess Ahnabin, enjoyed the lifestyle afforded by their status. Some would say she was quite spoiled and a contingent of those might be of a mind to say she was no less than a brat. She wanted for nothing, as every desire was administered to by her parents and nursemaids. She had the best of tutors, the best clothing, the best food and drink. And, like any other child born into privilege, Ahna found her lifestyle to be normal and natural and saw nothing wrong with how she was treated. She also saw nothing wrong with getting what she wanted nor letting anyone know about it, even her parents. And even though her father was stern and in opposition, and her mother often relented, the king would frequently sneak little gifts to his only child. He was King of the Castle and a great and well-trained warrior, but he had a soft spot in his heart for his daughter.

AHNABIN LEFT THE STABLES after an afternoon ride, her blonde hair pulled back in a tight French braid, wearing brown flannel riding pants and a white silk blouse. Pushing the large wooden door aside slowly, she carefully peeked around the edge and, seeing no one in the room, she strode confidently into the entry of the keep and headed for the large staircase that led to the upper quarters.

"AHNA!"

The King's bellow startled her. Ahna stopped abruptly and turned to face her father.

"Ahna, look at you! What is this? You are a princess, not a stable hand. Certain things are expected of you and one of those things is looking the part of a princess."

"Poppa, I don't want to be all fluff and frills like a porcelain doll set carefully on a shelf. I want to be like the favorite rag doll, constantly loved and held and dragged along everywhere. And if being dragged along everywhere means I get a little dirty and thread-worn, then let it be so. I want to travel everywhere and experience everything. Frills and indulgence and the isolation of entitlement make no stories to tell."

"It is what stories might be told that I fear the most!"

"And what stories would they dare to tell? If they speak ill of me, then have them arrested and placed in prison. Maybe a short spell in the dungeon will teach them to hold their tongue."

"Ahna, I cannot be throwing everyone into the dungeon that has an opinion about your unconventional ways or lifestyle. It would certainly bode poorly to morale and the trust the people have in my leadership." He continued, half under his breath, "And I may just end up there myself."

"Poppa! I heard that!"

"Well, it is how I feel. You are a princess and, above all, my daughter. No father wishes their child, especially their daughter, to be ridiculed for not conforming to what is considered normal and decent, whether it makes sense or not. You are a beautiful girl and I would like the rest of the world to see you in all your splendor; hair down, a beautiful dress billowing beneath and behind you, powdered and pretty. If I had but one wish, it would be for you to look the part of the princess of this castle."

Ahna threw herself down into an overstuffed chair, arms crossed over her chest, a deep frown on her face, eyes glaring at the floor. She and her father stayed that way for what seemed an eternity, their skirmish at an impasse until Ahna quickly sat forward and blurted out, "I want to ride horses!"

"But Ahna, you have your horses. You can ride them every day."

She scoffed at her father. "But to please you, I would have to ride side saddle in petticoats and lace. What fun is that? You can barely keep your balance at a slow trot let alone a canter. I want to gallop. I want to ride at breakneck speeds with the wind in my face and the world at my back."

"And I wanted a giraffe when I was seven. Needless to say, I never got the giraffe and it did not make me any less of a man."

"Why must I be so prissy? I want to wear britches and ride just like everyone else."

"Not everyone else. Not your mother, not Lady Cantor of *eht Vilna Moht*, not your friends Prysia, Eveline, nor Anjelika. They all carry themselves as proper ladies, proper in dress, proper in actions."

"Proper by who's standards? A patriarchal aristocracy? And keeping women in frills and lace serves only to subjugate. All you men see a strong woman as a threat."

"I appreciate your candor, Ahna, and I even understand your point of view, but others may not. Speak your mind as such in public and you might just find yourself a very despised and lonely princess. You seek to change the world in one fell swoop, but change as radical as you desire must take place over time if the masses are to accept it as normal."

"It's not fair, Poppa! Am I any less a person than you or Lord Darden or even the lowly stable hand because I don't possess a penis?"

"Ahna!"

"But it's true! If I were a man instead of a woman, I would be treated entirely different. You think your strength comes from what hangs from your loins. Maybe you should try pushing a new life out through it!"

"AHNA! I think that is enough!"

Ahna turned her back to her father and began to walk away, arms across her chest in defiance. After a few steps, she quickly whirled around to face him again.

"Why must change be so unaccepted? Why must it take so long? Why can it not happen swiftly, like the changes in the desert during a sandstorm? Why can't...?"

Her diatribe was cut off by an alarm sounded from the parapet. Something outside the castle walls presented a danger to those within.

Maob looked upward towards the orientation of the alarm.

"It would appear that your wish for swift change may be upon us, Ahna, just not the changes you had desired."

A cry came from the watchtower.

"Dragons! Dragons! They are swarming over the horizon and headed straight for us!"

Guards scampered from their barracks within the towers, through the cloisters atop the ramparts, en route to the armory below to gather their weapons.

"Assemble the guards in the bailey! Prepare for our attack, just like we practiced!"

King Maob headed to the armory to outfit himself for the confrontation with the dragons. After putting on his armor and collecting his weapons, he mounted an immense black warhorse. As the leader of his people, he would guide them into battle.

A heavily armed contingent of men from *eht Vilna Antessara*, King Maob at the lead, rode at full gallop through the castle gates, out to confront the dark mass in the sky, growing every minute like an uncontrolled cancer, before it reached the castle. A small blonde head anxiously peered over the parapet, watching the cavalry ride off into the distance.

Ahead, King Maob could see fiery lightning streaking down from the dark cloud hovering over the land before them. He had prepared his men for this moment as best as he could and now it was upon them. He would defend his people to his last breath and he knew each of his soldiers would as well. Maob and his best men had devised a plan of attack that relied heavily on archers, the only form of aerial offense available to them. He would attack his enemy on their playing field, but not on their terms. To the best of his knowledge, such an offensive stance had yet to be employed against the dragons. They rode onward awaiting Maob's signal to attack.

One by one, dragons dropped from the swarm, targeting an object below and launching a ball of flaming bile to incinerate it. Lord Roga, on his dragon and positioned slightly above the rest, scanned the approaching army below, searching for the right time to focus his attack. Barking out orders, he regrouped his flight to change their targets. The drove of flying reptilians and their riders prepared for the annihilation of the approaching ant-like cavalry.

Maob ordered his men to dismount and begin their attack. As they had carefully practiced, the soldiers dismounted in unison, leaving their horses to wander alone. Each man nocked an arrow and, aiming at the enemy above, waited for Maob's order.

"Fire!"

Roga stared at what was unfolding beneath, perplexed by the sudden doubling of the targets below as each rider disconnected from their steed. For an instant he was unprepared, simply flying in a daze, until a thin missile whizzed by his head, quickly bringing him back to cognizance. This time the enemy was fighting back!

"Avoid the arrows!" he barked, warning his riders of the counter from below.

The efficiency of the dragon attack suffered greatly as they attempted to dodge the onslaught of tiny missiles that hurtled their way. No longer did every flaming belch find its target below. The lack of absolute domination was an annoyance Roga was not accustomed to. It slowly built up into a rage that needed to be quenched. Scanning the battlefield beneath him, he sought the commander of this army. Spying Maob, he correctly determined his quarry, sending his beast into a dive straight at the warrior, prepared to unleash all his rage at once.

Ball after ball of flaming bile rained down towards Maob as Roga's steed wretched every last drop of phosphor from her gut. The king attempted to deflect the fire with his shield, but it merely stuck to the surface and began melting the metal. Unable to prevent the infernal assault, he knocked his final arrow and took careful aim, releasing it as his body became enveloped in fiery draconian vomitus.

Roga watched as his target finally succumbed to his volley, but any chance to revel in the moment was lost as he spotted the arrow headed towards him. He instinctively leaned out of the way, feeling it strike his left pauldron. Reaching up with the opposite hand, he grasped the shaft of the missile and ripped it from his armor, tossing it aside in disgust. Although struck, he had dodged a fatal shot and decided not to press his luck any further.

"Retreat!" Shocked, many of his men turned to look at their leader. These were words they had never before heard him say. "I said retreat! Return to the caves!"

The swarm quickly gathered themselves and, following Roga's instruction, turned towards home, the warlord and his dragon flying slightly above. As he looked across the sea to Khorgia, he felt a warm drop on his hand. Blood! He reached up under his shoulder armor, finding a small rivulet of the bright red liquid trickling down his arm from a cut. Perhaps he had not been so quick as to avoid the Tendiran commander's final shot. His first true battle scar. The Tendirans would pay dearly for this during the next attack!

AHNABIN SCANNED THE horizon from the watchtower, searching for any movement. She had been stationed there for hours. Many of the archers had returned. Queen Vivien approached from behind and gently placed her hand on her daughter's shoulder.

"Ahna, it is done. Too much time has passed. The dragons are no longer visible in the air, there are no more streaks of flame lighting up the sky. Those few survivors have already returned. Now the wind carries but deathly silence. I fear no one else will return."

Ahna slapped her mother's hand away. "No! Poppa wouldn't leave us here alone!"

Vivien took her daughter's head and cradled it against her chest. "Your father fought to protect us, to protect you, and all in this castle. He had a plan and it must have worked, for the dragons never made it to *Antessara*. From all accounts, this is the first kingdom to be spared the wrath of the demons, and I choose to believe it was your Poppa's doing. Come. Come with me. We do no good to anyone huddled up here weeping like two blithering fools. We need to put up a strong face for the rest of the castle. We need to gather them together and remove ourselves from here. This is not a safe place any longer. I need you to be strong. Be strong for me. Be strong for yourself. Be strong for your Poppa. He would have expected nothing less from you."

Ahna pulled her head from her mother's chest and wiped the tears from her face, shaking her head in agreement. "I can do this. I can be strong. I will lead what remains of our people from this place and make my Poppa proud."

"That's my girl. Your father would be very proud of you. Now, let's make haste. We need to leave this place before the dragons decide to return."

Queen Vivien took her daughter's hand and began to lead her towards the stairwell. Ahna abruptly stopped, jarring the Queen to look back at her.

"I will make Poppa proud, Mother. I will make them pay for what they did to him. I will avenge his death."

The Queen reached out and cradled her daughter's cheek in her hand. "I know you will. If ever there was a daughter capable of such a feat, it is you, my dear. And I will be the first to support you as you seek to attain your goal. But quickly, we must gather the rest and escape from here."

Ahna and the Queen made way to the bailey below, quickly calling together the few men, women, children, and elderly that remained in the castle. The Queen directed them to collect only the most necessary of belongings and supplies. They loaded everything onto wagons in preparation. Ahna scanned the contents of the tiny caravan.

"My dresses, Mother, I need my dresses!"

"Ahna, quickly, gather what is necessary and let us be on our way. How you dress as you flee from danger is not a concern. You have never before regarded the wearing of a dress to be of any import, why would you be concerned with dresses at a time such as now?"

"No! I promised Poppa I would be a princess, his princess. He said that was what the world expected of me. I cannot break my promise, Mother."

Vivien smiled. "You are right, Love. Go get your favorite dress, but nothing more. We have little time and there will be little room for luxuries in the wagons."

Ahna collected her best dress and a few simple accessories and mementos and placed them in a small chest which she then carried to the front of the keep. With four wagons loaded with provisions and possessions and another four with the remaining survivors of the castle, they left their home behind, heading south to find safety.

ROGA SAT UPON A LEATHER divan in his office, his trusted servant, Minarik, stood behind him cleaning his wounded shoulder and attempting to apply a dressing.

"Please, my Lord. If you would just hold still for a moment, I can finish bandaging you and you can get back to what you were doing."

Roga huffed loudly, crossing his arms and reluctantly relinquished control, for the moment, to his impromptu nursemaid. "Damned lucky shot! One would have expected the turbulence of dragon wings would have disrupted the arrow's flight. I daresay this will be the last time I fall victim to any counter from a Tendiran worm!"

"Quite lucky, indeed, my Lord. I'm sure you will be better prepared for the possibility going forward."

"Indeed, I will! I shall not fall victim to the likes of that degenerate lot again."

A knock came from the door.

Roga beckoned his visitor to enter. "Come!"

Marshall Octrall appeared from the hallway

"My Lord, I come to report on the latest attack." Marshall Octrall stood in the doorway to his master's study. Roga, motioned him in with a wave of his hand. Octrall made his way before Roga's desk. "I have casualties to report, my Lord."

Roga looked up at him, not necessarily shocked at what he had just heard based upon his own experience. Octrall noticed the Minarik attending to his master's shoulder wound but wisely chose not to mention it.

"No deaths, my Lord, just injuries. Seven dragons and one rider. Nothing life-threatening. All made the journey back to the mountain. Apparently, the result of the arrow counterattack."

Roga answered, staring stone-faced forward. "I saw the arrows but did not believe one could pierce the scutes of a dragon."

"Lucky shots, my Lord, between the scutes, and one through a wing membrane."

"The arrows, they were a shock to me. I was not prepared for a counter. Perhaps I had underestimated the Tendiran vermin. Apparently, they do have a little fire in their bellies and a few claws on their grubby little paws." Roga looked up at Octrall. "And what of the vermin?"

“There is no accounting of survivors on the field of battle, my Lord, as the attack was interrupted by their counter. The castle was not completely obliterated due to the casualties we suffered, but the potential survivors could only be minimal. Certainly, less than a score, possibly two.”

Roga turned to look at his assistant. “Two score? And you find this acceptable?”

Octrall snapped to attention. "No, my Lord, not acceptable, but certainly not completely unexpected. I must ask you, with all respect, did you honestly believe we could come away completely unscathed from every attack?”

Minarik quickly interjected before Roga could enter another verbal tirade. “What is important is that we have lost no one, and those Tendirans that may have survived will certainly fall during a future attack."

Roga brought his hand to his bandaged shoulder and sighed. “You are right, Minarik, as always. It is because of your honesty and ability to keep me grounded that I consider you a trusted advisor and friend. So, in light of current events, Marshall, how do we proceed? What can we do to prevent a similar outcome in the future? I prefer not to suffer further casualties and I certainly do not want survivors.”

Octrall relaxed. “I fear casualties are a consequence of battle that no preparations can serve to sufficiently avoid, my Lord. Even the use of armor cannot guarantee against injury and a fully armored dragon would be severely limited by encumbrance. Limitations to mobility may serve only to increase the odds of injury during battle.”

“Agreed. It would be foolhardy to armor the dragons. We have made a number of incursions to the mainland and have suffered minimal and entirely non-lethal casualties. The odds are certainly in our favor. We shall continue to attack in the same manner as we have to this point. How long before we will be prepared to launch another attack?”

“A good day’s rest or two and all but the seven should be ready for another flight. We could be at full complement in three, maybe four, days. The rider’s injuries should not keep him from battle.”

“And what of future attacks and the possibility of survivors?”

Minarik spoke up once again. "Again, I must implore you to consider that survivors, in numbers small enough to count on your hand, are always a possibility. One can never be certain that the target has not burrowed deep into the ground to avoid attack from above. It is not out of the realm of possibilities."

Roga scoffed. "Far be it for me to disagree with you on that account. This Tendiran filth surely would be at home slithering through the ground with the worms, as if they were brethren. If that is the game they choose to play, then we will determine a mode of attack that renders hiding in burrows ineffective. Octrall, put our best strategic minds on that problem immediately. I want a scheme to counter that in two days."

"As you wish, my Lord."

"And what of the vermin that survived our last attack?"

"Any survivors would most certainly move towards the nearest inhabited area, in this case to the south. Our attacks have all but made the northern provinces uninhabitable."

"Good. Plan another attack in four days. I want a full flight. And I want you to find and exterminate any of the vermin that survived our last attack."

14
THE PROPHECY UNRAVELS

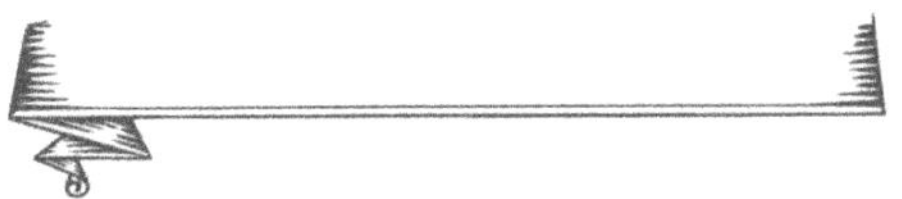

ROGA SAT ALONE IN HIS study. The room was dark, save for one large oil lamp hanging above his desk. Leather-bound books filled the shelves along one wall. A large map table filled the end of the room opposite the desk, various maps and parchments laid out on top. Centered on one wall, what appeared almost as a mini-chapel, was a single large tome, *eht Olheb Ahnan*, the Book of Beginnings, resting on a pedestal. The leather binding was very old, cracked and worn, the title embossed on the spine in flaking gold leaf. On the desk, beneath the lamp, was a large glass bowl of tropical fish. Roga sat in his chair, quietly watching the fish as they swam about the bowl.

Minarik coughed to announce his presence and entered the room. "My Lord, I have news from De'Aarna. We seem to have..."

Without moving his gaze from the bowl, Roga raised his hand toward his manservant and cut him off before he could continue. "Aren't they interesting? I had them brought in from every corner of the planet. I acquired the first specimens from one of our raids on the mainland. Young Ursen presented them to me. So very peaceful and calming to watch." He motioned to his assistant. "Come, my old friend. Take a closer look."

"Yes, my lord." Minarik approached tentatively and spent a few moments watching the fish move gracefully about the bowl. "Very relaxing. Very beautiful, too."

"Beautiful?" The notion caught him peculiar. Roga stared at the bowl intently, his brow furrowed, cocking his head to one side and then the other, and then shrugged his shoulders. "Beautiful. I dare say you may be right. I would never have looked at them in such a manner, but, after considering your comment, I would have to say you are correct. One could be persuaded to consider these creatures rather... beautiful. A fine observation, Minarik. Surely, your keen eye is one of the reasons you have remained in my employ for all these many years."

The assistant clicked his heels and bowed slightly, nodding his head. "Yes, my lord. Thank you."

Roga sat back in his chair, bringing his fingertips together before him.

"So, what is it that you have come to tell me, Minarik? Did I hear you mention De'Aarna?"

Minarik tensed a little. The moment of friendly banter with his master was now gone and the news he had to tell was not the most pleasant.

"It is my unfortunate duty to inform you that the people of De'Aarna have chosen not to accept our delegate, Canthus, as their governor, my Lord. He was not a popular choice. They have chosen, instead, to elect a council of royals from the surrounding kingdoms that have sought refuge there from the dragon attacks. Canthus was driven out of the city. They have barred the gate and have heavily fortified the walls. Everyone attempting to enter or leave is being questioned and searched. Only citizens and those with definite verifiable business in the city are being allowed past the gate."

"How can this be? The Prophecy of Korham tells of a single Gatekeeper, who shall open the gates of Korham for *Eyieritu*, the Chosen One. No council, no royals. One. Singular." Roga started to scan the room, presumably in search of answers. "Nothing is going according to the plan! This is not how the teachings have declared it will be! We are supposed to have a ruling presence in the city and control the gates, to delay the entrance of the Chosen One! We ***must*** control the gates of Korham!"

Roga was livid. He rose from his desk and began pacing the room.

"Damn it! What did I miss? Did I misinterpret something from the readings? How could I? I have studied every word, every phrase, every page. There is nothing I could have overlooked!"

Roga continued to traverse the room, more violently now, as his furor increased.

"I have read the prophecies, the songs, the teachings! I know every book cover to cover! I have studied their meanings, in depth, and have deciphered every parable! The timeline and events are clear and I have positioned myself to be in the right place at the right time!" Roga angrily beat his chest. "It is my destiny!" He grabbed a small tome off a shelf, ripping it open and violently fingering through the leaves until he reached his goal, stabbing at the page and holding it up for Minarik to see. "See! Here! It is written in the words of the ancient tomes! *The victorious leader shall come from across the sea and sit as the ruler of Korham. His arrival shall be heralded by the Gatekeeper and the doors to the city shall be opened to him.* I am that leader! I cross the sea regularly, victorious in our battles against the Tendiran vermin! I am to sit as the ruler of Korham! Who dares to say otherwise! I have studied these manuscripts for years on end and I know what they portend! I will be the victorious leader and no one will stand in my way!"

Minarik had shrunk back slightly at his master's outburst but felt compelled to interject. "Master, I trust in your knowledge of the ancient writing and I am sure you are to be the leader, but nowhere does it say the journey shall be easy. Nowhere does it give an exact timeline of events. Many battles are fought and won on the journey to the ultimate victory just as battles can be fought and lost. The war still rages on, my Lord. Your opportunity has not yet come to pass."

Roga seethed but did not respond. He knew his trusted servant was correct. A war is not won and lost by one battle. He would have to be patient.

"I want you to send parties to all corners and round up the most learned and holy of men to sit in council and verify my interpretation of what is foretold."

"And if they do not wish to serve on this council, my Lord?"

"Then *persuade* them! Their presence is not requested, it is commanded! I will have them all here within the week or you might be in the need of a holy man yourself!"

Once again, Minarik snapped to attention and clicked his heels. "Understood, my Lord, understood. You shall have a council of the most learned and most holy of men seated by the end of the week."

Minarik quietly left his master to his brooding.

ROGA STOOD SILENTLY in the darkness facing the bier of his Master. A deep voice rumbled in the cavern.

"*Your valet is correct, my most faithful apprentice. One battle does not determine a victor. And the parables can be read and interpreted any number of ways. They offer predictions of the future. They do not dictate the minutiae of how it will transpire. Gather those wise and learned, as you have suggested, and question them on alternative meanings of the prophecies. They may not come to the same conclusions as yourself, or perhaps they will determine a different path to the same end. Consider your options and plan accordingly. Even the most dismal of all predictions has an equally positive alternative. The ending may be dictated in what has been prophesized, but the journey is chosen by the likes of those that travel the path. The routes you may follow are truly numberless.*"

"I understand, Master. Minarik is correct and I need to be open to possibilities I may not have considered. I must learn to be more flexible in my expectations of the predictions I have made from my knowledge of what the ancients have foretold. The destination is ultimately what matters, not the steps we take to get there."

"*Well said, my son. Go. Seek counsel with the group you are assembling and learn from them what you may. Open your mind to new concepts regarding what you have learned from the writings of the prophets and you will begin to see the truth. The truth will lead you to ultimate victory.*"

"I shall go an enlightened man, my Master. When I return, I shall be far better prepared for what the future may hold in store. And I will remain focused on the ultimate goal, the destination. We shall prevail."

Roga bowed to his master and returned to his office.

FORTY-THREE CLERICS and wise men were crowded into the Great Hall of Oro, among them Gorem, the Elder from Ukiah, Pearsin of De'Aarna, Judah and Elimnem from the lands beyond the Oryon headwaters, and Benn Garra from the foothills north of the Souliban. Guards posted at the doors prevented any from leaving. The loud murmur of at least a dozen angry conversations hung heavy in the room, none intelligible outside of the immediate participants. The flailing of arms and the shaking and nodding of heads clearly indicated the level of agitation amongst the members of each group. All the while, a single old man sat quietly in a chair in the corner, his hands resting on a walking stick, watching the chaos unfold before him. The uproar stopped abruptly as the doors opened. Lord Roga entered the room flanked by Minarik and the young intern Ursen. Everyone in the hall turned to see who had entered. Roga addressed the group, almost shouting to ensure everyone could hear him.

"Good day, my revered guests. My name is Lord Roga, warlord, and leader, of the great and powerful Khorgian Empire. I have summoned you all here for a matter of great importance."

"*Summoned*?" Pearsin was incredulous. "I was accosted in my own home and brought here against my will. I would say it was more likened to a kidnapping than an invitation."

A cacophony of similar retorts rose from the others and quickly digressed to chaos, clearly causing the warlord to become agitated.

"Silence! Enough! I will tolerate no more of your insolent complaints. I have gathered you all here together to discuss a matter of great importance, so act like the learned men that you are, not like the whining toddlers you resemble at present. Do you not possess the common decency and courtesy to act accordingly when you are brought before a great and powerful leader?"

"A great leader? Are you to suggest that we are to show reverence to you because you are a *great leader*?" questioned Judah. "And by the judgment of what officiant has such a title been bestowed?"

Roga approached the cleric and stood nearly nose to nose with him, answering through clenched teeth. "You and forty-two of the finest minds on this planet, outside of my own, have been brought together, be it willingly or by force, to this room by *me*. No one else in the history as we know it has ever accomplished such a feat. By that, you have borne witness to the power that I possess. If you care to openly defy me once again, I am sure we can manage with only forty-two."

For a moment, you could hear a pin drop. From the corner of the room the silent old cleric loudly tapped his walking stick on the floor, attracting the attention of everyone, and calmly, quietly, spoke.

"Gentlemen, a physical altercation, even under the most chivalrous of terms, serves us no purpose in this particular moment. If we are to attend to the questions that we have been gathered to address, we must not occupy ourselves with aggression. It is not a means by which problems are ultimately solved."

Judah swallowed hard as Roga's eyes pierced through him. Backing away, and bowing slightly, he responded quietly. "I beg your forgiveness, my Lord, but the circumstances surrounding my attendance at this conclave have been somewhat upsetting. I shall put aside my feelings and gladly attend to the task you have gathered us for."

"Good!" Roga's voice echoed over the throng of clerics. "Before we continue, are there any more hurt feelings that need to be addressed? Egos that need to be stroked? Does anyone want their *mommy*? Hmmm?" His eyes quickly scanned the crowded room. "I thought not. Now, back to the matter at hand. I have brought you all together to discuss the events that we are experiencing now and in the few months that surround the present time. It would appear that a timeline has been put into motion, a timeline that clearly conforms to the events foretold by the Prophecy of Korham. I have read the tomes, the songs, the parables, and they all parallel the events that have been occurring in the present. It is clear to me that a certain chain of events has been set in motion and certain events shall follow. Apart from a minor occurrence that I had been unprepared for, the timeline has unfolded exactly as I had predicted. But it is this one minor event that has me baffled and has sent my thoughts off in every possible direction trying to resolve the order of events that I may have failed to recognize. I seek the influx of your wisdom and understanding to bring the truth of this reality to light in the context of what has been written. I seek an alternative point of view that might shed light on the potential inconsistencies in my understanding of the parables and teachings. No single man, no matter how powerful and learned, can have the answers to everything, but the conjoined intellect of some of the finest minds in history should be far more capable of delivering the truth. I have bet the success of my predictions upon it."

"And what has gone awry, my Lord?" questioned Benn Garra. "What has been your prediction of the chain of events unfolding before us as we speak?"

"I may have knowledge of events that you do not, but believe me when I tell you that certain conditions of the prophecy have been met and the time for the arrival of *Eyieritu*, the Chosen One, is nigh. The stories tell of a

Gatekeeper who will open the way for *Eyieritu* to enter the city of Korham, now De'Aarna. The teachings speak of a Gatekeeper, singular, but the people of Korham have determined the need for a governing council, not a single leader, to direct the affairs if the city. A council, even of just a few, fails to fit into the context of the teachings. *A victorious leader shall come from across the sea and sit as the ruler of Korham*'"

Elimnem countered the warlord with a novel idea.

"The number of potential interpretations of the ancient words exceeds all comprehension. Probability might steer towards a particular outcome, but no single understanding of the parables can be determined to be correct until after the moment has passed. And what of this moment you speak of? The clock by which the stories unfold has no definite period. What seems to take a moment in the context of that which has been prophesized may require days or years to unfold in our time. A blink of the Creator's eye may take centuries in our own."

Roga was taken aback by this line of reasoning. He had not considered the potential for temporal anomalies in his understanding of the teachings he had studied for years, and the potential intrigued him.

"You make a very valid point. Nowhere in the writings is there a mention of the passage of time, only the order of events. Indeed, events that have occurred in centuries past appear in the paragraphs that immediately precede the stories that tell of current events. Time, like a river, meanders and then rages throughout the texts, but I failed to consider that potential in my own predictions. Clearly, it is a factor that must be accounted for."

The cleric from beyond the Oryon continued his discourse with Lord Roga.

"And what other factors might not be accounted for? I care not to question your reasoning but to offer more alternatives for consideration. If memory serves me correctly, your predictions place the current time in the context of a '*victorious leader shall come from across the sea and sit as the ruler of Korham*'. I find it hard not to assume that you see yourself as that leader from across the sea. But the Prophecy of Korham does not definitively identify "Lord Roga" as the leader nor "Khorgia" as the place across the sea. You must beware the fallacy of concurrent realities that satisfy many of the conditions mentioned in what has been taught but do not produce the true final outcome."

"How does one avoid following a false prophecy?"

"Identify the verifiable facts. '*A victorious leader shall come from across the sea and sit as the ruler of Korham.*' We know the future ruler of Korham will not be of the mainland for he has come across the sea."

Gorem the Elder interrupted. "But what if the future ruler of Korham was actually from the mainland but was victorious in a battle that took place off-shore? One could certainly interpret the parable to fit that reality as well."

Roga looked back and forth between the two clerics, imploring. He had never considered so many alternative realities to the prophetic teachings. Confusion furrowed his brow. A swirl of conflicting possibilities clouded his mind. Clearly rattled by the multiplicity of potential outcomes, his face turning a bright shade of burgundy, the warlord was, once again, becoming quite agitated. A hand gently placed on his shoulder startled him.

"Relax, Lord Roga." It was the old cleric from earlier. "You will send yourself into a stroke and that will surely do nothing to ensure the ultimate outcome of the words as you have interpreted them."

Roga stared at the old man intently. "I cannot shake the feeling that we have met somewhere before, but I cannot place where."

"My Lord, I cannot say where we might have crossed paths before. I am sure our travels may have placed us in proximity on more than one occasion, either in this life or in any one of several previous lives, and our souls shall surely meet again in the future. Should the exact time and place of our previous acquaintance make itself known to you once again, I would be very glad if you would make it known to me so that I might enjoy the opportunity to relive that moment with you. Alas, I cannot recollect a previous encounter at the present time. Mind you, I would be most incapable of accurately enlightening you on my evening meal from four days past."

"How strange that I am less certain about the events that I have lived and the people I have met than I am of the events foretold by all I have read. Perhaps it is indicative of the larger picture and signifies the triviality of our individual lives in relation to the whole of all history."

"Do not minimize the experience of a single life in relation to history. Any individual can make an impression that endures far beyond their mortal life. Is not history the compilation of every individual's experience?"

"Again, my conclusions are proven wrong. Can I believe any predictions that I have made?"

"Certainly, the majority of your forecasting has become truth. I find it highly unlikely the whole of your remaining predictions to be incorrect."

Other clerics began to interject, shouting their own thoughts on the matter across the room.

"But what of the one incorrect prognostication? Is it not significant? Could not the ultimate determination be incorrect as well?"

"And it could just as well be correct."

"Could the entire context be indicative of a past occurrence? Does the line in the parable not speak of Korham? And does Korham no longer exist?"

"But the scribes and prophets could not have known that Korham would now be known as De'Aarna."

Roga attempted to redirect and regain their focus.

"Please, please, there must be a consensus that can be reached in regards to the coming events. A single truth must exist. Whether willingly or not, you are all gathered here at present and a question has been placed before you. My wisdom and my library are at your disposal. My assistants, Minarik and Ursen are at your command to retrieve any tome you may require. My library is most extensive. I would dare to say there may not be a page known to man that discusses the tenets which I do not possess. If you require food or drink, they will gladly provide. My suggestion is that you avoid the wine. There have been those who have preceded you that did not take too kindly to it. But this is where the pleasantries must end. I expect an answer. I expect some positive direction that will lead to a much clearer prediction of the events foretold in the words of the ancients and I insist that no one leave until I am satisfied with the answer to my questions. I will leave you to your task as I have other business to attend to. Good day."

Roga turned and left the room, the two large doors closing violently behind him. After a silent moment of disbelief, the murmur of multiple conversations erupted, quickly reaching a fevered pitch. Ursen and Minarik stood in disbelief of the spectacle before them, so many different discussion and arguments coexisting and entwined, like a ball of fishing worms. One could not make sense of where one argument ended or where the next started. From the throng, a single mage approached the two. It was the calm older cleric that Roga was certain he had encountered in the past.

"Lord Roga offered your attendance to our needs. I seek a particular tome, *eht Loritaid Turega*, the Silent Songs. It is but a small book, just a few verses, but it holds the answers to many questions and will certainly solve the problem I am befuddled by. It is very rare, only a few known copies exist. Certainly, it can be found in Lord Roga's collection. And a glass of wine, red if you have it. Your master may not believe it to be suitable for present company, but I'd just as soon make that determination for myself."

Ursen and Minarik stood frozen, baffled by the calm, matter-of-fact nature of the old man standing before them as the remainder of the clerics engaged in chaotic discussions. The wise man looked back and forth between the two, a kind smile on his face. Finally, Ursen broke the impasse.

"The book, what was its name? The Silent Songs? I am sure I can find it in the library. Minarik, some wine for the old man?"

Minarik responded as if broken from a trance. "Uh... certainly. Red wine." He looked to Ursen. "And you'll get the book." The two turned to leave, the old gentleman watching, the same smile on his face.

Ursen went to Roga's office to get the book that the wise man had requested. Scanning the shelves, he sought a small or thin book. The mage had said the book had but only a few verses. He reached for a book on an upper shelf and, pulling it away from the shelf, nearly lost his balance as the bookcase pivoted away to reveal a dark chamber behind. Wide-eyed, Ursen peered into the darkness. Carefully, he wedged the book into the bookcase to prevent it from closing and entered the space. Deep in the darkness, he heard what sounded like voices. Fascinàted, he continued into the darkness. Slowly, a dim light began to appear before him and, as he moved closer, the back of a man became evident followed by what appeared to be another, prone on a high bed. Ursen hid behind the corner and watched intently.

"Master, the wise men have taken on my challenge to develop a consensus regarding the Prophecy of Korham. I am assured that they can arrive at the most likely interpretation of the parables, although I am not certain that the most likely interpretation shall be the script that history chooses to follow."

"My child, have faith in the collective intellect of the men you have gathered. As one, they possess the knowledge necessary to decipher the riddles hidden within the words. Heed their cipher of the parables."

"Wise men they might be, but I am not fully confident in their abilities to solve the simplest of riddles. The bickering and contradictory conversation do not seem conducive to determining any singular outcome. I am uncertain any one of them could calculate the time of tomorrow's sunrise and, as a whole, whether or not the sun shall even arise."

"Indeed, there is one among them that has power beyond the sum of the others. I cannot identify this powerful cleric, but I sense his presence. With his guidance the group will develop a most eloquent interpretation of the ancient teachings that will confirm your findings."

"I trust in your senses, Master, and I will await their consensus."

Ursen was confused by what he was seeing and hearing. The body on the bed did not move, but his voice filled the room like smoke from a smoldering fire, booming, enveloping the entirety of space touched by the light.

"I believe I can identify the cleric you speak of, Master. We had the pleasure of meeting, face to face, in the hall. He seems to be quiet but I also sensed he has abilities belied by his outward appearances. He has been the voice of reason amongst a sea of bickering old men. And I believe I may have encountered him at some point in the past, but I cannot place the moment. With such a countenance, one would think I could place him, but for some reason, I cannot."

"Worry not if you can identify him. If your previous encounter with him is meant to be known to you, it will become known to you. What is of import is that he is here among the wisest and will aid you in finding the truth in the prophecy. Once you are satisfied with what the future holds in store, then you can lead us to victory. We will have power beyond anything you have ever imagined."

Ursen soaked in everything he was seeing and hearing. He had learned during his short military career that every detail could be important later. What he was seeing and hearing now could prove particularly beneficial in future dealings with Lord Roga. Sensing the conversation would soon be coming to an end; he backed away and quickly returned the way he had come.

As the young recruit turned to leave, Roga felt a presence behind him. Turning to look over his shoulder, he caught movement in the shadows but could not make out what it was. He took a step in the direction of the movement, but a voice halted him.

"*Let him go, my son. He has neither seen nor heard anything of consequence and what he has seen may just make him a stronger ally in our camp. He may be a valuable asset in the future.*"

Ursen returned to the hall, *eht Loritaid Turega* in hand, and sought out the cleric that had requested it. He found him, sitting alone in a corner as the remainder of the group was engaged in heated discussions.

"Sir, the book you requested." Ursen presented the small, thin volume to the old man.

"Thank you, young man. I think this is exactly what I was looking for." The cleric accepted the offering from Ursen and, standing up his perch, he placed the thin book beneath one of the legs of his chair. Sitting back down on the chair, he wiggled about slightly and then smiled back at the young soldier, now pleased with the stability of his perch. "Perfect! I knew it would be the proper size. Thank you! I shall wait here for your cohort to arrive with my wine."

Ursen stared slack-jawed at the cleric, in total disbelief.

ELDEN AND ZEPHRAIM awoke well rested and energized, ready to take on another day in the city. Hopefully, De'Aarna would prove to be full of eager recruits, ready to take on the scourge of the dragons and regain the peaceful way of life they had become used to. They replaced the skins they had used for bedding and awaited Jonas' return.

After exchanging pleasantries with Jonas, the two men headed off into the city, stopping wherever men would gather. After a visit to the inn and a small tobacco shop, Elden and Zephraim had drummed up interest in about a dozen men. With luck, they would draw the interest of those they spoke with and the numbers would continue to grow. As they left the tobacco shop and headed towards the other end of the city, a familiar face caught Elden's eye.

"Quoregg! How good to see that you made it! And only a day behind Zephraim and I. You made good time. And what of the others?"

"We arrived but an hour or so ago, shortly before they closed the city. We were the benefactors of a merchant with a wagon that agreed to ferry the cleric here. With the old man aboard, we were able to move at a much faster pace without him. I only hope the merchant and his wagon made it through the gates prior to them being barred. I fear the cleric unable to fend for himself in the slum that has grown outside the walls of the city. Many unscrupulous individuals have congregated there."

"We shall keep an eye out for him as we do business about the city. Would I be correct to assume that you have yet to find a place to settle down?"

"You are correct, we have not. The farmer and the cook volunteered to remain in an alcove just outside the marketplace, protecting the space for us. The remainder has fanned out to seek shelter and provisions. How have you two managed?"

"We have found a place to stay and a reasonable supply of foods. We could inquire about providing accommodations for the rest of the group if you wish. I am sure Jonas would not see any harm in it."

"That would be much appreciated. And how do we repay such kindness?"

"Jonas allows us to spend the night in his stall at the marketplace. We keep an eye over his wares in the off hours in exchange for space. More eyes would provide more security. I think we could work out proper arrangements."

"The group is to come together in the next hour or so, back at the alcove. What should we do in the meantime?"

"Zephraim and I have been recruiting. We would gladly accept your company and assistance. Will you join us?"

"Certainly. Is it not the reason we have all come to this place, to collectively generate the power and prowess to defeat the dragons?"

"That it is, Quoregg."

The three men walked together, seeking out small gathering places and speaking with the men they encountered there. After an hour had passed, Quoregg led them back to where the rest of the group had gathered. After a moment to reacquaint, the group followed Elden back to the tanner's stall where he secured accommodations for all.

The men eagerly assisted Jonas in rotating his stock, pulling skins that had not seen the light in quite some time up to the top of the pile. Their conversation soon turned to the task of training a large army of men with which to defend the mainland against the dragon attacks.

"There is a place just beyond the city walls, the Tantallon Forest, that might prove to be a good place to train men. The canopy is thick and high, and the terrain below is relatively free of underbrush. A few hundred men, if not a thousand or more, could easily make camp there and not draw attention from above. May I suggest that as an appropriate location to gather your army?"

"Much appreciated, Jonas. You have been a fountain of information and assistance. When the current situations have come to pass, you must remind me of my indebtedness to you. Perhaps a dragon skin or two would fetch a few gold coins."

"That they might, Elden, but simply removing them from our skies and bringing calm and peace back to our homes would be payment enough. Business has been slacking since the attacks. No one knows what to expect next, so no one is buying anything but the barest of necessities. Stop the dragons and business will boom."

"We will see what we can do."

15
THE SECOND MEETING

DE'AARNA WAS A SPRAWLING port city. Once known as Korham, the ancient city was built on the highest point in the delta where the Oryon River met the Touphorus Sea. It had been a bustling center of commerce for centuries and now was no exception. Having been somehow spared the wrath of the dragon attacks, the city had become a magnet for refugees, an unlikely safe haven from the maelstrom that had been decimating the surrounding land. All the streets and alleys were teeming with humanity from every station and walk of life. The walls of the city were hard pressed to contain the vast number of people that now sought refuge. The heat and stench of so many in such close quarters bordered on intolerable, but no one dared to complain. The conditions inside were far better than the conditions experienced by those living outside the city. For reasons unbeknownst to the residents, this was a sanctuary, bereft of the scars of war and the pall of destruction that had overtaken nearly everything beyond the city walls.

But change is inevitable and ultimately affects all. De'Aarna was no exception. Once an open city where citizens and travelers alike were free to enter and exit the city and roam its streets at any hour without restraint, the gates were now closed and guarded. All who asked to come or go were questioned and searched to ensure nothing of danger made its way within the walls and nothing of import made its way out. The conditions of the world outside the city walls were now dictating the conduct of the inhabitants within.

Elden was seeking supplies and men, gathering the requirements for a battle against an enemy that appeared to be unbeatable. It had been days since he first entered the gates of De'Aarna, but he was still short of materiel and recruits. Walking through the marketplace, he scanned for weapons and armor and non-perishable foodstuffs, all the while sizing up every man that crossed his field of vision. He had already secured some swords and knives from a blacksmith and dried hantaberry fruit from a local farmer. Encountering a purveyor of salted fish, he approached to arrange a purchase.

"Fishmonger, is this the extent of your inventory?"

"I have stores elsewhere. Why do you ask? What would you need with such a large amount of my fish?"

"I am gathering supplies for the Tendira Confederacy. We are preparing an army to counter the dragon attacks. Your fish would be a welcome addition to our supplies."

"I can easily supply your army with one hundred barrels from my stores and, if your requirement is larger, twenty barrels more every week until the end of the season. Of course, our transaction shall be contingent upon our negotiating a fair price."

Elden raised an eyebrow. "And what is a fair price?"

"I think five gold per barrel sounds fair to me."

Slightly displeased, Elden frowned. "And what is a fair price for your life?"

"I'm not sure I like your tone, stranger! You will find that I do not take kindly to threats nor do I accept them as a form of payment."

"Forgive me if I came across poorly. It was not intended as a threat, but I wish that you would consider where your fish will end up and for what purpose. It could help to save your business... or your life. Is it possible we can work out a deal that is more amicable?"

The fish vendor sized Elden up. "I'm still not sure I like you, but I do have a business to run and supplying the militia to assure some protection could be potentially good business." He pulled at his beard. "I am willing to accept four gold per barrel, but you have to guarantee a purchase of at least two hundred barrels in total from me."

Elden stared directly into the fish monger's eyes, hoping to get a sense of how firm the vendor was on his price. "Four gold? Two hundred barrels minimum? And you have one hundred barrels for the taking immediately, correct?"

"Yes, one hundred barrels as soon as you want them."

"I pay for what I take, as I take it, no more, no less?"

"No more, no less."

"And if your catch falls short and you cannot provide the twenty barrels promised each month?"

"Then I will sell you what I have for three gold and two silver each barrel."

Elden extended his hand to the vendor. "I think we have a deal. I can have my men pick up the first shipment in the morning. Where should I send them?"

The vendor shook Elden's hand, sealing the deal, and then pointed out towards the port. "I have a building out on the main wharf, maybe halfway down. The wharf is wide enough for a wagon. Have your men ask for Rulon. He will assist them. And make sure they come with four hundred gold or the deal is off. I will honor my end of this bargain and I expect the same in return."

"I would expect no less. The name is Elden. It was a pleasure doing business with you, sir. May the Fortunes smile upon both our endeavors."

"As I am sure they will, Master Elden. I am known by Kaleb. Please feel free to stop by my shop again, if you should need more supplies."

As Elden turned to leave the fish monger's booth, he was trampled by a blur of pastels and lace. The impact knocked both him and his assailant to the ground. Quickly gathering himself up, he stood and confronted the whirlwind that had just laid him out.

"Clumsy buffoon! Why don't you watch where you are going?" Elden peered at the mass of silk and lace bunched up on the ground and the lovely young woman that lay amidst it all. His demeanor changed immediately. "Excuse me, M'lady. I did not realize...." He extended a hand to help her up.

"Hands off, you oaf! Maybe it is *you* who should watch where he is going!"

"Please, M'lady, let me offer my assistance."

Swatting his hand away, she rebuked him. "I am quite capable of righting myself on my own."

Irritated, Elden remarked sarcastically. "Well, then. Let's see if the lady can accomplish it without exposing her petticoats to everyone in the market square." Elden took a half step back while bowing slightly and opening his arms to the sides in mock servility.

She flashed a stare his way that would have killed a dragon in mid-flight. After first trying to roll to one side, then the other, she pulled her legs beneath herself and got herself up on both knees. Finally, and with far less grace than she would have liked, she wobbled her way up on one leg and then the other. As she stood, she attempted to brush away some of the dust and straw from her dress.

"Uncouth, disrespectful lout!"

"Begging your pardon, M'lady, it would appear we were equally at fault. Perhaps we can exchange pleasantries and be back on our separate ways."

"How dare you place blame upon me! It was you that turned without so much as a glance and walked directly into my path. And you think I should apologize?"

"It would seem the logical thing to do. Surely you are not placing the entirety of the blame upon me."

The lady quickly snapped back at him. "And surely you are not suggesting that a member of the aristocracy goes about willy-nilly bumping into the peasantry in the market square. How dare you!"

Incredulous, Elden simply stared at her for a moment, slack-jawed.

"Well?"

"How dare I? How dare *you*! Maybe it is time you were knocked from your pretty pink high horse and forced to take responsibility for your actions!"

A frail older man seated on a bench across from the fishmonger's shop smiled as he watched their banter. Quite enjoying their discourse, he finally spoke up. "Ah, young love." He stood and approached the quarreling couple. "How strange and wonderful a thing, love, to be equally apparent in both intimacy and confrontation."

Elden and his feminine adversary stopped mid-epithet, turning their attention towards the commentator.

"Begging your pardon, old man. No disrespect to yourself, but the only lust I possess at the current time is the lust for dragon slaying. Currently, I have no time for any woman, let alone... *her royal highness*."

Elden's sarcasm did not go unnoticed, and the lady quickly chimed in. "And I would sooner accept employ as a scullery maid than be subject to the affections of such a vile and uncouth beast!"

The old man laughed. "I sense a bit of tension betwixt and between the two of you. Are you not a couple?"

Elden scoffed. "A couple? Miss high-and-mighty and myself? I should think not. I find her arrogance and serpent tongue rather revolting. And her acidic personality falls second only to flaming dragon's bile."

"How dare you! I am Lady Ahnabin, daughter to Maob of *eht Vilna Antessara*. As a member of the ruling family at Antessara, I expect to be treated with the respect I deserve!"

Elden was taken aback. "Maob? Maob of Antessara was your father?"

Lady Ahnabin thrust her chin into the air slightly, responding with a quiet sadness. "Yes, he was."

Elden bent forward at the waist in a curt bow. "Forgive me my indiscretions. M'lady. I had no idea. I have heard the details of the attack on your castle. Your father was an accomplished leader and warrior, selfless and true. His bravery is legendary and has come to be known throughout the land. I have the utmost respect for him and any member of his family." Elden straightened himself and held his arms out by his sides. "If I may present myself. I am Elden, grandson to King Olen of the castle *Vilna Sahnah*. It is a pleasure to make your acquaintance."

"You are of the *Sahni*? Your grandmother, Queen Isella, is well known to me and greatly respected. To most, I am Lady Ahnabin, daughter to Maob of *eht Vilna Antessara,* but those that know me address me as Ahna. Your kind apology is graciously accepted. Perhaps I was not paying particular attention to where I was going. It is quite possible that I should shoulder a portion of the burden of blame." Ahna looked Elden up and down. "I must say, to my defense, one would not easily mistake you for *Sahni* royalty."

Elden dusted himself off. "I prefer not to take advantage of my station at these times. We are at war and I am far more valuable to the people as a warrior than a figure of royalty under the current circumstances. It is far easier to gain the respect of my comrades when I approach them as an equal."

"A fair evaluation, M'lord. If I might be so bold to ask, what takes you from *eht Vilna Sahnah* and brings you to this city? Surely your castle has not fallen to the attacks?"

"The Beacon Castle still stands, but I fear it may not always be so. I have traveled here not to seek asylum, as have many, but to procure provisions and men. It will take a large and capable army to turn back the dragons. They are a unique and particularly formidable adversary."

"I would find it quite unlikely for you to peruse the whole of this marketplace without finding that which you are seeking. I daresay that I have encountered items beyond my imagination in the short time I have been a guest here. I would also assume that recruitment is going well?"

"Alas, recruitment is slow. We have begun gathering soldiers for training in the Tantallon Forest. The dragons have so far avoided burning it to the ground. It provides fair cover from overhead and there is little sign of human activity to attract the attention of the dragon riders. For the time being, at least, it is as safe a place as any to assemble and train an army."

After watching and carefully absorbing everything the couple had been saying, the old man finally spoke again. "I dare say I was correct. If you were not before this day, you surely shall be known as a couple before my time here has passed."

Elden responded to the old man with sarcasm. "It would appear we have a professional prognosticator amongst us?"

The old man chuckled lightly. "If only that were to be true, kind sir. I am known as Taygen. I am merely a simple conjurer, cast out from the Black Castle when it was overthrown in days past. Like many of the residents of De' Aarna, I am a refugee of the dragon attacks, a man without a home."

"But there is something about you, old man, something that is more than what meets the eye. I can feel it in my soul."

Taygen chuckled once again. "And now who appears to be a professional prognosticator?"

Elden laughed with him and patted him amicably on the shoulder. "You have made your point well, old man. But I cannot help but feel you are more than what you appear to be. I sense a high level of intelligence, avid observation skills, and a clever mind. I would guess your humility is harboring a grand secret. Perhaps your skills as a conjurer and prognosticator are far more advanced than what you dare tell."

"Ah, were it to be true, I would smite every dragon from the sky and provide you with the answers to all your challenges before you even encountered them. Unfortunately, I have no control over the evil that man or beast may do, nor the events of the day. What little I do have control of serves me well as entertainment for whatever audience I may have at my disposal." Reaching slowly for Elden's ear, he questioned. "If I may, young sir?"

Elden nodded his assent and watched with some trepidation as Taygen ran a cupped hand over his left ear and produced a rare desert lily flower. He handed it to Ahna. "I believe that this young man has been withholding this from you. Perhaps he is more bashful with the fairer sex than his countenance reveals."

Ahna smiled and accepted the flower from Taygen. "Perhaps he will be less bashful the next time we bump into each other." Her gaze returned to Elden. "Should I expect to see you once again in the marketplace?"

"I cannot say for certain, M'lady. Perhaps, after we have rid this land of the scourge that is the dragons, but, for now, it is neither in my best interest nor the interest of these people if I engage my efforts towards the fairer sex. With all due apologies to the lady, I have committed myself to a far more challenging mistress; an end to the peril brought upon us by our deadly foe from above."

"That is by far the noblest of all commitments. I only wish I could be of some service. The death of my father pains me so. Revenge would not be a very bitter pill for me to swallow!"

"Fortunately, for us men, battle is no place for the fairer sex, M'lady, but if it pleases your heart, I will gladly avenge your father's death by plucking a score of dragons from the sky with my bare hands."

Ahna giggled. "Your gesture is most kind, Master Elden, is it not Taygen?"

"If I dare say, yes, most gentlemanly. But do not minimize your own abilities, young lady. I am sure you shall find your own way to avenge the death of your father most satisfactorily."

"I shall take that under advisement, but for now I must excuse myself. Master Elden, Sir Taygen, it has been my pleasure bumping into the both of you this fine morning. Elden, I wish you well in both your search for supplies and men and in the battle against the dragons. May you always be strong and true. Taygen, I would hope that we shall meet again in the market on a later date. Your wisdom and discourse would make for a very stimulating afternoon, possibly over tea? For now, I must be on my way. I have other business I need to attend to." Ahna gave a very proper curtsy to both men, flashing them both a very enthusiastic smile, and headed back on her journey across the market. Both men fixed their gaze upon her as she left.

After Ahna had moved beyond his sight, Elden turned to Taygen. "I t is time I get back to my task, Taygen, sir. The success of our fight against the dragons may well depend upon it. It was a pleasure for me, as well, to meet you, old man. If there is more than a simple magic trick hidden beneath your cloak, I would ask that you grace our army with its advantage. We could surely use any assistance to ensure we are victorious."

"I will most definitely say words for you this evening, Elden. May the Fortunes look kindly upon you and your army."

"Your blessing is most appreciated. Now I must be on my way." Elden offered Taygen a very proper bow and started off on his way.

The old man turned and walked slowly back to his seat on the bench. Sitting in the same spot as before, he continued to quietly observe the activity in the market.

AHNA SPENT THE EVENING deep in thought. Her mind was stuck on what Taygen had said about finding her own way to avenge the death of her father. Was he fool enough to think she could do something that would somehow punish the adversaries that had taken her father's life? Surely there was nothing a princess could do. Vengeance was the pleasure of a warrior and a warrior she was not. Still, the words of the conjurer repeated in her mind, over and over again. This was certainly not the first time she entertained thoughts of engaging in activities more accustomed to the robust physique of a man. Perhaps a princess *could* take a more active role in defending her people and the legacy of her father.

THE SUN HAD BARELY risen above the horizon. The evening dew hung delicately on every branch, frond, and flower. Elden was up early, on his way to meet his men at the fishmonger's warehouse. As he made his way down the main wharf, he noticed a familiar figure seated on a wooden box outside the entrance to the warehouse.

"Sir Taygen? Is that you?"

The old man opened his eyes and looked up. "Master Elden! Good morning. You have caught me in my morning meditation. Such a pleasure to see you once again. Are you here on business?"

"Yes, I am. I am to meet with some of my men to procure provisions I purchased yesterday. In fact, this here is the place I was told to present myself to collect my purchase. And what brings you to be exactly where I was headed this morning?"

Taygen chuckled. "Who is to say what the driving force is that guides the everyday movements of men? I simply go where the Fortunes steer me and rest where they provide me repose. Perhaps we are meant to meet here or maybe our paths have crossed without consequence, a mere quirk of time and space."

"Well, whatever the reasons may be, it is certainly a pleasure. Your conversation and anecdotes intrigue me."

"I am pleased to hear my stories have not fallen on deaf ears. I enjoy most enthusiastically engaging in conversation with others, whether it be an early morn on the wharf, an afternoon in the market or an evening around the campfire. What makes the moment is the company."

Elden shot a quick knowing glance at Taygen. "That's it! I knew there was something about you, but I could not put my finger on it. The campfire! I met you with a group of travelers on my way to De'Aarna. You are the cleric that spoke so eloquently about the past. We shared a fire and an encampment overnight and engaged in conversation during our travels the next morn."

A rather large grin spread across Taygen's face. "I daresay you are correct. It would appear as though the Fortunes have something in mind for us, having placed the two of us in such close proximity on so many occasions. Our paths seem to be woven together. Perhaps there are grander things in store for us."

"I can think of no grander event than the fight against the dragons. Maybe there is a trick or two hidden within your cloak that will afford advantage to myself and the troops."

"It can only be so if trickery and sleight of hand are all that is required to confuse a dragon and his rider into submission. Perhaps the prayers and thoughts of an honest man will be all that is necessary to beg favor for you and your army from the Creator. If that be the case, then I have all that is required at my disposal to ensure that favor."

“Well, I certainly welcome any favor you may be capable of bestowing upon our ragged assemblage of fighters. It would take months of training to mold them into an elite fighting force, but I dare say, we do not have the benefit of time.”

Presently, a wagon rolled up, pulled by two strong draught horses. Two men were seated at the front.

“Elden. Is this the place?”

“Good morning, Conor. Yes, it is the place, but I have yet to see the attendant. The fishmonger assured me he would be here and that they could provide one hundred barrels today. Perhaps he is inside.”

Elden pounded upon the two large doors at the front of the warehouse. Sounds of movement within could be heard and then the doors parted. A mountain of a man, head shaved bald, appeared in the opening.

“Can I help you?”

“I am Elden. My men, Conor, Sammi, and I are here to collect the fish I purchased from the fishmonger, Kaleb, yesterday. Are you Rulon?”

The man offered a hand the size of a frying pan. "I am. A pleasure to do business with you. Is this your only wagon? You're going to need more than one trip with that."

“Yes, this is our wagon. We know it will require several trips. It’s not a problem for us if it is fine with you. We have all day.”

“Not a problem with me. Let’s get to loading this carriage.”

Elden motioned for the men to begin loading. Rulon began rolling barrels out the door and Elden’s men hefted them into the bed of the wagon. In relatively short time, twenty barrels were occupying the back of the wagon.

“I believe that is all we can accommodate for this trip, Rulon. We shall deliver this load to our encampment and return for another. You will wait for us?”

“I have no other place to be. I shall await your return. For how long should I expect you to be gone?”

"We must travel to the Tantallon Forest, perhaps thirty minutes out. I would expect us to be back in just over an hour."

"I will be here, in the warehouse. Knock and I will be ready to assist again."

Elden mounted the wagon, Conor beside him with Sammi astraddle the barrels behind. He addressed the magician.

"Perhaps you would care to join us, Master Taygen. It would be presumptuous of me to suggest that you brandish a weapon, but your wisdom would certainly be graciously accepted by the men. I am certain there is much that could be learned from interacting with you."

"I will have to pass on this occasion, but far be it for me to deny that we may be working together for a common cause in the not-too-distant future. Be on your way, young Elden. The Fortunes have brought us together once again for reasons we do not yet understand. It is not a stretch of the imagination to speculate that fate has already arranged for the two of us to meet again."

Elden nodded to the old man and, giving the reigns a quick snap, egged the horses onward. Taygen watched as the wagon disappeared beyond the wharf and slowly made his way back to the market. As the night previous, the marketplace was bustling with people, nearly shoulder to shoulder. The wise man made his way to the spot he had occupied when he encountered Ahnabin and Elden. As if mimicking the scene he had observed with the young couple, he himself experienced an abrupt meeting with another, bumping into a tall, dark figure of a man as he sought his perch alongside the market path. The figure caught the old man as he fell to the ground.

"Begging your pardon, young man. It would appear that I no longer move at a pace that is conducive to traversing such a populated area."

"I should place no blame upon you, sir. The marketplace is crowded beyond capacity. Even the most observant would find himself bumping into his neighbor. No harm has been done. May I provide escort to your destination?"

"That is most kind of you. I seek a spot across the marketplace, a place of rest for a weary old man. I appreciate and accept your kind offer. If I may be so bold to ask, you are not from these parts. From which kingdom have you been driven from to seek refuge in this place?"

"Unlike many here, I have no kingdom. I am an orphan, adopted into a band of vagabonds that roam the forests between the northern kingdoms. I have left to seek my own way and have found myself drawn to this city. Apparently, this is the place from which I shall make my fortunes."

"The opportunity to make one's fortune certainly resides in this place. There are many needs to be administered to, including your own."

The tall young man offered his arm to steady the old man and the two of them slowly wedged their way through the crowded marketplace, eventually coming to a spot not far from Kaleb's fish stand.

"I believe this is my destination. I thank you for the escort... I don't believe we exchanged names. I am Taygen, originally from *eht Vilna Moht.* "

"And I am known as Oran. I suppose De'Aarna is now my home."

"Master Oran, it has been my pleasure. Perhaps we shall cross paths again."

"Perhaps. Enjoy your day, Taygen, and please use care when crossing the marketplace. Although they mean no one any harm, the crowd has no patience for those less nimble. It would be a shame if someone as wise and as kind as yourself were to come to be the victim of the mindless swarm of humanity that occupies this space for hours on end."

"I shall exercise the most caution when my day is done and I must return to my bed. Please, be on your way. You will lose the day if you tarry with an old man the likes of me."

Oran quickly bowed to the elder in reverence and made his way through the throng.

ROGA HURRIEDLY MADE his way back to the Great Hall. Ursen had brought word that the conclave of scholarly men had come to a consensus regarding Lord Roga's quandary. His entire person literally tingled with excitement. He burst through the door upon arrival.

"My assistant has informed me that you have come to common consent. Pray, tell me the product of your conjoined intellects."

Gorem, the Elder, spoke for the group. "We have taken everything you and your assistants have offered as information and come to a conclusion.

You have enlightened us that the gates of the city have been barred. You were concerned that this did not play into your understanding of the Prophecy of Korham and did not fit well into your plans. Is it not a requirement for the gates to be closed for them to be opened? And can they not be opened from the outside just as well as from the inside? The Gatekeeper must open the gates of Korham for the Chosen One. If your understanding of the parables is true, then we can only deduce that ***you*** are *Eyieritu*, the Chosen One. We find no phrase written that can deny this to be true. And the Gatekeeper will be one familiar to the city, for he must be known to secure admittance. We cannot place him, for we know not the faces and names of those within your trusted circle, but the Gatekeeper must be someone known to you, possibly a presence from the mainland. He does not need to be in the city but he must be capable of commanding that they be opened for you."

"So, you are saying my predictions were correct?"

"Indeed, we are. The preponderance of evidence would lead us to believe that your predictions are indeed correct. Your only error was assuming the council of royals was the end. They are but a placeholder. The Gatekeeper cannot open gates that are not closed. It is a small detail, but crucial to the events that must play out."

ORAN HAD BARELY DISAPPEARED from Taygen's view when a familiar figure approached him, the cloaked man.

"Master Oran. I am glad to have found you. I have news that might be of interest. You have come to De'Aarna to seek your fortune, but your fortune might just lie across the sea. My master, Lord Roga, seeks an audience with you. He knows of our encounter in the forest and how we have become reacquainted here in the city and is most intrigued by your story."

"And what would your Master want with the likes of me? I am no one of status. He cannot know anything about me."

"Ah, but that is where you are wrong, Oran. Master Roga knows. He is a student of all that has been foretold. He has studied the tomes page by page, word by word, and has knowledge beyond that of any other man I know.

Something in your story has caught his interest and he has requested that I beg of you to journey to Khorgia and meet with him."

"But I have no means by which to make such a journey. I have no money to speak of. I would not be capable of securing safe passage across the Touphorus Sea."

"Your mode of travel has already been attended to, Oran. Lord Roga has addressed that detail. He has sent an emissary to meet you and accompany you on your journey. You must simply choose to go and your journey is assured."

Oran stared at the cloaked man for a moment, still unable to make out his face. "I..." He hesitated and fidgeted. "I don't... I suppose..." He let out an exasperated sigh and shrugged. "I have no better options currently. Perhaps Lord Roga has insight into my future. I surely have none. I place my future in his most learned and capable hands. Lead me to my transport. I pray it is not a dragon. I am unsure of how I would react to flight."

"No. I do not believe a dragon would find its way, unnoticed, to the shores of De' Aarna. Come. Follow me. My Lord has prepared a vessel for your journey."

The cloaked man led Oran to the port where a small but visibly sturdy ship awaited. Three rather surly characters occupied the vessel, apparently the crew. As they approached, the cloaked man hailed a fourth man.

"Ahoy! I have returned with Lord Roga's guest. You will take him to the port in Oro where he is to be directed to the Lord's valet, Minarik. Mind you, he is to be considered precious cargo. His Lordship would be greatly displeased if any mischief were to become of Master Oran. I dare not need to tell you the fate you shall endure if he were to be delivered in anything less than perfectly unharmed condition."

The man presented himself to Oran. "I am Bengt, representative of his Lordship, Master Roga. I have been sent to ensure your safe journey to Khorgia." He turned to address the cloaked man. "His Lordship need not worry himself. No one knows the channels and currents of the Touphorus better than the captain and his crew. They would be comfortable ferrying *Ahlok* himself from here to Oro and beyond. His safe journey is assured."

"Oran, you have heard it from the Master's emissary; your journey is assured. Apparently, looks can be deceiving." The captain snarled slightly at the remark. "Make yourself as comfortable as possible. It is not a long journey for a skilled crew, but the Sea can be less than favorable at times. I will send word ahead to Minarik to expect you. He shall ensure your accommodations once you have reached Khorgia. I bid you safe journey. May the Fates be with you."

Oran extended his hand. "I thank you for all you have done although we have barely been acquainted. May I call upon you when I return to De'Aarna?"

"I cannot portend what the future has in store for either of us. I often find myself in a different location the following day. If we are to occupy the same city in our future, then I would expect nothing less than to have you call upon me. I am at the command of my Master. Perhaps he shall inform Lord Roga of my whereabouts and arrange for us to share company once again. For now, enjoy safe journeys."

Oran climbed into the ship and watched the cloaked man fade into the crowd as the crew prepared to push off from the mooring.

16
THE APPRENTICE

THE DOOR TO LORD ROGA'S office opened and the warlord stood in the opening, motioning for someone to enter.

"Please, my son. Make yourself comfortable."

A tall, well-proportioned, dark-haired young man entered the room. Oran. "Lord Roga. It is an honor and a pleasure to finally meet you." He scanned the room, becoming instantly attracted to the two small lizards occupying a section of tree trunk on a pedestal in the corner.

Roga approached his desk and sat down, examining the papers and books before him. "I gather that your trip was satisfactory."

Oran hesitated a little before he answered. "Y... yes, quite satisfactory. Bengt and the crew attended to my needs as best as can be expected."

"Good. I am pleased you found it so. And I hope your stay with us will be equally enjoyable." Not looking up from his desk, Roga continued, almost as if disinterested. "You may be wondering why I brought you here. Look around you, around us." Roga waved his hand about the room without breaking his stare from the top of his desk. "I am a student of the ancient manuscripts. I have studied every one of these tomes and hundreds more. They speak of a time when the way of the world will be turned on its side. A time when evil will once again permeate the hearts and minds of men, allowing those who desire it to rise to greatness and power. By all accounts, this is that time. And the words tell of a leader, a Chosen One. The Chosen One, *Eyieritu*, shall come to the great city of Korham, that which we now know as De'Aarna." As the warlord talked, Oran wandered closer to the tree trunk and its occupants. Oblivious to the motions of his guest, Roga continued talking. "The Prophecy of Korham speaks of a man, the

Gatekeeper, who shall open the gates to allow the Chosen One to enter. You may ask why this is important, why should you even care? Well, as the Fates would have it, you are a perfect match to fulfill the exigencies of the Gatekeeper of Korham. You are familiar with the city, you are from the mainland, you now know of me and will be prepared to open the gates of De'Aarna so I may enter the city. It is possible you do not know, but you have a cousin, the son of your mother's sister. All that has been written by those learned speaks of the spawn of sisters and how one will pave the way for the Chosen. Everything about you is written in the ancient books."

Roga looked up at his guest and smiled. Oran had been oblivious to his words, lost in his admiration of the warlord's two lizards. "Ah, you have found my pets. *Motaurotsyiclaes arboretum*, the tree dragon. They are..."

Oran quickly cut in. "Small."

"Small?" Roga looked perplexed but then chuckled to himself. "I suppose from your perspective, they are. Your experience has only been with the large fire dragons. The tree dragons are indeed small, but more significant than most could possibly understand."

Oran turned to face his host. "How so?"

Roga stood from his desk and walked towards Oran and his pets. "It was from these small tree-dwelling reptiles that the massive rulers of the air, which you are more familiar with, were born. Years of meticulous selective breeding created the aerial flame-throwing behemoths you know from these timid little tree climbers. It is an accomplishment all Khorgians can be proud of. We created the ultimate aerial military platform, *Motaurotsyiclaes ignus*, the fire dragon. Would you like to see one, up close?"

"I would be honored for the opportunity, my Lord."

Roga motioned for Oran to follow him. "Come. My business here is done for the moment. I will take you to view my personal creature, the queen herself."

The two men exited the office together and headed deep within the mountain to the dragons' warren.

The warlord continued to discuss the dragons as he led Oran through the intricate maze of the mountainside warren to the creatures' den.

"Unlike our society, the dragons' society is matriarchal. The dominant female rules the roost. And unlike most other creatures, the queen dragon is the sole breeding female, supported by and cared for by neuter workers. As the sole source of procreation, she breeds with a handful of male consorts to maintain the roost. She is like the queen bee in a hive. Ants, termites, bees; they have been in existence for eons. Their familial organization has stood the test of time and I am confident the same will hold true for the dragons."

As they continued towards the warren, Oran felt the air turn warm and moist, almost uncomfortable. A low rumbling could be heard coming from the area beyond. As they entered the main rookery, a cavernous room at least three stories high and sixty feet across, Oran was in awe of the hundreds of small caves that dotted the walls. Betwixt and between, spaced randomly about the chamber, hallways led off to other areas of the warren. Oran could see numerous dragons in their caves, some alone and sleeping, others being tended by their riders.

"Does each dragon have its own rider?"

Roga chuckled. "I find it quite interesting that you have worded your question as you have. Yes, each dragon does have its own rider and, in fact, in many cases, the dragon chooses its rider, or more so, chooses who will *not* be its rider. Young recruits are required to tend to the unhatched eggs and newborn efts. The efts typically bond with one of them. Sometimes they reject their first recruit, but it is a rare occurrence."

"So, they have a bond from an early age. How long will they remain bonded? Until death?"

"The bond between rider and dragon will last a lifetime. A young recruit of about sixteen years will be selected by an eft. After about four peels, usually two years, the eft will sprout its wings and finally become a fully-fledged dragon. Another year to strengthen and learn to use its wings and the two will become a finely-honed aerial team. And that team will stay together until death, usually forty or fifty years, sometimes longer."

"And if either rider or dragon dies prematurely, what happens then?"

"If the rider dies early, while the dragon is still an eft, there is a slight possibility it will accept another rider. I have seen it happen, but it is very rare. If the dragon is male and fails to accept another rider, we can use it for breeding with the queen. You see, the rider imprints upon the dragon for the animals have far better senses than our own. Another rider fails to have the same feel, the same sounds, the same smell. If the beast is neuter and fails to accept another rider, it is put to rest. A dragon requires care and a dragon without a rider has no means to provide for itself."

"And if the dragon perishes?"

"It is quite possible for the *aryatoemi*, a rider that has lost his dragon, to imprint upon a new dragon. A rider, more often than not, finds being dragon-less to be unbearable, most often choosing *ahnemi shah*, 'the final walk,' a trek into the forest from which they will never return. But I have seen riders late in their career lose their ride and choose to mind the eggs and efts in the hopes of being chosen by another. It is not commonplace, but far more common than a dragon accepting a new rider."

"Care for a dragon must occupy most of a rider's time."

"That is an understatement, Oran. A rider spends every moment with his dragon. It is for that reason why the vast majority of our riders choose not to marry. They are betrothed to their steed and have little time for much else." Roga motioned down a very large hall. "Come, the queen resides here."

Oran could feel the heat emanating from the end of the hall. As they approached, a vast cave opened before them. There, bedded down on a raised platform, was a dragon nearly two and one-half times as large as the dragons he had passed along the way here. Dark steel gray scales larger than a man's hand covered her body, twinkling in the torch light that illuminated the room. A low, almost inaudible rumble vibrated the room with each breath she took. As the two men entered, the beast opened one eye to stare at her rider.

The warlord walked up to his beast and gently began rubbing her shoulder. The low rumble raised in pitch as she felt her rider's touch. Roga motioned for Oran to come closer.

"She will not bite, not as long as you are here with me, although I'm sure she would fancy you a tasty morsel."

Oran stepped closer and put his hand out. "May I?"

Roga grabbed his wrist and slowly guided his hand to the same shoulder he had been rubbing. Tentatively, Oran began to gently stroke the shoulder scales of the queen dragon. The queen purred deeply at his touch. Oran relaxed at her reaction and continued to rub her shoulder. The beast slowly cracked open the other eye and stared at him for a moment and just as slowly closed the eye again.

"She is at ease with you, no fear. Her acceptance is a signal of trust. If my ride holds you in high esteem, then so do I."

"Her scales, they are so soft to the touch. I had imagined them to be hard as a stone. One would think them to provide no protection."

"Soft to the touch, yes, but still strong enough to deflect most weapons easily. More difficult to penetrate than oil-hardened leather armor. And every detail and characteristic that makes the dragon the ideal fighting machine were created by man through a very selective breeding process. The weir masters spent lifetimes developing the creatures, leaving no detail unattended. You will be hard pressed to find a creature in the wilds capable of the feats the fire dragons are capable of."

"She is beautiful."

"Yes, she is. I fail to see the beauty in most things on this planet, but I shall never doubt the beauty of these magnificent creatures. If I were to come back in my next life, I would hope it to be as a fire dragon."

Oran continued to rub the giant beast's shoulder scales. The queen continued to rumble softly as he did.

"I believe she may just like you. Perhaps I should be concerned that she might decide that you are a more suitable rider."

"I find that highly unlikely. I find it hard to believe that I might be so superior to you, my lord, that your own beast would abandon you. And I haven't the first notion on how to ride."

"Be that as it may, I would think you to be a most desirable riding candidate for any newborn eft, possibly even the new queen."

"A new queen? I thought you spoke of a single queen in the rookery."

"Indeed, there shall only be one mature breeding female in the warren. But she is getting up in years and may soon become barren. A potential replacement must be hatched beforehand, so, as nature often does, the queen will produce a fertile female offspring during her later years for the continuation of the warren. It takes a very special person to be selected by a waiting queen. You could easily be that person."

"But I am too old."

"Nonsense! *Aryatoemi* much older than yourself have successfully imprinted on an eft and you have far superior wit and character. The eft seeks a connection. Age plays no factor in it."

"May I be so bold as to request an opportunity to tend to the nursery?"

"I highly encourage it, but all in good time. You have much to learn about why you are here, and we have a particular task that must be attended to first. Come. We must get back to my office. There is so much more we need to discuss."

Oran slowly removed his hand from the queen's shoulder. She responded with a long, high-pitched sigh at the loss of contact but settled herself for a long rest.

"DID YOU ENJOY YOUR tour of the caverns?"

"Quite. I am amazed by the number of dragons that live within this mountain and by how large the queen is."

"She is an amazing creature. They all are. A true testament to man's ability to shape the course of nature. Even more amazing is the fact that man's breeding them to their current configuration satisfies what has been written in eons past. '*And terror will rain down from the sky as balls of lightning, signaling Eyieritu, the Chosen One is near. For it is he who opens the Gates of Korham for the Chosen that will be showered with the riches of Ahlok, never to want again.*' The dragons surely fit as the 'terror in the skies.'"

"But who is the Chosen? And who is he who opens the gates to Korham?"

"Had you not been distracted by my little pets earlier; you would know the answer to your inquiry. Surprisingly, the answer to one of your questions is much closer than you could know. '*The sister stars of dusk and dawn shall bring to life, one praised, one scorned, cousins lost but bound by fate. Who shall live to guard the gate?*' I knew you were the one as soon as I saw how relaxed my queen was when you touched her today. Beasts have excellent intuition. They can read people well and her reaction to you matches what I have predicted from my studies. It would suggest that you and your cousin are excellent candidates to fulfill the Prophecy of Korham."

Oran looked perplexed. "Cousin? I have no cousin."

"Ah, but you do, my son. The mother and father that you know, the ones that raised you from a child, are they not your adoptive parents?"

Oran glared at Roga. "How do you know all of this?"

Roga laughed. "I know everything about you; your adoptive parents, Timmol and Maricol, the clan of nomads, the fight with Timmol and how you left the clan. Your journey and ultimate destination, De'Aarna. Nothing escapes my sources."

The two men locked stares for a moment before Oran pulled a chair to Roga's desk and sat down.

"Tell me more."

IN A COLD AND DAMP cave, a single dark figure lay motionless upon a funerary bier, the outline made discernible only by the glow of luminous phosphorescent algae clinging to the cave walls. Although unmoving, a booming voice, as deep and strong as the rumble of a swollen river but as soft and silent as a zephyr passing through an open field, emanated from the figure and filled the darkened space.

"*He hides himself well, but I can now sense his presence. His cousin acts as an antenna, attenuating his energy so I can feel him. He is somewhere in Tendira and the only way to be certain he is destroyed is by the complete devastation of everything on the mainland.*"

Roga addressed his Master. "But the teachings tell of one spilling the blood of his own on his way to becoming the Gatekeeper for the Chosen. Why would we expend the time and effort if the path has already been dictated?"

"*You are very wise, my child. You have studied the teachings of old well and learned the very details that will be the difference between victory and defeat. Trust in your knowledge. Follow your well-informed intuition. Prepare the young man Oran for the encounter with his cousin. He must be ready, for it will be his victory that lays the cornerstone for all that we have worked for. His victory ensures the gates to Korham are opened for Roga, the Chosen.*"

ORAN SAT AT ROGA'S desk, just as intrigued by the fish in the bowl as he was by the tree lizards. The warlord had the most amazing pets!

The office door opened, startling the young man, and a recruit clad in dark riding leathers entered.

"Good evening, Master Oran. I am Ursen, apprentice to Lord Roga. I have been sent to assist you with your needs and to show you to your quarters. I see you have noticed the master's fishbowl."

"Yes, indeed. They are most fascinating, as are the tree dragons."

"I presented the first few fish to his lordship as spoils from a raid. The others he has had brought in from all corners of the known world. I would say he admires them nearly as much as he does his dragons, both large and small."

"Master Roga told me of the process by which the fire dragons were created from the tree dragons. Imagine breeding a dragon for the sea. Certainly, that is one realm not exploited yet by the likes of man. The riches of the sea are boundless. Controlling that resource would open up so many possibilities."

"Perhaps that could be a project we can take up in the future, you and me, together. Lord Roga would be pleased to see two young recruits with such great ambitions working towards the improvement of the entire weir. But I need to get you situated in your room first. Come. Follow me. I will show you to your accommodations and help you with provisions. We can talk more on the way."

Oran followed Ursen out of the warlord's office, taking one last look at the tree dragons before carefully closing the door behind.

17
THE MAKING OF A WARRIOR

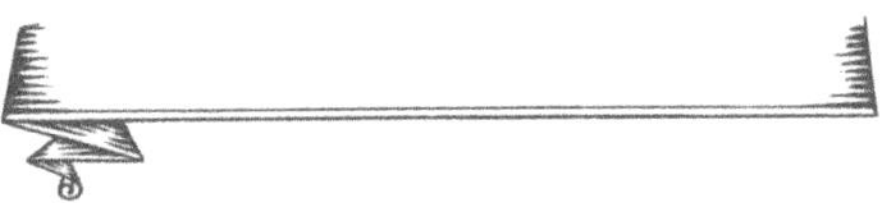

ELDEN WATCHED INTENTLY as a group of fresh recruits practiced with their longbows. The army numbered in the hundreds now and filled every corner of the Tantallon Forest. He slowly walked up to one of his trainers.

"Quoregg, the new men are shaping up rather well. It shouldn't be too much longer until they will be ready for battle."

Quoregg was Elden's key advisor and Man-at-Arms. They had met on the journey to De'Aarna and found a common bond in their desires to rid the land of the menacing demons that rained flaming terror upon their people. Both men were trained in the fine arts of warfare, a pursuit engaged in by many of the elite and more learned, even though the need had not been apparent for generations before the dragons appeared. Together, they had developed a comradery and a plan to build an army with which to defend their homeland.

"Indeed, Master Elden. They have learned well and are very eager to confront the Khorgians. I am unsure if we can defeat them outright, but it will be a victory just to slow them down and show them some resistance. If we can simply turn them back once, it will give us more time to build our own defenses."

"Quite so. And what is our compliment at the moment?"

"There are nearly three hundred men training here at the camp. If we include every man trained in the art of warfare across the land and residing in the various kingdoms, we may add half again that number."

"Those numbers will have to do for now but keep your men on the lookout for more recruits. We can use every man we can find."

As they spoke, a tall, slender man approached Elden and Quoregg.

"Zephraim, how are you today?"

Zephraim extended his hand to each man. "I am fine, Elden, Quoregg. I am bothered by something, Elden. Could you spare a few moments?"

"Certainly. Quoregg, if we may?"

"By all means, sir. I have recruits to attend to in the meantime."

Quoregg excused himself and walked away.

"Tell me, what is troubling you, Zephraim?"

"When we first met, back at *eht Vilna Sahnah*, you promised me an opportunity to exact revenge for my losses. Since we arrived at De'Aarna, I have watched as recruits have made their way here to the forest. I have watched them train and prepare, all the while as a spectator. It is time I become engaged and take an active role in preparing for this confrontation."

"You are right. I had promised you an opportunity for battle. I fear I have been so involved in recruitment that I have failed to consider your personal involvement. We can remedy that presently by having you properly outfitted."

Elden led Zephraim to the armory. Inside the tent, swords and battle axes were lined up in neat rows, shields were stacked in piles, and various types of armor were hanging from pegs.

"Please, take your time to find what suits you. The armorer can assist you if you are unable to find what you need. I must get back to the men, but I look forward to seeing you on the training fields. Good luck."

Zephraim walked about the tent, carefully examining the items available for his selection. The armorer watched him closely. He selected a pair of leather and iron greaves to protect his lower legs and strapped them on over his boots, slapping them heartily to assure himself of their protection. Next, he went to the far corner where he saw numerous pieces of iron and leather plate armor. There he found a vambrace of oil-hardened leather and placed it on his right forearm, followed by a leather and iron rerebrace that he placed loosely on his upper arm. A leather pauldron and a steel gardbrace for his shoulder finished the set. Carefully fastening the pieces together and tightening them to his arm and shoulder, he smiled and began to walk away. The armorer approached him.

"Sir, those items come in pairs. Do you not want armor for both sides?"

Zephraim held out and rotated his arm, carefully examining the armor. "No, I think this will suit me just fine. But thank you." Zephraim turned to leave.

The armorer called after him. "Please, sir. I daresay you may be laughed out of camp if you show up wearing armor on only one shoulder. And I should be laughed at, as well, for letting you leave my tent in that condition. Please, let me properly outfit you. Why, you haven't even a weapon."

Zephraim turned and chuckled. "But I do." Shifting his tunic aside with his right hand, he produced a sinew rope from a tie on his belt.

"A little rope, sir? And what do you think you shall do in battle with a length of string?"

With a quick flash of his wrist, Zephraim sent the rope following a shiny, conical metal dart, straight by the armorer's head and into the tent pole, at eye's height, beside him. "I assure you; the pole was my target. Were it you, there would be a place for an extra eye in your forehead."

The armorer stammered. "I... I have never seen such a weapon! Where did you come by it?"

Zephraim tugged at the sinew to dislodge the dart from the pole and began coiling it back up. "It is of my own design. It was originally intended as a toy, actually. I used it for target games, but the more I played with it, the more it became evident how deadly a tool it could be if properly utilized. I have yet to have the need beyond the occasional serpent or scorpion on the Souliban, but I assume a true need will be soon at hand."

"An amazing weapon, if I must say so. May I?"

"Certainly." He handed the coil to the armorer. "It takes some skill to learn how to use it, and one must use care as the sinew sometimes breaks. Otherwise, it is a very capable tool."

The armorer carefully examined the dart. "Fine craftsmanship." He bounced the dart gently in his hand. "Hefty, too. I daresay it would easily pierce the strongest leather armor and may do a bit of damage to iron. Is your skill the design of weaponry?"

Zephraim laughed. "No, quite far from it. I am a beekeeper by trade."

The armorer examined the coil of sinew attached to the dart. "Have you ever considered replacing the rope with a chain? I would reason it to be less likely to break." He handed the dart and coil back.

Zephraim carefully examined the returned coil. "No, I have never thought of using a chain. I assume it would be much more conducive to a battle situation. Could you attach a chain to the dart?"

The armorer smiled. "It would be my pleasure, sir. Return in two days and I will have a suitable chain affixed to the dart. That will make your unique weapon most battleworthy." He extended his hand to Zephraim, who accepted it gladly.

"Two days it is. I look forward to what you might be able to come up with." Zephraim turned to leave.

"Are you sure you won't humor me and allow me the opportunity to provide armor for the left side, sir? It all comes for the same price."

Zephraim chuckled again. "No, I think it is fine the way it is. My weapon requires speed and agility, and the extra armor would only weigh me down. Besides, I will face my quarry from the right side and I have no intent of allowing anyone to come at me from the rear."

"I understand, sir, but if you would be so kind as to humor me." The armorer rummaged about the tent for a few moments and came back with something. He held out a buckler to Zephraim. "Please, wear this on the left side. It is small and light and can easily be used to ward off an arrow or a blade in close quarters."

Zephraim took the small shield and fastened it to his left forearm. "I must agree with you. It is easy to handle and does not inhibit my use of the dart. It may be of use in close combat. Thank you."

"My pleasure, sir. It is what I do. I endeavor to make this army as battle ready as possible. And I am yet to be done with you. Be sure to return in two days' time for the chain."

"I will." He turned to leave but stopped. "I am called Zephraim. I did not catch your name."

"I am called Eroniaetus. I fear my mother was wont for the aristocratic. Those close know me as Eron and you may call me the same if you so wish."

"Eron, I will see you in two days." With that, Zephraim pushed the tent flap aside and exited the armory. Elden was outside waiting.

Elden carefully looked him over. "All kitted out, I see, or something to that effect."

"I assure you, Elden, the armorer is quite satisfied with my choice of armor. I believe when you see what I am capable of, you will agree."

"Well, then, let us introduce the new you to the rest of the camp. Quoregg will oversee your training. He will make sure you know everyone of import, as well as the men you are to fight with. Listen well and train hard. I fear we have little time to prepare before we are forced into battle."

"I will not disappoint you, Elden, sir."

Both men smiled as Elden walked Zephraim to the training field to present him to Quoregg.

THE FOLLOWING MORNING, the men were up early. Breakfast had been eaten and they were hard at it, carefully training for what was inevitable: battle with the Khorgian Dragon Guard. As Elden watched the men train, he noticed a familiar blur of pastels and lace out of the corner of his eye. Lady Ahnabin approached along the path leading from De'Aarna. She had found a driver taking supplies to the forest for the army and charmed her way upon his wagon as a passenger.

Elden met Ahnabin on the path. "Lady Ahna, this is a very pleasant and unexpected surprise. To what do we owe the pleasure of your visit?"

"I have come to volunteer."

Elden helped Ahna down from the wagon and offered her his arm. "That is very good of you, M'lady. There is always a need of a helping hand in the kitchen or laundry. Your skills may even be of use to the seamstress. Allow me to introduce you."

Ahna stopped in her tracks, nearly jolting Elden off his feet. "Kitchen? Seamstress? You are quite mistaken, Master Elden. I have come to volunteer as a recruit. I want to learn how to fight in battle. I want to help smite dragons from the sky." Ahna pushed herself up into Elden's face and started tapping on his chest to emphasize her every word. "I am here to avenge the death of my father."

"Surely you jest, M'lady. Battle is no place for a woman, let alone a princess."

"If a prince the likes of you can shed the trappings of royalty and become a warrior, then a princess can leave her womanhood behind and do the same. Are you prepared to stand in my way?"

"But M'lady, please! As a prince, I have trained in the fine arts of warfare since childhood, but you clearly have not. Far be it for me to allow the daughter of Maob to commit to something as suicidal as entering battle without the benefit of any formal training."

"I have taught myself to ride like any man and most likely better. I can catch Oryon trout as well as any male angler. I even bait my own hook! Far be it for you to try and tell me what I can and cannot do. If you are not going to help me, then I guess I will have to see to it myself." Ahna hiked up her dress and petticoats and stormed towards camp.

Elden ran after her. "Wait, Ahna! And where do you think you are going? You don't even know with whom to talk." He grabbed her by the arm and stopped her. "Fine. As you wish. I will introduce you to my Master-at-arms, Quoregg. I'm sure between he and I we can work this all out."

"There is nothing to 'work out.' I am here to volunteer and volunteer I will. *Sibu* save the man that decides he will stand in my way."

Elden knew this was not going to be easy. It was unprecedented for a woman to go into battle, let alone a princess. He could only hope that she would quickly grow weary with the physicality of training and withdraw. With any luck, this charade would be over in the matter of a few hours. Elden led her towards the training field where his Master at Arms was watching the men.

"Wait here. Let me go explain this to Quoregg. He will need to know how important this decision is to you and that I am in agreement. This is certainly *not* the norm for him."

Elden left Ahna behind and approached Quoregg. She watched intently at their animated discussion.

"This is unheard of!" Quoregg was adamant. The last thing he wanted or needed was for some spoiled princess to disrupt the training regimen of his men. The time for battle was far too close at hand for any distractions. "Am I to be babysitter to a princess, now, as well as a trainer of men?"

"Humor her, Quoregg. She is the daughter of Maob from *Antessara*. Let her train on the field with the newest recruits. I predict she will remove herself in defeat as soon as she dirties her hands. We can only hope she does so quickly and relieves us of this annoyance."

Quoregg let out a long sigh. "For you, Elden, and for the memory of Maob, I will comply with your wishes. I only hope you are correct in assuming the princess' training will be short-lived."

"Look at her." Elden motioned toward Ahnabin. "All satin and lace. Do you really think she will last more than a day or two?"

Quoregg laughed a little. "I would say not, but I will humor *you* for but a day or two. After that, she becomes your issue!"

Quoregg approached Ahna. "M'lady, I am Quoregg, the Master-at-arms. Follow me. Let us see if we can find you some suitable clothing. I am afraid your frills are not proper apparel for battle."

Ahna followed Quoregg as he led her to the tailor's tent. "Sir, I would prefer that you not address me as a royal. I want to be treated the same as any recruit. I am simply Ahnabin, or Ahna if you prefer. That is what my father called me."

Quoregg stopped and turned to face her. "I am quite familiar with your father, M'la.... excuse me, Ahna. If you wish to be treated the same as any recruit, then I shall abide by your wish. I only hope you fully understand the consequences of your request."

Ahna looked the warrior straight in the eye. "I am *very* aware of the consequences, sir."

"So be it, then." He motioned to the flap of the tailor's tent. "You will find Bennet, the tailor, and his seamstress within. They will help you find proper battle attire. I will await your return outside."

Ahna entered the tent. Inside were clothes of every imaginable shape and size, enough to dress a company of men. The tailor approached to greet her.

"Good day, your Ladyship. And how can we be of assistance today? Have we been graced with your hands or are you seeking a piece for someone special?"

"It would appear that you have assumed incorrectly, sir. I am neither here to sew nor to select a garment for a loved one. I am here to find something for myself, something more suitable for battle than this gown and these petticoats."

The tailor's jaw went slack. "I beg your pardon, your Ladyship. Did I hear you correctly to say that you wish to be outfitted for battle?"

"Yes, that is quite correct, kind sir."

The tailor stared blankly at Ahna for a moment, obviously wrestling with the notion of a woman in battle garb. Finally, his eyes twinkled and a little smile came over his face. He leaned forward, close to Ahna, as he whispered, "Ah, I understand now! You require an outfit for a little bedroom charade. I'm sure I can come up with an outfit that will transform you into quite the lascivious ..."

Ahna cut him short. "Obviously, you do NOT understand. I am in need of proper attire for battle. Master Elden and Master Quoregg do not believe I will be capable of engaging in battle in this gown. Indeed, Master Quoregg is awaiting my return outside. Should I get him for you?" Ahna started towards the tent flap.

"No, no, no, your Ladyship! If Master Elden has sent you, then it is my duty to... dress you." The tailor was becoming obviously uncomfortable. " I have not had the... uh... the pleasure of outfitting a woman for battle before, let alone a lady of your obvious stature. I must confess that it makes me rather uneasy."

Ahna motioned towards the seamstress. "Perhaps your seamstress will be kind enough to assist me?"

Feeling the pressure of the situation being suddenly diverted from himself, the tailor quickly agreed. "Yes, yes, yes! A fantastic idea! Lady Ezra will be glad to assist you. Ezra, please, assist the lady with..." The tailor swallowed hard. "Battle attire."

The seamstress approached and gave a quick but polite curtsy. "At your service, ma'am."

"Please, address me as any other recruit. I cast off my nobility to enter this battle." Ahna looked back to the tailor. "Is there a place where a lady could undress in private?"

The tailor went pale. There was typically no need for a private place for the men to change. His mind began to whirl until, finally, he came upon a solution. "Allow me a moment, your Ladyship." Grabbing two leather hides off a pile and stringing a rope between tent poles, the tailor hung the hides over the ropes to form an impromptu dressing area. “Does the lady find that to her liking?”

Ahna nodded. “It shall do just fine. Thank you.”

The tailor nodded and motioned for Ahna and the seamstress to their private corner. “I am sure Lady Ezra can find what you are looking for.”

Ahna and the seamstress entered the corner, hidden from view. Ahna turned her back to Ezra. “If you would be so kind as to untie me. I believe it would be best to be rid of these beforehand.”

The seamstress helped Ahna untie her gown and corsets. Ahna stripped herself of petticoats and undergarments and stood naked behind the leather blind. “Now, to dress me for battle. What would you suggest?”

“Allow me a moment, child. I believe I have exactly what you need.” The seamstress left the blind and returned after a few minutes with a pair of leather pants and a cotton tunic. “I believe these will do. Here, try them on.”

“Riding breeches! If only father could see this!” Ahna pulled the leather breeches up over her hips and tied them around her waist. They were itchy, stiff, and very uncomfortable. “Rather stiff and rough on the skin. Certainly not what I am used to wearing.”

“They will become more pliable and comfortable as you wear them, child. Just a few days of training and they should be as supple as a second skin. In the meantime, grab yourself a pair of thin cotton riding breeks from that pile over there. You can wear them underneath.”

Ahna picked a pair of britches, removed the leather pants, and stepped into them. The feel of the cotton was far more to her liking. As she returned, the seamstress stared at her naked torso. "Those are certainly a problem I haven't had to deal with before.” She leaned in towards Ahna and whispered in her ear while motioning in front of her chest, “Well, some of the older recruits... you know.” The two had a little private chuckle. “We’ll have to come up with something that will keep your bosom from getting in the way, because I’m quite sure there will be no ladies-in-waiting to cinch up your corsets on the battlefield.” She looked about the tent for some cloth. Finding a length of cotton, she wrapped the cloth around Ahna’s chest, binding her breasts tightly to her torso.

"This will have to do, for now, kitten. Come back to see me tomorrow. I will sew you a binding to keep them in place, something you can do up yourself." Finishing with the wrap, she tucked the end underneath. "That ought to do it for the time being." She stood back to admire her handiwork. "Quite clever if I should say so. Now pull on this tunic and then we shall find you some boots."

Ahna pulled the cotton tunic over her head and pulled the lacing at the neck closed. The two women exited from behind the makeshift blind, Ahna hopping along behind Ezra as she attempted to pull on her leather breeches. It was time to complete Ahna's transformation from noblewoman to battlefield recruit. On a pile of clothing outside the blind, a leather vest caught her eye. Picking it up, she looked to the seamstress. "May I?" she questioned.

"Certainly, child, take it if you find it suits you. Come, try these on." She placed a pair of knee-high leather boots in front of the girl. Ahna threw the vest on and sat on a small crate to pull on the boots. She pulled the laces tight and tied them, tying up her new vest as she rose.

"It looks like you are ready to go, my child. Are you sure this is what you want?"

Ahna smiled at the seamstress. "Sounds like someone has been talking to that big guy out there." She gestured to Quoregg outside the tent. Turning back, she addressed Ezra with a kind smile, "Yes, I know what I'm doing. I have thought this out very carefully. I am going to honor the memory of my father. He gave his life for me and everyone in our castle. Now it's my turn to give back."

The seamstress placed her hands on Ahna's shoulders. "May the Fortunes watch over you, my dear child." Placing a kiss on Ahna's forehead she turned and went back to her work.

Ahna gathered her things to leave. As she picked up her gown, she held it up and examined it closely. She looked over at the seamstress, already back at her work, and approached her with the gown in her hands. "I fear I have no further use for this. I figure that we are nearly the same size. Please, take it. It is yours now."

Astonished, the seamstress protested. "I... I couldn't."

"Lady Ezra, please. I have no need for it now. You have been so kind and helpful. Take it. Every woman deserves a pretty gown. It is yours now."

The seamstress took the gown from Ahna and held it up against her, admiring the exquisite tailoring and lacework for a moment. "I shall not forget this, my child. And I shall not forget you. When this is all done, come back to De'Aarna to find me. I will sew you a new gown to celebrate your return, a gown the likes that this land has never seen before."

"I will, I promise. Again, thank you for all you have done for me."

"The pleasure has been all mine, child."

The two women embraced, and Ahna left the tent.

She met up with Quoregg again outside the tent. "I presume this apparel is much more fitting a warrior?"

"Yes, much more fitting. I must say you look the part."

"Does that surprise you?"

Quoregg huffed and started walking again. "Follow me. We need to get you kitted out at the armory."

Ahna followed close behind, tugging at her breeches, still not used to the stiffness of the leather. Pants were going to take a bit of time to get used to.

At the armory, the armorer stared, wide-eyed in disbelief at the young lady, fully kitted out in battle wear accompanying Quoregg.

"Sir?" he questioned.

"It is the request of master Elden that this recruit be provided with whatever armament desired. See to it that his request is honored."

The armorer bowed his head deeply. "It shall be so."

Ahna was given free rein to select the weapons of her choice. She pored over the piles of arms and armor. Finding nothing to quite match her size, she simply grabbed the smallest short sword and a round shield and flung them over her shoulder. Somehow, she would learn how to handle them properly. She also grabbed a pair of hardened leather greaves and vambraces. She sat upon a bench and fastened them to her arms and legs. Standing up, her arms extended, she called to the armorer. "Would you suggest anything beyond this?"

The armorer looked her over carefully. "I can offer you a shirt of chain mail. It is fairly light and moves well with the body, not at all constricting or limiting. It provides excellent protection from blades and all but the smallest of pointed weapons. Not very good against bludgeoning weapons, I'm afraid, but no armor is suitable against all weapons of war."

"May I?"

"Certainly." The armorer grabbed the smallest mail shirt he could find and handed it to her.

Ahna grabbed the chain garment from him, surprised at how light it actually was. She put her sword and shield on the floor and pulled it over her head. The chains jingled as the shirt rested on her shoulders and settled on her body. It was baggy, almost like a potato sack.

"Not the best fit. Perhaps I can find you a belt. That might help to keep the shirt closer to your body and make movement easier."

An idea quickly came to Ahna. "I think I have a way to keep this shirt in place." She removed the mail shirt and then her leather vest. She placed the mail over her head again and then put the vest on. Tightening the ties of the vest, the mail compressed and formed to her body beneath. The lower portions extended beyond the vest but were not an impediment. "That ought to do it, don't you think?"

"Very well done, M'lady, very well done. That should provide you with adequate protection and still be relatively comfortable. And the vest will keep the mail relatively silent, a very important factor in battle."

Ahna grabbed her shield and sword. She thanked the armorer for his assistance and left to meet up with Quoregg once again.

"Master Quoregg, I believe I now have the necessary accouterments for a battle-ready recruit. Shall we begin my training?"

Quoregg sighed audibly. "It would appear you have all that is required of a recruit," continuing under his breath, "almost."

"Excuse me! Almost? And what would you say I lack?"

Quoregg's frustration with the situation finally burst through. "Balls! Every recruit I have ever had the pleasure of working with possessed balls, M'lady."

Ahna wheeled around to confront Quoregg face-to-face. "First, must I remind you I have renounced my royal status? You will address me by my given name as you would any other recruit. Second, if by balls you are referring to testicular fortitude or courage, you may not wish to judge me quite so quickly. If you are referring to your anatomical danglies, keep in mind that I will never need to worry about anything catching in the crotch stitching of my britches nor will I ever be brought to my knees by a well-placed boot. You may wish to keep the latter in mind."

Quoregg quickly changed the subject. "I think we need to get you out to the training fields with Conor. He will be assisting me in your training. I believe some time on the obstacle field would be in order. We shall see how well you fare at that task."

Ahna took full notice of what Quoregg was insinuating and responded defiantly. "Yes, you will, Master Quoregg. Yes, you will."

On the training field, a flight of archers was practicing their craft. Elden stood to the side, watching intently. Arrow after arrow went flying past, almost all striking their target across the field. As each successive flight approached the firing line, Elden carefully watched each archer and noted their progress. But as the next flight approached, something looked out of place. One archer took his place upon the line without a bow. It was the beekeeper, Zephraim. Elden approached him on the firing line.

"Zephraim, it is good to see you have joined us." Elden extended his hand again, which the beekeeper accepted enthusiastically.

"It is good to be part of a group with such an admirable goal. I feel quite at home here."

"We are pleased and fortunate to have men the likes of you within our midst. I am certain you bring great courage and fortitude to us all. You have me puzzled, though. I see no bow or quiver, but you are in flight with the archers. Am I missing something?"

Zephraim smiled. "By all accounts my skills are a quandary for most everyone here. I have a targeted weapon of my own design the likes of which no one here has seen before. Even the armorer was perplexed. Would you care for a demonstration?"

"Indeed! You have me curious now. Show me this marvelous new weapon."

Zephraim removed his coil and metal dart from his belt and held it out for Elden to examine. "I originally designed it as a toy, for target practice. It was while using it to scare away a serpent that I realized the deadly potential of its employ. With practice, I have become quite skillful in its use."

"Please, Zephraim, show me." Elden motioned for the remainder of the men to step aside. "The field is yours."

The beekeeper stood at the line, a target thirty feet away. With a sudden flick of the wrist, the dart quickly sailed towards the target, the sinew string trailing behind. With a metallic thump, the dart struck a near-perfect bull's eye. He gave the sinew a quick tug to dislodge the dart from the target, but the string broke. "Unfortunately, that is the main weakness. The sinew is prone to break after repeated use. The armorer has agreed to fashion a chain to attach to the dart. He believes it will make the dart a very battle worthy weapon. I must return to him today to see what he has created for me."

Elden was intrigued by the dart. "I am quite impressed with your weapon and your skill. I would suggest you take time now to see the armorer about your chain. Tell him that I have sent you and that I will be coming to see him later in the day. I would like to discuss the possibility of generating more of your impressive dart for other men to use in battle. Would you be considerate of the opportunity to train in the use of the weapon?"

Zephraim looked at him quizzically. "You wish to outfit men with my dart for use in battle? Are you sure?"

"Quite sure. It could be a tactical advantage to have men trained in the use of such an unusual and unexpected weapon."

"Of course I would entertain the opportunity to train them. It would be an honor!"

"Then it is done. Go to the armorer and get your dart repaired. I will go to see him later in the day to discuss fashioning more darts. Then we will recruit a few men to begin training in their use."

"I will inform him. If I may take my leave, sir?" Zephraim motioned towards the armorer's tent.

"Of course. I will find you tomorrow and introduce a few recruits. You can begin training them immediately."

"Tomorrow then." Zephraim nodded towards Elden and left to see the armorer.

As the beekeeper departed to carry out his duties, Elden noticed a recruit fall from the log wall and into the mud. Shaking her mud-plastered hair from her face, Elden was surprised to see it was Ahna.

Elden walked up to her, laughing. "Have you had enough yet?"

Ahna glared at him and pulled herself up from the mud. "I most certainly have not! If you think I am going to quit and give you a chance to gloat, then you are most sadly mistaken! I will not allow you, this training regimen, or a dragon to defeat me!" Returning to the front side of the log wall, she successfully scaled it. Staring back at Elden, she shouted at him. "I can, and will, do anything you are capable of doing, mark my words!"

Ahna turned to continue her training as Elden, somewhat defeated, walked over to his Master-at-Arms.

"Quoregg, keep pushing her. She'll either give in or become the best fighter we have. Either way, this is a win-win situation for us."

"Things will be much easier if she gives in. I'm not so sure the rest of the men will take well to a female soldier. Today, it's a novelty. Tomorrow, they may not see the humor in it."

Elden smiled as he began to walk away. "Well, then, like I told you, push her!"

THE CLASH OF STEEL on steel echoed off the cavern walls punctuated by the occasional grunt or groan. Two figures in fencing gear occupied an abandoned dragon's lair, engaged in mock combat. Roga and Oran circled the room, facing each other, each with an epee in hand.

Oran was breathing rather heavily as he attempted to speak. "I am quite surprised, Lord Roga, that you engage in swordplay. Are not the dragons formidable enough that hand-to-hand combat is not a concern?"

"No rider ever expects to need the skill of swordsmanship to be effective in battle." Roga's breathing was far less labored than his opponent, although the strenuous activity had some effect upon his speech. "Fencing provides more of a competitive outlet for the riders. It is a chivalrous activity that engages the competitive spirit and sharpens their decision-making skills. The level of strategy required to be successful with a sword is equal to the strategy required to defeat an enemy in battle. Each decision made could mean the difference between victory and defeat."

Oran made a hard lunge at the warlord as he was speaking, hoping he would be distracted by his thoughts. Roga blocked the thrust with his blade, nimbly stepping to the side to prevent contact. "You may not be capable of easily prevailing over my skills at this time, but you are rather proficient with your blade, Oran. Have you trained?

"Not at all. I have never possessed a blade outside of a poniard and a skinning knife, which I will admit to being quite skilled with. Not much for battle, but useful in close quarters."

"Then I am very impressed with your skills. I'm sure with a bit of practice you could become as proficient as I. If you are passionate about it, I daresay you may put me to task."

The two men continued to circle the room, trading thrust and parry as their conversation continued.

"I appreciate the encouragement, my lord. I find this exercise quite enjoyable and would be very receptive of the opportunity to practice again with you, or any rider for that matter."

"I can arrange for any number of riders to be available for your continued practice whenever you desire and I would be happy to entertain the possibility of squaring off with you again."

"That is most generous of you, master Roga. I believe I am going to enjoy my time in Khorgia."

"I believe that I, too, will enjoy your stay here. I can appreciate a good fencing challenge and you have the ability to become quite the formidable opponent. I may just have to work on my skills some to ensure you do not dispatch me too easily."

Oran smiled as his heart burst with pride. A compliment from a warlord was a much unexpected bestowal. In the moment he broke concentration and Roga saw his opportunity. Quickly deflecting one of Oran's thrusts, Roga deftly stepped slightly to one side and snapped his blade beneath Oran's chin, barely touching his throat.

"I fear today will not be the day that the tide turns in your favor. You let your emotions get the best of you today. You must learn to separate from your emotions in battle or your prowess will be compromised. Celebrate your victories, but only after they are well in hand."

Oran extended both arms out to his side and dropped his epee in submission. "Fortunate for me this is not the battlefield and I shall live to see another day, and another chance to improve my skills at the hands of a most learned mentor."

"Flattery fails to move me, but I have great interest in your future as a member of our community. We are of like mind, you and I. In fact, you remind me much of myself at your age. If that is true, then there is greatness in your future. Come. Let us prepare for dinner. We can continue this conversation over the table."

AHNA SAT ALONE OUTSIDE her tent working on her armor. Although the smallest she could find, the short sword was still very cumbersome for her. The shield was also a bit unruly and difficult for her to handle. Zephraim was walking back to his own tent when he noticed her perplexed look. He approached Ahna cautiously.

"You look annoyed. Is there something I can help you with?"

Ahna barked back at him. "I am quite capable! Just because I am female does not necessarily make me any less of a warrior!"

"Begging your pardon, but I was not questioning your abilities. It just seemed you were trying to work something out and it wasn't quite proceeding as you would wish."

Ahna sighed. "Forgive me. It's this damned shield and sword. They were the smallest that I could find in the armory, but they are still too much for me to handle efficiently. They keep slowing me down."

Zephraim extended his hand. "If I may be so bold? Please, hand me the shield and stand."

Ahna gave up the buckler and, taking Zephraim's hand, pulled herself upright.

"The sword may take some doing, but the shield is a bit easier to alter. Like this. See?" Zephraim adjusted the arm straps. "If you alter how the straps attach to the back, you can wear it over the shoulder and quickly bring it back to defensive position. That way your arm is free to help maintain balance or to climb or grab other items." He slid the newly-adjusted buckler over her arm and onto her back. "Try it."

Ahna shrugged her shoulders a few times and then looked closely at the shield on her back. Twisting around, she was able to slide the shield off her shoulder with some effort and onto her forearm.

"Not graceful, but certainly approaching effective."

"I'm sure I can master it with a little practice. I thank you for your help." She gestured towards her sword. "I don't suppose you have as quick a fix for that now, would you?"

Zephraim bent down and retrieved the sword. "Your blade may take a bit more work, work that is well outside my proficiency, but I do believe I know someone who has the expertise necessary to alter your blade. I am on my way there as we speak. Would you care to join me?"

"Most definitely! If someone can do something with this blade and make it more manageable, I would be greatly appreciative."

Zephraim continued his way to the armorer, Ahna in tow.

The armorer looked up as the flap to his tent opened, revealing a smiling Zephraim. He rose to greet him. "Master Zephraim, it is a pleasure to see you again." Ahna entered behind the beekeeper. "Ah, I see you have brought a friend. I have had the pleasure of making the young lady's acquaintance earlier in the week."

Ahna nodded her greeting. "Zephraim has offered to better fit my sword to my stature. He has already reworked my shield for fit and utility."

Eron looked towards Zephraim. "It may appear that you missed your calling, Master Zephraim. First, you design a most impressive weapon and now you are fitting arms and armor."

Zephraim chuckled. "I think I will leave the more complex aspects of armor to the experts. Minor adjustments to a buckler are the extent of my prowess."

"Well, then, what can I do for you?"

Zephraim held the short sword out for the armorer to see. "The sword is unwieldy and too heavy. It needs to be shorter and lighter if my lady friend is going to use it properly. Can you do something with it?"

Eron took the sword from the beekeeper's hands. "I can easily shorten it and decrease the breadth. That will take some weight away. Did you have anything else in mind?"

"Can you remove some steel from the center of the blade? Hollow it out? That would reduce weight and decrease resistance to the air."

Examining the blade closely, Eron hesitated. "It is not something I have ever done before, but that does not mean it cannot be done. I have some experience working steel. I will give it my best."

Ahna thanked the armorer. "That is all I can ask of you, sir. Anything you can do will make it easier to handle."

"I will need a day, possibly two. It certainly isn't going to be the easiest task. And you will need a replacement for training." He motioned towards the rack of swords. "Pick whatever you think you can handle. Master Quoregg would not smile upon you if you arrive on the field without a blade."

"Thank you, sir. I look forward to seeing your handiwork come the morrow."

"Please, m'lady. Anyone dear to the heart of the beekeeper is dear to mine. Call me Eron."

"I think you have misjudged our relationship. I have just met Master Zephraim this morn. He has been kind enough to offer his assistance and I am sure we shall form a bond as strong as any between two kindred warriors. I will be happy to call him friend."

Eron responded apologetically. "Excuse my presumption. I meant no insinuation nor insult by it. In my short acquaintance with Master Zephraim, I have found him to be a gentleman in all aspects. Whatever form of relationship you two may cultivate, I would expect it only to be the most honorable. As for myself, I still prefer Eron to any number of titles I have been addressed by, a score of which I would never repeat in present company. Regardless of the extent of your relationship with master Zephraim, you may address me as friend."

"Thank you, sir. I will hail you as requested, but you must call me by my given name as well. My father called me Ahna. A woman finds few comrades in a camp of fighting men. I am most happy to add you to the short list. It will be a pleasure to meet with you again upon the completion of your work on my blade. I will take my leave as soon as I have chosen a temporary replacement. I understand you and Zephraim have other business to attend to. I will leave the two of you to it."

"It is a pleasure, Lady Ahna. I will have your new blade ready for you as quickly as my talents allow."

Ahna nodded to the two men and made her way to the swords.

Eron turned to Zephraim. "I have your chain. Would you care to examine it before I add it to your dart?"

"Most certainly, Eron. And I have news for you. Master Elden has had the pleasure of seeing the dart and was quite impressed. He requested that I inform you that he will be requesting more darts be made to outfit a squad of men. He wishes that I train them in its use. He believes it will provide a strategic advantage."

"Well, I have a surprise for you as well. I took it upon myself to fashion a dart of my own design, very similar to yours but fluted with a hardened point to better penetrate metal armor and chain mail. It should function the same as your design but with better incursion. I hope you will forgive my liberties with your design. I think you may be suitably impressed."

"Please, show me your design. I may want one for my own."

Eron pulled a leather wrap from beneath his workbench. Carefully placing it on the bench, he unwrapped it to reveal a polished steel dart. Four flutes extended from the base to the point and a double-linked chain attached to a ring on the base.

Zephraim's eyes opened wide. "It is... beautiful! I am impressed. And the chain is of impeccable design."

"The double-link allows for superior strength without compromising flexibility. It should function quite well."

"May I try it?"

The armorer handed it over to Zephraim. "It is yours. If you wish to try it, you can do so as much as you wish. But, please, I prefer not to be as near to the target as I was previously."

The beekeeper looked at him in shock. "For me? I cannot accept such a gift. This dart is incredible."

"And what use would I have for a dart? My reward is a well-equipped army that is capable of defending the homeland. If you are willing to defend me, I am willing to relinquish my first dart to your skilled hands."

"Then, my dear Eron, I accept your gift. It will be a pleasure to use it in securing your defense. But first, let's see what it can do."

Zephraim coiled the chain and hooked it and the dart to his belt. Then, in one smooth and swift motion, he threw the dart at the tent pole he had targeted the previous day. The hardened point sank deep into the post.

"Impressive! You have created a very balanced projectile. Will you be capable of producing more to meet the request of Master Elden?"

"It will be my pleasure. I shall make enough for a squad by week's end. Will that be timely enough?"

"It will be fine. The men can get acclimated to the basic skills by using a stone dart attached to a string." Zephraim tugged at the dart's chain, but it was firmly buried in the pole. Tugging harder, the dart finally released. "The chain is quite impressive. No sinew would have withstood that effort. This is truly an impressive weapon now."

"You designed it."

"And you improved upon it. I am not so arrogant as to hoard credit when I can claim only half honestly."

The two men shook hands. Zephraim bounced the dart in his hand.

"Go! Get out of here! Go to the training fields and get familiar with your new dart. Besides, I have work to do if I am to outfit a squad with these by week's end and create a light but strong sword for Lady Ahna." He patted the beekeeper on the shoulder. Zephraim snatched up the dart and quickly made his exit through the tent flap.

THE MEN HAD BEEN TRAINING for weeks. Zephraim was proud of his squad of dartsmen. The number of target hits had increased to a level where most men were hitting at a rate of eighty percent or more and the hits were becoming more and more solid, requiring more than a little force to remove them from the practice target.

Ahna had continued her training along with the others, oftentimes excelling at the tasks presented to her. Although not fully accepting of the thought of a woman as a battle partner, she had earned the respect of most of the men as a more than competent recruit. In fact, in most mock battle exercises, she was feared for her agility, balance, and tenacity. Her skills had become so refined that she nearly always finished these practice battles as the victor, a point her adversaries would be reminded of constantly by their comrades. She had become a force to reckon with.

Part of her skill could be attributed to Eron, the armorer. From the short sword she had chosen, he had fashioned two impressive weapons; a sleek short sword, shortened and lightened by the removal of small sections of the blade's breadth to minimize weight and reduce air resistance, and a dagger constructed from the steel that had been removed from the sword. The blade of the dagger gleamed in the light, highly polished and razor sharp. In contrast, the blade of the sword became much harder to see due to the open spaces along its length. Eron had purposely failed to polish the blade to further conceal it.

Elden and Quoregg had divided the men up into seven small fighting forces, one for each of the six remaining kingdoms and another for those kingdoms that had been lost. Zephraim and Ahna, along with several wandering mercenaries, found themselves attached to the Forces of the Lost Kingdoms, clearly the elite among the others, comprised of soldiers determined to avenge the loss of their families and friends, as well as their homelands. Their common bloodlust was easy to discern from the looks on their faces during training. Their resolve would make them a most formidable force to be reckoned with. From atop a small knoll, the two generals admired the small army they had built. They were as ready as they would ever be. It was time to set their strategy in motion.

LORD ROGA HOVERED OVER his cartographer's table, an aged and stained map of the mainland stretched out before him. Marshall Octrall stood by his side. The two men were intently discussing the next attack.

"We have laid the most of the coast bare, apart from De'Aarna, my Lord. We must begin to make sorties further inland. Where do you wish to focus our efforts?"

Roga's eyes wandered across the parchment. Pointing to a spot, he asked, "And what is this river that feeds De'Aarna?"

Octrall looked closer. "I believe that is the river they call Oryon. It flows to the sea at the De'Aarna delta from the mountains much further north. The headwaters spring forth close to the Wailing Mountain."

"I see it as a natural causeway, either by boat or by foot. Laying waste to the land surrounding may not result in many deaths, but it surely will lay open the area surrounding the river like a gaping wound. Without any cover, travel along its length would no longer be hidden. It is far easier to control a location when you know who or what is coming in and out. In fact, without the benefit of cover, many will likely choose *not* to travel to De'Aarna. Fewer people in the city plays to our advantage."

"So, we open up the banks of the Oryon. How far upriver?"

"As far as we can travel comfortably in a day and return to the rookery. If we meet little resistance and expend our efforts pruning back the underbrush, we might be capable of denuding nearly a third of the way to the mountains. Three attacks in relatively short succession will make a slash in the countryside from mountains to sea. If we follow that incursion with an expeditionary foray into the mountains, we may potentially locate a spot for a mainland rookery. A mainland bivouac for our superior aerial forces could all but make us indomitable."

"I will prepare the men. When should we begin our attack?"

"Within a fortnight. We must prepare well, as this will be our first incursion deep into the mainland. Discuss all potential issues and prepare for the worst. These attacks must be successful and not fraught with casualties."

"As you wish, my Lord. I will prepare the men." Octrall clicked his heels and spun quickly around and out the door. Roga continued to pour over the map, a strategy continually formulating in his mind.

18
A CALL TO ARMS

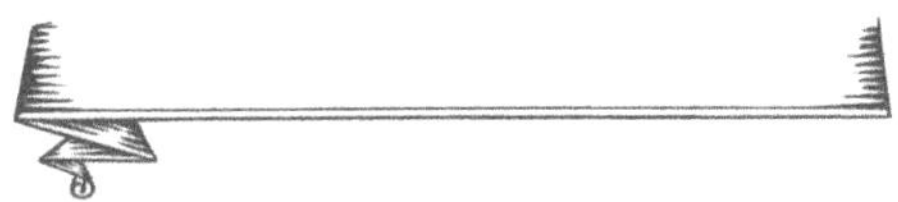

ELDEN AWOKE TO A RUCKUS. People were clamoring about outside, rushing to accomplish something of unknown import. He rose, quickly dressed, and stuck his head outside his shelter. He reached out, stopping one of the villagers as she rushed by.

"Maiden, what is all the noise? What is happening?"

"Lady Isella, her Highness, the Queen, from *et Vilna Sahnah*. She has arrived this morn and others are expected. A conclave of the Confederation. They have come to discuss the attacks. Please, unhand me. I must go about preparations."

Elden released the woman's arm and gazed at the people rushing about. His grandmother had arrived without notice. She had promised to wait until he had time to gather an army. She had broken her promise. For that, she would have a good reason. Had there been more attacks, as of yet unknown in De'Aarna, or was she simply flexing her diplomatic muscle, showing her grandson, and the Confederacy as a whole, who was still boss?

Elden stopped another villager rushing by. "The Queen, where is she? Do you know where she is staying?"

"They are preparing the Governor's manor as we speak. She is seated in Council Chambers."

Elden composed himself and headed towards the Governor's manor.

In light of the recent attacks on neighboring kingdoms, Queen Isella had quickly called upon the seven kingdoms of the Tendira Confederacy to defend themselves. Members of each royal family, along with a military contingent as an escort, had been sent to De Aarna for safety. To date, the city had not been attacked and, if it did, its proximity to a permanent water source offered the most logical defense against the flaming acidic bile of the dragons. The leaders and military minds from the members of the Tendira Confederacy were beginning to arrive at the Governor's home. Two of the nine tables arranged in a circle were already taken. Several contingents were commiserating in the hall but had yet to find their seats. The last contingent, the representatives from *Linnaea Gomerra*, the Gomerran Kingdom, were just arriving in the plaza and were expected in the hall momentarily. Word of the conclave had reached those lands surrounding the seven member kingdoms of the Confederacy and representatives of those lands were arriving as well.

Although nearly everyone from the Confederacy knew of one another diplomatically, not everyone was on particularly friendly terms. Not that there was animosity between kingdoms, but most were simply acquaintances, a name, possibly a face, but nothing more. The Confederacy was a union built to promote peace and prosperity, not to foster deep friendships. It had been formed during the reign of Elden's grandfather and had quietly remained intact through many decades of calm. Now, for the first time, the Confederacy was facing a crisis.

Representing *eht Vilna Sahnah*, Elden sat at the table with Zephraim and Taygen, directly across from a low dais with a single throne-like chair. To his right, the contingent from *eht Vilna Copa*, to his left, *eht Vilna Turega*, had already occupied their places. An empty table and two tables of representatives unknown to Eldan flanked the throne. Representatives from *eht Vilna Tumehr* and *Linnaea Gomerra*, presently arriving in the hall, completed the conclave.

As the remaining members of this council were getting to their seats, Queen Isella entered the hall, and approached her chair, a large wooden throne with no cushions. The chair was not at a particular table but was set separately between two tables, as if the seat of a moderator. The members of the conclave stood to address the Queen.

"Gentlemen, I appreciate your attendance at such short notice, although not quite short enough." The Queen pointed to an empty table to her right. "As you can see, representatives from *et Vilna Antessara* are not with us today. It would appear they suffered the same fate as the Souliban and *et Vilna Moht* just a few days past. From all accounts, there were few survivors, further proof that this gathering is necessary. We have also been joined by representatives of this fine city, De' Aarna, who have been kind enough to offer both their hospitality and protection during this meeting. With six contingents of the Confederacy represented and two from the outer regions, we have an even number. I shall reserve the right to decide any deadlock. Shall I assume that meets the approval of everyone?"

"But does that not give your kingdom two votes in these proceedings? Your grandson occupies a seat with the contingent from *et Vilna Sahnah*. Is that not an unfair advantage?" It was Amari, king of the Gomerran Kingdom, a large flat province at the base of the Silver Mountains. Similar to what was once known as the Souliban, Gomerra was one of the few kingdoms without the benefit of a castle, a fact that was typically looked down upon by other kingdoms.

"I recognize your concern, King Amari, and I offer you this in response. My husband, King Heidel, was instrumental in forming this union, and as much as he was the leader of our kingdom, he kept the needs of the entire Confederation in his mind always. I have no intentions of doing otherwise. I value the strength we have as a united people and will pass judgment as the arbiter of the whole. I would hope that matters for the good of the whole shall be decided by unanimous vote, but if that should prove to be a fanciful expectation, I am confident I can act as an unbiased judge. If anyone here doubts my ability to act fairly and just, please enter your concerns now."

Everyone looked back and forth amongst each other, but no one spoke against the Queen.

"I remove my comment and offer apologies, Lady Isella. I meant no offense."

"Amari, no offense is taken. I appreciate your candor and concern. It is a stressful time for us all and we seek what is best for our own. Please trust in my word when I state, unequivocally, that I watch over the entire Confederacy as if it were my own. And can I not but reiterate that we all seek the same end: a stop to the attacks that have brutalized our land."

The Gomerran nodded his consent, and the remainder of the conclave began striking the tables with their fists in a vote of confidence.

Isella raised her hand to calm the group and addressed them. "Is there any other business we need to attend to before we discuss the subject at hand?"

Elden rose to address the conclave. "Would the contingent from *Tumehr* please remove their animal from the hall? He reeks of wet canine and the odor has permeated the entire room. It is making me nauseous."

"My dog is not wet, nor is he afoul!"

"Perhaps I am mistaken, Lord Dolphus, and it is *you* that reek of wet."

Dolphus rose to confront Elden but was held back by the table he was sitting at. "How dare you...!"

Queen Isella, standing, interceded. "Gentlemen, enough! Dolphus, this is intended to be a conclave of warriors and men. Would you kindly remove your animal from the proceedings? I sincerely doubt he has much to offer to our discussions today."

"Why is it that your grandson can have this charlatan as a representative at his table, but I must remove my most trusted companion?"

"This *charlatan*, as you call him, is a trusted advisor to both myself and my grandson, and not only does he have considerable knowledge to offer at these discussions, he has yet to lift his leg to relieve himself on the pillars of this house, Master Dolphus. The same cannot be said for your beast. You are a guest in this house for these talks. So, unless you can prove to me that the dog can provide counsel, I have asked you to remove your beast, and you shall respect my request."

Dolphus, obviously flustered, turned to his son. "Derrick, take the dog outside and mind him well. It is not my desire to insult the Lady or the conclave." The Tumehrian turned and nodded towards Queen Isella. "My sincerest apologies for the behavior of my animal."

Isella nodded in return. "Your kind apology is accepted. I'm certain your beast was simply marking newly-found territory. Unfortunately for him, I believe all the territory in this house is spoken for." Isella turned to address her grandson. "And you, Master Elden. Have you any other issues with the attendees of this conclave? Or possibly the hall? Is it too dark for you or too cold? Perhaps you have a need for milk and cookies?" Her stare and sarcasm cut straight through him.

Elden quickly demurred. "No, my Queen. The hall is quite comfortable and the members of the conclave are to my satisfaction."

"Good! I am sure it pleases everyone that you are pleased." A chuckle quickly went around the room. "Are there any other issues or pettiness we need discuss before we attend to more important matters?"

The entire group stared silently at the Queen, a direct acknowledgment of her leadership at this gathering.

"Enough of the pleasantries, gentlemen. It is time for something a bit more serious." Isella sat back on the throne. "I have called you all together to discuss the dragon attacks. These attacks have obviously affected all of us in one way or another. So, as a group, we need to bring together all our knowledge and experience to develop a clear course of action."

Dolphus spoke up. "So, what do we know about our enemy?"

Elden responded. "The dragons come from the sea. They have been seen on the horizon as they appear. Wherever they come from must be beyond the horizon, across the Touphorus Sea."

A quiet voice spoke up from *eht Vilna Copa* table. "Khorgia." All heads turned to face the owner of the voice. It was Pennik, chief minister and trusted counselor to Prince Horace, the reigning authority at *eht Vilna Copa.* "It is an island nation some fifty or sixty myriameters beyond the shores of Tendira. Possibly further. We have encountered their people very infrequently over the decades, fewer times than the number of fingers on a healthy man's hand. To my knowledge, there has never been any particular animosity between our lands. Why they would suddenly choose to attack us eludes me."

"Whatever the reason, they *are* attacking and there is no sign of them stopping any time soon. They fly in on their dragons, lay waste to a tract of land and retreat. No prisoners, no troops left behind to occupy the lands they have taken. It is all very unconventional, but, yet, they keep coming. We sent an envoy to Khorgia by sea, but they never returned. We must do something. We can't just sit around and let them destroy everything we know."

"And what would you suggest, Elden? Word is that Maob turned his archers on the swarm and may have slowed them down somewhat. It was the first castle that was not destroyed and ransacked. Perhaps targeted ground to air weaponry would work. More archers or possibly ballistae could be used to wage a defense."

"We have yet to show any attack that caused them casualties. I have not heard of a single dragon being struck down. Would an attack from the ground prove to be effective in the least?"

The men began questioning amongst themselves, a loud murmur filling the room.

The Queen raised her hand to bring order to the group once again. "Do you have a better plan, Elden, as Master Pennik has asked?"

"Indeed, I do. We attack them on their homeland."

Dolphus quickly responded to Elden's suggestion. "On their homeland? How?"

"We cross the sea. We take the fight to them. I would suspect they have no reason to believe that we are capable of such a feat. Not only would it be a surprise, but they are certainly less likely to incinerate their own homeland."

"Are you mad? We have no navy, nor do we possess knowledge of the sea. I would hazard to guess that we would be hard pressed to find a handful of seafaring men in all the Confederacy. This plan is destined to fail."

"And you have a better plan, Dolphus? Do you truly believe a defensive stand is the best way to battle this foe? Look how well we have defended ourselves thus far! Thousands dead. Entire villages destroyed. Whole landscapes laid to waste. And not a single dragon or rider has fallen from the sky. At this rate, there will be no Confederacy remaining as we turn the next year."

"Without knowledge of ships and the sea, any attack by water is a suicide mission."

"And simply waiting for the next attack by an enemy we have yet to stop, in any manner at all, is a thousand times more suicidal. We must attack! We surely are unable to defend ourselves on our own land. Quite possibly, by bringing the fight to them, we can gain an advantage. As complacent as we have been so far, an attack upon their homeland might just take them by surprise. It could be the one advantage we are looking for."

"I understand the logic behind your strategy, Elden, but we have no expertise on the open water. We might all perish before reaching their homeland."

"Is it better to perish attempting to defeat our enemy or to simply await our own certain death?" Elden gazed around the room. "We can learn how to sail a ship. Bring anyone in the Confederacy with knowledge of ships and the sea here to De'Aarna. I am sure we can devise some means of a vessel that will be seaworthy.

Taygen spoke up. "I have designed and built model vessels that would float about the waters of *Berwyn Gosta*. I'm sure I could come up with a design that would ferry men across the Touphorus."

"Toy boats are a far cry from a naval vessel, old man."

"My models do not take on water. If care is taken when scaled to a vessel capable of carrying men, there is no reason they cannot be seaworthy."

"It is a moot point if we have no one with the expertise necessary to sail them, let alone build them."

"There are merchants that sail the coast on a regular basis. Someone had to build those vessels. Speak with those merchants and find that expertise."

"And when they are built, who is going to sail them?"

"A man can be taught to ride a horse or shoot a bow. That is something we do on a regular basis. Why can we not teach a man to sail a ship? We do not need to be experts, just proficient enough to keep the vessels afloat long enough to reach the dragons' homeland."

A murmur spread through the room as the group openly considered Elden's suggestion.

Following a brief period of deliberation, the Queen spoke. "Does anyone have a better plan for consideration?" The room became silent. "It is settled then. Have the cleric design a seafaring vessel to carry troops to Khorgia. Find someone with the knowledge required to build them and the skill to sail them. Assemble carpenters and craftsmen to help build these ships and loggers to harvest the timbers necessary to produce them from. Is there anything else we need?"

Elden responded matter-of-factly. "Men. We need troops to fill those ships if we are to defeat the Khorgians. Even without the dragons, their numbers exceed the meager forces we have accumulated."

The Queen made a plea to the other kingdoms. "Send word back to your people. Have them send all able-bodied men, young and old, to serve in our fighting forces."

"We have been training for weeks in the Tantallon Forest. The men can join us there. All are welcome."

Queen Isella addressed the men seated before her. "Have we come to a consensus? Is there anything else we need to discuss?" Her questions were met with silence. "I declare this conference closed, gentlemen. Design and build your ships, train your captains to sail them and send your men to train as soldiers in defense of the Confederacy. Elden, you have overseen the training in the Tantallon Forest, so I suggest you remain in command. Pennik, I request your assistance in finding a shipwright. Surely someone in your kingdom, as it borders the sea, has built a seafaring vessel at some point in their lives. I pray *Ahlok* looks over you all with favor and the Fortunes smile on your actions. We are counting on you to rid us of these attacks. Do not fail your people."

The group watched in somber silence as Queen Isella left the mansion. The time for talk had ended. It was time now for action.

TAYGEN APPEARED THE following morn with a small wooden model of a sailing vessel. The hull was long and narrow in beam, obviously designed for speed. It had but a single deck with storage below and an odd single mast at the stern of the vessel.

Taygen placed the miniature on the table before Elden. "This is the ship you should build."

Elden looked at the wizard in awe. "This? In one night?" He picked up the model and examined it closely. "A master shipwright as well, Taygen? And what other wondrous skills do you possess that you have not been forthcoming with?"

"Even a simple magician has time to dabble in things beyond his occupation, Lord Elden. And with the library of a castle at one's dispense, the potential subjects a man can gain knowledge of are innumerable."

"The design appears to be simple but seaworthy. But what of this mast at the rear?"

"Trust me, Elden, you will come to understand in due time. Just trust it is necessary."

"I will leave it to you and the ship builder. Pennik has found a shipwright that has built for local merchants in years past. He can introduce you to him and you can present your model. Work with him to ensure our needs are met. The vessel needs to be capable and quick to build. You can find Pennik in the Governor's mansion."

"I will go to him presently. It will not be much longer, Elden. You will bring this fight to the Khorgians and see how they react. An end to this evil is within our sights."

"Yes, it is, Taygen, yes, it is. Go. See the shipwright and get some transports built. We avenge our brothers and sisters, family and friends, as soon as we can set sail."

19
THE JOURNEY

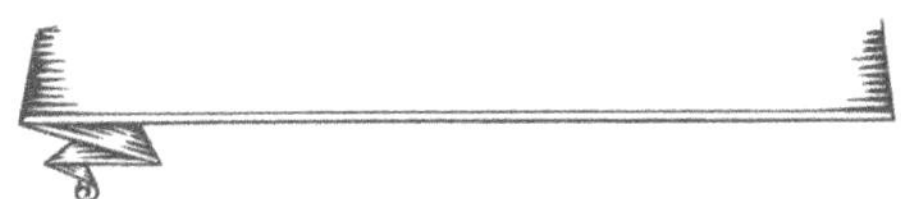

TWO MONTHS HAD PASSED since the conclave. Several boat builders had been hard at work churning out the small ships designed by Taygen. They filled the harbor and beach at De'Aarna, ready for their call to duty. Men continued to train in the Tantallon Forrest, preparing for the battle that would soon be upon them. And the dragons continued to attack, three times along the coast. The time for an offensive strike was nigh.

Elden approached Quoregg on the forest training grounds as the sun dipped below the tree line. "It is time, Quoregg. Have the men gather their things and start moving supplies to the harbor. We leave the Tantallon at dawn and prepare for our sea voyage."

"Of course." Quoregg turned towards the encampment and shouted out new orders. "Pack it in, everyone! Pull your things together and bed down. Get yourselves a good rest tonight for tomorrow we prepare to sail!"

THE BEACH WAS A BEEHIVE of activity. Warriors laden with supplies were preparing the twenty small cutters for a journey across an unknown sea. Wagonloads of supplies and scores of men were slowly packing each ship to capacity. Food, water, arms, and armor occupied every available inch below decks.

As each ship was fully outfitted, the crew began to unfurl its strange, singular sail. Presently, Taygen arrived on the beach.

"Elden, I see you have managed to assemble a most formidable flotilla. I am impressed."

"Thank you, Taygen, and all built as you suggested. A unique configuration. Are you sure it will work?"

Taygen chuckled slightly. "Of course it will work, young man. Would I ever steer you wrong?"

Elden placed his hand upon the magician's shoulder. "No, dear magus, I don't believe you ever would. So, what do we owe the pleasure of your presence this morning?"

"I came to offer a blessing on your fleet. I'm sure you could use all the help you can get from the higher powers."

"Is that an indication of how confident you are in your ship designing prowess or in the preparedness of our army?" Elden began to chuckle.

Taygen laughed along. "No. No, I have every confidence in the training of your army and in my design for the sails. More confidence than I think you realize, for both." Taygen motioned towards the ships on the beach. "Look at them. Look at the sails. Such simplicity of design. Minimal rigging, large surface area. Simply exquisite!"

Elden gave his little navy a quick glance over. "I see what you are saying but why blue? I may not have seen many but never in my days have I seen a ship with blue sails."

"Ah, blue." Taygen hesitated a moment before continuing. "A dark color will attract the heat from the sun, which will in turn warm the airspace beneath the sails. Hotter air rises, so that will help to keep the sails up off the deck and available to gather the wind, and blue mimics the color of the sea helping to camouflage the vessels."

Elden gave the fleet another long gaze. "Ingenious. You missed your calling, magus. You should have been an engineer or a designer. A builder, maybe. Imagine the incredible things you could have created?"

Taygen scoffed at what Elden had just said to him. "You forget, Elden, that I am simply a conjurer. Simple sleight of hand and a fair amount of observation have been the tools that made me what you see before you. It is amazing what one can learn by observing the wonders of nature, and even more amazing what you can devise by embracing its simplicity and putting its designs to use for yourself."

"Well, if this is an example of what can come of observing nature, then you are a master!"

"As long as they carry you to your intended destination swiftly and safely, then my job has been done. What happens when you arrive is for you and Master Quoregg to devise. I pray you have a well-constructed battle strategy?"

"We have, but all the best-laid plans cannot prepare one for the uncertainties of battle. It will inevitably be our flexibility in the battle plan that will lead us to victory."

"I advise and warn you, use care. The Dragon Lord is a most determined and devious adversary. He has not shown mercy to man nor beast. Were I not to know it a physical impossibility, I would proclaim the man has no heart. He is one to prepare carefully for and never to underestimate."

"I am prepared for whatever he and his dragons can bring to bear upon us. My mind is clear and focused. I have said goodbye to all my weaknesses and put aside all that I have regretted. My resolve knows no bounds. Nothing shy of my own sacrifice will stop me from bringing the Dragon Lord to his own demise."

Taygen placed his hands upon Elden's shoulders. "My prayers and blessings go with you and your men. Go confidently in the fact that you have prepared well and have the force of an entire people behind you. We trust in your abilities and will await your victorious return."

The two men quickly embraced. When they separated, Elden returned to the task at hand, directing the preparations for a journey by sea to battle an adversary that was, on most accounts, a complete unknown.

AS THE LAST OF THE supplies and men were placed upon the flotilla of small ships, Elden and Taygen once again met on the beach.

"Master Taygen, please, I ask of you a blessing on our fleet."

"With pleasure, Elden." Taygen turned to face the fleet and addressed them in a voice that seemed to fill the air. "Hoist your sails!" Slowly, two hundred blue sails unfurled and filled with the cool ocean breeze. Taygen raised his arms high above his head, his hands open to the sky. "*Ahlok*, Father of all Creation, maker of all that we see, *Sibu*, Mother of the Land, provider of all that we need, look with favor upon these vessels and the men that they bear. *Copaien*, Ruler of all the Waters, grant safe passage and still waters across the sea. *Gojabahn*, Lord of the Winds, fill these sails with strong but gentle breezes to propel them on their journey and the favor of fair weather. *Copai azulis ahmat cito peri ouvlis. Konduet spelshem fonorit elibior ohndayid. Wipnoticar mindion gojabhi Khorgo. Selbit!*" Suddenly a calm but strong breeze filled each sail as an ethereal shimmer gleamed across the light, blue fabric. From above, the sails seemed to blend in with the water below, all but obscuring the small craft beneath. As if by magic, the fleet was nearly invisible to the unknowing eye.

"Thank you, Taygen. Until we return." Elden turned towards his fine new flotilla. "Hoist anchor and push off!" He leaped to the bow of his boat as it slid gently into the Touphorus.

Slowly, the fleet made its way from shore and out to sea. Taygen watched from the beach until the last ship drifted beyond sight. Turning to leave, he whispered to himself. "Fear not, for I am with you."

TEN SCORE WATERCRAFT, gunwales a mere hand's breadth above the surface of the sea, cut slowly through the swells against a steady headwind, gossamer ceilings all but blotting out the twin moons above. Huddled beneath, quiet in anticipation, twenty men per craft waited patiently for land to appear from the darkness, only the soft sounds of the swells lapping gently on the bow, like a metronome, tapping out the time as it passed.

Suddenly, a series of guttural shrieks pierced the silence, focusing the attention of every man towards the lead skiff.

Elden approached the beekeeper, head hung over the side of the ship. "Are you ok?"

A very pale Zephraim peered up at him. "I have never been on the water before. There isn't much of it in the Souliban. The sea, it moves the vessel in ways I have never felt before."

"Indeed, it does. Fear not. It will pass in time, and time we have. I suspect two, maybe three more nights before we reach the shores of Khorgia."

"I believe I shall be fine for the remainder of the journey. The denizens of the sea have received all my belly has to give and more."

"May your impromptu offering please *Copaien* and purchase safe passage to Khorgia. Coupled with Taygen's blessing, we are sure to make landfall without incident."

Elden left his comrade to recover from his heaving as a quietude encompassed the fleet once again.

Guided by twin moonlight at night, the rising and setting sun by day, and propelled by a stiff sea breeze, the Tendiran armada skimmed the surface of the deep, swiftly eating up the distance to the source of the dragons. Taygen's unique design provided protection from the sun for the army during the day, helping to maintain their comfort and morale as the voyage extended day upon day. In solemn silence, anticipation and confidence grew with each passing hour. If they could survive the vastness of the ocean, they would certainly fare well against the Khorgians.

Hours accumulated into days, followed by nights, two, then three. Blessed with fair weather and mostly clear skies, the trip was predominantly uneventful. Early on the fourth morn, the silence was broken once again.

"HO!"

The call came from high above the deck. Land! The long journey across the Touphorus Sea was finally over.

Elden approached the mast.

"Where? Is it Khorgia?" he shouted up to the sentry.

"Due east, sir. It is more than a tiny isle. I can see what appears to be a mountain range and the land extends as far as I can see. If I were to guess, I would say it is Khorgia."

"Signal the others to close ranks as we approach the island. We must anchor far offshore and lash the ships together, one behind the other, to maintain as small a profile on the horizon as possible. We must remain unseen if we are to maintain any advantage."

It had been a long journey. Four days at sea, sailing towards the unknown. An armada of seafaring vessels piloted by more experienced captains might have made shorter work of the trip, but the entirety of the inexperienced Tendiran navy managed to complete the journey. Elden ordered the anchor dropped and signaled the call to cluster. The ships slowly came together, one after the next, each lashing itself to the other, forming a line two wide and ten deep, facing directly towards Khorgia. As the final ship tied on, Elden sent word across the entire group.

"Prepare a single ship and gather the expeditionary crew. We will scout the area and then return. Have the men rest. We must be prepared for what is inevitable."

Elden gathered his commanders together to prepare for the coming days.

"Quoregg, I leave you in charge of the flotilla. Keep the ships lashed together and anchored far enough offshore so as not to be seen. I will lead the expeditionary crew to get a feeling for the lay of the land. Once we have a decent feel for what lies ahead for us, we will send a man to tell you to meet us on the island."

"Understood. How long should we wait for word to rejoin you?"

"I suspect we will need at least two days. If we have not returned in four, return to the mainland. It will most certainly indicate that we have been found out and either taken captive or put to death. No need to subject the entire army to that fate. Better to return to De'Aarna and work on another strategy."

"But..."

"No buts. That's a direct order, Quoregg."

THE SUN HAD SHORTLY drowned itself in the sea and the first of two moons silhouetted the Khorgian Mountains as it rose from behind. A single ship had been prepared, stocked with everything the small group would need for four short days on the island. Elden, Ahnabin, Conor, Dorian, and fourteen of their seafaring comrades, climbed over the gunwale.

"Remember, Quoregg, four days. On the fifth, if we haven't returned, pull anchor and head to the mainland. If we've been captured or worse, the Confederacy will need every possible man to defend the homeland."

"It shall be as you wish, Elden. But I have confidence in our mission. I will see you four days hence and we will rejoin you on the island. Go. Find a place for our invasion force to land and become familiar with the terrain. We will only have a short time to land the fleet and make our move before the Khorgians make us out. We need the veil of surprise on our side if we intend to beat the dragons."

The two warriors shook hands and quickly embraced. The crew unlashed a single boat from the others and pushed off, unfurling the dark blue sail overhead. A gentle sea breeze filled the canvas, slowly but steadily propelling the craft towards shore. Quoregg watched as the ship sailed into the darkness and out of sight.

"May the Fortunes smile upon you all, for yourselves and for the good of all of Tendira."

20
THE KISS

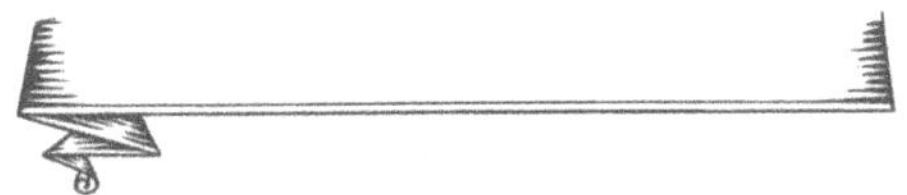

A KNOCK CAME AT LORD Roga's office door.

"Come!"

Minarik appeared at the opened door. "A sentry from the island's western perimeter, my Lord."

Roga motioned to let the sentry advance. Minarik stepped aside. A leather-clad soldier stepped through the door, assuming a position of attention before the warlord's desk, clicking his heels as he did.

Roga croaked at him impatiently. "Speak."

"Yes, my Lord. I bring news from the western perimeter. There have been some unusual movements from the forest, movements that are unexplained and do not make sense."

"Unexplained movements? What kind of unexplained movements?"

"Trees moving against the breeze, a flock of birds scattering without apparent reason. Just... movements."

"And what is making these... these "movements"?"

"At present, we do not know, my Lord. Our patrols investigate anything we see that is unexplained, but we have yet to determine a source."

"Is there any danger to the kingdom?"

"There is not enough information for us to determine that as of yet, my Lord."

Roga, annoyed, looked up at the sentry. "So, you have come here and disrupted my evening to inform me that "movements" have been noticed along the perimeter that you cannot adequately describe, generated by a source you are unable to identify, posing a danger that you cannot quantify or qualify."

"I... I guess... When you put it that way... it does sound rather... silly, my Lord."

"*Silly*?" Roga cocked his head to one side, looking away from the sentry. "And should we next play monkey-in-the-middle and have biscuits and warm milk before our afternoon nap!" Roga slammed his fist on his desk and glared at the sentry. "Impertinent idiot! I do not abide "silly"! Get out of my office before I call Minarik and have you drawn, quartered, and fed to my dragon! You are wasting my time with this foolishness! I loathe foolishness! Annoy me any further and the next "movement' you experience will soil your leathers! Let me make a less than silly suggestion, no, a command! Leave my office. Gather your men together. And do not present yourself before me again until you have something of significance to report!"

The sentry nearly fell over himself as he scrambled for the door, doing his best to leave quickly while avoiding further scorn from the warlord. The door remained ajar as the sound of his heels on the stone hall floor echoed into silence.

"Minarik!" Roga beckoned for his assistant to come to his desk.

"Yes, my Lord?"

"Tell Worren to initiate random dragon patrols of the forest between here and the western perimeter. The sentry may have been spouting gibberish, but even the most unlikely of reports needs to be followed up and, apparently, my own troops are incapable of handling this on their own. Something may be amiss in the forest, and I intend to find out what it is and ensure it does not cause me any further annoyance."

"I will attend to it immediately, my Lord." Minarik turned to take care of Roga's command.

"Oh, and have the sentry sequestered in the dungeon until such a time as his hallucinations have been disproved. Even then he may continue to be a recipient of our fine hospitality. It's the least I can do to repay the annoyance he has caused me this evening. And bring him a fresh pair of leathers. I do believe he may be in need of them."

"As you wish, my Lord." Minarik bowed slightly and left the warlord's office, closing the door silently behind him.

THE SHADOW OF A DRAGON floated along the forest canopy. It crisscrossed above the treetops, its rider searching below for anything unusual. Part of the dragon patrols initiated earlier that morning by Lord Roga, the rider and his winged steed had yet to roust anything unusual out of the cover of the trees. Perhaps the reports from the perimeter guard were merely tricks of the mind born from hours of monotonous scanning of the horizon and the anticipation and anxiety of the next offensive on the mainland. The eyes and the mind can play tricks when focus is displaced by random thoughts.

The rider turned his dragon to make one last circle before returning to the roost, gaining altitude before diving sharply towards the forest canopy, leveling off at the last moment. The dragon's belly scales clipped the few twigs courageous enough to extend themselves beyond the sea of green that delineated the border between the arboreal and terrestrial. Each beat of its mighty wings created waves that extended out along the surface of the leaves, just as a brisk wind blows up waves upon the ocean, leaving a leafy wake behind. A quick scan as the beast skimmed over the treetops revealed the same - nothing unusual. Satisfied with his reconnaissance, the rider reined his beast towards the roost. If there was anything to be found in the forest today, one of the other riders would certainly find it.

Elden appeared out of the forest and half ran into camp.

"Is everyone here?"

Conor responded, "Yes, sir, everyone is here. Well, everyone but the girl. She went to the river. To take a ***bath***!" The rest of the group started to chuckle. "I told you from the beginning it wasn't a good idea to bring a female along. What's next, painted toenails and perfume?"

Elden placed a hand on Conor's shoulder. "Conor, I think we all agree that you would look a damned sorry sight with pink painted toenails and smelling like a De'Aarnan *pista*."

Stifled belly laughs and snickering chattered in the air. Elden quickly changed tone.

"Enough of this jocularity, me included. We need to get serious, and quickly. The Khorgians are on the move. I saw a dragon patrolling the sky just a few moments ago. Put out the fire and scatter everything amongst the leaf litter. Make sure everything is well hidden. Then hide yourselves. I will go find the girl and return her to camp."

Conor nodded his understanding and started barking hushed orders to the remainder of the group. As the men broke camp, Elden headed off towards the river. It was just like Ahnabin to get all the men in an uproar. He had told everyone to stay in camp until he returned. Maybe it had been a mistake bringing her along. But she had been so insistent, so convincing, and the Tendirans needed every capable fighter they could find. She had trained well and was as good or better than almost any of the men. If there was one thing that could be said about Ahnabin, she was definitely a fighter!

Elden made his way to the river, anxiously scanning the treetops as he went. It was a good five hundred paces or more from the encampment. There was a waterfall that emptied into a small pool a few hundred more paces upriver. That would be the most likely bathing spot, so he headed there first. As he neared the water's edge, he came upon the female soldier's leathers, boots and sword nearly hidden in a pile beneath a tree. Scanning the water, he saw her head break the surface near the waterfall.

"Ahna! Quick! Get out of the water and back to camp!"

Ahnabin could not hear him shout over the roar of the waterfall. Elden shouted again, but she still did not hear. The shadow of a dragon swept across the forest.

Elden quickly stripped off his armor and his boots and placed them in a pile beside Ahnabin's clothing. He removed his sword and propped it against the tree. Taking one last look into the sky, he dove into the pool, fully clothed, and crossed most of the distance to his stubborn female soldier completely beneath the water, and surfaced just a few feet away from her. He quickly swam the remainder of the way and grabbed her by the arm. Startled, she began to flounder a bit. He grabbed her beneath the armpit to keep her afloat. She poked her head back up from under the water, shook her hair out of her face and began punching and slapping at the air, trying to connect with her assailant. As the water cleared from her eyes, she looked up to see who it was that had grabbed her. Before she could focus on his face, another dragon shadow passed.

"Quickly! Under the falls!" Elden grabbed her by the shoulders and pushed Ahnabin towards the curtain of water. They both swam under the waterfall, finding a hollow behind in which to hide.

Ahna punched and slapped at him. "What's your game, huh! What the hell do you think you're..."

Another shadow passed over the waterfall.

"W... what was that?" Ahnabin looked up into Elden's eyes, imploring, frightened.

"A dragon. The Khorgians are on alert. I think they might be aware that something is awry. I dispersed the camp as soon as I returned from scouting the area. But ***you*** weren't there, although I gave specific orders for ***everyone*** to stay put while I searched the surroundings. Why do you have to be so reckless? Why can't you just obey orders like everyone else? Your stubborn strong will is going to be the death of you! I just hope you don't take anyone else with you when it happens."

Elden gave Ahnabin a quick scan, lingering for a moment at her chest. Noticing his gaze, she sank lower in the waist deep water and looked away. She was embarrassed by her lack of clothing and the awkwardness of the situation with her present company. She also knew she had made a grave error in judgment coming to the river and it nearly cost her life.

"I'm sorry", she whispered, turning her back towards him. "It won't happen again."

"See to it that it doesn't. I cannot afford to lose good soldiers."

Ahnabin turned to look at him, surprised by his evaluation of her. Another dragon shadow darkened the sky. They both scanned the rear of the waterfall, attempting to make out what was happening on the outside.

"I wish those damned things would just go away!"

"They're probably going to search until darkness falls. I fear they suspect our presence in the forest. We will have to proceed with care from this point on."

An hour or so had passed since they had ducked behind the waterfall. Ahnabin had begun to shiver, having been in the water, unprotected, for quite some time now. She was cold, but could not allude to that fact for fear of showing vulnerability to Elden. However, her chattering teeth and the little ripples her quivering body made in the water gave her away.

"You're cold. Here, take my tunic."

"No," she replied, "I am fine. Any warrior handles the situations presented to her with determination and dignity. I am not going to let a little water get the better of me." Ahna wrapped her arms around herself and sank deeper into the water, keeping her back to Elden.

"Self-sufficiency is one thing; foolishness is yet another. A warrior also knows when to take advantage of the resources at hand. Keeping warm, dry, and fed are first and foremost on the list. Take the tunic."

She turned her head towards him and glared. "Your tunic is soaked through. A true warrior knows wet clothing sucks body heat away from her. It is far better to remain submerged."

The shriek of a dragon pierced the air immediately beyond the waterfall, loud and angry, like the horn of a runaway locomotive. Ahnabin startled and jumped backward, right into Elden's arms. He wrapped his arms around her, holding her up.

"Relax," he whispered. "They can't see us behind the falls."

"I'm not afraid," she responded adamantly, twisting against his grasp to push away. She looked up at him. "It just... startled... me. I'm... fine." Her voice trailed off. She stopped struggling and stared up at him, quiet. She became very aware of his arms around her naked body, his chest against her chest. "I'm fine." She allowed herself to fall into his embrace.

Elden kissed her, hard and passionately, squeezing her closer to his body. She did not resist, kissing him back with the same fervor. They were soon lost in the moment, lost in each other. Lips kissing, hands groping, only the roar of the waterfall masking the sights and sounds of their passion from the rest of the forest.

DARKNESS HAD ENVELOPED the forest when Ahnabin and Elden reappeared from behind the waterfall. They swam to the shore, and she quickly dressed. Elden grabbed his armor and boots and strapped his sword back to his waist.

"We need to get back to the men. I need to find out what happened while we were hiding behind the waterfall." Elden sat to pull on his boots.

He looked up and she was standing there beside him, her clothing clinging to her wet skin, hugging every womanly curve.

"And what about what just happened, behind the waterfall?" she asked quietly.

He stood up and pulled her close with one arm. "What happened behind the waterfall is between the two of us. The men cannot know of it, or it will change how they perceive you and me. That won't be good right now. Just be confident in the fact that what happened behind the waterfall was real. My feelings for you are strong, Ahna. I just cannot allow our emotions to interfere with the task that is currently at hand. And I cannot allow the men any reason to let their confidence in me waver, even for a moment."

Ahnabin reached up with one hand and stroked Elden's cheek. He pulled her toward him and kissed her, holding her tight. This would be a difficult time, not being able to show affection for her, but it would be an awkward situation if any of the men were to know. They would have to make the best of it until the war was over.

Elden broke their kiss. "Come. We need to get back and muster the men. Hopefully, we had no losses." Ahnabin reluctantly released her embrace and grabbed her sword as Elden led the way back into the forest towards the encampment. In her mind, she tossed about the events of the last few hours. "*My soul has been claimed by his.*"

As they approached the place where the camp had been, Elden signaled with a whistle. Within moments the forest seemed alive as fourteen men came out of hiding. The first to greet Elden was Conor.

"Elden, are you okay?"

"Yes, Conor, we're fine. We've been hiding behind a fall in the river for hours. The dragons kept flying overhead. I was sure we would be seen. By the grace of *Ahlok*, we managed to evade detection." Elden looked around at the men. "Is everyone here? Did we make it through without any losses?"

"I wish I could respond in the affirmative, sir. Dorian went missing. There is no sign of him at all. I can only assume he was taken. We have scoured the area well, but there is not a trace of him anywhere, not so much as a hair."

"Well, they are sure to know we are here now. Dorian is a good man. Let's pray he can withstand whatever means they intend to employ to get him to speak. Come. We need to set up camp somewhere so everyone can get a little rest. We leave before dawn."

"AHHGH!" DORIAN SCREAMED as he felt the brand, hot against the sole of his foot again. The acrid stench of burning flesh filled the air. "There are seventeen of us! I have told you! Only seventeen!" He was gasping for breath, sweat collecting on his brow. He could barely move, for Roga's men had tied him down well. His right foot was strapped to a low stool, exposing the bare sole to the torture of hot steel.

His Khorgian captor questioned him once again. "Seventeen?"

"Yes, seventeen."

"I find it quite difficult to believe that your leaders would only send seventeen men on a journey this far. It serves no purpose."

"We were sent to gather intelligence and return so that a proper battle plan could be created. A larger unit would have more easily attracted attention."

Roga stopped his man for a moment and looked at Dorian. "Hmm. There might be a ring of truth in what you say. I have received no word of any seafaring vessels being found on the shore and none of my riders have reported any vessels at sea. A single vessel might be easily hidden, but the number of ships required for an invading army would most certainly attract some form of attention."

"Yes! See? I have told you the truth. There is only our small group."

"You could very well be telling me the truth." Roga made a motion with his hand and his torturer placed the brand against Dorian's foot again. He screamed in pain. "But, then again, you could be lying. How many of you were there again?"

"Seventeen! Seventeen!"

"Seventeen, you say." He motioned to the torturer again. "Are you certain?"

The brand burned into flesh again. There was little left to the sole of Dorian's foot, burned to the point where not a nerve remained to feel the pain. He sensed that this was the case and kept his wits enough to use it to his advantage. He screamed as if in pain, tugging at his bonds, although he could no longer feel it.

"Seventeen! I am sure of it!"

"Take our guest back to his cage. Give him something to wrap up that foot. I certainly wouldn't want him to catch his death while under our watch."

Roga walked away with his torturer, whispering to him. "Bring him back tomorrow afternoon. We can work on the other foot. Let's see how consistent his story remains. Who knows, maybe he will crack or maybe he already has. Either way, continuation of his torture shall keep me entertained until we have secured the remainder of the intruders."

21
THE VISITOR

ELDEN STIRRED FROM his slumber. He opened his eyes and let them adjust a moment to the darkness. It was past midnight, but the morning light had yet to filter into the evening sky. A wisp of fog hung in the air, illuminated by the columns of light passing through the canopy from the two moons hanging in the cloudless sky. A figure stood before him. A long flowing cloak, thinning white hair beneath a snug cap.

"Taygen?! How...?"

The magician placed his finger to his lips and whispered to the young warrior.

"Arise, Master Elden. Do not awaken the others. Come and walk with me."

Elden picked himself up out of his bedding and began to gather his things. As he reached for his sword, the old magician stopped him, gently touching him on the arm.

"There will be no need."

Elden looked up at him and then at his blade for a moment before placing it back down on top of his bedding. Standing, he followed as Taygen slowly walked into the forest.

"It is good to see you, magi, but I do not understand. How is it that you come to be here, in the Khorgian forest? Did you choose to follow us in another of your vessels?"

"That is of little matter. What matters is that I have come to speak to you, to counsel you on the events of the coming days. As you must know by now, the Dragon Lord, Lord Roga, is aware of our presence here in the Khorgian wilderness. He may not be aware of who exactly is here and how many, but he knows that Tendiran soldiers are on the island, and he will stop at nothing to find them and protect his interests."

"That has become profoundly evident to me. One of our party, Dorian, is missing. We assume he has been taken. Is there something you can do to help us; some spell or prayer?"

"There is nothing I can do to alter what is predetermined to be. I may have the power to adjust the course that is followed, but there is nothing I can do to supplant the final destination. What *Ahlok* has decided for each of us is woven into the fiber of the universe, never to be changed by the hand of man."

"If you cannot alter what is ultimately to be, why have you traveled here? What assistance could your counsel possibly provide?"

"It is quite justified for you to feel I can be of no assistance, for there is much you do not understand. Although the ending shall be what the Creator has intended, how you reach the ending, what losses you may endure, and what advantages you might be able to create on your journey will come from the choices you make. Analyze every step, every opportunity, and choose your moves as for a game of chess. Think ahead at what may be the result of your decisions and how those results may reveal other opportunities. What may seem like folly at first glance may create advantageous opportunities in the future."

"I question every detail of this journey. Do we have enough manpower to defeat the Khorgians? Can the dragons be stopped? Have we trained enough? Have I brought the right people? Is the girl bad luck?"

"Do not regret your decision to bring the girl along. No matter what your comrades may think, she will become a very valuable team member to your mission. Her physical and mental attributes are key elements in what is to come." Taygen stopped and turned to Elden, staring directly into his eyes. "Beyond that, she makes you happy."

"Wha... How did...?"

"She is meant to be here."

"If only I could convince the men of that now. The tension is high in the camp. Although she has shown extreme promise in training, I am unsure if our comrades trust in her abilities under pressure. And her going missing at the river didn't help. Her rebellious nature causes unease in a time of warfare.

Personally, I do not doubt she is capable. It is the remaining men on this journey that she needs to persuade."

"She may surprise you yet, Elden, and your men as well. And the beekeeper. His knowledge and intuition shall prove invaluable. He speaks from a vast experience outside of the training of a warrior, an insight that neither you nor your generals have access to. Conventional warfare is not the path to victory."

"Fighting an aerial army from the ground an ocean away from home is quite possibly as far as one could get from what is most commonly considered conventional warfare, Taygen."

"Very true, Elden, but how one contends with an aerial army whilst it is not airborne shall seem even more unconventional."

Elden stopped and stared quizzically at the mage, who simply smiled, turned, and continued walking. After a quick moment, Elden hurried to catch up.

The two walked deeper into the dense forest, guided only by the dim moonlight that managed to reach the ground through the high canopy.

"If you cannot change what is to come, if it is set in the fabric of the universe, are you able to portend what is inevitable? Can you tell me what I am to expect to happen?"

"It does not work quite the way you are asking, Elden. The paths you may follow are innumerable. There are too many possibilities to offer a script of the events to come."

"But no matter how varied and wide the various paths may be, eventually they all come back to one event, to one destiny. That being true, common events must occur, at least as the outcome approaches."

'Very true, Elden. Along each path, there are minor conditions that must be met, conditions that are shared no matter what path you choose. Think of them as milestones. In most cases, these are the moments that steer you to that goal."

"But can you elucidate in regard to the final outcome?"

"I am here to provide insight into the events that are to come. Even I know not how it all ends. You must experience the journey on your own. I can only speak in generalities."

"Well, generally speaking, what can you divulge to me in respect to the coming battle?"

"I can tell you many shall perish, but that is the nature of battle."

"That is understood without the benefit of your counsel, Taygen, but who shall win? What are the prerequisites for victory?"

"Victory shall come through the shedding of your own blood. You will find that your adversary is, in fact, one of your own."

Elden stopped in his tracks. "One of my own? Which one of my men would turn against me?" Taygen continued walking.

"I cannot answer that, Elden. It is not for me to say."

"Not for you to say? Taygen, you come to me tonight and offer me all this information that answers no question but only generates more. You said that you have come to me to provide counsel, but you speak to me in riddles. Why can't you just tell me what you have come to tell me?"

Taygen stopped walking and turned back to face Elden. "My son, I am only a conduit for the contrivances of destiny. I cannot change them, I cannot challenge them, nor can I decipher their meaning for you. What the Fortunes have determined to be your path is for you to experience, not for me to reveal. All will become clear to you when the time arises."

The two continued to walk, Elden eagerly listening to the riddles posed by his mentor, soaking in every word.

As if by design, the two found themselves back at the encampment, apparently completing a large looping journey back to where they had started. All the others were still fast asleep.

"I feel as though we have been away for hours, but the sun has yet to rise."

"The concept of time does not relate when one is intent on other things. What may seem as minutes are actually hours and hours may pass only as minutes. The passage of time was not relevant to our conversation, so it is as if it had stood still."

Elden looked at the magician oddly. "Do not dwell upon it, Elden. It is not that important."

"Surely you will stay with us for the remainder of our campaign, Master Taygen? You have traveled all this way to counsel me. It would seem foolish for you to return to De'Aarna."

"I'm afraid I cannot. Just as you have come this far without me, you must travel the remainder of this journey without me. Take care, Elden. Fear not, for we shall meet again, in another place and time not too far from the present."

The two men shook hands and embraced. Elden watched as Taygen disappeared into the late evening mist and then lay himself back in his bed.

ROGA TOSSED AND TURNED in his cot, unable to sleep. His mind swirled with thoughts of the Tendirans. Even his beast was uneasy, shuffling about and circling her bedding like a skittish dog. Somehow a group of Tendirans had made their way to the island without being found out. How could a vessel have crossed the Touphorus Sea to the shores of Khorgia and not be noticed? Had he and his most trusted military men become arrogant and, as a result, complacent? What other possibilities had they either discounted or not even considered? Could they have focused too deeply on the offensive and failed to consider the defensive? And now that they were here, what could be done to stop them, to incapacitate them, to destroy them before they acted against his own army? Could a force of a score or less even be a threat?

The warlord pulled himself up from his cot and started towards his quarters.

"Minarik! Minarik! Get me my riding clothes! Ursen! Prepare the Queen! I intend to be airborne at dawn!"

A groggy Minarik appeared in the hall and headed towards Roga's office, nearly colliding with an equally sleepy Ursen as he headed towards the rookery.

"Be quick in preparing his ride. He will not be pleased if he is made to wait."

Roga bellowed from the hallway ahead, "Minarik!"

"Coming, my Lord!"

ELDEN AWOKE WITH A start and carefully looked around. The first rays of the dawn were filtering through the trees, enough that he could make out the objects around him. He was lying on the ground in the same place he had originally fallen asleep, still wrapped in his bedding. His sword was close to his side, in the exact same place he had left it last night. His mind went quickly back to the events of the previous evening. He had been awakened by Taygen and had gone for a walk with him, discussing all that was to come in the near future. They had walked long and deep into the forest and had talked at length about recent events and what he could expect during the next few days. But he could not remember coming back to camp or saying farewell to his old friend or climbing back into his bedding. He did not remember falling back to sleep let alone waking up in the first place. Was it all true? Did it all happen? Or was it just a vivid dream?

22
RECONNAISSANCE

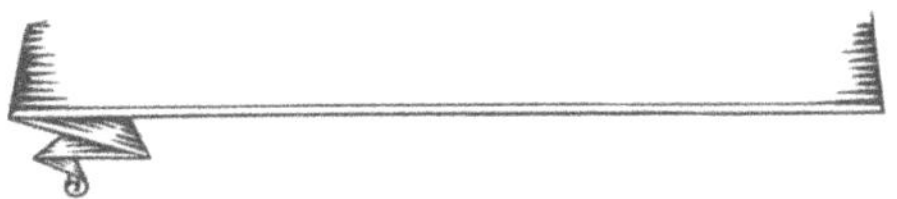

AS THE EARLY MORNING light struggled to filter through the treetops to reach the forest floor, Elden had already awakened from his fitful slumber. Everything was covered with a thin film of dew, an ethereal mist rising from the forest floor. Scattered about him under well-camouflaged mounds, fifteen men were asleep in their bedrolls. Even the most well-trained eye would have been pressed to have picked this location to be a camp. The events of the night still fresh in his mind, Elden determined it was time to make a move. He gathered his things together and started to rouse the men. As each man was awakened, they quickly packed up their belongings, carefully concealed their presence, and congregated by a large fallen tree. The sun had not yet fully pierced the canopy when Elden began to speak.

"After yesterday, I believe it is in our best interest to survey the situation again today. The Khogians have Dorian. There is no telling what devices they may use to try to draw information from him. If they have been successful, I wouldn't put it past their leader to be planning an ambush against us." Elden turned to Conor. "I need two men to help me. The rest of you, break up camp, remove any evidence that we were here, and scatter the men into the forest again. Hide yourselves well. We need to scout the area, to see if Roga has any surprises in store for us." Conor nodded his acknowledgment and called out two of his men, Arun and Gregor. The remainder of the men started to break up camp.

"You!" Elden grasped Ahnabin by the shoulder. "You are coming with me this time. Someone has to keep an eye on you before you get someone killed." Although it was a simple ploy to have Ahna by his side, Elden was also well aware that none of his men wanted to have her in their group. Not only was she female, she was also seen as a liability, mostly due to her headstrong nature. She glared at him, angry that he would make a fool out of her in front of all the men. He motioned for the two other men to work their way to the south before heading north with Ahna.

"Expect us back in an hour. If we are gone much longer than that, regroup and head for the ship. It probably means we have been captured. Get everyone out of here, off this infernal land, and return to the remainder of the fleet. Pull up anchor and head back home. The advantage of surprise must be on our side if we wish to defeat the Khorgians."

Once they had walked out of earshot, Ahna slapped Elden across the back of the head. "Ow! What the hell did you do that for?"

"For making me out as a fool in front of everyone back at camp! A fine way to show me how you feel about me. How dare you treat me like that! I am not a little girl, you know."

"Yes, I do know. But you and I cannot afford to allow the men to know what has happened between us. I need to treat you as I have all along, treat you the way they expect, and after your escapade in the river, they expect me to be harsh with you."

"It's not fair! Why does something that feels so right end up being so wrong?"

"No one says it's wrong, Ahna. It's just not right at this time, for the current situation. The men need to focus on the events that are at hand. ***We*** need to focus on the events at hand. Any distractions could cause someone to lose their life. That's a risk I cannot take right now, for you, for me, for the men. We've already lost Dorian. We need to stay focused on this mission so the rest of us can all go home safely. Only then can we live our lives the way we want."

Ahna cast her eyes towards the ground. "I just want to be with you," she said softly. She looked up into Elden's eyes. "But I understand. It is what it needs to be. This time will be short compared to the rest of our lives. And it is a sacrifice I am willing to make, to make our lives and the lives of our families easier, to avenge the death of my father. Come. We have work to do."

Elden stared in shock as Ahnabin started to walk deeper into the forest. For all the controversy she could create, she was still an amazing woman.

A LONE DRAGON FLEW high above the canopy, a single rider on its shoulders. Roga steered his beast in large lazy circles, scanning the land beneath them for movement. He knew the Tendirans had a group of men down there somewhere and he was determined to find them.

This was a task Roga abhorred, long, tedious, and boring. He diligently guided his perch in a spiral, one circular path bisecting the next. The course did not quickly cover much ground, but it did offer a thorough view of the landscape below. He scanned the areas between the treetops for any signs of life below, spotting the occasional bird or animal and quickly discounting it. His search had been fruitless so far, but he continued on. The prisoner, Dorian, had divulged the presence of a small expeditionary force on the island and the warlord was determined to find and destroy them.

Then, out of the corner of his eye, he spied some movement on the ground. Unable to immediately determine what it was, he turned his dragon in a wide arc, circling back to the spot to get a better look. Carefully examining the landscape below as he made another pass, he saw nothing to attract his attention. A third pass produced the same results. Maybe it had been an animal, a falling piece of vegetation or even his own wishful thinking. Whatever it was, it was no longer there. Returning to his previous flight pattern, Roga continued his search of the forest below.

ELDEN AND AHNABIN LAY perfectly still, face down in the underbrush. Elden had spied the dragon high overhead and quickly made for cover. They both had held their position as the dragon and rider made two more passes above. It had been nearly five minutes since it had last flown over. Elden looked over at Ahna and nodded. The danger had passed. They both pulled themselves up out of the underbrush.

"That rider knows someone is out here. It is inevitable after yesterday." Elden offered Ahna a hand. "Let's get back to the men. If they are searching by dragon wing, it is unlikely they have men searching for us on the ground.

If we are all careful, we should be able to make progress on the ground without being seen."

"Let's get back to the camp, then," Ahnabin suggested. "The sooner we are on the move, the better. A moving target will be harder to find."

"Agreed." Elden put his hand on Ahna's back as they moved out of the clearing. She looked up at him and smiled. Then, just as they reached the edge of the clearing, she saw something in the sky.

"Dragon!"

Elden looked up at the sky. Low, just over the canopy, a dragon and rider passed by the opening in the treetops. He pushed Ahna ahead and dove behind her into the underbrush.

ROGA SAW A FIGURE DIVE into the forest below. His plan had worked! After two forays above the clearing, he had decided to move from the spot and return a short time later, just in case he had actually seen something, giving that "something" time to regain a comfort level and be on the move again. Keeping low to the canopy top, he circled back on his dragon minutes later, silently riding the air currents, to sneak up on whatever had been in the clearing. He had found his quarry!

Signaling his beast to gain altitude, Roga prepared for an attack on the clearing. Reaching a height hundreds of feet above the forest floor, he turned his dragon into a dive. Wings tucked back; the flying lizard gained speed. Roga lay flat on the beast's back, holding onto its scutes as tight as possible, the air whipping by him nearly sucking his breath away. As it approached the treetops, a tactile command triggered the dragon to spew forth flaming acid into the clearing. Within a heartbeat, every piece of dry vegetation burst into flames. The clearing became instant chaos. Birds flew up out of the clearing. Beasts of all shapes and sizes scurried to keep out of the flames. Roga was hard pressed to find his quarry amongst all the movement. Smoke started to billow up out of the clearing, further inhibiting his search. His dragon pulled up from its dive with seconds to spare and glided across the tops of the trees. Roga turned her in a wide arc once again to make another pass at the clearing.

ALL ABOUT THEM, THE clearing became an instant inferno. Birds and animals scattered in every imaginable direction. Those not fast enough burst into bouncing balls of flame. The dragon's phosphoric bile devoured everything in its path as if it were bits of dry tinder. Even the ground and boulders lay scorched by the attack.

Elden grabbed Ahnabin by the hand and began to sprint deeper into the forest. The Khorgian warlord knew they were there, and he would stop at nothing to either kill or capture them. Their only chance of escape was to find a path through the dense underbrush that would conceal them from sight and allow them to change direction without detection. The dragon could be used to methodically scorch the forest floor below, but a carefully planned route might avoid the next segment to be set ablaze.

ROGA PUSHED HIS BEAST to the extent of her ability to maneuver. He could feel the creature balking at his tactile commands but pressed harder to persuade the animal to continue. He was not going to miss this opportunity to eliminate an adversary. But, unlike any previous raiding party, this was one dragon against a small fast-moving target. On every previous raid, the targets were numerous and the dragons were many. The targets were typically out in the open. It was almost impossible to not hit something on each individual skirmish. This attack was far more challenging, for both dragon and rider, and Roga relished the challenge. The forest served to provide cover for the Tendiran. Roga pushed his steed into a steep turn as it dove towards its quarry.

Suddenly the dragon lurched to one side. Her right wingtip had clipped a branch on one of the taller trees. The beast immediately drew both its wings in against its body in an attempt to protect them and itself. Striking the limb had produced a slight spin in its trajectory that quickly became a spiral as it streamlined its profile for protection, becoming, now, a projectile. Roga hung on with all his strength. He knew this was going to be a wild ride. As she began to lose altitude, the trees began to impede the creature's descent, buffeting it from both sides with branches and leaves. Roga kept his body as flat as possible against the beast's leathery scales, trying his best to maintain as low a profile as possible to avoid injury. Ten feet from impact, a branch finally caught him, stripping his grasp away from the dragon and flinging him down to the ground about twenty yards from the where the fallen beast was coming to rest. He tumbled for a few yards and then settled in a pile of leaf litter. He paused a moment, gathering his wits and bearings, and checked to make sure he hadn't sustained any serious injury. He glanced at his beast, which was cautiously doing the same. Neither appeared to be the worse for wear after their tumble out of the sky.

Roga scanned the area where he thought he had last seen his quarry. At first, he saw nothing. Then, out of the corner of his periphery, he saw the warrior climbing up onto a small stone outcropping to escape to the other side. Much to his surprise, Elden stopped, turned, and, lying on the rock, stomach-down, extended a hand to another person. Roga had not reasoned that another person was with him, having had no information to support that theory. Roga watched intently as Elden grasped the hand of what first appeared to be a teenage boy. But when the boy turned around to look back, Roga could clearly see that a teenage boy it was not! Despite the small, slender frame, the curves of a young woman were apparent.

"So, the Tendiran warrior has himself a pretty, young harlot traveling with him. Certainly, she will become a distraction and a liability that I can use to my advantage. What fools these Tendirans. Do they not know that females only cloud a warrior's intellect? To bring one to battle is beyond nonsensical. Fleshly pleasures do nothing but sap the strength and distract the mind. Females and the pleasures they provide should only be made available for victory celebrations."

Elden and Ahnabin scaled the outcropping and scurried out of sight. Roga picked himself up and tended to his mount, making sure all was in order. He stroked the dragon's neck, ensuring the creature that all was fine and then climbed back onto its shoulders. Applying pressure to the animal's side with his heels, he signaled for it to leap back into flight for the trip back to the caverns. This would be an interesting return trip. There was much new information to process and share with his men back in the weir.

23
THE DRAGON SMOKER

AROUND A LOW GLOWING campfire, the Tendiran leader and his generals gathered to discuss strategy for the impending attack, surrounded by the remainder of the expeditionary force clustered in small groups of two or three. The conclave had been discussing strategy for hours but had yet to come to a consensus on a plan. It had devolved to the presentation of every absurd notion for consideration in the hopes that something would either spawn a useful idea or become the answer to their dilemma. Frustration and disgust boiled up from within, erupting in shouts, pounding of fists, stomping of feet, and the occasional pushes and shoves.

From the back of the group, a voice rose above the clash of egos. "You need to look at this from a different angle if you expect to gain an advantage."

The shocked leaders turned to see who dared to speak. Conor was particularly irritated.

"Who said that?"

Zephraim stood up. "I said it."

"Who are you? And where do you get along trying to discuss military tactics? Do you have command experience?"

"No, but I..."

"Then what do you have to offer? I would think it in your best interest to continue taking orders and let those of us in command work out the strategy."

Elden interjected, "Please, you know this man. It is the beekeeper. Let him continue. He certainly cannot bring forward anything more absurd than those ideas already suggested by the likes of anyone gathered around this fire."

The commanders were in shock. It was true that none of the strategies discussed so far seemed very plausible, but what could a common man come up with that could provide a military advantage to their cause?

Elden called back to Zephraim. "Tell them your plan."

"Thank you, Elden." Zephraim continued. "For those of you that may not have come to know me by name, I am known as Zephraim. I have come to join you from the Souliban. I have joined your group to avenge the loss of my family, my friends, and my countrymen. I have no intention of losing this battle. For that reason, I offer my thoughts. You need to think outside the normal military tactics to gain a significant advantage here. Take them by surprise. The leader of the Khorgians is obviously a well-educated military tactician. He will not be easily taken by surprise, but his dragons may not be so fortunate. It has been my observation that most animals have a natural fear of fire. I used that inclination to my advantage when I was still capable of performing my chosen profession. As a beekeeper, whenever I opened a hive, I first doused the opening with smoke, making sure to pump it well inside. The bees are made to believe the hive was on fire and they would flee. They would eventually return, but, by that time, I would have completed my work, opening the hive, removing the honey, and making repairs if need be. I would believe it to be a reasonable expectation that the dragons will react in the same way. Their "hive" is the caverns that they use as a rookery. Just like a beehive, there must be a large area within where the dragons rest and eat, with a small, single opening to enter and exit. Pumping smoke inside wouldn't be that difficult and the fear it would instill in the creatures should cause them to flee."

"I find your manner of thinking to be quite unique and ingenious, but I question if we will have the amount of time necessary at the cave entrance. The Khorgians will not just allow us to walk right up and light a fire at their front door."

"You will not need to go to their front door." Zephraim approached the group. "Creatures that big could not survive in an enclosed area without the benefit of fresh air. There must be vents to provide airflow. We just need to find one of those vents."

The group began to listen more carefully to what the beekeeper was saying.

"I would think that the small entrance would be very easy for them to defend, as you said, but as advantageous as that might be for defense, it can also be a disadvantage. It isn't sizeable enough for easy egress. If there was a way to make the animals believe there was a real fire inside, we could potentially neutralize the entire dragon horde. The beasts would certainly panic. The ensuing bedlam might generate an atmosphere so chaotic as to result in the incapacitation or demise of many the animals within, as well as many of the warriors. Such losses could be enough to tip the scales of fate in our favor."

The commanders looked back and forth at one another, murmuring amongst themselves. After a moment or two, Conor finally spoke up. "It appears I owe Master Zephraim an apology. His knowledge of the natural ways of creatures could work to our advantage. I say we discuss the details of such a plan. Beekeeper, please join us." He motioned to a seat at the fire. "I believe your expertise in such matters will be invaluable."

Zephraim looked about the group, uneasy with his new-found authority. He smiled meekly and looked at Conor. Conor nodded and the beekeeper cautiously took the seat.

Zephraim started to explain how he could crawl up one of the cavern vents with the supplies necessary to create a smoldering fire. The fire would produce smoke that would travel up the vent and fill the dragons' living areas.

"Beekeeper, please, leave the fighting to those trained in the fine arts of warfare. Your strategy is well conceived, and we are grateful. Only a thinking man with knowledge of the attributes of nature would be clever enough to devise such a plan. But you are far too eager. Leave the execution to those trained to do so." Although pleased with Zephraim's plan, Conor was still irritated that a layman had developed the strategy that he and his warriors would be counting on to negate the Khorgian advantage. He was trained as a warrior from the time he was a young boy. Was he now to subjugate himself to the orders of a beekeeper?

"I can defend myself!" Zephraim produced a rope dart from beneath his shirttail. In one swift motion, the weapon was from his belt, and he had it twirling about. A quick release and the dart sailed passed Conor's head and embedded into a tree beside him, eye height. Jaws dropped and Zephraim drew the amazed stares of many about the clearing. "My target was the tree, but it could have easily been your brow." A tug on the chain and he had the dart back in his hand. "Never underestimate the prowess of those less physically impressive than yourself. Even the mild-mannered beekeeper can deliver a sting that should be reckoned with."

Elden stifled a laugh. "Apparently, not everyone within our little band of fighters has been made aware of our dartsmen. I think the beekeeper has made his point. Quite clearly, I might add. I think it is time to shed your egos and recognize that those without years of military experience might be more physically equipped to carry out this plan than the rest of you."

Conor, still irritated, defended his skills. "You mean to tell me that there is someone among us that is more capable than me? I will outhike, outhaul, outclimb and outfight any man in this group! Who dares to challenge me?"

Elden patted Conor on the stomach. "No one challenges your strength, but I find it hard to imagine this physique making its way into a vent hole."

Conor turned to protest but realized he had been beaten. "And what would you suggest?"

"It's quite simple, Conor. We need the smallest members of our group. A slender frame is necessary for gaining access through a vent. And who is the slightest of all our army?" A murmur rose from the men as everyone quickly scanned the group, eyes eventually stopping on Zephraim and Ahnabin.

"Zephraim I can accept, but the girl...?" Conor was beside himself with disbelief.

Elden cut him off. "The girl that you and Quoregg trained so well that she quite capably passed every test and trial the two of you administered? Had you not done your job so well, she might not be so well prepared for such an important mission."

"Well, of course, she... I... We trained... She can do whatever any of..." Conor was obviously flustered.

"That settles it. We have the personnel and the plan. All we need now is the execution. Zephraim, what would be your suggestion?"

Still irritated, but clearly beaten, Conor did not continue to protest Elden's request of the beekeeper and the princess-turned warrior. Quite obviously, his expertise, and his physique, had limited value to an operation as unusual as this.

"We need a material that will smolder and produce thick smoke. Dry reeds soaked in sea water and lamp oil should work. We will need a sizeable amount if we intend to generate enough smoke to fill the caverns. I would say roughly enough to fill a wine cask."

"So be it. Conor, select a few men to collect the reeds. Bundle them tightly into fascines and soak them in the tidal pool. We should have some oil. Fill three or four wine skins. They will travel well and not break." Elden turned to Zephraim. "Do you have issues with your partner? It would seem she would not be the selection of most."

"No, I have no problem working with Ahna. She is very capable, and I am quite sure she will not have any issue with her ego on this assignment." He glanced around the camp, knowing his comment was not earning him many comrades, stopping his stare at Conor. "She was trained by the best, and well-trained at that." He paused a moment, and breaking his stare, he turned to Elden. "Don't worry, Elden. We will make this plan work."

"I have no doubts, Zephraim. Is there anything else you will need?"

"Ropes. The lowest vent intake may be high upon the mount. We will need to bring ropes to help climb if necessary. And a vent. We need to find a vent that is large enough for a man, or woman, to climb into. If you could deploy your best scouts to seek a suitable vent, that would be most helpful."

"Very well. Everyone. Let's gather up the supplies for this mission. Arun! Gregor! Prepare to scour the cliff face for a vent hole into the rookery. Tomorrow night we show the Khorgians who is truly superior."

BY THE COVER OF DARKNESS, Ahna crept unnoticed to Elden's bed. Placing a single finger across his lips, she roused him silently.

"Wha...? What are you doing?" he whispered. "The others will see!"

"Not if we're somewhere else."

"What are you suggesting?" Elden implored under his breath.

"Tomorrow, if we are successful, the Khorgians will most certainly be looking for a fight. We will not have a moment's rest from that point on." Ahna winked and smiles at Elden. "That being so, *we* have a moment *now*, and I am suggesting we take advantage of it."

From her tone it was quite evident to Elden it was less of a suggestion and more of a demand. Ahna took his hand to guide him deeper into the forest and the two slipped silently into the darkness.

After a few yards of careful, quiet creeping, Elden and Ahna moved, first, to a quick walk and then to a slow trot before coming to a small open space. The pair were immediately wrapped in each other's arms, lips locked, tongues entwined. This was the first time alone since the waterfall and Ahna was not about to let this moment pass. Grasping wildly at his clothing, she quickly removed his tunic and trousers and tossed him to the ground. Barely landing in the grass, Ahna was astride his hips and pulling her own shirt over her head. Elden pulled her down on him, mashing her breasts into his chest, once again bringing his lips to hers, his fingers entwined in her hair.

Ahna relaxed, feeling suddenly safe and secure in her lover's arms. She eagerly gave herself to Elden, suppressing her own advances and relinquishing control to his. Sensing the shift to his advantage, he deftly changed positions, assuming the dominant position over his partner. Uncharacteristic of the warrior within, Ahna surrendered to Elden, instantly becoming woman, lover, soulmate.

The two remained entwined, sharing each other's breath, hands groping, lips seeking lips. Elden's hands moved to Ahna's hips, hooking the waistband of her breeches, and helping her wriggle out of them. Repositioning himself on top, he wedged himself between her thighs, aligning his sex with hers and slowly pushing himself forward. Ahna caught her breath and tensed up as he entered her, then relaxed, feeling each inch sliding deeper within. She tightly wrapped her arms around his back, her legs around his waist, locking her ankles to ensure they remained connected, rhythmically matching his motions. Elden half supported his weight on his elbows, his fingers once again entangled in her locks, continued to kiss Ahna passionately as his hips pistoned forward and back in an ecstasy-fueled onslaught. His thrusting prevailed, increasing to a frenzied pace as, together, they approached release.

Ahna's breath quickening to a short staccato rhythm as his sex began convulsing within hers. A warmth from deep within spread throughout her entire body as her skin flushed. She pulled him in tighter with her arms and legs, seemingly attempting to make them one. After an eternity existing within a mere few minutes, Ahna released the strength of her grip upon him and he rolled, positioning them side by side. Elden pulled his love close, cradling her in his arms, soaking in what they had just shared between them.

After a few moments, Elden began to feel himself drifting off. He quickly sat up, startling Ahna.

"I do not wish to spoil this moment, but we need to get back to camp before we fall asleep here. It would not look very good if everyone woke to find the two of us missing. That would definitely raise some suspicions and most certainly divulge our secret." Brushing the grass and dirt off his body, he stood and began dressing. Ahna followed his lead. When they were both fully dressed, they each carefully inspected the other in the moonlight to ensure no vestiges of their tryst remained. Nodding to each other that everything was in order, Elden turned to head back. Ahna grabbed him by the arm and spun him back into her embrace, placing a long kiss on his lips.

"I love you, Elden."

"I love you, too, Ahna. This war will not last forever. Once we are back home, we can reveal our true feelings to the world. Until that time, we need to remain focused on the task at hand so we can both return safely."

"I know. Come. Let's get back before anyone notices we were gone."

Hand in hand, the two lovers headed into the forest, making their way back to camp and their respective beds.

AS THE LAST VESTIGES of the sun were setting into the ocean, Ahna and Zephraim stood, arms stretched out to their sides, as wet ash was rubbed onto their clothing, hair, and their exposed skin. Both threw two wineskins over one shoulder and two large fascines wrapped in dark cloth over the other. Each fascine was further wrapped in long lengths of rope for climbing. Everything they would need to successfully complete this mission hung tightly against their bodies.

Elden approached. "Have you memorized where Arun and Gregor found the vent? You need to find it quickly if you are to be successful before dawn."

Zephraim looked at Ahna and then back to Elden. "Either of us could find it with our eyes closed and one hand tied behind our back."

"I would suggest keeping all four of your eyes open and on the task at hand. May *Ahlok* smile upon you both, then. Remember, this is *your* plan, and it is a fine one. It is up to you and Ahna to execute it. Take your time and remain vigilant. Our fate as a people may not rest entirely upon this mission, but, if successful, it will turn the advantage away from the Khorgians and their dragons."

Conor placed a bed of charcoal on a flat of fresh leaves. Reaching into the fire with his sword, he removed a large glowing ember and placed it upon the charcoal, rolling the leaves into a loose bundle and then wrapping the entire package in pliable bark from a young tree. He handed the bundle to Zephraim and did the same for Ahna. "These should last an hour or two. You can add more charcoal or a rope of dried grass if you need more time."

"Understood. With luck on our side, we will not need more time."

Conor grabbed Zephraim's hand and pulled him close. "Forgive me if I doubted your ability to offer a valid strategy, beekeeper. Your plan is most eloquent and far more viable than anything anyone else had presented. I have full confidence in it and your ability to execute it successfully."

"Apologies are not necessary, Conor. These are tense times, and at times like these, we do not open ourselves to thinking outside the known. That you can accept my plan and have confidence in its execution are gratitude enough."

The men shook hands. Conor then turned to Ahna. "You have learned as well as any recruit I have ever trained. Your competence exceeds most every man in this army. I am fully confident in your abilities. Make me proud, young lady."

Ahnabin was shocked. "You will have nothing but pride to feel upon our return, sir. I have taken everything you and Master Quoregg taught me to heart. I will show everyone how capable a warrior I have become thanks to your tutelage."

Like two ghosts in the night, Ahna and Zephraim stepped into the forest, near instantly melding with the darkness of the forest and disappearing into the trees.

Two blackened soldiers silently approached the base of the mount, pushing their way through the heavy underbrush. Zephraim put his finger to his lips. "Shhh. If we have followed Arun's directions, we should be close.

Listen carefully. The lower vents should draw fresh air in from below as the hot air within the rookery exits from vents above. If we are close enough, we should be able to hear the rushing air in the stillness of the night." He placed his ear close to the rock face. After a moment he shook his head and pointed towards the north. The two moved along the base of the mountain, stopping occasionally to listen.

A few hundred yards along, Ahna's eyes grew wide. A smile curled across her face as she pointed up, whispering, "Here."

Zephraim scanned the cliff face for a way up. A ledge about ten feet above led to a large crack in the stone that ran up the stone façade. He pointed up and then squatted, his hands cupped in front of him. Ahna placed her foot in his hands, and he boosted her upwards. She grabbed the edge of the ledge and climbed up. Securing herself, she dropped a rope for her accomplice. Once both were settled, they moved towards the crack.

The crack in the rock was wide enough to wedge a body inside, extending hundreds of feet above. The sound of rushing air whistled above; its movement easily felt on the skin. The vent opening was clearly visible a reasonable climbing distance above. The two stopped and pulled the bundles and wine skins off their shoulders. Carefully, they soaked down the reeds, the smell of lamp oil surrounding them as the air current swept it up into the vent. Having prepared the reeds, Zephraim pushed Ahna ahead up into the crevice towards the vent, following close behind as she led the way. Wriggling up through the crack, they inched their way towards the hole eventually arriving at the vent opening. It was not much more than two feet across and even less in height. As she reached it, Ahna pushed her bundles in ahead followed by Zephraim's. She pushed the reeds further and further into the vent as she made her way behind them. At about twenty feet, the hole narrowed, preventing her from passing.

"It's too small. I can't go any further."

"Plug the passage with the reeds, but loose enough so the air will flow through the bundles. We need to keep the air flowing. It will carry the smoke into the caverns."

Ahna wedged the bundles loosely into the opening and reached for her ember carrier, carefully unwrapping it. Inside was only black. Her ember had burned out!

"It's out!" she hissed. "What do we do now?"

"Remain calm. I have one, too." He handed his bundle to her. "Use care not to allow the air current to blow it out. Here." Ahna held it close to her body, shielding it as much as possible from the breeze, and unwrapped it carefully. A single orange ember stared up at her from the charcoal like a demon's glowing eye. Continuing to protect it from the air rushing by, she carefully pressed it against the bundles. Slowly, a single reed began to smolder, then another and another. The glow of smoldering reeds filled the small space as the rushing air fed the burning mass and swept the black smoke it produced up through the plug of reeds towards the rookery chambers above.

"It is done. Quick, let's get out of here!"

The two scurried out of the vent hole like rabbits escaping a burning warren, dropping first to the ledge and then quickly to the ground. Satisfied with what they had accomplished, they turned and headed back to camp.

IT STARTED AS AN ODD smell and then a small wisp of black smoke, slowly curling up through an air vent in the lowest level of the caverns, unnoticed by any of the Khorgian warriors. Rather quickly, though, dark smoke was entering every level of the warren. The beasts were first to notice. What started as an uneasy rumbling quickly became confusion, anxiety, and then pandemonium. As their dragons began to panic, so did the riders. Fire in the caverns was the last thing any of them had ever expected. Thick, dark, withering smoke rapidly filled the air, making it hard to see and breathe. The frightened creatures began clamoring for the cave entrance in a desperate attempt to escape, but the portal quickly became blocked. Terrified, the dragons lashed out in the only manner natural to them, belching their flaming acidic bile at anything in their path. Bellows of fear and pain from the beasts, accompanied by the screaming of the Khorgian riders, filled the air as thick as the dark smoke. The smell of phosphorus, burning flesh, and sheer terror was everywhere. A single dragon and then another had managed to reach the apron outside the entrance and quickly took flight, escaping the chaos within. Subsequent beasts fought at the entrance, becoming wedged in the opening. Dragon carcasses accumulated at the single point of exit like cordwood, completely preventing any possibility of egress. In a vain attempt to assert her dominance and find a means of escape, the Queen vomited forth a stream of burning bile that quickly encompassed the entire rookery. Everything the phosphor came in contact with instantly burst into flames. The caverns became a literal hell on earth with fire and smoke and unbearable heat accompanied by the wailings of both man and beast. *Uglebdek* himself would have sought respite from this chaotic otherworldly incinerator.

THE SHRIEK OF A DRAGON echoed across the sea, loud and mournful like a funeral dirge. Quoregg jumped to his feet and ran to the bow to try to get a better look. A second roar and then a third followed. Straining to see, what appeared to be fireworks erupted from the top of the mountains. Something was happening and it did not appear to be good. Quoregg stared, anxiously attempting to decipher what was going on. He could only pray that his friends were fine, but the sound of dragons and the sight of flames did not bode well.

IN THE DISTANCE, THE agony of the rookery could be heard, wafting in on the evening breeze accompanied by the fetid odor of death. Like the howl of a wolf high on the mount, the roar of the beasts within emanated from the once-gaping maw of the catacombs, stifled by the dead bodies that blocked the way, but still clearly audible. Their torment could be heard by the Tendiran troops both at sea and on land for what seemed like hours, the volume slowly decreasing until only the occasional muffled shout could be heard. Zephraim's plan had, obviously, been a success. How successful would not be known until a later time.

THE PUTRID STENCH OF burning flesh filled every corner of the cave system. Lord Roga's chambers were no exception. Behind the closed door to his chambers could be heard the results of his developing rage. The breaking of glass, the smashing of wooden tables and shelves, the thumping of fists on the walls and the near-constant bellows of outrage.

Within the room, books and papers littered the floor. Two tree dragons clung ferociously to their log perch, desperate to blend into the wood. A fishbowl lay in pieces on the floor, smashed as it impacted the wall during Roga's fit of rage, water enveloping the shards, numerous scaled bodies flopping aimlessly on the floor.

"How could anyone choose to bring harm to such regal creatures!" he screamed, not truly expecting an answer. "What sort of depraved monster does such a thing! Cowardly, insolent degenerates!"

As Roga proceeded to rant, Minarik stood motionless, staring helplessly at the fish on the floor, opening and closing their mouths, frantically trying to suck life-giving oxygen from the dry air with their gills. He dared not move to help them for fear of becoming the focus of his master's rage.

"I want every guard that survived the fire brought to me at once! I want an explanation of what happened!"

"Yes, My Lord!" Minarik took full advantage of the order and quickly excused himself from Roga's office.

"They will pay for their ineptitude!" Roga hissed through his teeth as he shifted the weight of one foot from the heel to the ball, unwittingly crushing a goldfish beneath his boot with a nauseating *pop*.

Minarik knew the warlord's furor would subside with time, so he would take his time gathering the guards for their interrogation. If he were to present them to the warlord in his current condition, heads would literally roll. The Master was not very accepting of events that did not follow his plans. This blow was definitely NOT according to plan.

Minarik approached Octrall in the hall. "The Master wants all the guards that survived the attack to appear before him. Gather them together in the barracks and call for me. I will prepare them for what is sure to come. Haste will not be to their advantage, but we cannot make him wait too long or he shall surely become infuriated again. We want to allow him time to calm his anger, but not so much time that he angers again."

Octrall clicked his heels. "Understood. I will gather them as you requested." He headed off into the catacombs.

THE SNAP OF A TWIG brought all men's eyes to the edge of the trees, alert and ready to defend. The attack and deathly screams that had come from the mount had everyone hyper-vigilant. Swords raised as a branch moved aside, a hand and an arm becoming visible and then a face, smudged in soot. It was Ahna! Immediately behind, Zephraim. They had returned!

"It is done," Ahna announced, a white, toothy grin gleaming against her blackened face. "And from the sounds and the smells coming from the mountain, I can only assume the results were as much as we could ever ask for."

Elden and Conor and the rest quickly gathered around them, exchanging handshakes and hugs and slaps on the back. To a man, Ahna was welcomed back with admiration and respect. Conor spoke up above the clamor to quiet them for a moment.

"Ahna, Zephraim, if any of us ever doubted your abilities or your importance to this mission, you have given us pause for thought. Your actions tonight prove that we all have important parts to play in this, and certain physical attributes or mindsets do not prove useful for every circumstance. You have proven yourselves tonight and your contribution to this fight will not be forgotten. I believe I speak for all when I offer my gratitude and respect. We can view you as nothing more than equals from this day forth."

A cheer rose up from the group.

"Enough of the merriment," Elden interjected. "It is time for us all to come back to reality. We are still at war and there will most definitely be a battle ahead. We must call for the others to make landfall and under the cover of darkness. Tonight, before the sun rises, we should send a message that they make preparations. Enjoy this moment, but realize we have only won this battle, not the war."

24
PREPARING FOR BATTLE

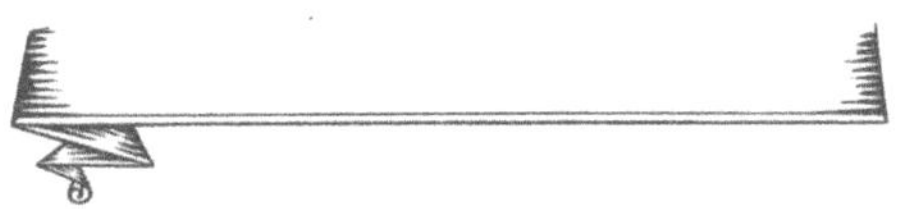

ROGA SAT AT HIS DESK. His rage had finally subsided. Minarik's diversion had functioned as expected. The Master's temper was not as strong when he addressed the guards and no one was executed. Now it was time to prepare a counterattack.

Minarik approached the warlord from behind, stopping just behind him and to the right. He coughed to signal his presence.

Roga spoke without acknowledging his trusted assistant. "How many were lost?"

His assistant questioned him. "Men or dragons, my lord?"

"Both. It cannot be expected that one survives without the other, can it?"

"No, my lord, I should think not. As far as the dragons are concerned, three remain in the caverns. Seven are unaccounted for, assumed to have flown away. Whether or not they will be found or will return on their own is unknown. The remainder have perished, some trampled at the ledge opening while they attempted to escape the smoke in the caverns, many others exterminated when the queen reacted to the situation. We are hard at work to remove the carcasses. A respectful internment is planned. The men fared much better. We have twelve known missing and three hundred and seventeen known dead. That leaves seven hundred and forty-two men, either in the caverns or on the ground."

Roga sat in silence for a moment, staring blankly into nothingness. This was a loss he did not take lightly. Never in his wildest dreams had he expected the Tendirans to be able to exact such a terrible blow to his forces with as few as a score of men. Hundreds of dragons had perished, a number beyond his comprehension. There had been one disadvantage to the safety and shelter provided by the caverns and Tendirans had exploited it. It had come at a great cost.

Minarik broke the silence. “Master Oran survives. He was a pillar of strength during the mayhem that ensued during the attack, my lord. His attempts to calm the beasts and rally the men together were admirable. His actions may not have had much effect upon the results, but he was willing to sacrifice his own life for the security of the rookery. You would be proud of him, my lord.”

Roga turned to face his trusted servant, head cocked slightly, one eyebrow raised. A moment passed.

“Will there be anything else, my lord?”

Roga looked at him, suddenly and strangely sentimental. “It would appear that your opportunity to ride may have been taken from you by those filthy bastards, Minarik. There are not enough beasts for you to imprint upon and establish a pairing, I fear. As soon as things have settled a bit, we will need to find this band of vermin and exterminate them. I want a few scouting parties organized to ensure they can be located. Then, we will attack!”

"It shall be as you wish, my lord." Minarik turned to leave but stopped before closing the door and leaned back into the room. "My lord, do not despair for my lost opportunity to ride. Once the Tendirans have been dispatched, surely my opportunity will present itself. I have faith in your abilities, as a leader, as a warrior. You will rise above this and, with you, our people. We have not come this far to be beaten back so easily."

Minarik left his master, quietly closing the door behind him.

Roga sat silently in his chair for a moment, trying to process everything his faithful servant had brought to his attention. Barely audible, he whispered, “You shall ride, my most loyal companion. Your time to ride will come.”

BY THE COVER OF AN overcast evening sky, scores of Tendiran vessels made their way to the shore. The weather had provided the perfect cover at the most advantageous time. The Khorgians were still reeling from the smoke attack on the caverns and were not in the mental state necessary to be hyper vigilant. Each ship offloaded all but a minimal crew, along with weapons and supplies. A flurry of activity on the beach followed, toting the cargo to the concealment of a sparsely wooded area, thinned by the constant sea spray, a few hundred yards off the shoreline. Elden watched intently, supervising the operation, carefully gauging the materiel and manpower that was present as well as the time remaining to sunrise. Everything had to be in hiding and the ships back to sea before the first light.

Quoregg approached. "Not to bring bad fortune to this mission, but it would appear things are going quite to plan, Elden."

"Agreed, Quoregg. We need to maintain this pace if we expect to offload everything and everyone before the sun rises, though. We cannot afford to trip up anywhere. Do you estimate enough cover in the woods to hide us all?"

"The trees should afford some cover for everyone. It is not the perfect place to hide, but it will have to do for now."

"Make sure the men arrange themselves in units as they disembark. Being more organized from the beginning will help to maintain order and facilitate our attack. The Khorgians are in disarray, and we need to strike before they can regain composure. I want to be fully prepared for battle before the sun is high."

"As you wish, Master Elden. I will see to it." Quoregg turned to attend to his task.

Elden called back to him. "Quoregg!"

"Yes, Master."

"Quoregg, you and Conor have done an admirable job with these men. You fashioned a fine army from nothing in an exceedingly short time. I would feel comfortable leading them into any battle and am confident of their ability to defend our land and my life. You should be proud."

"Thank you, sir. From you, such words carry the full weight of truth. You can count on me and these fine men to give their all for you and the defense of our homeland."

"I have no doubt about that. Let's get ready in preparations for the day. Our destinies await."

Quoregg turned once again and headed towards the beach, directing his men into action. Like a perfectly choreographed tango, two ships would land to be unloaded while the previous drifted back into the sea and the next slowly glided in from behind. The offloading became quicker and quicker as the number of men increased with each vessel's landing. Baskets of food and casks of morel, a mixture of mead and water used for sea voyages to prevent spoiling, waterborne parasites, and illness, made their way to the trees along with crates of weaponry and armor. Each man quickly found his unit and gathered only the supplies they would require for the next day. All excess was placed in a hidden location for later use.

Elden and Quoregg watched with great relief as the last ship drifted back to sea, far ahead of dawn.

"That is the last of them, Master Elden, and with time to spare."

"Use that time well, Commander. Ensure everyone is well organized and prepared for battle. I fear the moment of confrontation is nigh. Do your best to get everything under cover. Once we are found out, we will lose any advantage of surprise. Depending upon how successful the smoke attack was, the Khorgians certainly outnumber us easily two to one."

THE SCOUT STOOD NERVOUSLY before Roga's desk, wringing his hat in his hands, and quietly shuffling his feet. Roga looked up at him and the two locked eyes.

"Are you sure about this?"

The scout stammered. "Y... yes, my lord. Very sure. They have assembled just northwest of the Dordurn Plain. Scores of them, maybe hundreds, hidden in the forest, heavily armed and organized. I have seen them myself."

Roga was incredulous. "How? Where did they all come from? They multiply like vermin copulating in a grain bin. Our intelligence concluded there were not more than a single score of men as early as two days hence."

"There is evidence of a large disturbance overnight on the western shoreline, footprints and drag marks, but we have yet to locate a single vessel, even out to sea. It would be foolish to believe that the Tendirans are some form of mermen, so some manner of seaworthy transport must have been employed."

"Whatever form of transport they utilized matters little now. Somehow the Tendirans have amassed a formidable army upon our shore, right under our noses. They have annihilated our aerial offensive capabilities by their cowardly attack on our dragons. It is time we regain the advantage once again." Roga stood up from his chair and began pacing the room. The scout stood motionless, tracking the warlord's movements to the extent his eyes could follow without moving his head. "The Tendirans are surely quite full of themselves, having scored a few easy victories, but the Khorgians shall retake the advantage. Take a message to Octrall. Have him assemble the men as land forces in preparations for battle in the forests east of the Dordurn. We may still be capable of surprising the Tendiran warrior and his little army." Roga turned to face the scout. "What are you standing there for? Quickly! Be off! And tell the Marshall to send Oran to my study immediately. Surely he will wish to be informed of our plans."

The scout stumbled over himself as he rushed to get out the door. The sound of his footsteps running down the hall echoed and drifted off. Roga sat on the corner of his desk contemplating strategy for the attack. He reached back behind for something and, finding it not there, turned to scan the top of his desk. His shoulders fell, remembering his fishbowl was no longer there. Sheepishly, he called for his aide.

"Minarik!"

Near instantly, the door to his office opened. "You called, my lord?"

Roga sat quietly for a moment, staring ominously at nothing, a blank look on his face. Without acknowledging his aide, he quietly spoke as if a child.

"I need more fish."

"ORAN, THE TENDIRANS have managed to amass an army on our shores west of the Dordurn Plain, from all accounts numbering in the hundreds. I would say that your swordsmanship skills will be put to the test. Are you prepared to do battle?"

Oran sat across the desk from Roga, blackened and blistered skin evident on one side of his face, up and down both arms, and on his hands. A bare patch stood like a beacon on the side of his head where dark hair once sprouted.

"I am as prepared for battle as any one remaining in the caves. My injuries are superficial, and I am still breathing and vertical. I am prepared to stand beside every other Khorgian warrior as one of them until the last breath flows across my lips. These are my people, now, and I intend to support them in every way that I can."

"Without question, you are one of us now, and I would proudly consider you as an offspring. The riders are gathering in preparation for an attack. I would like you by my side when the fighting begins. Go. Gather your gear and report with the rest of the men. We will find a tactical position by cover of the pre-dawn hours. Today we engage the enemy for the protection of Khorgia!"

THE DORDURN PLAIN LAY west of the Khorgian Mountain Range, bordered by a thick forest between. A sparsely forested seaside rise edged by ledge and cliffs as the coastal border moved southward. The plain itself was a patchwork of grassy flats and knolls interspersed amongst rocky outcroppings and gravel rises. Patches of sea grass and small bushes dotted the land. Every aspect of terrain was represented in this relatively confined area. A small hill rose from the grass just east of the central meadow, providing an excellent view of the entire plain.

Hundreds of Tendirans had encamped in the thin coastal tree line overnight, quietly awaiting the morning light and the call to battle. Nearly twice as many Khorgians had made their way down from their mountain home in the early hours of the morning, amassing under cover of the foothill forest. Oddly, neither army was surprised by the other's presence. The hiding and waiting were mere posturing, more a means to raise tensions to the breaking point than a necessity. That and the fact that neither commander wanted to expose the size of his army and lay their cards on the table first. Sooner or later, someone would have to budge.

The hazy sun rose and hung heavy in the sky, a portent of the ensuing clash of humanity expected at any moment. Every so often, a slight sea breeze rolled quietly across the plain, stirring the shin-high grass and small brush as it went. Just beyond the sparse tree line at the seaward side, the Tendirans gazed out through the cover of the leaves. Quoregg and Elden scanned the plain and the trees beyond for any sign of the enemy. Entry into the open plain would quickly expose them and the size of their army, an action that, if not executed at the right time, would certainly play right into the Khorgians' hands. Carefully seeking inconsistencies in the trees, Quoregg estimated the size of the Khorgian army.

"I estimate somewhere around twice as many men as we. I suspect those numbers will balance out the hand-to-hand skills they surely lack as a primarily aerial military. And I make out no dragons. That would suggest the smoke attack was more than successful. If we can quickly take advantage of our skills, we may just steal the balance of power. Do you agree?"

"Agreed, Quoregg. Send the word out to be prepared. We will rush from the trees on my order. Archers to the rear, but they should not expend their quarrels before we have engaged. We need to save as much firepower as possible for the later stages of battle, or if we have overestimated our smoke attack and the dragons are still in play. Tell them to let fly only when their quarry is certain. I will give the order after each unit has responded."

Quoregg relayed the message along the front line in a barely audible whisper. Minutes passed as the anxiety grew thick and heavy in the still air. Elden and Quoregg waited patiently. The heartbeats of every man within earshot were nearly audible. A whispered response returned. All the Tendiran troops were prepared, awaiting the call to...

"***ATTACK***!!"

The coastal tree line burst into an explosion of humanity as the Tendiran army charged onto the plain.

25

THE GREAT BATTLE

NEARLY FOUR HUNDRED Tendiran warriors charged onto the Dordurn Plain, a battle cry emanating from every throat. Feet pounded the ground, weapons beat at the air, and armor creaked and clashed. The sound was deafening, rolling out ahead of the advancing army like a tidal wave. The Khorgians calmly awaited their adversary on the opposite side of the vast open space, carefully hidden behind a tree line and a rock outcropping. Confident in their substantial numerical advantage, the marshals held back their forces, hopeful that the charge across the plain would tire the enemy and make them an easier quarry. Fighting as a foot soldier was an unfamiliar task for the majority of the Khorgian forces, always relying heavily on the dragons to handle the enemy from above the ground. This would be a very different fight.

A cloud of dust billowed up in the wake of the advancing Tendiran soldiers, following them like a shadow and obscuring the sea behind them from sight. As the Tendirans edged ever closer, the Khorgians continued to remain still, their numbers hidden behind the tree line, patiently awaiting the order to attack.

Roga commanded his forces to hold steady. "Wait for my signal! Wait for it!"

As the Tendirans approached the tree line at the edge of the plain, a shouted command came from the forward position as Roga released his army, and all of nearly eight hundred Khorgian soldiers erupted from the trees, charging headlong at the advancing enemy. Within the matter of a few moments, the two sides met with a great clash and clamor of metal, as swords and shields and armor of one army were brought to bear upon that of the other. The Khorgians were far less proficient with their weaponry, but close quarters combat and sheer numbers played heavily to their advantage. If a Tendiran dispatched one Khorgian, there was likely another behind to take his place. The dust cloud kicked up by the charge quickly caught up with the Tendirans and enveloped the point of attack, obscuring all but the closest of objects, friend and enemy alike. The fighting continued as the dust storm wafted through, neither side missing an opportunity to use the limited visibility to gain an advantage.

INTENSE HAND-TO-HAND combat in close quarters proved devastating to both sides. The air was soon thick with the smell of death, the ground covered with blood and bodies, some struggling to survive, others given way to the promiscuous hand of death. The Dordurn Plain had quickly become a red, swampy cauldron of slaughter.

As the number of combatants decreased through attrition, more room for engagement led to an intensified battle. A quick shiv up under the ribs was replaced with blocking shields and parrying swords. What had initially been no more than a massive rugby scrum now became a brutally truculent ballet, warrior circling warrior, deftly sidestepping a corpse or puddle of blood to find a secure foothold. The roar and murmurs evolved into a more orchestrated opera of metal clashing against metal, timed by the percussion of shields blocking weapons, and punctuated by the staccato of arrows jetting through the air with some ultimately finding their mark. The deadly opera of battle was being belted out in full voice.

FROM BEHIND THE TREES, as the dust cloud dispersed, a single dragon erupted into the sky with an ear-piercing screech. Perched on its shoulders was Minarik, Roga's trusted assistant. The warlord had promised him the opportunity to ride and afforded him one of the few dragons to survive the smoke attack. Without the normal opportunity for rider to imprint upon his beast, the union of the two was tenuous at best. Many of the

Tendirans hesitated at first, fearing the waves of aerial assailants they had become accustomed to, but were quickly relieved when they saw but one dragon in the sky. Even under the less-than-proficient direction of Minarik, the attack of a dragon could wield a heavy toll on the warriors below. He nudged and coaxed his reluctant aerial steed in an erratic flight above the battlefield, occasionally managing to coax his ride to vomit a burst of flaming bile onto the armies below. Although not skilled in the arts of aerial warfare, just his presence above, flitting about like a honeybee zigzagging from flower to flower, was enough to keep many of the Tendirans and Khorgians on edge, turning one eye to the sky as they came face-to-face with the enemy on the ground.

ZEPHRAIM MOVED WITH a flight of archers from the rear of the Tendiran attack. He required the room to utilize his rope dart, so being in the midst of the initial attack made no tactical sense. Only after the initial crush began to disperse did he move forward, keeping five to ten yards of space between himself and the onslaught of Khorgian warriors. He carefully targeted his quarry and, with a subtle flick of his wrist, launched his deadly projectile. Each target was caught completely by surprise, not expecting an attack from a short distance. His first victim stared cross-eyed at the dart as it struck the bridge of his nose, a look of total astonishment glazed over his face, a trickle of blood dripping along the side of his nose and across his lip. Zephraim snatched the dart back, extricating it from his adversary's skull in one smooth movement. The Khorgian fell to his knees before hitting the ground, face first. The next Khorgian reacted similarly as the dart penetrated his leather breastplate and sternum, piercing his heart. Blood sprayed in bursts through the wound around the dart's flutes like a crimson fountain as the dart made its way back to its owner. Again, and again, Zephraim struck his target, either in the head or torso. Again and again, a shocked and perplexed adversary gazed in disbelief as the dart pierced flesh and bone with fatal results, quickly succumbing to the deadly accuracy of Zephraim's well-practiced aim.

Zephraim's rope dart afforded an additional advantage; by engaging his opponent at a distance, his exposure to the dangers of the blade and hand-to-hand combat was all but eliminated. Most perilous to him were the arrows released by the few archers employed by the Khorgians, but they were infrequent and rather poorly placed. For the most part, Zephraim casually walked his way through the Khorgian lines. So unexpected was his method of attack, nearly every foe he encountered was struck before they understood what was occurring. His unusual weaponry placed the advantage squarely in his hands. The same held true for his unit of dartsmen. Although not as proficient as Zephraim, each had been carefully trained in the weapon's use and had amassed hours of practice. Coupled with the element of surprise afforded by their non-traditional weaponry, the dartsmen were a formidable force on the battlefield, striking down scores of Khorgians before suffering a single loss. It was this uncharacteristic hand-to-hand combat that would quickly reduce the Khorgians' numerical advantage and even up the odds.

AS THE TENDIRAN CHARGE advanced towards them across the plain, Oran felt the surge of adrenaline course through his veins. Finally, a battle of classic nature, man-to-man, face-to-face on the battlefield. This was much more to his liking. Glorious hand-to-hand combat. No more hiding behind the security of a dragon. Their destiny would lie in their own hands now, each man the master of his own fate.

Oran heard Roga's call to advance as the Tendirans reached a small knoll three-quarters of the way across the plain. In unison, the Khorgian army emerged from the edge of the forest, clamoring over a stone outcropping like an avalanche of humanity crashing onto the plain. As the foot soldiers swept onto the battlefield, a small contingent of Khorgian archers, hidden within the forest, let loose a volley of arrows, attempting to scatter the oncoming army.

Oran found himself just behind the initial push, slightly right of the center of the plain. The deafening Tendiran battle cry filled his ears moments before the first combatants clashed. The roar became mixed with the rhythm of marching footsteps, the clatter of metal on metal, and the sickening sound of steel parting flesh. Cries of pain and victory pierced the air, thick with the stench of battle.

Oran engaged his first Tendiran and quickly dispatched him with a sword to the torso, pushing him aside like a sack of wool as he marched forward. Although never classically trained as a warrior, Oran continued to move through the battlefield with the competence and grace of a seasoned veteran, drawing upon his sparring practice with Lord Roga, and the inner strength and physical prowess bestowed upon him by his parentage. Within him, he felt the presence of his Master, Sahk Tett, coursing through his body, bathing him in a calm confidence. He strode along the plain, always making the right move at the right time, offensively and defensively, as if every moment had been carefully rehearsed. Tendiran after Tendiran fell to either side as his sword cut a swath through the battling mass of humanity until no one stood before him. Oran scanned the death-strewn battlefield, seeking out another enemy fighter to engage. It was then he saw him. Elden. He was on one knee, hunched over a recent victim. Here was his chance to eliminate the heart and soul of the Tendirans! What glory would be his!

Oran locked eyes on his quarry and began to work his way towards the Tendiran leader. He roughly pushed aside everything and anything that managed to get in his way without bothering to engage. Anything that resisted was met with a steel blade and quick death. Nearly halfway on his journey to Elden, as he pushed aside another Tendiran warrior, he was strangely compelled to lock eyes with the man. It was Seamus, the watchman!

Oran hesitated a moment, staring intently into the man's eyes, sensing an unknown familiarity with him. Seamus stopped his attack as well, returning the gaze, recognizing the battle-enticed yellow eyes. His own eyes widened, and he shrunk back slightly in fright. For some reason unknown to him, Oran was compelled to let the watchman pass, dropping his weapon to his side, and motioning for him to pass peacefully. Seamus relaxed his own weapon slightly and cautiously made his way past, keeping one eye on the Khorgian soldier. As each turned to continue elsewhere into battle, a queer feeling came over them. Each recognized the strangeness of the moment but also, deep within themselves, the importance. It was a moment of reckoning that was unfortunate enough to be quickly brushed aside by the ensuing battle that surrounded them.

MINARIK STRUGGLED DESPERATELY to hold on to his aerial steed as it lurched and sputtered in the air erratically at the unpracticed beck and command of its novice rider. Even functioning as a less-than-precision battle platform, the dragon still created a distraction for the Tendiran forces below. Minarik successfully coaxed his beast to belch the occasional ball of flame, reminding the troops below that their adversaries still command the air above. Unfortunately, his untrained piloting and targeting skills caused the Khorgian foot soldiers to be as likely a target as the Tendirans, suffering the same effects of the acid bile as it streamed to the ground. The collateral friendly-fire damage was easily offset by his presence overhead. With a dragon in the sky, the Tendirans would still have to remain vigilant.

AS THE TWO ARMIES CLASHED, Roga found himself happily towards the rear. Better those of a lower status absorb the brunt of the initial clash than himself. Far be it for him to take the traditional place front and center of his forces, and put himself at a defensive disadvantage. He was only interested in combat with the elite of the Tendirans, the likes of Elden or possibly the blonde concubine he had foolishly brought to battle. Once his forward forces dispatched the Tendirans, Elden and the whore would be much easier to locate in the melee.

During the fighting, Roga pushed his own soldiers before himself as blocks or shields for protection from the enemy, conserving his energy and keeping his body from harm. It would be much easier to fight when the area wasn't as crowded and he could not be so easily encircled or attacked from his blind side. He clearly had no value for any life but his own. Occasionally, an enemy combatant managed to get around his mortal defenses and Roga was forced to employ his terrestrial military skills. Although unpracticed after years of training on his dragons, Roga was sufficiently skilled in swordsmanship and the arts of warfare to thwart each assault. But this was not the form of combat Lord Roga had grown accustomed to. With each encounter, he became more and more annoyed.

"Vile, tenacious beasts, these Tendirans!" He shouted at his warriors before him. "Stop them! Don't allow them a step closer! You are Khorgian warriors! Do not let these insolent creatures beat you!"

As wave after wave of Tendirans marched upon his shield of warriors, Roga slowly pushed along behind them, occasionally thrusting his sword forward to pierce the flesh of an adversary already engaged with a Khorgian soldier. Eventually, the crowded battlefield began to clear as the swirling hurricane of humanity dwindled, a victim of itself. As his human blockade dispersed before him, Roga found himself wading through a sea of death, occasionally engaging an enemy warrior. As he removed his blade from his latest victim, he looked up to scan the battlefield for his next opponent. It was then that he first saw her. The blonde! Elden's little concubine! He began walking towards her, stepping over the dead and pushing aside comrades and adversaries alike. His sole focus was the female warrior. Nothing else mattered to him at this moment except engaging Elden's lover in battle and vanquishing her. Only the head of Elden himself would be a loftier trophy, and he would seek out the Tendiran warrior as soon as he finished dispatching the girl.

AHNABIN HAD SIMPLY moved with the onrushing horde of Tendiran warriors as it began its charge across the plain. Nearly oblivious to what was happening around her, she found herself unconsciously whisked along by the river of humanity. Her mind and body had taken control of her actions, innately performing the motions required to attack and defend out of sheer repetition on the training fields of the Tantallon Forest. As Ahnabin regained conscious control of her actions, she noticed the bright red on her blade. She had evidently meted out her own fair share of revenge on the Khorgians during the hazy early moments of the siege. But as the battle drew on, she would need her wits as well as her reflexes to stay alive. This would be her moment to show the mettle she was made of. She would make her father proud.

Wielding her special-made sword before her, Ahna purposefully marched ahead, battling every warrior she encountered with the fervor of a berserker. Her blade whistled as it cut through the air, creating melodic eddies as the atmosphere wove its way through the holes in the hollowed blade. The sound often distracted her opponent, so unlike anything else heard on the battlefield. Even more distracting than her weapon was her appearance. A female on the battlefield was never heard of. When her visage filled the eyes of her adversaries, there was a moment of disbelief that offered her a distinctly favorable position, a position that she took full advantage of, carving a path through the throng. She had truly become a warrior, not afraid to profit from any situation that presented itself as advantageous. Each fallen Khorgian boosted her confidence and made her feel all the more powerful and capable. This was her time; she was the master of the moment.

In the middle of the bloodied battlefield, she saw him. The Khorgian Warlord. His eyes were trained upon her like a jackal lining up his prey for the kill. The blood of his vanquished adversaries spattered his uniform, like a grotesque trophy. A perverse smile was chiseled into his face. She was most definitely chosen as his next target, and she prepared to engage him. Roga was casually but intentionally walking towards her, set on his quarry, oblivious to the death that surrounded him. She prepared herself for this battle.

THEY SQUARED OFF ON a small knoll, slightly elevated above the remainder of the battlefield like a stage, which suited Roga just fine. This was to be a confrontation of epic proportions and he wanted it to be center stage. What would happen during this particular conflict could quite possibly be the defining point of the entire siege.

He continued walking toward her, his sword in his right hand by his side. As he approached her, he smiled and addressed her, feinting as slight bow. “Ah! The golden boy’s little slut! Let me introduce myself. I am Roga, the Khorgian Warlord. It will be such a pleasure to offer you a slow tortuous death and let your souteneur witness your agony before I do the same to him!” He drew his sword up in one fluid motion to engage her, bringing it quickly down upon her. Ahnabin skillfully defended the blow with her own blade, steel clashing against steel. Using the momentum of his attack, she deflected his weapon to the side and nimbly wheeled around into a defensive posture.

Roga laughed sarcastically. "I see the courtesan fancies herself a dancer. Dancers and pretty little whores have no place on the battlefield. Before I am done with you, you will wish you had never left the comfort of your lord and master's bedding."

Ahnabin advanced, her blade like a windmill, slashing four times at Roga. "You fancy me a whore, do you? Well, not only will I prove myself a woman and a warrior to you, I will assert my superiority over such a useless and cowardly excuse for a man, the likes of which you are."

Roga pushed each stroke of Ahna's blade off almost nonchalantly. "A warrior? I have endured fiercer attacks from the likes of a mosquito and its whining in my ears was far less annoying than yours."

"And like that mosquito, I shall draw from you your life-giving blood." Ahna swung hard, waist high, as Roga deftly jumped back, barely missing his mid-section. "You shall feel my sting yet."

Ahna pressed forward, relentless in her attack. Each lunge was quickly followed by another and then a strike from above or the side. She easily struck four or five times for every counter from the warlord. She was definitely the aggressor in this fight.

"Feisty little bitch. Are you only your master's whore or are you shared for the entertainment of all the troops? It would seem you possess the energy required to satisfy them all."

Ahna felt her blood boiling within. She had heard all she wanted to hear from this disgusting arrogant ass, but she could not let it show. She could sense he was well trained, not only in the intricacies of warfare but also the fine art of reading a person from their reactions. If he sensed he was having an effect upon her, getting into her mind, he would find a way to use it to his benefit. She would not give him any sense of superiority, even if his outward appearance was that of supreme confidence.

"If I were you, I would be more concerned with how my energy will wear down an old man like yourself, driving you closer to defeat."

Roga ducked a straight thrust, Ahna's blade whistling past his ear.

"Even your weapon whines like a bitch in heat as it sweeps through the air. A male warrior would never abide the use of a sword that whistles a lullaby during the throes of battle. Even more reason women should remain at home, ready to submit to the victorious warriors that return to them, or to those that conquer their men in battle."

Ahnabin quickly jabbed back at Roga's head.

"Any strong, confident woman would strip you of your testes before allowing herself to become servile to the likes of you, that is if she could find them. Men like yourself choose to be arrogant and self-serving to compensate for their obvious deficiencies in other areas. Are you displeased with your lack in the manhood department?"

Roga managed an offensive thrust in answer to her slight on his manhood.

"I remember my mother having a lap dog like you. The little bitch was all mouth and nipping at your heels. Nothing a swift kick couldn't easily get rid of." Roga lifted his foot and kicked her in the stomach, pushing her backward. Ahnabin stumbled but quickly regained her footing. She had to focus on his movements and not be distracted by his words. She had to be prepared for his tactical style, as well. Certainly, Roga was not averse to using less-than-honorable tactics. His concern was merely victory, not a chivalrous battle.

Undeterred by Roga's constant chatter and dirty tactics, Ahna fought on, sizing up her moments as the battle endured, carefully choosing when to attack and when to defend. Each successful strike or defense goaded at his ego. He was letting her prowess get the better of him and retaliated verbally.

"I fail to see how such a scrawny headstrong wench as yourself has attracted the attentions of a valiant warrior the likes of your man. Maybe it's your boyish appearance that makes his blood boil. It wouldn't surprise me in the least if he were to fancy the likes of little boys." Roga chuckled.

"How dare you! Elden is far more a man than you could ever wish to be. And his affections towards me are beyond anything you could ever comprehend. I suspect there is no fairer sex waiting impatiently in the catacombs for you to return. A heart so vile lacks the ability of attraction."

"Ah! Elden, is it? Now I have a name to put with his face when I meet him in battle and when I recall the story of my victory with my colleagues and their families. Perhaps I will carve his name on a stone to mark the place of his demise. Every deceased warrior deserves a monument."

Their fighting intensified, sparks flying as steel struck hard against steel, ringing out as if singing the notes of a Gomerran death song, Ahna's blade whistling in accompaniment. Thrust met counter and riposte followed parry, again and again, as the two remained fully engaged.

Their battle finally brought them in close proximity, each grappling quickly with the other. They stood, nose to nose, staring at one another, arms and swords entangled between them.

Roga stared directly into her eyes. She could feel his hot breath on her face. "I hope you are well prepared to die."

"It will take more of a man than you'll ever be to outmatch the likes of me, you filthy murderous beast!" Ahnabin spat in his face.

Roga pushed her away, freeing his arms and sword, quickly wiping the spittle from his face with his sleeve and followed with a lunge. Ahnabin deflected his attack and sidestepped around him, positioning herself for the next assault.

"Ah! You are a nimble little bitch, aren't you? I'm sure your master finds your gymnastics particularly pleasurable in the sack."

Ahnabin defended his thrust. "If you must know, he is not my master, but my equal, and he finds everything about me pleasurable."

"Oh, I'm sure he does!" Roga let loose with a little laugh.

"Your heart and mind are infected, perverse and malevolent."

"My heart and mind and soul radiate with the confidence and strength of a warrior. If that is perverse or malevolent, then so be it. Those that are weak, bullied, and pushed around shall always fall to those that are confident, dominant leaders. Only the strong survive, little girl. The weak get pushed aside as will soon be your fate."

This was the most protracted of any skirmish either had engaged in during the entire battle. With no rest, the effects of constant combat were beginning to show. Sweat beaded up on Roga's brow, trickling down his face and releasing into the air with every blow. He found himself circling his quarry, taking a more defensive approach, and allowing his body to rest as he sought out an opening. Each attack was now not much more than a short burst or even a single well-placed thrust. How much more important was it now that he had spared himself the aggravation of becoming occupied in skirmishes in the earlier stages of the battle. Had he done otherwise, he might have already succumbed to the youthful energy of Elden's little wench.

Ahna's hair stuck to her face from perspiration. Her arms felt heavy, and every muscle burned from exertion. She struggled to hide the effect this fight was having on her body. Using the same grit and persistence she had during her training back in the Tantallon Forest, she pushed herself through the pain. She had made it this far, proven her worth and abilities to her comrades, and was now in combat with the leader of the Khorgian people, the leader of the dragon raids that had taken her father away from her. Her opportunity to avenge his death was nigh and she would not allow fatigue to take this chance away from her.

The two continued to dance in a spiral, closer and closer, each watching for an opening to strike, conserving what remained of their energies. Both lunged at precisely the same moment and, again, Ahnabin and Roga found themselves in a clinch. Roga took advantage of the opportunity to compose himself and catch his breath. She was a far more resilient and formidable adversary than he had ever considered. He would need to unnerve her somehow to gain the advantage. Keeping their weapons and arms entangled, he pulled her as close as he could. "Maybe I should try some for myself and see what Elden finds so satisfying about you." He stuck out his tongue and licked her, leaving a trail of spittle on her cheek. Ahnabin wrenched her head back in disgust. Roga laughed smugly at her reaction, but his laughter was short lived as a knee squarely found his groin, knocking the breath out of him. He released his grip and Ahnabin took advantage and pulled away. Roga hunched over, trying desperately to regain his composure and his breath.

"I see that a female warrior possesses one particular advantage you men shall never have. Unlike you, I will never become a victim of my manly bits."

Sensing a sudden strategic edge, she prepared to deliver the fatal blow. She raised her steel to shoulder height and slashed at the back of Roga's head.

But the warlord recovered much more quickly than she had expected. He caught her off guard as he defended her strike by blocking it with his own blade. Then, standing swiftly, with two hands, he quickly spun his sword around hers, torquing the pommel from her grip and disarming her. Ahnabin watched as the blade pinwheeled away from her, a shrieking whistle chasing it through the air. Roga swiftly moved towards her.

"It sounds like even your weapon is screaming surrender. I would suggest you do the same. Beg me for your life, you little wench!"

"Never!"

Roga slashed his sword at her and she sidestepped, deftly avoiding the blade.

"Think hard, little whore. Maybe now is the time to beg, to offer up your body to me in exchange for your life. Your stamina and agility are impressive and have strangely brought me to wanting for a little taste."

Ahnabin kicked Roga in the side of the knee, staggering him again. "I am no man's whore, least of all yours!" She jumped out of the way, again, as Roga grabbed at his knee. "And I would never give you the pleasure, not that you could manage, you impotent coward!"

Roga screamed and lunged at her. "Foul little bitch! We will see who the coward is!" He slashed at her again, barely missing her as she moved to avoid his blade once again. "My pleasure will be in seeing you die! Your scrawny little ass would provide no more than a very uncomfortable ride. That has no appeal to me."

Roga feinted a lunge, but came across low with his foot, catching Ahnabin by surprise and tripping her up. She fell hard to the ground, striking the back of her head. For a moment, everything went fuzzy, but, keeping her wits, she rolled away from his strong side.

"Right where you are most comfortable, I see. Rolling around on the ground. Although I'm sure you must feel rather overdressed." Roga laughed as he chased her down. With no weapon and no time to scramble to her feet, Ahna was trapped. Her mind quickly evaluated her options. Whatever she would do would have to be quick, as Roga possessed a distinct advantage.

Roga quickly made up the space between them. He hovered over her like a vulture, legs straddling her body, hands clasped on the hilt of his sword high above his head, the point facing down towards her chest. Winded from the battle, he hesitated for a moment, reveling in apparent victory.

"I cannot begin to tell you how much pleasure this moment brings to my heart! Your defeat and ultimate death will energize my being, and the effect it will have on your dear Elden will work well to my advantage."

Roga raised his hands higher above his head, preparing to thrust his sword into Ahnabin, claiming another victim. "Take one last look around before you die. See how futile your attempts to stop us have been. How many of you Tendiran scum lay dead upon this battlefield?"

As he reversed direction, bringing the sword point downward, Ahnabin quickly rolled to her right. Roga's sword struck the rocks that were previously beneath her with a flash of sparks. But what caught his eye was a different flash. As she had rolled and repositioned to a crouching pose, Ahnabin had removed Eron's small dagger from its hiding place in her vest. The well-polished blade glistened in the fading sunlight. Like a lightning bolt, it flashed up at Roga, finding its mark across his throat. He released his grip on his sword, which clattered to the ground, and brought both hands to his neck. Bright crimson seeped from between his fingers. He stared down at Ahnabin in total disbelief. He opened his mouth to utter one last cynical witticism, but only bright red liquid flowed from his lips. He dropped to his knees as his life drained through the wound. Ahnabin rolled to the side, out of his reach, just in case he had enough strength to muster one final attempt on her life.

"I avenge the death of my father and the hundreds of other fathers lost to your hands. Let my voice be the last thing you hear and impress upon your pathetic and misguided soul. I am no man's whore! I am a woman warrior! Take that truth with you to *Uglebdek* himself!"

Roga's blank stare remained focused straight in front of him. He teetered forward slightly, his motion hanging in space for a moment before falling face first to the ground, his body bouncing slightly before coming to rest beside the sole meadow flower left untrodden on the battlefield, the impact startling a single honeybee from within the petals. This battle was now over.

A DARK FIGURE ON A bier in a cave far, far away snapped open its bright yellow eyes in a sudden moment of disbelief. The leader of the movement had been taken away, lost forever. The voiceless, motionless figure sobbed silently in its own mind. A faithful servant and diligent pupil had given his last breath for the cause.

AHNABIN CRAWLED PASSED Roga's body where she found his blade and picked it up. Using the weapon as a crutch, she pulled herself back to her feet and rested for a moment on the hilt of the sword, trying to catch her breath. Slowly, she raised the sword high above her head with both hands, like a trophy, and let all her emotion pour forth from her body in one thunderous victory cry.

A searing pain entering her lower right side and exiting through her left lung, punctuated her celebration. Had she been hurt more seriously than she thought during the battle with Roga? Looking down, she saw the wavy blade of a flamberge had entered her side. Blood was already flowing towards the hilt. She followed its flow, to the hands that held the sword and scanned up the arms and to the face of the person that had directed it to violate her body and claim her soul.

ELDEN TOOK ON EVERY aggressor he encountered as he made his way across the battlefield. Not being well trained in the intricacies of earth-bound conflict, the Khorgian soldiers were, often, quickly dispatched. It was the sheer numbers of assailants that were nearly overwhelming. Leather-clad Khorgian replaced leather-clad Khorgian like the teeth of a shark, a seemingly endless number of foot soldiers. They approached from the left and the right as well as directly, forcing him to keep his senses heightened to detect any eventuality. Elden faced off against each assailant as they came at him, never looking them in the eye but simply focusing on their weaponry and defenses, analyzing his quarry, and quickly terminating the conflict. He had easily put down two scores of attackers in the first few minutes of battle and they continued to appear, relentless in their commitment to the fight and their master. Elden found himself appreciative of their dedication, but failed to allow emotion to cloud his mind. He would not lose focus on the Tendiran objective of stopping the Khorgian scourge that had devastated the mainland. He was like a machine, sizing up the next antagonist before the lifeless body of the previous reached the ground.

As he paused to catch his breath from the last skirmish, Elden felt a presence over his shoulder. The glint of a sword blade held high above the head of a dark figure entered his periphery. His ears filled with the figure's deep guttural battle cry. Elden reacted quickly, turning to his left and thrusting his sword up into his attacker, piercing leather and mail, following through until the blade exited the far side of the chest cavity. His victim's blood spilled out and down the sword, onto his hands. Exhausted, he did not immediately pull the blade out. He uncharacteristically looked up, into the eyes of his enemy, something he never did, preferring to have the identity of those whose death he had caused remain anonymous. Their eyes met and Elden felt the life's blood within him turn cold. He could now associate a face with this kill, a moment in time that would haunt him forever.

AHNABIN BEGAN TO SLUMP forward, quickly losing her battle to remain alive, Elden's huge flambard run through her body, the gaping wounds pouring forth crimson red. Her eyes met his, a tear forming on her cheek. He stared back at her in horror. She managed a small smile and mouthed an otherwise silent question. "Why?"

Elden released the grip on his blade and caught her in his arms as she fell. Cradling her close, he brushed the hair from her face, rubbing the blood and grime of battle away from her skin. Tears welled up in his eyes. "Wha... what have I done?" Ahnabin grabbed him by the sleeve, staring up into his eyes.

"Please, don't leave me Ahna. What am I to do without you?"

Unable to speak, she struggled to smile despite the pain. She could feel her life slipping away. Mustering all the strength she had within her, she spoke one last time. "It wasn't your fault, Elden. I love you."

"I love you too, Ahna."

Her eyes fluttered and one last breath passed through her lips as she expired in his arms. Elden held her close, sobbing uncontrollably. He was beyond despair. How could this have happened? How could he have killed the woman he loved? A mixture of sorrow and rage flooded his entire being causing him to shake uncontrollably.

Pulling himself together, Elden carefully removed his sword from Ahnabin's lifeless body and began to gently set her down upon the ground when he heard the familiar voice of his mentor, Taygen, echo in his head. "Turn! Now!" Elden responded to the command, re-arming himself with his flamberge and, in one swift motion, turned quickly to defend himself as Oran's sword came down from above.

26
THE GREAT BATTLE ENDS

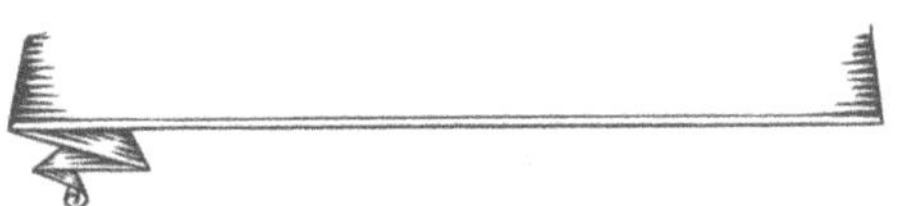

THIS WAS THE BATTLE Oran had been hoping for: he against his cousin, the hero of the Tendiran army, face to face in singular combat. Around them, the main battle was wearing on with no true victor. The clash of metal against metal could still be heard, but the frequency had diminished significantly. Exhaustion was beginning to set in. What would transpire here between these two leaders would determine the victor of the battle and, most likely, dictate whether or not the war would come to an end.

Oran carefully walked up to Elden from behind. A smirk appeared upon his scarred face as he noticed his cousin holding the lifeless body of his lady friend in his arms. He thought, "How perfect. With one swift blow, I can ensure their happiness together in the afterlife." He raised his sword above his head, preparing to deliver the deathblow on the unaware Tendiran warrior. As he began to bring his sword downward, Elden turned, as if in response to some inaudible cue, defending himself against Oran's attack. In shock, Oran was easily pushed away.

Tumbling away from his intended target, Oran righted himself and prepared to face off. "It would appear Tendirans have eyes in the back of their heads. I shall keep that in mind from this point forward."

Elden assumed a defensive posture and waited for the next offensive from his attacker. "Perhaps Khorgians are too clumsy of foot to set a proper sneak attack in motion. You might want to keep that in mind from this point forward as well."

"That may very well be true for Khorgians, but I cannot declare that as my birthright."

All around the two champions, the fighting was coming to a halt. Warriors from both armies were now standing, exhausted, side by side, to watch the battle between their two leaders.

Infuriated by the insult, Oran charged, striking a blow at Elden. The Tendiran skillfully deflected the attack and deftly turned to face his adversary as they both regrouped. Oran approached more slowly this time, carefully contemplating his next move, finally swinging his mighty sword at Elden. A flurry of flashing steel and the clash of metal against metal followed as both paladins attacked and defended. Sparks flew and the dust came up about the two as they circled and engaged each other. Periodically, both men would take a moment to rest and regroup, all the while circling each other in a strategic waltz. Oran, the aggressor, broke each recess with a well-calculated attack and, each time, Elden was up to the task of defending against it.

After several failed attempts to overcome his adversary through swordsmanship and brute force, Oran changed tactics, attempting to gain advantage by engaging Elden's psyche through conversation and compliments.

"You are quite the accomplished swordsman, cousin. I would not have expected anyone capable of handling such a large blade as skillfully as you do. It would seem that prowess in the arts of warfare run in the family."

Elden looked at Oran, confused by what he was saying. Suddenly realizing his inability to comprehend what he had just said, Oran laughed aloud.

"Perfect! How utterly perfect! It appears that you had no idea." A huge smile appeared on Oran's face. "Let me enlighten you on one of the more sordid details of our little family. You are apparently quite ignorant of them. I am your cousin, the bastard child of your mother's twin sister, long since passed from this world, son of the snake demon, Sutek. Our grandmother, the *lovely* Queen Isella, had me cast out of the castle as a newborn, thrown out over the parapet like the contents of a chamber pot and left to die in the wilderness outside the castle walls. But, as you can quite clearly see, the son of a demigod is not so easily disposed of. The creatures of the natural world saved me and brought me to my adoptive family and, ultimately, I arrived here to study under the tutelage of Lord Roga and our master, Sahk Tett." All the while, Oran continued to circle Elden, occasionally sparring with him.

Finally, the truth of the situation hit Elden. "So, this is what Taygen meant by my adversary being one of my own. Not one of my warriors, but of my own family, my own blood." He lunged quickly at Oran, who defended with his sword and stepped deftly to the side.

"Where have you been all these years?"

"I have been to the four corners and beyond. I have slept beneath the stars and huddled in thickets for warmth from the winter wind. I spent my early years with the *borundahli* and have since sought repose with great leaders of men. But, if you truly wish to know where I have been for all these long years, you can follow the trail of my tears."

The two men clashed steel once again, each stepping to the right to avoid the other.

"Tears? You look no worse for wear. Your story sounds no different than any one of a thousand of the men on this battlefield. Everyone is born with their own curse. You are not alone in this."

Oran flushed with anger and lunged. Elden narrowly escaped being pierced by steel.

"Everyone born with a curse? And what curse have you had to endure, cousin? Did the maid fail to fluff your pillow at night? Or did the footman fail to serve your pheasant at the proper temperature? Try surviving on what little you can steal from the royal fields and spending your nights asleep on the ground under a deerskin tent."

"Why did you not come back to the castle?"

"Come back to the castle? For what reason? Our grandmother had me cast out, banished me. I was not welcome as an infant. Why would I even imagine I would be welcomed as a man? I ***will*** return to the castle in due time and my return will be as a victorious conqueror. This time, it will be the lovely Queen Isella that is cast out into the wild!"

Elden blocked a parry from Oran with his shield. "That, dear cousin, will only happen if you can get through me."

"Then I suppose I should stop toying with you and start fighting." Oran stood up straight, took a deep breath, and reassumed a battle-ready pose. "Prepare yourself, cousin. Your time to die has come."

Oran charged his cousin once again. Elden engaged his blade with that of his aggressor, wrapping him up so the two were drawn together, nose to nose.

Deciding it was now time to turn the psychological element to his advantage, Elden began to taunt Oran. "So how am I, a mere mortal, supposed to vanquish the son of a demigod?"

Oran disengaged and pushed Elden away. "Being the offspring of a union between mortal and demon doesn't necessarily guarantee immortality, but rest assured that the demon resides within me. I was not blessed with the supernatural powers of my father, but his contribution afforded me great physical strength, superior stamina, and fierce determination; from my mother, intelligence, and a boundless capacity for learning. Their union imparted the qualities that have made me what I am today, a formidable warrior, the champion of the Khorgian Dragon Guard, and your worst nightmare!"

Oran made another charge at Elden, his blade thrashing through the air like a windmill, pushing his cousin back with every parry. Although on the defensive, Elden was able to deflect every blow while giving only what little ground he thought he could reacquire. Amazed by his cousin's tenacity, Oran took pause to re-evaluate his strategy. This was obviously not going to be a quick victory.

The battle continued, neither gaining more than a moment's advantage. Steel crashing steel, lunges deflected, and attacks defended and countered. The minutes ticked on but neither adversary faltered or tired. Both fighters forged on, fueled by strong will, superior training and skill, and maintained by adrenaline-fed stamina.

After what seemed like hours of impasse, an opening finally presented itself. Elden lost his footing on some loose gravel, slightly losing his balance and his focus. Oran saw the slip and seized the moment of opportunity. As Elden was attempting to regain his balance and composure, Oran lunged at his distracted and unprotected quarry, a primal scream erupting from his lungs, the yellow eyes of his father appearing as his own. His sword entered Elden's chest just below the sternum and ran straight through, exiting just to the left of the spine. Elden let out a gasp and dropped his blade. Oran pulled his sword back out of his cousin's torso. Blood wept from the wound, but not profusely. The blade had somehow missed his vital organs. Gasping, Elden looked down at the wound, then he slowly raised his eyes to meet Oran's. Their gazes locked, and for a moment Oran felt a pang of pity for his cousin.

Sensing this moment of weakness, Elden grabbed the wrist of Oran's sword arm with both hands. Oran struggled to loosen Elden's grip of his wrist, but his cousin held firm. He pushed away and Elden stumbled backward a step. Oran noticed how close to the cliff's edge he had pushed him.

Eyes still yellow with fury, Oran addressed his cousin for what he assumed would be the last time. "Say hello to *Uglebdek* for me. Surely the Master of the Dead has set aside a place for you in readiness." Dropping his sword, he gave one last triumphant push.

"I believe you will have the opportunity to tell him yourself." As Elden allowed his body to go over the edge, Oran realized that the chain mail of his sleeve and gauntlet were entangled in the mail of his cousin. He frantically struggled to free himself, but the dead weight of Elden's body began to pull at him, jeopardizing his balance. Oran teetered on the edge of the cliff, gaining a few inches to his advantage, only to lose the same to the loose gravel beneath his feet. The battle for his balance seemed to last for hours, although it was, in fact, mere moments. Oran struggled to free his armor from his cousin's, while Elden did not struggle at all. He hung like a dead weight, resigned, but at peace, with his fate. His only movements came while addressing his cousin, which he continued to do.

"A very smart man once told me that 'victory shall come through the shedding of your own blood.' I was of the mind, at the time, to believe that the only way to victory was to bear the scars of battle, shedding one's own life's blood to secure victory. I see the true meaning of that statement now. My victory shall come from your death, cousin. You are family, the blood of my blood, and with your death, I shall make my cause victorious." Elden's breathing was becoming labored as the effects of his wounds began to take their toll.

Oran laughed. "And how do you intend to shed my blood, cousin. You have no weapon; you are all but exhausted. You are hanging perilously over the edge of a cliff, a few tangled links of mail temporarily delaying your most certain death. It is only a matter of moments before I disengage the mail, or it breaks under the weight of your body. Either way, your moment has come, not mine. In the end, I shall be the victor."

With his last breath, Elden looked up into his adversary's eyes and smiled. "'Between life and death, good and bad, there is no true victor. For just as life springs forth anew in the birth of all things, death begets the final outcome.' So, the ancient words say. My end has come, dear cousin, and, of your own free will or not, you will join me in it." Elden looked Oran directly in the eyes and smiled. Then his eyes rolled back into his head and his free arm released its grip on Oran's, falling limply to his side.

Unnerved by Elden's last words, Oran finally lost his battle with gravity, breaking his toehold on the edge of the precipice and fell over the edge, into the fog, attached to his cousin to the end.

In disbelief, Tendiran and Khorgian soldier alike lowered their weapons and inched toward the edge of the precipice, crowding one behind the other. To the eyes of those near enough to see over the edge, neither leader was in sight, the location of their fallen bodies obscured by the mist. Looking back on the remainder of the men shaking their heads, it was clear that this battle, and this war, was over. There would be no more fighting today, or in the foreseeable future.

Dusk started to settle in as they began walking away. Tendirans and Khorgians alike gathered amongst their own, all in somber silence. Weapons, valuables, and the bodies of those vanquished were collected as each army slowly went its separate way. There would be no spoils of war after this battle, and no champion's body would be left for martyrdom.

High above the battlefield, a lone dragon flew away towards the horizon, a dark shadow hovering between the two rising moons. The rider did not look back. The last Fire Dragon of Khorgia and its rider disappeared into the night.

IN A DARK UNKNOWN CAVE, an unheard scream echoed in silence. The carefully cultivated plans of the evil one, Sahk Tett, had been dashed. The process of releasing himself and the essence of all evil from the enchanted bonds put in place so many centuries before would have to begin once again, although the taste of evil had been added to the palate of all men; to some, a very bitter medicine to swallow, but, to others, the sweetest elixir of all. It was a taste that would not soon be forgotten by either.

27

A NEW BEGINNING

A PEACEFUL SENSE OF order had once again settled over the land.

In a castle high up on a hill, with an enormous outer palisade hiding everything within from view of the outside world, the occupants were preparing to welcome another life into the kingdom. In the castle keep outside the main sleeping quarters, a young nobleman paced nervously outside the door. Prince Averon impatiently awaited word from within. Inside the room, countless nursemaids and a midwife were assisting his young wife, Princess Myra, with the birth of their first child.

Inside the room, the princess was a fright. She had been in labor for nearly the entire day. Her nightshirt clung to her body, soaked in perspiration. Her hair was matted in places, stray locks stuck to her face by sweat. Leaning forward on the bed and supported from behind by a nurse, she puffed and panted with exhaustion.

"Push, m'lady, bear down and push!"

The princess responded in complete exhaustion, rolling her head back and whining. "I can't. I can't. Please, do not make me do it again. I cannot."

"But, M'lady, you must. Certainly, the baby cannot stay where it is, and I feel quite confident that you do not want it to stay there either. Here, take my hand, grip it firmly, take a deep breath, and *push*!"

"Let the little bugger find its own way out. I have not the strength to continue."

"Shall we tell the babe that you do not care whether it is born or not? Shall we tell your child you care not if it makes it into this world? Is that how you would prefer it?"

"That's not fair. You know I want this child. I am just so tired, so weak. Why do you shame me so?"

"If to shame you I must in order to get you in the proper frame of mind, then shame you I will. The babe must be born and only you can ensure that it happens. You need to push. Are you ready? Can you push some more for me?"

Reluctantly, the princess replied in the affirmative. "Yes, I am ready to push again. But be prepared, for once this child is born, I can assure you I will need plenty of assistance caring for it. And I believe I have a perfect candidate in mind."

The midwife laughed. "You may be exhausted, M'lady, but you haven't yet lost your sarcastic wit. Your child will be well attended to, but first, we need to bring it into the world." She helped the princess into position. "Are you ready? What do you say? Let's make a baby."

"That's what he said to me to get this whole fucking mess started!"

The princess lay back against one of the nursemaids and, grabbing her knees, she pulled herself forward to give one strong push. The pain was almost unbearable, the effort nearly impossible. Puffing and panting followed more pushing until the princess lay back once again, exhausted.

The nursemaid at her head applied a towel to her forehead, desperately attempting to mop up some of the perspiration and keep her cool.

"You are so close, M'lady, so close. Just one or two more pushes."

Princess Myra sat up once again, grabbed her knees and pushed harder than she had yet.

"Ahhhhhhh! It fucking hurts!" Myra, panting, took a moment to catch her breath. "I love you, he said. Let's start a family, he said. All romantic and touchy-feely, whispering sweet nothings in my ear, and making me feel so good, so loved. But he doesn't have to deal with this part!"

"The exact reason this doula never sought the pleasure of a man."

Myra glanced at her nurse incredulously.

"And you decide to tell me this now? Where were you nine months ago?"

The nurse quickly changed the subject to the task at hand.

"Almost there, M'lady, almost there. Push!"

The princess pushed again, with all the strength she had, screaming at the top of her lungs. "It's ripping me in half, like I am shitting a pumpkin!"

The crown of a head appeared, already covered in thin wisps of flaxen hair, then a face. The midwife carefully rotated the baby, exposing a shoulder.

"The head is out! One last hard push, M'lady."

The princess took a few quick short breaths and bore down one last time, pushing the shoulder out followed by the rest of the body in one fluid motion. As the child exited the birth canal, the princess slumped back in sheer exhaustion.

“It’s a girl!”

The nurse at her head patted her forehead down with a towel. "Well done, M'lady, and look, you didn't even tear. A blessing you will be much happier about later, I'm sure."

The midwife deftly tied the umbilical cord off with two pieces of fine silk thread and, with a sharp knife, cut the sinuous cord in half. She wiped the remnants of the birth away with a linen cloth, carefully wiping the eyes and ensuring that the mouth was clear. To the pleasure of everyone’s ears, the baby began to wail loudly.

“Ah, strong and healthy. Ten little fingers, ten little toes and everything else where it belongs. You did a fine job, m’lady.”

As the midwife wrapped the babe and placed it on her mother’s chest, she noticed a movement in her lower abdomen. Palpating the princess’s stomach with her hand, she felt something within. “Merciful Mother! There’s another.”

Exhausted, the princess, newborn in one arm, strained with the other to prop her head up to see the midwife. “Another? Another what?”

“Another child, m’lady. You carry twins.”

“Twins? Another child? No, it cannot be. I could not possibly bear down one more time if my life depended upon it.

“But you must, m’lady. Not only does the life of the little one depend upon it but, indeed, your life as well.”

One of the nursemaids came to retrieve the first-born from her mother. The princess reluctantly released the babe to her, forlorn eyes watching as her child was removed from her view.

With the help of another of the nursemaids, the princess sat up slightly and prepared to push. Exhausted, it was all she could do to muster the strength to sit up. Again, the nurse supported her from behind. She began to feel the telltale pressure below. Pushing herself up into a more seated position, she prepared to begin bearing down. The nurses and midwife coached her through the contractions, instructing her when to push and when to rest.

"Don't fight it, M'lady. You will almost certainly make it worse. Give in to your body and the baby, and it will happen quickly."

The pain was nauseating, pressure rising from her tailbone and radiating through her groin, the accompanying pain like the stabbing of a knife.

"Push again, M'lady, push!"

The princess felt like a wet rag doll, no strength in her arms or her legs, completely soaking in her own sweat.

“Please, princess, you need to push!”

With help, Myra sat once again, and with great determination, brought all her remaining strength to bear upon the babe within.

“I hate him! That inconsiderate bastard! He did this to me! Twice! TWICE! I hate him, I hate him, I hate him!” she screamed at the top of her lungs.

Finally, another head appeared, and with a deft twisting of the infant’s shoulders, another perfectly formed newborn plopped out into the midwife’s hands. Once again, she expertly tied off the umbilical cord and severed the babe’s last permanent connection to its mother.

“It’s another girl!” The midwife quickly cleaned the new babe as the first and wrapped her in a thin silk cloth.

Princess Myra could see that her head was crowned with light wisps of flame-red hair. Redheads were common in her family, so it came as no surprise that her child would be one. Although, it was far from common for a woman to bear twins of both ginger and flax.

As the midwife handed the babe to one of the nursemaids she began to wail. The nurse chuckled while wrapping her in a warm cotton blanket, “I think she prefers the warmth of within.”

“I believe she may just be hungry.” The midwife took the child from the nurse and laid her on her mother’s chest. Still wailing, she began to root around like a tiny pink piglet, trying to find the breast.

One of the nurses took the princess by the hand. “Like this.” She guided her hand, moving her breast and nipple to rub against the infant’s mouth.

Eagerly, the infant took the nipple and began to suckle. As she calmed and settled in to feed, her older twin was brought to take the other breast. As before, the nurse coaxed the first twin to take the nipple as had her sister. While the two newborns engaged in their first feeding outside the womb, the nurses all gathered around to view the sight. Finally, a sense of calm and normalcy had replaced the chaos that had been the birthing room. In unison, everyone in the room expressed relief and joy at the precious sight before them.

"Awe!"

The second born infant, startled at the sound, disengaging from the nipple, and gazed up at the crowd of nursemaids exposing two piercing yellow eyes!

28

BALANCE

AND FROM SISTERS THAT are indeed the same
Both good and evil shall be born.
Each will work to pave the way
For Eyieritu to bring Ahnálian.
Blood shall war against blood
And the victor shall throw open the gates
With fanfare for the New World Order
And all shall begin anew.
Good and evil shall forevermore coexist
In a tenuous balance forever.

No longer would Xerses experience the singularity of ambivalence. The powerful counterweight of evil would once again provide a counterpoint, creating a dichotomy of experiences unlike any witnessed for generations. The words written by the ancients abound with indications of twin sisters playing pivotal roles in the future of Xerses. But which twin sisters do these verses speak of? Are those in one verse identical to those in another? Or do the songs speak of multiple identical pairs?

The birth of a child is but a stage in the cycle of life, a stage that begins a slow journey towards an inevitable death, although death, in and of itself, is but a fleeting moment in time. It is the journey that lasts a lifetime. And even those that might offer no reason but to believe that they have met their demise may indeed find ways to cheat the hand of death. Life and death achieve relevance from but a point of perspective; a position that, if changed, may divulge an unmaterialized reality.

Both Roga and Oran had proven to be formidable adversaries for Elden and the Tendirans, but neither succeeded in establishing a permanent foothold from which evil could gain an advantage. Still, not terribly poor for a first attempt to reach beyond the eternal slumber that was intended to bind evil forever. Cracks had now appeared in the magical vessel that held all evil within. A few seeds planted had germinated but failed to take hold.

When would the next seed be cast and how successful would the next sown be? Only time would provide the answer.

GLOSSARY

AGNES ['ag-nəs] **daughter of the Beekeeper, Zephraim**

ah ['ä] **one**

ahla ['ä-lä] **morning**

Ahláan [ä-'lā-än] **firstborn twin daughter of King Olen and Queen Isella, mother of Elden**

Ahlok ['ä-läk] **Creator, the Father of Creation**

ahlot ['ä-lät] **witch**

Ahnabin ['ä-nä-bin] **daughter of King Maob, often referred to as Ahna**

ahnan ['ä-nän] **beginning**

ahsahn ['ä-sän] **awaken**

ahnemi [ä-'nā-mē] **walk**

Amari [ä-'mär-ē] **king of the Gomerran Kingdom**

antessaran [ȯn-'tes-,är- än] **fir tree**

Aramas [a-'rä-məs] **Khorgian officer in charge of sacking eht Vilna Moht**

arboretum [,är-bȯr-'ē-təm] **of the trees, forest**

Arun ['a-rən] **a member of the Tendiran reconnaissance**

Arvid ['är-vid] **survivor of the Khorgian attack on eht Vilna Moht**

aryatoemi [,är-'ē-at-ō-'em- ē] **a dragon rider that has lost his dragon**

Averon ['av-ər-,än] **husband of Princess Myra**

azulis [a-'zü-lis] **blue**

Benn Garra ['ben 'gär-ä] **cleric from the foothills north of the Souliban**

Berwyn ['bər-win] **lake along the Oryon River**

borundahli [,bȯr-ün-'dä-lē] **nomads**

Braeden [‘bra-den] **cleric whose eternal slumbering body was used as a vessel for all evil**

Conor [‘kän-ȯr] **a member of the Tendiran reconnaissance**

copai [‘kō-pī] **water**

Copaien [kō-‘pī-en] **Rule of the Waters**

Cora [‘kȯ-rə] **wife of the Beekeeper’s the Beekeeper, Zephraim**

Darden [‘där-den] **lord of eht Vilna Moht**

De’Aarna [,dā ‘är-nä] **city on the Tophorus Sea at the mouth of the Oryon River, once known as Korham**

Derrick [‘der-ik] **son of Lord Dolphus**

Dolphus [‘däl-fəs] **lord of eht Vilna Tumehr**

domae [‘dō-mā] **fire** (verb)

Dorian [‘dȯr-ē-en] **a member of the Tendiran reconnaissance**

Ebby [‘eb-ē] **Queen Isella’s best friend and lady-in-waiting**

eeja [‘ē-jä] **before**

eht [‘et] **the**

eis [‘ās] **my**

elāan [el-’ā-än] **star**

Elden [‘el-den] **son of Ahláan**

Elimnem [el-‘im-nem] **cleric from the lands beyond the Oryon headwaters**

Eos [‘ē-ōs] **primary moon of Xerses**

Eroniaetum [‘er-ōn-,ī-et-əm] **the Tendiran armorer, often referred to as Eron**

Eyieritu [ī-,yi-er-‘ē-tü] **chosen, the Chosen**

Ezra [‘ez-rä] **the seamstress**

Friederick [‘frēd-er-,ik] **Lord Roga’s wine steward**

gojabhi [gō-‘jäb-hē] **winds**

Gojabahn [‘gō-jäb-än] **Lord of the Winds**

Gomerra [‘gȯm-ər-ä] **a large flat province at the base of the Silver Mountains**

Gorem the Elder [‘gȯr-em] **cleric from Ukiah**

Gosta [‘gōst-ä] **lake**

Gregor [ˈgre-gōr] **a member of the Tendiran reconnaissance**

Gudtahn [ˈgüd-tän] **God**

Heidel [ˈhī(-ē)-dᵊl] **king of eht Vilna Sahna, father of Olen**

Horace [ˈhȯr-əs] **prince of eht Vilna Copa**

ibu [ˈē-bü] **rise**

ibuta [ˈē-bü-tä] **rising**

ignus [ˈig-nəs] **fire**

Ilsinga [il-ˈsiŋ-ä] **sorceress at eht Vilna Sahna**

Isella [is-ˈel- ä] **queen of eht Vilna Sahna, wife of King Olen, mother of Ahláan and Shahláan**

Jonas [ˈjō-nəs] **tanner in De'Aarna, brother of Mican**

Judah [ˈjü-də] **cleric from the lands beyond the Oryon headwaters**

Kaleb [ˈkā-leb] **fishmonger in De'Aarna**

Khorgia [ˈkȯr-jə] **island east of Tendira, home to the dragons**

konduet [ˈkän-ˌdü-ət] **travel**

Korham [ˈkȯr-ham] **city on the Tophorus Sea at the mouth of the Oryon River, once known as De'Aarna**

linnaea [lin-ˈā-ä] **kingdom**

loritae [ˈlȯr-it-ī] **song**

Maob [ˈmā-äb] **king of eht Vilna Antessara, husband of Queen Vivien, father of Ahnabin**

Maricol [ˈmer-i-ˈkōl] **wife of Timmol, adoptive mother of Oran, referred to as Mari by her husband**

mena [ˈmēn-ä] **judge** (verb)

Mican [ˈmī-ken] **council foreman at De'Aarna**

Minarik [mə-ˈnar-ik] **Roga's assistant**

moht [ˈmōt] **black**

Montfort [ˈmänt-fȯrt] **a member of King Heidel's court and one of his closest advisors, Earl**

more [ˈmȯr-(ˌ)ā] **great, large**

Motaurotsiclaes arboretum [mō-ˈtōr-ˌōt-ˈsī-clēz ˌär-bȯr-ˈē-təm] **tree dragon**

Motaurotsiclaes ignus [mō-ˈtōr-ˌōt-ˈsī-clēz ˈig-nəs] **fire dragon**

Myra [ˈmī-rə] **wife of Prince Averon**

nohn [ˈnōn] **dark, evil**

Nyx [ˈniks] **second moon of Xerses**

Octrall [ˈäk-träl] **one of Roga's generals**

ohndayid [ōn-ˈdā-id] **safe**

Olen [ˈō-len] **king of eht Vilna Sahna, husband of Queen Isella, father of Ahláan and Shahláan**

Olenitur [ˌō-len-ˈi-tür] **Prophecy**

oleb [ˈō-leb] **book**

Oran [ˈȯr-en] **son of Shahláan and Sutek, adoptive son of Timmol and Maricol**

Oro [ˈȯr-ō] **Khorgian city, birthplace of Roga**

pada [ˈpä-dä] **truth**

Pearsin [ˈpir-sin] **cleric from De'Aarna**

pendiro [pen-ˈdir-ō] **speculate**

Pennik [ˈpen-ik] **chief minister of eht Vilna Copa**

pista [ˈpēs-tä] **servant, slut**

Quoregg [ˈkȯr-ig] **Elden's Master-at-Arms**

razha [ˈrä-zä] **battle**

Razha [ˈrä-zä] **war**

Roga [ˈrō-gä] **Khorgian warlord**

Rulon [ˈrü-län] **Kaleb's warehouse man**

sahk [ˈsäk] **sleeping**

sahnah [ˈsä-nä] **beacon, light**

Sammi [ˈsam-ē] **a member of the Tendiran reconnaissance**

Seamus [ˈshā-məs] **Master of the Watch at eht Vilna Sahna**

selbit [ˈsel-bit] **ordain, decree, literally "it shall be so"**

shah [ˈshä] **last, final**

Shahla [ˈshä-lä] **Evening**

Shahláan [shä-'lā-än] **second-born twin daughter of King Heidel and Queen Isella, mother of Oran**

shahnan ['shä-nän] **ending**
shuh ['shú] **now**
Sibu ['sē-bü] **nature, Mother of the Land**
siclaes ['sī-clēz] **ride**
Souliban ['sü-li-,bän] **desert land north of Tendira**
spelsham ['spel-shem] **grant, authorize**
Sutek ['sü-tek] **the Snake Demon, father of Oran**
tauron ['tȯ-rän] **dragon**
teht ['tet] **sorcerer**
tahla ['tä-lä] **sorceress**
Tantallon ['tan-tə-'län] **forest northwest of De'Aarna**
Taygen ['tā-gen] **magician from eht Vilna Moht**
Tendira [ten-'dir-ä] **area south of the Souliban**
Timmol ['tim-ōl] **leader of the borundahli, husband to Maricol, adoptive father of Oran**
toemi [tō-'em-ē] **lost**
Tophorus ['tō-fȯr-əs] **the Sea east of Tendira**
Tumehr [tü-'mər] **hilltop**
Turega [túr-'ā-gä] **silent, quiet, calm**
Uglebdek ['ü-gleb-dek] **Master of the Dead, the Collector of Souls**
ur ['úr] **mind**
Ursen ['úr-sen] **apprentice to Lord Roga**
Vidro ['vē-drō} **member of the borundahli**
Vilna ['vəl-nä] **castle**
Vivien ['vi-vē-ən] **queen of eht Vilna Antessara, wife of King Moab, mother of Ahnabin**
von ['vōn] **speak**
vona ['vō-nä] **speaker**
Wilhem ['wil-em] **son of the Beekeeper, Zephraim**
Worren ['wȯr-ᵊn] **Roga's Man-at-Arms**

Xerses [‘zir-sēz] **planet in the Triangulum galaxy, home world of the Tendirans and Khorgians**

Yockeff [‘yäk-ef] **son of Vidro**
yul [‘yül] **year**
Zea [‘zā-ä] **Governor of De’Aarna**
Zephraim [‘zef-ram] **the Beekeeper**

About the Author

A native of nearby Connecticut, Tim has been a resident of Warwick, Rhode Island since 2007, shortly after meeting the love of his life, Colleen. After graduating from Killingly High School in 19... ah... a long, long time ago, Tim spent a year at Penn State, two years at Quinebaug Valley Community College, and two years at New England Institute of Technology before settling in to the world of manufacturing. With a little push from his wife, he finally received his Bachelor's degree from Eastern Connecticut State University at the age of 45 and his Master's from Harvard University at the age of 50. Professionally, Tim works as the Director of Safety for a large international cleanroom construction firm headquartered in Massachusetts and gets to travel North America, visiting job sites to ensure everyone is being safe. Although that pays the bills, Tim is most at-home at home, building, fixing, or creating something. Whether it is upgrading a bathroom, building a new deck, or installing a new linen closet, there is always a project happening at home. And when the home projects are finished, Tim can often be found at Tranquil Touch Mind & Body Spa in Conimicut Village, implementing one of Colleen's visions for her spa, or driving the back roads of Rhode Island and Connecticut with Colleen in their 1964 Corvair Monza Convertible (top down, of course).

In his spare time, Tim likes to dabble in several creative outlets. Author. Poet. Lyricist. Woodworker. Engraver. Rocket Scientist (OK, maybe not that one). Some might say 'Renaissance Man', but Tim prefers 'Jack of all, Master of none'. And, sometimes, he even sleeps.

Tim lives in Gaspee (Warwick) with his wife Colleen and three rescue cats, Ukiah (KiKi), Maleficent (Mally) and Luna (LuLu). Together, Colleen and Tim share four children, Trevor, Ryan, Tyler, and Kaetlyn, who are each out and about, living their own lives as adults. Tim and Colleen also have two granddaughters, Thea and Lilia, the apples of their eyes, that live nearby in Connecticut.

About the Publisher

45-1 Properties is the private publishing label responsible for production and distribution of printed and digital content written by Timothy E. Collins.

Milton Keynes UK
Ingram Content Group UK Ltd.
UKHW020825061124
450821UK00012B/871

9 798227 681621